Eleanor Ray is the author of the highly acclaimed novel *Everything is Beautiful*. She lives in London with her husband and three young children, and is currently writing her next book.

Also by Eleanor Ray

Everything is Beautiful

the art of belonging

ELEANOR RAY

PIATKUS

PIATKUS

First published in Great Britain in 2024 by Piatkus
This paperback edition published in 2024 by Piatkus

1 3 5 7 9 10 8 6 4 2

A CIP catalogue record for this book is available from the British Library.

ISBN: 978-0-34942-747-8

Typeset in Caslon by M Rules
Printed and bound in Great Britain by Clays Ltd, Elcograf S.p.A.

Papers used by Piatkus are from well-managed forests
and other responsible sources.

Piatkus
An imprint of
Little, Brown Book Group
Carmelite House
50 Victoria Embankment
London EC4Y 0DZ

An Hachette UK Company
www.hachette.co.uk

www.littlebrown.co.uk

For Roger, the best of fathers,
and Teddy, Violet and Clementine, the best of children.

Chapter 1

Grace Sayers sat on the park bench, clutching her paper cup close to her chin for warmth. She was watching the small coffee van parked across from her, enjoying the dramatic puffs of steam as the coffee machine exhaled, the smooth gliding of steel on perfectly fitted steel as the man slotted the filter into place, the sound of metal tapping on wood as he loosened the ground beans.

A woman about her daughter's age was chatting to the man making coffee. They were both laughing as she shook chocolate sprinkles onto the top of her drink and the wind swept them onto his counter. Near the woman's feet, a small boy was pushing a toy train along the tarmac while simultaneously sucking on a carton of juice. Grace watched as he temporarily removed the straw from his mouth to emit a loud 'choo choo', then reinserted it and sucked until his face and the carton both puckered up, concave.

The noise was too familiar, and it gave Grace a sharp pang, as if the paper straw were stabbing into her. She didn't think she'd let any sound escape, but the woman turned to look at her, so she must have done.

Not wanting to be seen as a silly old lady, Grace made a coughing sound to compensate. 'Coffee went down the wrong way,' she explained, with a theatrical tap to her chest. Her words must have been swept away by the wind, because the woman turned back to the truck and the sprinkles and the smiling man, and Grace realised, with embarrassment, that she was talking to the air.

The woman had brown hair, swept back into a bun in a style that Grace's daughter used to wear before she got sick of her long hair and cut it all off. Grace would never forget the time she'd come into her teenage daughter's room to see her hair sitting on the desk like a small rabbit, while Amelia stared at her defiantly, still clutching the scissors. Years of brushing that hair, teasing out the tangles, for it all to go like that, not even cut straight. Grace had wanted to cry, to mourn those silky curls, but Jonathan had told her to relax. It was Amelia's hair, he'd said, to do with as she pleased. And if she'd made a mistake, it would grow back. Worse things could happen.

He was right, of course he was. Grace didn't want to be someone who tried to control what her daughter did with her hair. She'd been a feminist in the seventies, for goodness' sake, or at least she thought she had.

These days, she made a point of complimenting her daughter on her still short hair, whatever it looked like, every time she saw her. Which wasn't often enough.

Grace felt the urge to phone Amelia bubble up inside her like the froth on her cappuccino. She suppressed the desire, putting her hand to her own hair, usually neat but today dishevelled by the wind. She had to be careful with Amelia. Even as a baby, she'd been easily angered, her little face puckering up with rage if she dropped her dummy or her nappy was inadvertently fastened too tightly. And then, after it happened, things had become even more fragile.

But she wouldn't think about that now. Grace took a sip of her coffee, swallowing it carefully in case life followed lies and it really did go down the wrong way. Amelia didn't like to be disturbed during the day, not when she was working. *I'll call you*, she'd said, sounding irritated, the last time Grace had tried to contact her. *When I have time.*

That was five days ago now, though Grace had promised herself she wouldn't be counting. Amelia was busy, that was all. Grace pulled her phone from her bag. No calls. She tucked it back in again. She knew what it was like to be busy at work, with children, with life. It had been years since she'd felt like that, the type of busy that made her feel important and stressed and hurried and efficient, all at once.

The kind that meant she missed things right in front of her nose.

Grace bit her lip and turned her attention to the boy. The carton was now completely flat, sucked of all air and juice, and he was pulling on the hem of his mother's coat. 'Pop it in the bin if you're done,' the woman said, barely glancing his way.

There were no cars in the park, of course, but it didn't mean that bikes, scooters and the occasional large dog didn't charge along, and Grace watched nervously as the boy ran, without looking, across the path to the bin that sat next to her bench. Scraped knees, bloody noses, cut elbows came to her mind.

The right kind of inflictions for childhood, the kind that could be mended with antiseptic, plasters and kisses.

She tried to catch the child's eye and smile, but he was reaching to the bin, carton in one hand, train in the other, absorbed in his task. It was too high for him, and he had to stand on tiptoes, his arm raised like a crane as he released the carton to join the rest of the rubbish.

'Nice train you've got there,' ventured Grace. He was a cherubic little thing, maybe three years old, with just a few smudges of what must have been his breakfast still clinging to his chin. The remnants of a dippy egg, perhaps, or maybe dried yoghurt. Hard to tell. Grace wished she had a napkin to give him a good wipe, but of course she couldn't, even if she did. She was just a stranger in the park.

'The train goes very fast,' the boy informed her, rather sternly. 'The wheels go round and round.'

'That will be the pull-back mechanism,' said Grace. 'Inside the chassis.'

He frowned at that news, then dragged the train backwards along the concrete path, several times, rather roughly. He released it and it travelled forward a few centimetres before coming to a rather pitiful halt.

'Broken!' he exclaimed. Grace looked at him, then the train. He was right on the brink of tears. She hesitated. It really wasn't any of her business. But then again …

'Here,' she said, holding out her hand. 'Perhaps I can take a look?' The boy stared at her, suspicion clouding his features. 'The internal coil spring is probably jammed. I'll fish out my tweezers …' Grace located them in her handbag and held them up for the boy's inspection.

The tweezers clearly endorsed her credentials in the boy's mind, and he handed her the train.

'There we are,' said Grace. 'Look, that bit of the chassis is misshapen. It really isn't a very good design. If it were me, I'd have built in a better suspension system. Right, I'll pull this out here … There you go.'

She passed the boy the train and he snatched it back, pressing it to his lips.

'Oops, I've dropped the tweezers,' said Grace, squinting at the paving. 'Can you pass them up to me, please?'

But the boy only had eyes for his train. He pulled back the toy and shrieked with delight when it went charging off along the path. He chased after it like a dog with a ball.

Grace sighed and creakily crouched down to pick up her tweezers. They were her favourite pair, just right for adjusting miniature fishplates. She grabbed them and then took a little moment near the ground, steeling herself to get up again. Gravity seemed to have a much stronger hold on her since she'd passed seventy. She put her hand to the ground to steady herself, then noticed that her coat was trailing in a puddle, soaking up the dirty water.

'Bother,' she said, her voice coming out rather more loudly than she'd expected.

'Oh my goodness, you poor dear.' Grace looked up to see the boy's mother descending on her. 'You've had a bit of a fall.' She felt arms around her shoulders. 'Stefan, can you help me get her up?'

'No, really, I'm quite capable . . .' began Grace, feeling horribly embarrassed.

'Must be an awful shock,' said the boy's mother. To Grace's dismay, she found the coffee man's hands in her armpits, heaving her back to her feet with a rather bigger grunt than really seemed necessary.

She took a moment to regain her balance, then let the full horror of the humiliation sink in. 'Thank you,' she said politely to Stefan, who to his credit slunk back to his van with a gentle nod of acknowledgement.

'There you go,' said the woman. She smiled at Grace. 'Maybe you'd better have a sit.'

'I'm fine,' said Grace.

'Of course you are. It's lucky I was here.'

'Not really,' said Grace, feeling flustered at being manhandled. 'I didn't fall.'

'Oh my goodness,' said the woman. 'You slipped on Felix's train, did you? I told him to keep it close, that it can be such a hazard for the elderly, but he just does what he wants. Boys will be boys, won't they?'

'I hardly think his gender has anything to do with it,' said Grace. 'A girl could just as easily—'

'Let me buy you one of Stefan's muffins,' said the woman. 'To apologise.'

'No, really . . .'

'Oh my goodness, is that the time? Felix, we're late for our mother and toddler yoga class. Come along.' She pressed a coin into Grace's hand. 'For your muffin,' she said.

'I can afford my own muffin,' exclaimed Grace.

'Yes, of course, but with the price of heating, it must be *so* hard.' The woman smiled benevolently. 'You just never know what people have to deal with, do you?'

'No,' replied Grace, as she supposed that was true. No one ever did know, not really.

The woman hurried off, Felix in tow. He looked back to Grace, and she thought she saw the words *thank you* forming on his lips, before he turned around and ran after his mother, the train flying through the air at the end of his outstretched arm.

'So, a stranger gave you a pound for a muffin?' Ava's voice was loud, echoing around the toy museum, and several members of the Merrington Miniature Club looked up from their tiny chalet kits, paintbrushes paused mid-stroke. 'I bet that wasn't enough, not at Stefan's coffee van.'

'No,' said Grace. 'It wouldn't even buy one of those vegan bars that inexplicably taste of leather.'

'Those are great for your digestion,' said Ava. She paused. 'Did she think you were homeless?'

'What? No,' exclaimed Grace, wishing she hadn't said anything about the morning's incident. 'Of course not.' She paused. 'She just thought I'd fallen over her son's toy train.'

'So she gave you a pound?' queried Samir.

'That's hardly recompense,' said Ava. 'You could have sued her.'

'But I didn't fall,' insisted Grace. 'I was picking up my tweezers.'

'Is that what you were wearing?' asked Ava. 'You should let me take you shopping.' Grace watched as Ava cast a judgemental eye over her comfy M&S elasticated-waist trousers with a warm cardigan over the top. It hardly looked as though she were on the breadline, thought Grace, even if she did have a little mud on her coat and her hair was in disarray from the wind. The cardie was cashmere blend, for goodness' sake. Though when she looked back at her friend's rather more colourful and much less comfortable home-embellished sequin-encrusted ensemble, she did feel rather drab. Perhaps some people could still convincingly pull off sparkles past the age of seventy. She wasn't sure she was one of them.

'I don't think you look homeless at all,' contributed Toby. 'You look very nice.'

Ava tutted at him. 'Trust you to stick up for her,' she said. 'In your corduroy.'

Toby looked at his corduroy trousers as if he hadn't noticed them before. Then his eyes went back to the chalet he was trying to decorate. 'I do like your snow recipe, Grace,' he said. 'But my consistency doesn't seem quite right.'

Grace looked over. 'Yours is a bit too thin,' she said. 'You need to add more plaster-of-Paris shavings. If it gets too thick, add more talcum powder. The paste, two parts glue to one part water, should hold it all together.'

'To think I've been buying snow ready-made online for all these years,' said Samir. 'And it still doesn't come out as nicely as this.'

'You should manufacture this snow,' suggested Toby. 'I'd stock it.'

'It's nothing really,' said Grace, though she was flushing with pleasure. 'You just need the right ingredients, in the correct quantities. A little like baking a cake. Or fusing an alloy.'

Grace settled back into the task at hand. She'd joined the club almost four years ago, when she found herself alone again, and it had quickly become the highlight of her week. The toy museum closed early, the children shooed out to be replaced by the motley assortment of OAPs she could see surrounding her now. Toby was the founder and organiser of the club, using kits from his shop, and they took it in turns to make the tea and provide the biscuits. The museum gave them the hall, and in return they paid a small hire fee and donated some of their best creations to the displays.

Some of the members, like herself and Toby, were genuine enthusiasts with working model railways at home. Others, she suspected from the crookedness of their constructions, were here out of boredom, loneliness perhaps. Ava came because she was determined to find a boyfriend to liven up her sunset years, but the endeavour had been disappointing to her so far, as she'd whispered to Grace rather too loudly over a cup of tea and a Jammie Dodger the first time they'd met.

'I was thinking,' said Toby, 'of installing a ski lift in my alpine section.' He looked at Grace for approval.

'I was thinking the same,' she replied.

He smiled at her. 'I've ordered rather a nice kit into my shop,' he said. 'Perhaps you'd like to come and see? Something similar might work for you.' He paused a moment. 'I could even help instal it, if you'd like? I'd love to see your models.'

'Is that what they call it now?' smirked Ava, never one to miss an innuendo, even if it did come from a retired septuagenarian sporting elbow patches and with Rich Tea biscuit crumbs in his greying beard.

'I'm going to build the lift myself, I think,' replied Grace, pretending she hadn't heard Ava. 'The pulley system shouldn't be too hard to replicate, and then I could construct the lifts with wire loops.'

'That's ambitious,' said Toby.

Ava stifled a yawn. 'Yes, yes, Grace is a genius. Now, I'm too young for all this stairlift chat. How's your lovely granddaughter?' she asked. 'Did she like those clothes I made for her?'

'She loved them,' replied Grace, though she'd received no acknowledgement at all. The outfit had been rather more sparkly than anything she'd ever seen Charlotte wear, but Grace had been touched when Ava made it for her, and so she had packed it up, sent the parcel, and hoped that it would be well received.

She glanced around the museum, uncomfortable with her lie, and noticed Hector staring at her. He was a large, extremely old teddy bear that sat in one of the glass cases. He inspected her disapprovingly from his one remaining eye and Grace imagined the horror he must cause to the poor children who visited the place. She went back to her snow. It was fine and white and it made her wish for Christmas, even though the last one had been rather lonely. Perhaps if she added more glue, she could fashion a tiny snowman.

She'd done some rather lovely decorations for Christmas in her diorama, not bothering to decorate the real house. It would have just been for her sake, as Amelia and her family had gone skiing. 'You don't mind, Mum, do you?' her daughter had said, clearly expecting her to say it was fine. 'It's just with Tom's business, my job and Charlotte's school, it's the only time we can go.'

'But it's Christmas,' Grace objected, feeling like a petulant child.

'It's just a day like any other,' Amelia replied. 'We'll celebrate together once we're back. You know how much travel we missed in the pandemic.'

'OK,' Grace had replied. It wasn't just travel that had been sacrificed in the pandemic. It was time with her daughter and granddaughter too. She knew they had to stay away for all those months to keep her safe, but regular visits had never really resumed in the same way. It was such a minor complaint, after everything that had happened, that she hadn't said anything. 'Do what's best for you,' she conceded instead. 'Of course you need a holiday.'

'Like I said, we'll celebrate properly once we're back,' Amelia had replied, a concession to the sadness in Grace's voice. 'It will be even better. You can buy the presents in the sales.'

Except when they were back, they became busy, and now a month had passed and she'd eventually packed up their presents and sent them in the post. Next year perhaps she'd invite them earlier in December, maybe even November, before they got busy. Now, when would the shops start selling turkey?

Grace stopped herself. It was only February, and she was planning Christmas already! When had life become quite so devoid of events to look forward to? Perhaps she should book a holiday. For a moment, her thoughts were filled with sunny cafés and walks on the beach, before practical concerns at what to pack and travelling alone and whether she'd be able to lift her suitcase took over and she sighed with imagined exhaustion.

'My snow!' exclaimed Ava, as a cloud of talcum powder rose from her chalet. 'I hadn't mixed in the glue yet. You've sent it everywhere. Breathe on your own chalet!'

'Sorry,' said Grace, but she caught Toby's eye and they smiled at each other. Ava was coated in a white talcumy shroud.

'It looks like dandruff,' she declared, brushing it off her lap in disgust. She grinned. 'Do you dare me to sprinkle some on Samir's shoulder?'

'No!' exclaimed Grace, looking at poor Samir, his remaining length of unnaturally black hair pasted carefully across his forehead as he frowned through his glasses at the skiing figure he was attempting to paint.

'Spoilsport,' laughed Ava, putting down her chalet and stretching. 'I'm done for today. Who fancies the early-bird special at Luigi's? If you smile at him, he throws in a glass of red.'

'I'm not sure he'd do that for me,' said Toby. 'But yes, I'd love to.'

'Grace?'

'Maybe next time.'

'That's what you always say.' Ava stood up. 'Samir?' He ignored her, so she walked around to his good ear and waved at him. 'LUIGI'S?' she shouted.

'YES,' replied Samir. 'AND THERE'S NO NEED TO SHOUT. I'M NOT DEAF.'

Ava mimed speaking at him, and he frowned, fiddling with his hearing aid.

'You're awful,' said Grace, trying not to giggle.

'He likes the attention,' replied Ava, with a smile. 'And remember what I said about shopping. I'm here to be your stylist any time you need. De-hoboing you would be a treat. Now, you're sure you won't come with us?'

'I've got to get back,' said Grace. 'Amelia might call.'

Chapter 2

Bins had been Charlotte's downfall today. She watched as her mother stabbed a fork into a sausage from the frying pan and waved it at her. 'I'm sorry, but they were all out of the veggie ones at the little Tesco's, so I had to get pork.'

'But you lied,' ventured Charlotte, holding the empty packet that she'd found in the bin. 'You said they were plant-based.'

'I'm sorry,' said Amelia, sitting down next to her. 'That was wrong of me, especially after you've been a vegetarian for three days.'

'Four,' corrected Charlotte.

'Of course.' Her mother smiled at her. 'The fourth day makes all the difference. But seeing as how your dad was meant to be home by now and making dinner so I could catch up with work, could you eat it just this once?' Charlotte could hear a pleading tone in her voice, a hint of despair. 'The pig isn't coming back to life now, in any case, so perhaps you could bend your principles just this once, for me?'

Charlotte allowed the sausage onto her plate, but the sight of it, with juice oozing from the holes where her mother had pronged it, made her feel sick. Maybe she could eat her mash and peas without looking at it, then smuggle it into the bin later.

The bin. That's where she should have left that slip of paper.

But no.

She'd fished it out while trying to confirm her sausage suspicions earlier and had carelessly left it on the counter, where her mother had found it. It had meant nothing to Charlotte, something official from the bank, numbers on a page. But her mum had turned whiter than the paper it was printed on when she had seen it.

The phone rang. Amelia looked at it and sighed. 'It's your grandmother,' she said. 'I told her I'd call when I had time. This is all I need.' She looked at Charlotte. 'Do you want to talk to her?' Charlotte shook her head. They both sat and looked at the phone, which continued to ring with a guilty insistence.

They heard a familiar rattle at the door, the jangle of keys, and thankfully the phone stopped ringing. 'Dad's home,' said Charlotte. Sometimes the return of her father put her mother in a good mood. She had the feeling that today might not be one of those days.

'About time,' said Amelia, glancing at the kitchen clock as he came through the door. Charlotte heard the way she greeted him, her voice much more brittle than usual.

Charlotte reached out to hug him, feeling his stubble graze her cheek. He smelled a little stale and beery, and she braced herself for an argument.

'How's your day been, kiddo?'

'She's eleven years old,' said Amelia, frowning at her husband. 'Not really a kid. And where have you been?'

'She'll always be my princess, won't you, sweetie?' he replied, ignoring the question.

Charlotte nodded and hoped her dad wouldn't get too near to her mother.

But Amelia was already sniffing the air. 'Have you . . .?'

'Just one beer,' her dad replied. 'You can't build a business without a couple of drinks with suppliers.'

'But it was your turn to make dinner,' said Amelia. 'We agreed this morning, remember? I have to get that fundraising plan finished for tomorrow.'

'Sorry,' said her dad. 'I forgot.'

'Anything else you forgot to mention?' Charlotte watched her mother's hand hovering over the paper she'd pulled from the bin.

'If there is, I've forgotten it,' he replied, with a wink at Charlotte.

Charlotte turned her attention to her dinner, trying to tune out what she knew was coming. She took a forkful of mashed potato and popped it into her mouth, then proceeded to prong peas with her fork, sending several flying onto the table. She watched one roll to a stop right by her mother's hand. Luckily for the pea, her mother didn't notice.

'After dinner, maybe you can go to your room, Charley,' said Amelia. 'There are a few things I need to discuss with your father.'

'That sounds ominous,' said her dad with a laugh. He was misjudging the situation, making light of this. Charlotte closed her eyes, bracing herself for an argument.

Her mother brought her hand down to the table with a thump. Charlotte opened her eyes and watched as the pea ricocheted up in response, then landed and rolled to the edge. It paused for a minute as if in indecision, then toppled over.

Amelia didn't say anything, and they all looked at one another. Charlotte heard the kitchen clock tick.

'Your mother clearly has something she wants to say to me,' said her dad, his voice still light, but strained now at the edges like fraying fabric. 'Maybe if you're not going to eat your sausage, princess, go and do your homework.'

'She's going to eat her sausage.'

'I'm not,' said Charlotte. 'I'm vegetarian.' She sat and looked at her mother.

'Fine,' Amelia replied. 'I'll eat the damn sausage.' She stabbed it with her fork and took an aggressive bite. Charlotte seized her opportunity and escaped to her room, muttering something about homework.

Grace sat at her kitchen table, staring at her phone.

Still no call from Amelia.

She looked at the time. Seven thirty in the evening.. That was a good time to call, it must be. Or would they be eating?

She thought for a moment of a family meal, her daughter, son-in-law and granddaughter sitting around the table, chatting about their day. What harm could it do to call? She felt a little thrill of excitement and picked up the phone to dial.

Dial.

That wasn't what it was any more. No spinning the rotary dial with your index finger. That had seemed simple at the time, but she still remembered the joy she'd felt when she'd bought her first phone with the innovation of pressable buttons. Buttons on phones had been relatively short-lived, though. She missed them; the satisfaction of a quick, firm press. Perhaps a rewarding clicking sound. Now it was simply a silent tap to the screen and the phone knew what you wanted.

Easier. Quicker. Progress.

She focused on the screen, listening to the hopeful tone of the phone calling out to her family. Maybe they'd put her on speaker, perhaps even on video, propping her up on the pepper shaker, like they had on her birthday in lockdown. It had felt like they were all eating together.

Her hopes faded as the phone rang out. She watched it for a moment to see if her daughter rang right back. Maybe she'd been in the middle of cooking something elaborate. No, that wasn't like Amelia. More likely she was still at work, or trying to fry a sausage while dialling into a conference call. Grace felt a flash of pride, as she often did when she thought about her daughter. Head of marketing for a major cancer research charity. Of course she was busy. What she did mattered.

No call came back.

Grace tried not to be disappointed. Dinner. That was what she needed. She opened her fridge and peered in. Half a block of cheddar, two eggs and a packet of greying ham looked back at her.

Caring about food had been an interlude in the later years of her life. After she'd retired, she'd turned her skills to cooking for herself and her husband Jonathan. To her surprise, she found she rather enjoyed it. Combining the ingredients and applying heat, watching the consistencies change and the flavours develop was rather a satisfying way to spend her time. Jonathan, for all his progressiveness, liked his food traditional, and Grace had indulged him with pies and potatoes in all their forms.

But then towards the end, he hadn't been able to eat much. She'd made him soups and spoon-fed them to him, lukewarm and bland.

Once he'd gone, it seemed such a waste to cook and clean just for herself, and gradually her repertoire had faded to sandwiches, supplemented by the occasional piece of fruit. She still couldn't bring herself to eat soup.

It hadn't always been like that. Grace thought back to the seventies, to a hurried lunch eaten in the Concorde canteen, devoured quickly so she could get back to building her engines. Some of the men lingered over lunch, chatting about football or girls or whatever it was they were into. Grace rarely joined in; the men found her something of an oddity. A woman who, at the time, didn't want to settle down and have a family. 'There's no point you working so hard,' she remembered one of them saying. 'You'll have to give it up when you have kids.'

'No I won't,' she'd replied, to their amusement.

'Feel sorry for your husband then,' he'd said.

Grace found herself hoping that Amelia never had to listen to comments like that. She couldn't imagine her daughter putting up with it, and felt another moment of pride.

Pride was quickly overshadowed by hunger. Ham sandwich, cheese sandwich or egg sandwich? She debated the merits of each in her mind. She went to the bread bin but found the loaf cultivating light bluey-green spots. It was a struggle to get through even the smallest loaf each week on her own; her appetite wasn't what it was. She wondered for a moment if the ducks in the park would like it, then remembered the sign that told her the ducks should only be fed oats, and grapes cut in two. Even they had gone health-mad, it seemed. She tossed the loaf into the compost bin and bent down to get a pan from the cupboard. Omelette it was.

Grace sat at the table, eating her omelette alone.After years of trying – and often failing – to get home from work in time to eat as a family, it was mealtimes when she missed them all the most. She should have gone to the restaurant tonight with her friends. Maybe next time she would.

For now, she put the TV on for company. Then she turned it off again when it was the beginning of that terrible teen show that would be rotting the minds of the youth of today. She wondered whether Charlotte liked it. She had always seemed a curious, introspective sort of girl. Not like her mother. Much more like . . .

Grace stopped her train of thought and finished her omelette, then found herself yawning. She didn't miss everything about being young, but she did miss the deep slumbers of her twenties. Now she was lucky to get a couple of hours at a time, light sleep that led to tired days and frequent naps that overtook her at inconvenient moments. Back in the seventies, as she'd drifted off in her single bed, she'd have been thinking about the day's challenge.

The optimal angle for a turbine, the velocity of a rotor blade. Not whether she'd annoyed her daughter or got the texture of the snow wrong on her chalet.

Her chalet.

She put her dishes in the sink and carefully lifted the small structure she'd made earlier, carrying it with her as she left her kitchen and walked through the garden to her shed. She heard the neighbour's dog barking, the sound dancing on the breeze like a sycamore seed. She took out her key and slotted it into the lock.

As she opened the door, she felt the memory of the lonely meal slip away from her.

Now she was home.

Charlotte sat in her room, wondering what to do. She would even quite like some more homework, just to distract her from the argument she could hear in the kitchen. But she'd mastered her fourteen times table, completed a short story she'd written about elephants and packed her school bag for Monday. She'd turned on the second half of *Love Shack*, the show she knew all her friends would be talking about, but she found it boring and couldn't bring herself to focus on it. Leaving it on in the background, she got out a dog-eared copy of *Five on a Treasure Island* that she pretended she'd grown out of and opened it at her favourite section about Timmy the dog. She could still hear the fighting, but now it was muffled through the door, giving her scope to imagine what the quieter words might be.

It had been happening more and more recently, an evening in her room so her parents could swear freely at each other. Six months ago, her mother had taken on a promotion at work, and her parents had sat her down and explained that her mum would be busy but would still make time for her, and her dad would come home early more often instead.

But he hadn't. He'd been as busy with his business as ever, and Charlotte had watched as the bags under her mother's eyes darkened, her mood following suit.

And whatever was on that paper would be adding more fuel to the fire. Charlotte wished again that she'd put it back in the bin where it belonged.

She felt that, under the circumstances, she would be justified to ask again for a puppy – it seemed all the more essential now that she was so often alone, though somehow she wasn't sure that her parents would see it that way.

Not alone, she reminded herself, putting down the book to peer into the tank that sat on her desk. One stick insect peered back at her. The other ignored her, nonchalantly munching on a wilting privet leaf.

Her parents' argument was reaching a climax and Charlotte could make out more of the words.

Unforgivable. That was her mother, who had told her she should always forgive people if they apologised nicely.

Then her father, a full sentence, shrill and panicked. *Not everyone thinks I'm such a loser.*

Well, you are. Her mother again.

It's the people who care about you even when you screw up. They're who matter.

And what's that supposed to mean? I don't matter because you've been lying? And God knows what else?

Charlotte opened the window and leaned out. The evening air was fresh and she took a deep breath, enjoying the feeling of it cooling her lungs. She caught the song of a city blackbird, floating on the breeze. Then she heard the front door slamming. It seemed the whole house shook.

This was new. She hadn't known one of her parents to actually leave the house before. Usually they'd argue, slam some cupboard doors, and perhaps there'd be some tears, but they both stayed put. There was silence now, and Charlotte wondered which of her parents had left. If it was her mum, she might venture out in search of the pot of chocolate mousse she'd seen in the fridge. But if it wasn't? Not a risk worth taking, not after she hadn't eaten her sausage.

She shut her window and looked back to her stick insects. One was waving his slender leg in the air as if dancing. The other was determinedly scaling the glass of the tank to the very top, perhaps searching for the freshest leaves. Charlotte would pick some new privet for them tomorrow.

It was nothing to worry about, she decided, turning back to her book. Her parents would make up. They always did.

Chapter 3

Amelia sat at the kitchen table. Days had come and gone, bringing fresh revelations and whispered arguments. She couldn't quite believe he'd done this to them. Not Tom. He'd always been so open, so willing to talk about everything. It was refreshing; just what she needed after years with her mother. That was why she'd fallen for him, in the beginning. Well, that and his eyes, deep and blue as the ocean, like her father's.

Her promotion had put extra pressure on him, she knew it had. But he'd been so sweet about it. She'd told him she felt selfish, guilty for prioritising her career while Charlotte was still at school. He'd laughed, and told her that he couldn't think of anyone else who would feel bad for wanting to spend more time raising funds for a cancer charity.

'I don't want to be like my mother,' she'd said. 'All career and no time for my daughter. I can't have Charlotte feeling abandoned.'

'You're nothing like your mother,' he'd reassured her, words she always wanted to hear. 'Plus you have me. We're a partnership.'

It hadn't felt like a partnership, not for a long time. His words had proved hollow; he was so often out late, claiming to be busy with work. Now she realised it was because his business must have been spiralling out of control. But he could have talked to her still, surely? She knew she could be a little abrupt at times, and that he could be a bit of a coward, and that when they were tired, which was often, they would argue. But they were Tom and Amelia. Amelia and Tom. They loved each other.

Or at least they used to.

'You really want to do this?' he asked.

She felt anger rise at that question. As if this situation was her fault, her decision. 'No,' she said. 'I don't want to do this. I didn't want any of this. But I didn't get a choice, did I?'

He nodded. 'I know,' he said. 'I'm sorry.'

She felt herself softening as she looked into his eyes, and for a moment she wished she could just forgive him. But she couldn't. It wasn't so much the money he'd taken from their joint accounts. The debts he'd built up in both their names. Not even the secret remortgages that meant they'd lose their home. It was the lies. The deceit. He'd been doing this for years, it seemed, to hide the losses from his business.

And he hadn't confided in her. Not once. She felt so foolish, missing it as she had. Perhaps that was why he'd been so keen for her to take the promotion. Not because he cared for her well-being, but because he needed the extra money.

The thought made her feel sick, and she pushed it away and tried to speak in an even tone.

'We need to sell this house,' she said. 'That's not me talking, that's the bank.' She paused. 'I can't trust you. Not any more. It's best if we find separate places to live. For a while, at least, while we work out what to do.'

'Yes, but I . . .' He stopped. Amelia wondered if he was going to tell her he loved her. He hadn't said that in a long time. 'OK,' he said, instead.

'OK,' repeated Amelia, trying not to feel disappointed.

'Charlotte's been at her after-school club, but she'll be home any minute. We'll tell her then.' She paused, wishing there was a way her daughter didn't have to suffer in all this. But she had to be honest. She owed Charlotte the truth.

'How much will you tell her?' he asked.

Amelia looked at him, seeing his concern. 'Enough so that she understands,' she said. She tried to smile at him, but from the expression on his face, she could tell she hadn't quite succeeded. 'You're her father,' she said. 'She needs to know that you've made a mistake but that you still love her.'

'Of course I do,' he said. Amelia looked at him, waiting again for him to add that he loved her too.

He didn't.

Amelia stirred the jar of tomato sauce into the vegetarian mince she was frying. It sizzled reassuringly, but remained an unappetising grey colour that made her think she was doing something wrong.

She knew what she was doing wrong. She was putting off the conversation that she knew they had to have. Enough.

'Charlotte, Tom, come in here, please,' she said.

'Just a minute, I've almost finished my homework,' said Charlotte, flooding Amelia with love for her conscientious daughter.

Tom came into the kitchen and pulled a beer from the fridge. Amelia gave him a look, but let it slide. She could do with a drink herself.

Charlotte emerged and peered into the frying pan. 'It's meat-free,' said Amelia, holding up the packet as evidence.

'Thanks,' said Charlotte. Amelia watched as Charlotte looked from her father to her mother. 'You're both home early,' she said, her voice suspicious. 'And you're making my favourite dinner.'

'Please sit down,' said Amelia. 'We need to tell you something.'

She took a deep breath, and looked at Tom. He was concentrating on his beer can as if the ingredients list was fascinating.

'What is it?' asked Charlotte. 'Is it about the puppy?'

Amelia felt her heart break a little more than it had already. 'No,' she said. 'It's about your father and me. And you. And what we're going to need to do next.'

'Come on, let's ring Grandma.'

Charlotte looked with surprise at her mother; it wasn't often she made a suggestion like that. But here they were, sitting in their almost empty house, wondering what to do without the television. Not even three weeks had passed since Charlotte had found that letter, but her life had since been turned upside down and packed away. Some stuff was in storage, but the televisions and computer had been taken by a burly man with tattoos. Charlotte's mother had sent her to her room when he arrived. She and the stick insects had listened to the man whistling as he took their possessions, Charlotte's world crumbling while the insects munched on privet leaves.

'How come you get to keep your phone?' Charlotte asked. 'And I don't?'

'We're cutting back on luxuries and your contract is up,' said her mother. 'Like I explained. And mine is for work. I need it.'

'I need mine too,' said Charlotte. 'My friends . . .'

'You can still meet up,' said her mother. 'We won't move far.'

'Then why can't I stay at school?'

Amelia sighed. 'There was an issue with the fees,' she said. 'Your dad . . . made a mistake. We've been over this.'

'But I don't understand.' Charlotte looked around the house. It seemed bigger, dustier now it was empty, with lighter patches on the walls where their pictures had been, and rectangular areas of brightness on the carpets where the furniture had sat. She'd lived in this house for as long as she could remember, and the thought of leaving it made tears push at the edges of her eyes.

Her mum put an arm around her. 'I know it's hard,' she said. 'But you need to be brave.'

'It would be easier to be brave if I had a phone.'

'I didn't have a mobile phone at your age,' said Amelia, squeezing her a little tighter. 'And somehow I managed to survive.'

'I miss Dad,' said Charlotte. Her father would have let her keep her phone. She knew he would. 'When can I see him?'

'I told you,' her mother said. 'He's got lots of work to do, so he's living somewhere else for a while.'

'Don't you love him any more?' Charlotte couldn't work it out. Her dad had messed up something with money, and her mum was angry. Charlotte was angry too; she didn't want to leave her house and certainly not her school, full as it was of kids she'd known most of her life. But she loved her dad. Wherever they were going, he should go too.

'It's complicated,' said her mother. 'We need some time apart.'

'How long?' Charlotte ran her finger along a line on the wall where a wedding picture of her parents had once hung, the two of them laughing at something that they'd never been able to explain to her. 'Will he still be able to help me with my maths homework?'

'I'm better at maths than your dad,' said Amelia. 'I'll help you.'

'I know, but—'

'Come on,' said her mother, picking up her phone. 'Let's call Grandma.'

'I don't want to. She smells funny.'

'You can't smell her on the phone. Besides, there's nothing else to do.' Her mum smiled, a glimpse of amusement in her face. 'And you have to thank her for those rather fetching clothes she sent. Frankly, I can't believe the tattoo man left them behind.'

In spite of themselves, Charlotte and her mum both giggled, a crack in the tension. The clothes had surprised, baffled and then amused them, the sequins glistening through a mountain of misery. 'You talk to her first,' said her mother. 'Then I'll go in with our news. It's about time we told her.' She shrugged. 'She never did like your father. She'll probably say I told you so.'

'He didn't mean to,' said Charlotte, still hoping for a reconciliation.

Her mother's jaw set, the bone flickering dangerously at the bottom of her cheek.

'Yes. Well. Now's the time for her to dig up the family millions.'

'Family millions?'

'Here's hoping.'

It took Grace a moment to realise what the sound was as she blinked her eyes open. She hadn't meant to fall asleep at all, but here she was, half-eaten cheese sandwich in hand, eyes closed, dribbling on her armchair. When had she grown so old?

She didn't have time to think about it.

The phone.

She pushed herself out of her chair and hurried to her handbag, nearly falling over the dining table. She righted herself, muttered a quick warning to no one in particular to be more careful, and rummaged around in the bag, where her phone, despite its screen being lit, managed to evade her fingers.

Finally, she found it and answered.

Her granddaughter.

Grace smiled so hard she could barely speak, but of course Charlotte didn't know she was smiling, and the conversation dried up awkwardly. Her smile faded and she asked about the clothes, and thought she heard a small snort amid the thank you, which again ended in silence. Grace found that she'd started to prattle that she'd almost fallen over the table and how at seventy-two you needed to be careful about things like that because hips snap so easily as bone density is reduced and once you have a broken hip you'll be in a home and so often it's the beginning of the end and you don't leave the home until you're in a box.

She finally managed to stop herself talking, shaking her head. What eleven-year-old wanted to hear about that? Even Grace didn't want to hear about it. Ava would have told her to shut up as soon as she'd said the word 'hip'.

Silence.

More silence.

'Mum wants to talk to you,' said Charlotte finally, and Grace felt a flood of regret mingled with relief that the ordeal of the conversation was over. Amelia took the phone and told Grace sternly to wait while she went into a different room. Grace wondered what she had to say to her that Charlotte couldn't hear. Was Grace in trouble with her daughter?

No.

Her eyes found the wedding photo of Amelia and Tom that sat on her mantelpiece. She always wondered what they were laughing about in that photo, but no one was laughing now. She listened in disbelief. Amelia had looked gorgeous that day, all silks and lace and vintage-style flowers, whatever that meant. Grace remembered the ordeal of shopping for her own mother-of-the-bride outfit. Ava would have been helpful back then, but instead she'd had Amelia, popping out on her lunch break to inspect Grace's selections while busily taking work calls on her phone. They'd eventually agreed on a sky-blue linen dress with matching jacket to conceal the loose skin on her arms. It had wrinkled as soon as she sat down and she had spent the day wishing for an iron, but Jonathan had said she looked beautiful.

'All your money?' she repeated, not sure that she was understanding.

'Apparently he used the house as collateral to borrow for his business,' said Amelia, in her matter-of-fact way. 'He'd been losing money for some time,' she added. 'And covering it up by dipping into our accounts and borrowing at exorbitant rates all over the place. Then lying about it.'

Grace had never liked the husband her daughter had chosen; all overpriced flowers and fast cars that made her stomach turn and gallant kisses on her cheek that smelt of fancy aftershave. Jonathan had never felt the need to conceal his natural scent, and he drove in a way befitting the precious cargo in their family Volvo.

She clamped her mouth shut to avoid an *I told you so* creeping out. That was the last thing her daughter needed.

But what was the first thing?

Grace listened for the subtext of what Amelia was saying.

Money.

She needed money.

'I have some savings,' she said. 'You must take them.'

'That's very generous,' her daughter replied. 'But it wouldn't be enough.'

'We could remortgage my house?'

'I can't ask you for that.'

You could ask me for anything and I would give it to you, thought Grace. But it sounded rather sentimental and dramatic, so she didn't say it.

'Where will you all live?' she asked, getting back to practical grounds.

'Tom has gone already,' said Amelia. 'I don't know where he's staying, but it won't be with us, not for the moment. I'll find an Airbnb,' she added, leaving Grace mystified.

'Of course,' said Grace. 'Airbnb,' she repeated. It sounded like a floating hotel, but that couldn't be right. She looked back at the wedding photo. Her daughter's marriage over. Amelia looked so happy in that photo. Grace bit her lip. Losing a partner; there was very little that was worse. He wasn't dead, but still. It would be awful. 'I'm sorry,' she said, feeling the words horribly inadequate.

There must be something that would help.

She thought for a moment. Amelia needed to save money. And she'd be looking after Charlotte alone.

An idea started to form in Grace's mind.

Amelia needed somewhere to live.

And here Grace was, living somewhere.

Amelia could work from anywhere; the pandemic had proven that. And Grace's house was commutable to London too, just about, if needed. The nice little school Amelia had attended was still there and flourishing, a short walk from the house. Grace had two spare bedrooms, languishing unused, and here was her daughter, talking about sky hotels and mountains of debt.

'Come home,' she said.

A tut down the phone. 'That's what I'm saying. The house is being repossessed. We don't have a home any more.' Amelia was speaking more loudly now, and slowly, as if she was starting to doubt Grace's marbles.

'I mean my home,' said Grace, more assertively now the idea had taken hold. 'Our home. You and Charlotte should come and stay with me.' She paused, almost hearing the horror pouring down the phone. 'Just till you're back on your feet,' she said, to make it sound more palatable. 'Renting is money down the toilet,' she added. That was what Jonathan would have said, Jonathan who had always got along with her daughter so much better than she had. She paused again. 'Please.' No, that was wrong, it sounded desperate, like she'd be following Amelia about, begging her for attention. 'Just an idea,' she said, trying to sound casual.

'I'm barely at home anyway,' she lied. 'It's very busy, being retired. I almost missed your call.'

A pause.

'It's not the worst idea,' said Amelia.

Isn't it? thought Grace.

No. It wasn't.

She prattled on about the practicalities, schools and rooms and towels and meals, but she already knew that she'd won.

Her daughter was coming home, her granddaughter too, and without her son-in-law, it seemed.

They'd share meals, share a house, get to know each other again.

Grace stopped talking, sinking into her armchair as the potential for disaster set in.

What on earth had she done?

Chapter 4

'Does your daughter have a BO problem?' Ava, looking rather too sparkly for the John Lewis bathroom department, was frowning at her.

'No,' replied Grace, wishing she hadn't brought Ava along as she tried to decide between Egyptian and ultra-soft cotton. 'Of course not.'

'So she's not going to be showering four times a day?'

'No,' said Grace.

'Then why all the towels?'

Grace looked at the mountains of towels in front of her and decided on Egyptian cotton. 'It's nice to have plenty of fresh towels, don't you think? And I thought we could all use our own colour. I'll take the old ones, which are green. Amelia's favourite colour is blue,' she said, remembering vividly the summer when Amelia refused to eat anything that wasn't blue. Food dye had been Jonathan's friend for those months. She smiled to herself, thinking that she would stock up, perhaps cook a blue meal. Would Amelia remember, or would she think her mother had finally lost the plot?

'Only you could grin like that at a towel,' said Ava. 'Wait till you see the toilet brushes.'

‘What colour towels do you think Charlotte would like?’ Grace picked up a yellow that reminded her of butter, then put it back again. Perhaps something more neutral would be better. Safer.

‘She’d probably rather have some make-up,’ said Ava. ‘Let’s go to cosmetics.’

‘She’s too young for make-up,’ said Grace.

‘No one is too young for make-up,’ replied Ava. ‘And girls these days. They are much older than we were at that age.’

‘That doesn’t even make sense,’ said Grace, though she knew what her friend meant. Would Charlotte have a boyfriend? Surely not.

She should get some nice toiletries, though. She’d used most of her talcum powder to make snow. She had a vague feeling that powders were out of fashion anyway. No, she’d get some pots of moisturiser for her guests, in an assortment of flavours so they could pick their favourites. Perhaps even some nice soaps, the ones shaped like fruit.

‘Everyone likes fruit-shaped soap, don’t they?’ she said.

‘You’re going doolally,’ said Ava, pleasantly. ‘And everyone uses shower gel these days. Let’s go look at the clothes. You’ll need some new outfits so you don’t embarrass your cool granddaughter.’

Grace put down the towel. She hadn’t thought of that. In her plans to ensure she had plenty of sheets and towels and soaps, she’d not considered whether she might be an embarrassment.

But she would be.

Of course she would.

Charlotte wouldn’t want her to meet her friends, not her frumpy old grandmother who couldn’t even decide which colour towels to buy. A stranger had given her money for a muffin, for goodness’ sake. She glanced down at her coat, the mud from the puddle staring back at her accusingly. She still hadn’t taken it to the dry cleaner’s.

'God, I didn't mean it like that,' said Ava, looking at her in concern. 'I was only joking. I'm sorry. You look lovely.'

Grace picked up the towel again. 'I like the purple,' she said, her voice a little wobbly.

'Great choice,' said Ava. 'Reminds me of the Pope.'

'What do you know about the Pope?' teased Grace, trying to get the light-hearted feeling back to their excursion.

'I know he likes purple,' replied Ava. She nudged Grace affectionately. 'And don't worry,' she said. 'I'm here to be the surrogate cool aunt if you need one.'

'Great-aunt,' corrected Grace, though she was touched.

'Aunt,' replied Ava firmly. 'Now, cosmetics?'

'Homeware,' said Grace. 'I need to buy new plates. And saucepans. And a big roasting dish.' She smiled. 'I'm going to make a roast dinner for when they arrive,' she said. 'All the trimmings.' She used to make a roast dinner on Sundays. Back when Jonathan was alive, Amelia and Charlotte and Tom would come over and stuff themselves. But after Jonathan died, Amelia had said she didn't want her mother to go to all the effort. Then the pandemic began, and visits stopped. She was already looking forward to the smell of chicken warming her kitchen again.

'You're such a dinosaur,' said Ava. 'What's wrong with Deliveroo?'

Grace looked at her, puzzled. 'Deliver-who?'

'Never mind,' said Ava with a chuckle. 'And I don't think you need to worry about Charlotte being cool,' she added, giving her a gentle push to show she didn't mean any harm. 'She's got your genes. She'll be geeky and awkward. And fabulous.'

Charlotte knew the stick insects didn't like their tank to be moved. She was as gentle as she could be picking it up, but still, their world was shaken in a way they couldn't understand. Sure, in the wild, the trees in which they lived would blow in the breeze, perhaps there would even be a monsoon in their native India. But nothing as devastating as this. Nothing.

'Charlotte, come on,' her mum called up.

Charlotte hugged the tank close to her chest as she turned around to take a last look at her bedroom. It didn't look like it was hers any more; the posters, mainly a selection of rainforest animals to make the insects feel at home, had all been taken down, each leaving four little Blu Tack ghosts. Her bed was gone, her books packed. All that remained was the view from the window, the cherry tree still bare, although she knew it would be just a few weeks until it became covered in buds and then erupted into flower. If she opened her window, the petals would float in like confetti.

But it wasn't her window. Not any more.

'Charlotte, it's time to leave.'

'OK,' she said. She looked at Pickle, who had fallen from his leaf and was starting to make his way tentatively up the glass. 'You need to be brave,' she told him.

Her mother was standing in the doorway already, holding the keys to the small van she'd rented for the day. They didn't even need a proper moving truck, as many of the things they had left would stay in storage. 'You get in,' she said. 'I'll lock up.'

Charlotte didn't get in. She stood clutching the tank, watching her mother lock the door to their house for the last time. 'What's it like?' she asked. 'Grandma's house?'

'You've been plenty of times,' said her mother.

'I've never stayed there before. Not overnight.'

'It's comfy,' said Amelia. 'And you know your gran's a good cook these days.'

'What's there to do around there?'

'Not much,' admitted her mother. 'But we won't be staying for long.'

'Then why do I have to go to school?'

'Because it's the law.' Amelia's voice softened. 'It will be fine,' she said. 'You'll make new friends.'

'I don't want new friends. I want my old friends.'

'I know.' She gave Charlotte a hug. 'But we have to go.' She paused. 'Look, I've left a comfy spot on the back seat for the stick insects' tank.'

'I'll keep them on my lap,' said Charlotte, holding the tank tightly. 'Hugo and Pickle might get scared.'

Grace looked around her living room again, wondering what she'd forgotten. She'd picked some winter jasmine from her front garden, a flower that Amelia used to like to stick her nose in as a child, claiming it must contain honey. The chicken was slowly browning in the oven, filling her house with the smell of family meals, and filling her mind with memories of Jonathan.

Although she was still in the house they had shared for over forty years, there were a few things that reminded her too strongly of him. Roasts had been one. His armchair another. She'd had to give it away in the end. Seeing it day after day, sitting empty, the echo of his body still imprinted upon it. It had been too much. She'd put a new ficus plant where the chair used to be, but when she closed her eyes, the chair appeared again, with Jonathan sitting in it, smiling at her.

Grace blinked the memories away and got on with her chores. She put a few little snacks on the table, the fish-shaped cheesy biscuits Amelia loved as a girl, some carrot sticks for everyone's eyesight, and a big bowl of fiercely priced jellybeans, as a treat.

She'd laundered, dried and ironed the new towels and they were sitting, carefully folded, on the beds, which were adorned with the new sheets, also washed and ironed. She'd put Amelia in the bedroom she'd had as a girl, and then, with a flicker of hesitation, set up the spare room for Charlotte. She'd cleared the room out and repainted the walls years ago, but still, she'd stood in there a moment, remembering.

Only a moment, though, as there'd been so much to do.

Like closing up the shed. She'd put blinds up on the inside to cover the windows, and locked it, checking it twice. It wasn't that she minded if they saw inside, she told herself. She had nothing to hide. But maybe it would be better if Amelia just thought it contained a lawnmower, a few old cans of paint. Easier, for now.

She took a deep breath, inhaling the smell of the chicken again. She felt the activities of the last week starting to take their toll. She used to have boundless energy, at least that was what Jonathan said. One of the reasons he fell in love with her, apparently. When they'd met, she'd been up a ladder, investigating why a turbine had got stuck. She was leaning in, trying to disentangle a leaf from the mechanism, when she had a momentary wobble, before righting herself. She heard a cry from below and looked down to see a man gazing back up at her, clipboard in hand. He was about her age, with messy blonde hair scattered haphazardly over his head.

'I'm an aeronautical engineer,' she called down, aware that as the only woman on the team she was often mistaken for the secretary. 'So I'm fine up here.'

'I'm the safety inspector,' he called back. 'And no, you're not fine up there.'

She climbed back down, jumping the last rung. He reached out to catch her, dropping his clipboard in the process, but she'd landed with perfect balance.

'I was surprised to see you there,' he said, picking up his clipboard and wiping off the mud.

'I can climb just as well as any man,' she replied, taking umbrage.

'I don't doubt your climbing skills,' he replied. 'But doesn't that sign say "Danger, Do Not Climb"?'

Grace looked, and saw that it did. 'That's just advice,' she said. 'I was perfectly safe.'

'Because I was here.'

'Isn't that a safety inspector's job?' she asked.

'I put up the signs,' he replied. 'I like to think that even the aeronautical engineers will read them.'

She smiled at him, taking in his deep blue eyes and concerned face, furrowed into a frown. He'd be rather attractive if he smiled, she thought. She decided that what she would like to do most in the world right now was test that hypothesis.

'I read menus,' she replied, pleased with the line. 'I can show you, if you'd like to join me for dinner one night?'

He coloured; a deep pink that made her smile broaden. 'I suppose that would be OK,' he replied. 'As long as you don't clamber up any unstable ladders.'

'Not till after dinner,' Grace had replied, and the rest was history.

She blinked herself back into the present and glanced at the carriage clock on the freshly dusted mantel. They weren't due for another hour, and her daughter was often late. She'd have a sit, maybe close her eyes a moment, get herself ready. Meditate, that was what her yoga teacher called it. Mentally prepare.

Thoughts of her daughter flowed through her mind, but Amelia was a child again. Amelia was always a child when she closed her eyes. Home-baked biscuits and sticky fingers and board games and picture books and tantrums. Grace found herself smiling. She never slept well when her daughter was under another roof, always worrying about where she was, whether she was safe. It had been almost twenty-four years since Amelia had lived at home with her, and Grace felt those years acutely. Sometimes she thought she'd had better sleep when the girl was a newborn.

But now things would be different. Her daughter was coming home.

Grace flicked her eyes open. She could hear something. Not her phone.

The doorbell.

They were here.

She felt flustered, as she often did when she awoke from a nap. Her hand went to her chin, where sure enough there was a little patch of dampness. She'd been dribbling. She wiped it with her sleeve and heaved herself out of her chair just as the doorbell rang for a second time.

'You OK in there, Mum?'

Her daughter's voice. She probably thought Grace had taken a tumble and was lying prostrate on the bathroom floor.

'Absolutely fine,' said Grace, hurrying to the door to prove the veracity of that statement and swinging it open.

'Hi, Gran,' said Charlotte, who looked much taller than she had the last time Grace had seen her.

'You've grown,' she exclaimed, hugging her close. Charlotte didn't have anything to say to that, understandably, and made a sort of nodding shrug when she was released from the hug.

'Hey, Mum,' said Amelia, giving her a quick peck on the cheek.

Grace looked at her daughter. She was pale, with dark circles under her eyes. Grace felt her heart split in two for what she must be going through. What would make her feel better? She fished for words, unsure what to say. Should she bring up what had happened? Offer some comfort, some sympathy?

No, safest not to. Amelia might not want to talk about it.

'You know where everything is,' she found herself saying instead, then felt foolish. Amelia had grown up in this house. Of course she did. 'I've put out some snacks for us all,' she added, gesturing to the table. 'Help yourselves.'

Charlotte scooped up a handful of jellybeans and poured them into her mouth before her mother moved the bowl, taking it into the kitchen. 'You know the rule about sweets before dinner,' she said. 'And I bet they're not vegan either.'

'Vegan?' asked Grace, her mind on the chicken.

'Vegetarian,' corrected Charlotte, still chewing. 'And most jellybeans aren't made with gelatine.'

'You didn't say,' said Grace, turning to her daughter.

'I've had other things on my mind,' snapped Amelia. She looked at Grace, who in turn was looking at the kitchen with a panicked expression on her face. 'Sorry,' Amelia added. 'I forgot to tell you.' She picked up one of the fish-shaped biscuits and chewed it. 'I haven't had these in years,' she said.

'They used to be your favourites,' said Grace, pleased.

Then she thought of dinner, and panic set in. She took a breath, trying to be calm and relaxed about it. Chilled, that was what Ava said the young people called it. 'Well, I've made plenty of veggies,' she said, trying to sound jolly and chilled at the same time and rather disappointed with the effect.

Amelia and Charlotte didn't have anything to say to that. She found the three of them standing in silence. It wasn't going well, she could tell. Amelia was scowling at the new ficus plant and Charlotte looked as unhappy as a person who had just eaten a mouthful of jellybeans could.

What else to say? 'Your hair looks nice, Amelia,' she managed, finally. Her daughter took another fish biscuit. Grace turned her attention to Charlotte. 'You've grown so pretty,' she said. 'You've got Grandpa's blonde hair.' She reached out to touch it.

'It's like my dad's,' Charlotte replied, flinching a little at the touch. 'Does your neighbour still have that puppy?'

'He's not a puppy any more,' Grace said. 'He's all grown up since your last visit.'

'I'm sorry it's been so long,' said Amelia, her voice defensive. 'We just got so busy.'

'I didn't mean ...' began Grace, feeling the tension in the room start to build. She reached out to her daughter to give her an affectionate pat, but Amelia had turned around and was going outside to bring in more of the belongings that were piled in the front garden.

'Make yourself at home,' said Grace to Charlotte.

Charlotte looked at her, and Grace felt she'd said the wrong thing. 'We won't be staying long,' said Charlotte, her voice a little too loud, as if trying to convince herself. 'Mum said. It's just a break. Then I'll go back to my old school.'

'OK, dear,' said Grace, regretting the words as soon as they had left her mouth. They sounded so patronising, so ostentatiously grandmotherly. *Dear*? She was seventy-two, not ninety. This wasn't the fifties. She thought for a moment about how to counter what she'd said. Did she know any cool expressions to show her granddaughter she wasn't a frump? No, not really. Chilled, maybe? But how to work that into the conversation? Perhaps she should just swear.

Grace looked nervously at the front door, aware that her daughter would come back in at any moment. Did she swear in front of Charlotte? She certainly did in front of Grace. At least she used to. Teenage Amelia had been foul-mouthed.

Foul-mouthed? What an expression. She'd be suggesting washing out mouths with fruit-shaped soap and water next.

Safest to leave it.

'Do you want to see your room?' she asked Charlotte.

'Do you have a privet hedge?' Charlotte countered. Grace found herself blinking at the non sequitur.

'Not . . . not in your room,' she said.

Charlotte just looked at her.

'I'm afraid . . . I think it's more of an outdoor plant, isn't it?'

'One of your neighbours probably does. I'll find one,' replied Charlotte.

'I did pick some fresh flowers. Winter jasmine, your mum's favourite. It smells lovely.'

'Pickle and Hugo don't eat jasmine,' said Charlotte. 'It would give them bellyache,' she added, mystifying Grace. 'I'll help Mum bring in the suitcases,' she went on, already halfway out of the door as Grace tried to make sense of the conversation and wondered which one of them had lost their marbles. Odds on it was the seventy-two-year-old. 'We've brought a lot of stuff, but it's not because we're staying.'

Staying. The word had a permanence that pleased Grace and she tried to ignore that it had been used in the negative.

Jonathan hadn't stayed, not for good. Till death us do part had parted them. Not that it was his fault.

Dying and leaving were two very different things, though when she was left on her own, the result seemed the same.

No. When people left, they could come back. Like Amelia had. Amelia and Charlotte. Jonathan wasn't going to come home, though; she wasn't going to warm her icy toes on his legs as they lay in bed. Never again.

Loss was too much to think about, and Grace wriggled her toes. They were fine. She simply wore socks in bed these days.

Be practical.

That was the answer.

There was only so much sobbing a person could do before eventually she realised that it wouldn't help. She simply had to pick herself up from the bathroom floor and go and prune the rose bush.

Grace went into the kitchen and fussed with the potatoes, giving the not-at-all vegetarian chicken a dirty look. 'Stupid bird,' she muttered. She'd have to stop talking to herself, she decided, now that her daughter was here.

Then she smiled.

The chicken didn't matter.

Her family was home.

Amelia sat down on the single bed that she'd never intended to sleep in again and looked at the pile of bright-blue towels her mother had neatly folded for her. They looked suspiciously flat, as if they had been ironed. The bed was small. In fact, the whole room seemed to have shrunk; the ceiling closer, the shelves lower. She could hear her mother fussing with the chicken that was roasting guiltily downstairs, and the clatter of cutlery as her ever-helpful daughter set the table.

The smell of roast chicken made her think of her father. She'd barely eaten it since he'd passed away. He'd loved roasts, and they'd all loved their Sundays together. Her father always made Tom feel comfortable, chatting to him amiably about sport. His attempts to sound interested in Tom's business ventures made her heart swell with love. All her mother managed was thinly veiled dislike as she prodded at the bird in the oven and stirred her gravy. When Charlotte had been born, her father had been so delighted. He'd bounced his granddaughter on his knee in a way that brought back memories to Amelia that she couldn't even remember being formed. Visiting had been magical, her favourite part of the week.

When he died, she couldn't bring herself to come to her parents' house on a Sunday any more. Not for a roast. When she was at work or at home, she could sometimes pretend, just to herself, that her father was still alive. Pottering around the house, tending the garden, sitting contentedly in his chair. When she visited her childhood home, his absence was too obvious; his chair too empty, her mother too alone. She'd tried to be there for Grace, but then the pandemic had hit, and then she'd been so busy . . .

And now this.

Amelia opened her suitcase. Her clothes were crushed inside, the wrinkles in her suit reminding her of what a mess her life had become.

'Dinner is ready,' called her mother's voice. Even though she was hungry, Amelia felt a pang of sadness at the words. She wasn't even in control of the family timetable any more.

'Coming,' she called back down, feeling herself relinquishing her rights as an adult as she did so. She decided not to go down immediately, pausing to unpack a few more items of clothing, then felt ridiculous at the petty nature of her rebellion and came down the stairs, resisting the urge to stomp like a teenager.

'This looks delicious,' she said graciously instead, with what she hoped was a pleasant smile at her mother and daughter.

Grace beamed back at her. 'It's such a treat for me to have you staying with me,' she said. 'It's nice to have people to look after again.'

'I hope we won't be too much trouble,' replied Amelia, slicing into a roast potato. Perfect, as usual. Her mother had become much more domesticated after Amelia had left home. When Amelia had been Charlotte's age, Grace often got home too late for them to have dinner together. She'd rarely cooked, leaving that side of things to Amelia's dad. When Amelia was younger, of course, it had been different. Her mother had more reasons to be at home.

Amelia stopped her train of thought and chewed her potato. She sometimes struggled to even bake potatoes properly, resorting to bunging them in the microwave in a desperate attempt to create something edible.

'It's a pleasure,' said her mum.

Amelia was so far from feeling pleasure, she couldn't think of anything to say. They simply ate for a while, the sounds of cutlery on plates the only backdrop.

'It's lovely to eat as a family,' began Grace, again. 'It's like it used to be.'

Except it wasn't, thought Amelia. Not at all. Because her dad would have been here and her mother probably wouldn't. She glanced over to where he used to sit, and saw the small collection of rings on the table where he put his pint glass, always forgetting to use a coaster, no matter how many times her mother reminded him. The concentric circles reminded her of one of Charlotte's old Spirograph patterns. She looked at her mother, who was gazing at the other empty place. Amelia knew who she was thinking about.

'You've got rid of Dad's armchair,' she said, glancing at the large house plant that now sat in her dad's favourite corner of the room.

Her mother continued to chew, then swallowed carefully. 'Yes,' she said.

'Dad loved that chair,' said Amelia, trying to soften the accusation in her voice.

'He did,' agreed Grace. 'I thought a plant would liven up that corner. It's nice, isn't it?' she added, too brightly.

'It seems to be flourishing,' said Amelia, slicing a carrot in two and putting it into her mouth to stop herself saying more.

'These potatoes are so fluffy,' said Charlotte. She was eating more than Amelia had seen her do since Tom left. 'And I like the crispy skins.'

'I hope you have enough to eat,' said Grace. 'There are more roast potatoes and carrots in the kitchen if you want. If I'd known you were a vegetarian now, I would have made a nut loaf. I think I have a recipe somewhere. Nuts are very high in protein, and ...'

Amelia switched off from her mother's rambling. She wondered what Tom was doing now. He had told her he was staying with friends. He was probably enjoying the bachelor lifestyle: pizza straight from the box washed down with an ice-cold beer. Amelia prodded her delicious chicken, feeling miserable and not at all hungry.

'Is the chicken OK?' asked Grace, her voice anxious.

Amelia looked up, realising that she'd just been moving it around on her plate for the last few minutes. And her mother had noticed. What was next? Was she going to choo-choo the food train into the tunnel, complete the regression?

'It's lovely,' she replied, trying to suppress the annoyance in her voice. 'Really very good. A treat.' She made an attempt at a smile, but was pretty sure she hadn't succeeded. Instead she put a piece of chicken in her mouth and chewed, grateful to have a reason to stop talking.

Chapter 5

Charlotte sat on a bench in the school playground. She was doing her best to look like she was waiting for someone and wasn't so cold her fingers felt numb. In truth, lunchtime, previously her favourite part of the school day, now filled her with dread. She'd only been at her old secondary school for the few months since September, but starting there had seemed so easy. Most of her friends from primary school came with her, and everyone was new all at once.

Here, it was just her. Just her, friendless, eating alone.

In class, she could sit, inconspicuous, and listen to the teachers. Mr Brown, her form teacher, seemed really nice. In morning and afternoon breaks, she lingered in the classroom as the others left, then made her way to the loo and shuffled back, killing time until the bell rang.

Unfortunately, at lunch she needed to eat. She couldn't muster up the confidence to approach a group and ask to join; the very thought of it made her skin crawl. But she couldn't bring herself to sit alone at one of the tables either. She'd tried on Monday and the concentration required to *not* look like a loser meant she forgot how to chew and almost choked to death. Mr Brown had to give her a slap on the back and everyone had laughed as sandwich pieces flew from her mouth and splattered the table.

So now she huddled in the cold and ate outside, where she hoped to blend in, chameleon-like, with the bench on which she sat. They wouldn't be at her grandma's house forever, her mother had said, adding that the prospect made her feel ill. Just till she'd saved enough for a deposit on a flat back in London. Her dad had stayed in a location undisclosed by her mother, where he could get on with his 'work'. Whenever her mother mentioned her father's 'work' now, she made funny little air quote marks with her fingers and a scowl with her face.

At least it wasn't raining. Charlotte's contingency plan was to either go hungry and linger in the corridors, or lock herself in the loo while she stuffed a sandwich in her mouth.

Neither appealed.

A worried pigeon waddled towards her, away from the exuberant game of football that dominated the playground. Charlotte broke off a piece of sandwich and dropped it to the ground near her feet. The pigeon looked at the bread, then at her, suspicious. Charlotte tried harder to look like a part of the bench, holding her breath in an attempt at bench-like stillness. She passed the bird's risk assessment, and it came closer, picking up the crumb with its beak and flinging it in the air before hurrying after it again. Charlotte donated another piece of sandwich, and more pigeons flocked to the party. She watched as they pecked at the food, a sudden mass of life where it had just been her.

'They like Hula Hoops the best.'

Charlotte looked up. A boy she recognised from her class was standing in front of her, watching the birds. Clutched in his hand was a red bag of hoops; he plucked one out and threw it down. It bounced on the tarmac, then rolled towards the pigeons, gathering momentum on its way.

The birds went crazy, pecking ferociously at the hoop, then at each other. The boy sat down on the bench.

'I'm Sammy,' he said, holding out the bag. Charlotte noticed that he'd put potato rings on his slender fingers, as if he were a crisp emperor.

She took one from the bag and hesitated before popping it into her mouth and crunching it closed. She chewed for a moment, letting the salt stimulate her tongue. 'I'm Charlotte, but my friends call me Charley,' she said, painfully aware that no one had called her Charley since she'd moved.

'Hi, Charley,' said Sammy.

'I'm new,' she explained.

'I know,' said Sammy. He grinned at her. 'Do you like football?'

'No,' she said, glancing up at the game. 'Do you?'

'Of course not.' He paused. 'Do you want to see something cool?' he asked.

'Sure,' said Charlotte.

'Meet me after school,' he said. 'There's a great place I know. Are you free after school?'

Charlotte looked at him for a moment. He wasn't the gaggle of girls she'd been a part of in her old school, giggling and gossiping. He was small and thin and had a slight wheeze in his voice. But he was here, and he was friendly.

'Yes,' she said, and she released the first genuine smile she'd managed since she'd joined the school a week ago. 'Yes, I am.'

Amelia sat at the small desk in her bedroom. She was dialled into a Zoom meeting, but the people from the agency were spending far too much time presenting a research report that she'd already read. She suspected it was because they hadn't finished the concepts that she'd commissioned for the new fundraising campaign. She muted herself, turned off her camera and looked out of the window. The view reminded her of her childhood; the trees were a little taller and there were a few more buildings in the distance, but really, it had barely changed in thirty years. She could see the roof of her mother's shed dominating the garden, and thought for a moment of the time they had spent there, all together.

It must have been more than a moment, because when she looked back at her computer, the Zoom call had disappeared and the screen saver had popped up. It had somehow got onto a setting where it cycled through her photos, and today had selected a holiday shot of her, Charlotte and Tom by the sea in Crete. Looking at it now, she could almost feel the pleasant pain of Tom's arm draped over her sunburnt shoulder, the touch of hot skin on hot skin. Four-year-old Charlotte was oblivious to the proceedings, completely engrossed in the ice cream that was already smeared over much of her face.

Quickly Amelia reached for the mouse, making the memory disappear and bringing back the bored faces of her colleagues. She found herself closer to tears than she wanted to be on any call, albeit with her camera off. She couldn't deal with this emotional abuse from her laptop; she needed to change her screen saver settings.

And get back into the office. Working from home had been hard enough when her home was her own. Now here she was, sitting in her childhood bedroom. She knew she should feel lucky that she had somewhere to go, that Grace had so eagerly taken her and Charlotte in. But living with her mother at forty-two? It wasn't what she had planned. Her life with Tom hadn't always been easy, but at least she'd had her independence, her own space.

A knock sounded on her door. 'Would you like me to make you some lunch?'

'I'm on a call,' Amelia said, hoping that was enough for Grace to leave her alone. She didn't feel like talking. Not to her mother. Not now.

'Because I'm going to do some work in the garden in a bit,' said Grace, not taking the hint. 'So if you do want something, it's best to say now.'

Amelia sighed and opened the door a fraction. 'Thanks, Mum, but I can get something later. No need to go to any trouble.'

'It's no trouble,' said Grace, sounding hurt.

Amelia felt guilt creeping up on her. Her mother had done nothing but kindly offer to make her lunch, and she'd snapped at her like a grumpy teenager. 'I'm sorry,' she said. 'I'm just quite busy right now.'

'It's fine,' said Grace, though Amelia suspected that it wasn't.

She couldn't deal with this. Not someone else's upset as well as her own, especially when it was her fault. 'I've got to get back to this call,' she said, gesturing to the computer screen, from which a host of little faces in squares looked out. 'I've put myself on mute, but this campaign will be really important. I need to make sure the agency gets it right. Sorry.'

'It's fine,' repeated Grace, and she left, closing the door behind her.

Grace made her way downstairs, mystified by her daughter's job. Being head of marketing at a charity seemed to involve complaining about the broadband and talking to people through the computer screen, punctuated by the occasional cigarette that Amelia surreptitiously smoked out of the window as if she were a teenager.

She might not want lunch with her, but she was here. Grace allowed herself a big smile. Her daughter was back, living under her roof. And as Grace had hoped, she'd been able to get a place for Charlotte at the local school. That lent a sense of permanence to the arrangement, something she was going to add to right now.

She decided to skip having a lonely sandwich in favour of her next task. She'd been to the garden centre that morning, and she looked with delight at her purchase as she stepped outside. A woodpigeon was pecking at the soil in the potted plant she'd bought, so she shooed it out of the way. Taking up her shovel, she got to work.

The ground was still cold and the hole she had to dig was deep. The woodpigeon watched her from a respectable distance, and a robin, smaller but bolder, settled on a nearby branch, then darted down to snatch a wiggling earthworm from the upturned soil.

'Each to their own,' muttered Grace to the bird, but it reminded her that she needed to expand her vegetarian repertoire. Despite Amelia's assurances that the vegetarianism was a phase, Charlotte had showed no signs of relenting over the last week. Grace had made various pastas and roast vegetable combos. Perhaps she could find a recipe for a stuffed butternut squash, or maybe a mushroom pie? Jonathan would be turning in his grave at the thought of a pie without meat, she thought, as she continued to dig. Or he would if she'd buried him rather than cremated him. For a moment, she was struck by the memory of his ashes fluttering in the air as if they were disintegrating grey butterflies, before finally settling on the earth.

Maybe she would become vegetarian too. Solidarity. Or was that a cheap trick to bond with her granddaughter? That's what Amelia would think. Grace could practically see her rolling her eyes. But no. Grace had never liked meat, had always thought the idea of eating a dead animal rather absurd. Of course, vegetarianism wasn't really invented when she was younger; it was for hippies and Buddhists and people who couldn't afford sausages.

She straightened up and admired the hole she had dug. The robin cocked its head to one side, also impressed, then darted down for a second earthworm. The woodpigeon remained on the sidelines, interested but too timid to partake.

'Come on then,' said Grace to the new plant, turning it upside down to release it from its pot. 'We can't have Charlotte wandering the neighbourhood looking for the right kind of hedge.' She popped the privet bush in the hole and piled the earth back in around it. She was mystified by the alien-like creatures that Charlotte kept in the tank in her room, but if privet would make them happy, and they would make Charlotte happy, then so be it. She stepped back to inspect her planting, wiping her brow with what she realised too late was a muddy hand.

'I'm going into the office.' Grace turned around to see Amelia frowning at her. 'The new agency haven't understood the brief; they need a face-to-face meeting. I'll be back late; can you watch Charlotte? She knows her own way home from school, so you don't need to pick her up.'

'Of course,' said Grace, pleased that Amelia trusted her with the responsibility.

'Make sure she does her homework,' said Amelia. 'She's got a geography project due tomorrow.'

'Yes,' said Grace, though she'd already started planning a fun grandma–granddaughter evening; perhaps they'd even make some vegetarian sausage rolls. She'd pop out and get the ingredients once she'd watered the privet. 'Consider it done.'

Charlotte hauled herself up the fence and landed with a satisfying crunch on a pile of leaves left over from the autumn. Sammy scrambled up after her. She watched as he teetered at the top, then hurled himself down, landing awkwardly on all fours. He picked himself up, dusted off his hands and then turned to her. 'Nice, eh?' he said, gesturing around.

Charlotte looked at the wilderness in front of her. Bare winter trees were starting to bud, tight little balls of leaves ready to expand into a thick canopy. Sammy bent down and grabbed a brown sycamore seed, then threw it in the air. They both watched as it descended, spiralling like a dog chasing its tail. 'What is this place?' asked Charlotte.

'It's the wild land around the train tracks,' said Sammy, with a touch of pride. 'I'm the only one who comes here.' He smiled at her. 'Now you, too. Come on, I know where there are still a few conkers, left over from last year. Follow me.'

Charlotte walked along behind her new friend. New friend. Already she could feel the tension in her chest starting to dissipate, and she visualised lunchtime tomorrow, sitting with Sammy in the warmth of the lunch hall. Perhaps he'd even introduce her to his friends; maybe some of them would be girls who could eventually replace Charlotte's much-missed companions.

'So who do you hang around with?' she asked as they walked along. 'At school?'

'By myself, mostly,' said Sammy cheerfully.

'Oh,' said Charlotte, her dream receding. She tried to remain optimistic. 'Are you new here too?'

'Been at Fairbourne Park since primary,' said Sammy. 'My brothers are at the school too.' He looked at her, and Charlotte felt her face being read. 'There's four of us kids at home,' he explained. 'Quite nice to have some time to myself at school. And all most of the boys want to do is play footie. Not my thing.'

Charlotte nodded. She was enjoying not watching the programmes she used to have to watch just to have something to talk about. Not having to mould yourself to be like others was rather appealing, though she thought she wasn't bold enough herself. 'I hope you don't mind me being here,' she ventured.

'You're OK,' said Sammy. 'I can tell. Come on.' She followed him as he set off purposefully down a small dirt track.

He made a funny coughing sound, then stopped and rummaged in his backpack, eventually pulling out a plastic tube and taking a deep inhale. 'Touch of asthma,' he explained, leaning forward. 'In the cold, when I move too fast.'

'Sit down,' commanded Charlotte in alarm.

'I'm fine,' he said, taking another puff. He glanced at his watch. 'Conkers will have to wait,' he said. 'It's time for the 15.56 to Rochester. And here it comes, bang on time. Give me a boost, then I'll haul you up.'

Charlotte allowed Sammy to put his trainer-encased foot on her hand, and helped heave him into the tree. She didn't need his outstretched hand to get up; she was at least a foot taller than him. She took it anyway to be polite, though it actually made the whole manoeuvre rather trickier.

The sturdy branch of the horse chestnut provided a surprisingly comfy seat, and the two children sat looking out at the railway line. 'Shh,' said Sammy, though she hadn't said anything. 'You'll hear it in a minute.'

Charlotte couldn't hear anything. Until she could. It sounded like horse's hooves galloping in the distance.

'It's got the old Southern Rail livery!' said Sammy. 'That's unusual to see still, we're lucky.' Charlotte watched as a train came into view and powered down the line at a startling speed. 'I wish we could see it go through a tunnel, but there's none around here,' said Sammy regretfully. 'The nearest tunnel it passes through isn't until the North Downs.'

He watched transfixed. A trainspotter, thought Charlotte, her heart falling like a conker from a tree. Her first friend, and he had to be a trainspotter. The girls back home must never know. Charlotte would climb down the tree, be polite, and that would be the end of it.

But she was distracted by a woodlouse that had crawled onto her finger. She lifted it closer to her face and watched as it crept over her palm. Sammy coughed, and it rolled into a tiny ball. She smiled at it, tightly coiled around its vulnerable belly.

'That's cool,' said Sammy, peering into her hand.

'It's a pill woodlouse,' said Charlotte. 'Slater woodlice look very similar but can't roll themselves up in the same way.'

'How do you know that?'

Charlotte blushed. 'I read it in a book,' she said. 'I like reading about animals.'

'You're a bit different, aren't you?' said Sammy, inspecting her.

This was the last thing she needed. She had successfully hidden her interest in animals from her other friends, pretending to be as terrified of spiders as the rest of the girls, when in fact she'd rescue them from the corner of the classroom when no one was looking. She could already imagine the taunts of 'Lousy Lottie' that would echo around the playground when Sammy told.

'It's OK,' he said. 'So am I.' He smiled. 'I won't tell anyone.'

Charlotte felt relief wash over her. Maybe being a trainspotter wasn't so bad. They sat in silence for a moment, watching the trees swaying in the breeze. Deciding it was safe again, the woodlouse tentatively unfurled itself and proceeded to march across Charlotte's hand. 'Most people think woodlice are insects,' she said, carefully allowing it to descend to the branch, where it disappeared into the folds of bark. 'But actually, they're more closely related to crabs.'

'You're smart,' said Sammy. 'And you know about animals. You should be a vet.'

Charlotte beamed at him. 'Not much call for woodlouse vets,' she said, brushing off the compliment but feeling warm inside. 'And my mum won't let me get a puppy.' She paused, wondering if she could convince her grandmother.

'Are you going do something with trains when you grow up?' she asked.

'Drive them,' said Sammy with a grin. 'Of course. Shall we collect conkers now?'

'I have to get home,' replied Charlotte. 'I'm late already.' She paused, searching for the courage she needed. She visualised the train hurtling confidently along the tracks. Her old friends weren't here now. Sammy was. And as it turned out, she thought she might like him very much. 'Maybe we could have lunch together tomorrow?'

'Sure,' said Sammy with a smile. 'Sounds good.'

Charlotte wasn't home.

Grace looked at the clock on the mantelpiece, wondering whether to call her daughter. She didn't want to get Charlotte in trouble, but what if something had happened to her?

No, that was silly. Charlotte was minutes late, that was all. She took a moment to imagine the call, playing through the conversation with her daughter in her mind. Would she say that Charlotte was missing? That wasn't true. Not yet. She'd say she was late. But how late did she have to be to be missing? Grace was meant to be looking after her, and she'd disappeared.

No, she hadn't disappeared.

She was just late.

She looked at the clock again. Ten minutes. Ten minutes more, that was the difference between missing and late. Or was it? She could imagine Amelia's eyes rolling at her already, the motion somehow transmitting through the telephone wire. Except telephones didn't have wires any more. The signal made it through the air, floating on the breeze like dandelion seeds. No. She wouldn't phone Amelia, she decided. Not yet. Charlotte was fine. She'd make tea instead. Making tea was always a safe option. No one ever got fired for making tea. Was that the expression? It didn't feel quite right; slightly off, like milk that was on the turn.

She shook her head, as if that would help her to dislodge her thoughts. Lateness used to seem fun when she was young. She was so often late for her dates with Jonathan, back in the seventies. It was a sign that she had too much to do, was too much in demand. 'I'm so sorry,' she'd said, when she'd swept into the restaurant where Jonathan sat, an empty pint glass in front of him, the foam still clinging to the edges like lace. 'There was a leak somewhere and it took us ages to find and repair it.'

'It's OK,' replied Jonathan, standing up to accept the kiss she offered. He smelt yeasty, and as Grace sat down, the waitress brought another pint and set it down in front of him with a smile. 'Thanks, Brenda,' he said.

'A glass of Lambrusco,' Grace had said, trying to dispel the sense of intimacy the use of the waitress's name had created. 'Nice and cold.' She smiled sweetly to compensate for the clipped tone of voice. Brenda nodded acknowledgement.

'Anyway, I'm sorry,' said Grace. 'I won't be late again.'

'Grace, it's fine,' Jonathan replied. 'Your work is important to you. I know that.'

'But it's rude,' Grace said. 'My mum always said it was like stealing people's time, making them wait.'

'You're worth waiting for.' He'd looked at her with an intensity that made the corny words seem as though they'd never been so laden with meaning. Grace felt as if there were a tiny bird in her chest, flapping its wings a hundred times a minute.

She'd picked up the menu and turned the conversation to prawn cocktails, but his words lingered in the air until Brenda arrived and cut through them with a large glass of Lambrusco, ice cold.

Keys jangling at the door brought Grace back to the present. Thank goodness. It would be Charlotte. She went to the hallway to be sure, then at the last minute changed her mind and hurried back to the living room. She didn't want to be standing by the door when her granddaughter came through, like an over-eager dog waiting for its owner.

'Ah, there you are,' she said, lowering herself into her armchair as if she'd been relaxing there all along. No, that sounded like she'd been worried. Charlotte smiled at her. She'd got away with it. 'Your mum had to go to the office, so it's just us tonight.'

Charlotte nodded, and Grace was relieved that the girl didn't seem fazed by the prospect. 'I was with Sammy,' she said. 'He's my new friend.'

Grace smiled. 'I'm glad you're settling in,' she said, then wondered if that was the wrong thing to say. Charlotte had seemed so adamant that they weren't staying for long. 'I thought we could make sausage rolls,' she said, to cover her potential mistake.

Charlotte frowned at her.

'Vegetarian ones,' she added.

'Oh,' said Charlotte. She smiled again, and Grace smiled back. 'Thanks. I have a bit of homework to do . . .'

'It won't take long, I've got all the ingredients here. We just need to mix them up and then roll out the pastry. Homework after dinner?'

'Deal,' said Charlotte.

Grace felt better in the kitchen, busying herself with baking trays and pastry and chattering away. 'Sausage rolls are what I'd miss if I were vegetarian,' she told her granddaughter. 'I'm not sure how they'll turn out, with this meat substitute, but I thought we'd try. I've grated some extra cheese for moisture, and chopped fresh parsley for flavour.'

Charlotte looked at her. 'That's nice of you,' she said.

Grace stopped what she was doing, feeling startled at the compliment.

'Mum pretends she forgets,' said Charlotte. 'But I think she's just hoping I'll grow out of it. I won't.'

'Your mother has a lot on her mind,' said Grace, loyally. 'I'm retired.' She smiled, and nervously reached out to touch Charlotte on the shoulder. 'It's so nice for me having you here. I like to look after you. Both of you.'

Charlotte bit her lip, feeling uncomfortable at the papery hand touching her. She could see the sinews within, the dirt beneath the fingernails. 'Is it lonely, living on your own, without Grandpa?' she asked.

Grace was a little surprised at the question. 'I suppose,' she said. 'But I've got friends.' She found herself wanting to make her life sound interesting, fun, self-sufficient. 'We go out for meals sometimes,' she said. 'After the little club I go to.'

'That's good,' said Charlotte. She thought about whether to tell her grandmother more about her new friend. Too early, she decided. 'Friends are important,' she said, non-committally.

'And family,' countered Grace, who then wondered why they were speaking in platitudes. Next thing she'd tell her granddaughter that children were the future or some such nonsense. 'I planted some privet in the garden,' she said instead. 'I thought Hugo and Pickle might appreciate it. Pick as much as you like for them; privet is a robust plant, it won't mind.'

Charlotte didn't know why, but she found tears prickling the corner of her eyes. Unsure what to do, she flung her arms around her grandmother and put her head on her shoulder. Her grandmother smelt of earth and pastry and talcum powder.

Grace found herself in a hug. A hug that smelled of soil and trees and the fruity shower gel she'd chosen at the department store. She squeezed her granddaughter, surprised at how warm she felt. ‘It’s nice to have Hugo and Pickle to look after too,’ she added, just to have something to say that might prolong the moment. ‘Even if they do look like aliens.’

Chapter 6

'You're up early.' Amelia smiled at her daughter, already dressed for school and sitting at the kitchen table, red felt-tip in hand. 'What are you drawing?'

'Nothing,' said Charlotte. 'How was your meeting?'

'Fine,' replied Amelia. 'Is that a volcano?'

'Yes.'

Grace came in, still in her dressing gown. 'Morning, all,' she said. 'I'll pop the kettle on. Who'd like some scrambled eggs on toast?'

'No thanks, Grandma. I have to finish this.'

'Maybe porridge?'

'Finish what?' asked Amelia.

'My geography project.'

'How come you didn't do it last night?' she asked. 'That's not like you.'

'Oh, that's my fault,' said Grace. 'You see, we decided to make sausage rolls.'

'Sausage rolls?'

'Vegetarian ones,' said Grace, sounding nervous. 'They turned out fairly well, considering, but I think next time I might add more . . .'

Amelia wasn't listening. She was looking at Charlotte, hunched over in tense concentration. 'Mum, can we have a word in the garden?' She opened the kitchen door for her mother, who stepped onto the cold patio in her slippered feet.

Amelia closed the door behind them. 'I am grateful to you for looking after Charlotte last night,' she began, feeling the responsibilities of single-parenthood weighing down on her. She thought her mother, of all people, would understand the importance of education.

'It was a pleasure,' said Grace, shifting on the wobbly patio tile. Amelia watched her. When she was a girl, she used to love jumping on that tile. 'She's wonderful.'

'She is,' agreed Amelia. 'But I did ask you to make sure she did her homework.'

'I know,' said Grace. 'But like I said, we made vegetarian sausage rolls, and picked some fresh privet, and we had such a lovely chat that then it was time for her bath and I thought . . .'

'She's just started at the new school and she gets so anxious if she doesn't get her work finished in time.'

'I'm sorry,' said Grace. 'I'm not used to all this, and—'

The door opened. 'Are you talking about the homework?' Charlotte asked. 'It wasn't Grandma's fault. Did you know she's planted a privet bush for Hugo and Pickle?'

Amelia saw her mother and daughter smile at one another. She felt excluded, somehow. On the outside.

'But I'm doing my homework now,' added Charlotte. 'I've almost finished.'

'Good,' said Amelia. 'You carry on. Don't worry about breakfast, you can have a cereal bar on the way.'

'I'm sorry,' said Grace again. 'I don't know what I was thinking. Making her cook instead of doing her homework. I feel like I've set feminism back twenty years.'

Seventy, more like, thought Amelia. But she let it pass.

'You didn't make me, Grandma,' said Charlotte. 'And you taught me about the chemical changes in the pastry when heat is applied.' They both smiled again at the memory.

'It's cold out here,' said Amelia, watching them. She didn't have any memories like that with her mother; they'd rarely baked together, let alone discussed chemistry. 'Let's get back inside.'

'Who can tell me what dolphins and bats have in common?' Mr Brown put the question to the class, who were all shifting uncomfortably on the science lab stools, the peculiar smell from the Bunsen burners lingering in the air.

'They can both fly,' suggested Marlon.

'Dolphins can't fly,' said Nia, with a flick of her hair. 'They swim.'

'They leap up in the air,' said Marlon defensively.

'That's right,' replied Mr Brown. 'They can leap right out of the water, but they can't actually fly. It's not the answer I was looking for. Anyone else?'

Charlotte bit her lip. She'd been tense all morning after having to rush to finish her geography project, but she was starting to really enjoy the class now. And she knew the answer, but she didn't want to seem like a swot.

'I'll give you a clue,' said Mr Brown. 'Eeeeeeee,' he shrieked. The class covered their ears, laughing. 'Eeee,' continued Mr Brown. 'I'm not stopping until someone gets the right answer.'

'They're both annoying,' called out Kaval.

'EeeEEEE!'

'Make it stop,' said Nia.

Charlotte tentatively raised her hand. 'Charlotte?' Mr Brown said. 'Can you rescue your classmates' ears?'

'They both use sonar,' she said, feeling shy.

'You've all been saved by Charlotte,' Mr Brown declared to the class. Charlotte flushed, but she noticed Erica, next to Nia, turn and give her a smile. 'Dolphins and bats can emit and receive the echoes of sound waves that bounce off objects. It's like a special way of seeing, useful in the dark for a bat, and underwater for a dolphin. Whales do the same. Echolocation.' He paused. 'Right, I've got an echolocation exercise of my own invention for you. Get into pairs while I pass out these blindfolds and recorders.' He paused. 'Let's hope no one is in the next classroom, because this may get noisy.'

Mr Brown was right. It did get noisy, but Charlotte couldn't remember the last time a class had been so much fun. Now they were sitting down again, the recorders safely back in the music room, writing up their findings. She was engrossed in what she was doing and didn't look up the first time Sammy nudged her, so he poked her with his pencil. She took her eyes from her workbook and saw that he was pointing at something. A ladybird was climbing the window, seemingly unfazed by the transparent surface on which it found itself. Flies would throw themselves at the glass come summer, she knew, but this ladybird, enjoying the welcome warmth of the early days of spring, took it all in its stride.

Charlotte felt something, watching that ladybird.

Happiness.

That was what it was. She was astonished at the difference a single friend could make. She hadn't felt her usual anxiety when told to get into pairs, because Sammy had been right there, looking at her expectantly. She'd always felt like she needed lots of friends, safety in numbers, spares, but just this one boy had made life so much more bearable.

And her grandma. Charlotte looked at the lunchbox sitting by her feet that would be full to the brim with leftover vegetarian sausage rolls, her favourite seedless purple grapes, and home-made biscuits, punctuated by raisins.

'We'll take the ladybird outside with us at break,' she whispered to Sammy. He was busy drawing the creature, capturing its glossy dome with a firm stroke of his pencil. 'It will be happier in the playground.'

'That's very good, Sammy.' Both children looked up in surprise; they hadn't realised Mr Brown was standing behind them. He leaned to one side and opened the window. The ladybird opened its thin shell, revealing gossamer wings underneath. It spread them, paused a moment, and then flew out. 'But ladybirds are not one of the animals that uses sonar, unfortunately,' he added, closing the window again.

'Sorry, sir,' muttered Sammy.

'How are you getting along, Charley?' Mr Brown hovered over her workbook. 'Excellent,' he said. 'And you're absolutely right, sonar is only one of the many ways that dolphins communicate. Great work.'

Charlotte smiled up at him. It was the first time a teacher in her new school had complimented her, and it made her feel warm inside.

'Mrs Varga wants you, sir,' said Nia, gesturing urgently. Sure enough, Mrs Varga's pretty face was at the classroom door window, looking in.

'Keep going, everyone,' said Mr Brown, hurrying to the door. 'I'll be right back.' The moment the door shut, the classroom erupted into chaos. Sammy and Charlotte were the only ones who didn't burst from their seats. Sammy hurriedly finished his sketch, and Charlotte, buoyed by the praise, continued writing.

Ten minutes passed and still Mr Brown didn't return. Charlotte finished her work and put down her pencil. Marlon was doing a gorilla impression at the front of the class, Nia was

French-plaiting Anne-Marie's hair and Sammy was sketching a railway tunnel.

'Want some of my sausage rolls at lunch?' she asked him. 'I made them myself.'

'Doctor's appointment,' said Sammy with a grimace.

'Are you OK?' asked Charlotte, anxiety rising in her.

'Just my check-up,' he answered. 'I'll be back for afternoon lessons.'

Amelia watched as the screen in front of her froze, her colleague Sarah's face trapped in an unintentionally comical expression, her eyes to the sky and her mouth wide open. Amelia allowed herself a childish smirk before turning her own camera off and writing a quick apology for her connection. Her new role was hard enough without technology stepping in to make life more difficult.

She stood up from the desk in the corner of her bedroom and stretched, silently thanking whoever had invented the fake backgrounds in Zoom calls. She couldn't have her team see her bedroom, even if her mother had snuck in while she was showering earlier today to make her bed and take her laundry. It was helpful and infuriating all at once.

Her mobile rang.

Tom.

She looked at the screen, wondering whether she should answer. It was the first time he'd called in ages. She didn't want to talk to him.

Or maybe she did.

But he knew she didn't like to be disturbed during the work day. Not now that she had too much to do. She remembered in the early days, before Charlotte, when he used to turn up at her office, flowers in hand, to take her out for lunch, simply because he hadn't seen her since breakfast. She'd pretended to be embarrassed, but she'd loved it.

'Amelia Sayers,' she answered, relieved that she hadn't changed her name when she married.

'Hi, Amelia.'

His voice was the same. He could be calling to let her know that he'd picked up her dry cleaning on the way home from work. That he'd got a new client for his business. That he loved her.

It wasn't that, of course. They were on a break. 'What do you want?' she asked.

'I think some of my shoes went into your storage boxes,' he said. 'I need them for a meeting.'

'You can go barefoot for all I care.' The words escaped her before she'd even realised how angry she was feeling. The first time he'd spoken to her in weeks and the topic was shoes. He was the guilty party, for Christ's sake. He should be apologising.

'That's mature,' he replied.

Great. Now he had the upper hand. When had it become a power struggle? Amelia could hear her mother pottering around downstairs. 'You have access,' she said, keeping her voice quiet. 'Go pick them up.'

'I don't know how you've organised the boxes.'

Good God. Why had she been missing this man? 'You'll just have to do your best.' She paused, thinking of her daughter. Their daughter. 'You'll want to see Charlotte,' she said, forcing out the words. 'Shall I bring her to you, or do you want to visit her here?'

She listened as he mumbled something about it being a key time for him with work stuff, being on the cusp of turning things around.

'Where are you even staying?' she interrupted.

'In a flat,' he replied. 'In town.'

'Could you be more specific?' she asked.

'You remember Steve?' he replied. Amelia did. Steve and his wife had separated four years ago, and Tom had been out for a few consolatory beers with him before coming home and nuzzling her affectionately. He'd said he never wanted that to happen to them.

How things had changed. 'I have to go now,' she said, hanging up before he could hear the sadness she knew was breaking into her voice.

For a moment, she slumped on her bed, unsure why the conversation had been so painful. She'd had screaming matches with Tom, many of them. But now it felt like he didn't care about her any more. Not at all. He was more interested in his shoes.

She'd been the one to say they needed time apart, she reminded herself. And for good reason. She wasn't going to cry.

She was going to go to the office. That was what she needed. She wanted to concentrate on something else, something that mattered and that didn't involve her husband's shoes. The presentation from the agency would be much better in person rather than by Zoom. She'd ask Grace to look after Charlotte again so she could stay late. Perhaps that would make it up to her mother for snapping at her about the homework earlier.

Amelia sighed as she looked for less comfortable and more office-appropriate clothes to put on. She didn't want to upset her mother, but Grace was just so sensitive.

Was that the problem, or was the problem Amelia herself? She wasn't sure, and didn't want to think about it.

Work. That was the answer.

Charlotte took a deep breath as she stepped into the playground at lunch break. Sammy's mum had picked him up for his appointment at the doctor, and she felt self-conscious again without him by her side. She should have approached the other girls on a day when she had Sammy in tow; then she'd have a back-up when he wasn't there. She couldn't do it now, not on her own.

But it wasn't for long, she told herself. Sammy would be back soon. She just needed to find somewhere quiet, eat quickly, and then perhaps she could go back inside and linger in the classroom, pretending to be interested in the displays on the wall.

At least it was sunny, so she made her way to her favourite bench, a little sheltered from the rest of the playground by the overgrowth. She tugged her Tupperware from her bag as she walked so she didn't have to make eye contact with anyone. 'Oh,' she said, spotting when she was almost on top of him that Mr Brown was sitting on the bench, his head in his hands. 'Sorry.'

He jumped up. 'Sorry,' he echoed, seeming flustered. He attempted a smile, but his face looked puffy. 'I'm on playground duty,' he said. 'Just resting my legs a moment. You sit.'

'Thanks,' said Charlotte, doing so. Her teacher stood awkwardly, shifting his weight from one foot to the other as if trying to work out in which direction to go. 'There's plenty of room,' she offered, 'if you want to sit down again?'

He sank back down to the bench as if his legs weren't really giving him a choice. 'I'll be off again in a minute,' he said. 'I just need to collect my thoughts.' He looked down at his shoe, as if that was where his thoughts were kept.

Charlotte took a bite of her sausage roll, wondering what the matter was with her teacher. 'I liked your class today,' she said, the words feeling awkward as they came out.

'What?' replied Mr Brown, looking at her as if he couldn't quite see her. 'Oh,' he added. 'Thank you.' He paused. 'Great work.'

Charlotte smiled at him. She hesitated a moment. No one was watching them, and she had far more lunch than she could eat. 'Sausage roll?' she offered. He looked so pale.

'No thanks,' he replied. Charlotte felt mortified. Offering a teacher food. It was a weird thing to do. Of course he'd say no.

'I'm vegetarian,' he elaborated, as if sensing her embarrassment.

'So are they,' she said, pleased. 'And I am too.' She realised that the last time she'd eaten meat she'd been living in her old house and her dad had still been there. She felt a sharp pang, and wished it was her father who was sitting next to her right now.

'Really?' asked Mr Brown. He reached out and took one. 'Thanks,' he said, biting in. 'They are really very good,' he added, pastry crumbling onto his jumper. 'And nice to find a kindred spirit,' he added. 'Not enough young people seem to care about animals. It's all football and reality telly.' The food seemed to bring him back to himself a little.

'I want a puppy,' said Charlotte. 'But my mum won't let me, so I have stick insects instead,' she told him. 'Hugo and Pickle.'

'Good names,' said Mr Brown. He stood up, looking a little brighter. 'I should get back to my duties,' he said, brushing himself off. A pigeon waddled over to peck up the pastry flakes. 'Thanks, Charlotte,' he added. 'It was nice to talk to you.'

'It was,' Charlotte replied, but he'd already gone. She took another bite of her own sausage roll, then tore a piece off and flung it to the pigeon. More birds fluttered down to join their fortunate friend, and as Charlotte watched them, she couldn't help but feel less alone.

'This is brilliant work,' said Amelia. The account people from the agency looked relieved. The concept was just what the charity needed, and she felt excited, more excited than she had in a long time.

She stood up, drawing the meeting to a close. 'Remember the deadlines. I'd like to see a timing plan first thing Monday.'

'A few of us are going to the Crown,' said her colleague Paula, as Amelia emerged from the meeting room. 'Why don't you join us? You haven't been out with the team for ages.'

'I think they'll have more fun without me,' said Amelia. 'Having the boss around cramps their night out.'

'Why don't we go for one then, just us?' suggested Paula. 'That quiet wine bar that smells a little musty? We'll get a seat at least.'

'OK,' said Amelia. Paula worked in events, and was the only person in the team she felt she could relax with. 'Just one, though, then you can join the others. I want to get back before Charlotte's in bed.'

'Sure.'

Amelia packed her laptop and a pile of papers into the heavy bag she lugged around with her, and they walked a couple of blocks to the bar. The pubs nearby were overflowing with office workers, spilling into the street and smoking, drinking and laughing away the stresses of the day. Planters filled with tulips demarcated the island in the pedestrian crossing, and Amelia saw Paula pause to admire them.

They entered the bar; downstairs, dark and unpopular. Amelia tried to identify the smell, somewhere between mould and disinfectant. She got used to it after a while, and the wine wasn't bad, though hideously overpriced. She ordered two glasses of Sauvignon Blanc, and the women chinked their glasses.

'How's life with your mother?'

Amelia winced. 'She means well, I think,' she said. 'She's obsessed with Charley's latest phase and spends all her time wrapping soy proteins in pastry.'

'Nice that she's making the effort,' said Paula.

Amelia nodded. 'Perfect grandmother, apparently,' she said, then realised how bitter she sounded. Just because Grace hadn't been the best mother didn't mean she couldn't be a good grandmother. And God knows she needed the help.

'I don't mean it like that,' she corrected herself. 'I'm pleased they're getting on. All this has been tough on Charley, you know. She's always been sensitive. She was so settled at her old school, most of her friends had been with her since primary, and now she's been uprooted. At least she's got a lovely grandmother, even if she does have a rotten father.'

'She's got a good mother too,' said Paula.

'Hmm.' Amelia didn't feel like one. She loved her job and she loved her daughter, but balancing the two of them just seemed so hard. There weren't enough hours in the day, or enough energy inside Amelia. And much as she loved her daughter, Charlotte always seemed to get the scrag-ends of the day. The morning, tired and pre-coffee. The evening, tired and grouchy. Between her, Tom and after-school clubs, they'd just about been managing, but it hadn't been easy. Weekends and holidays were when they spent quality time together, the time when Amelia could relax and enjoy her daughter's company.

Now at weekends Charlotte had other places she wanted to be, and holidays seemed a distant memory. Amelia supposed her daughter would want to see less and less of her as she got older, and she took another sip of her wine, feeling guilty that she wasn't already on her way home.

Still, at least she was there for Charlotte more than her own mother had been for her.

'Have you heard from Tom?' asked Paula.

'One phone call, to ask where his shoes were.'

'What?' exclaimed Paula. 'He hasn't even grovelled?'

'He hasn't even seen his daughter.'

'Good thing you chucked him out.'

Amelia took a sip of wine, but the musty smell interfered with the taste, and she swallowed it so quickly it made her cough. She paused a moment, regaining her composure. 'I thought it was the right thing to do, to take a break after what he'd done,' she said.

'It was,' replied Paula. 'He stole from you and he lied about it.'

'Yes,' said Amelia. She swirled her wine around the glass, looking at the lines it left in its wake. 'But it's as if the break has taken on a momentum of its own.' She paused again. 'Not of its own,' she said. 'Of Tom's.' She hesitated, not wanting to voice her thoughts out loud. 'I think he's pleased this has happened,' she said, finally coming out with it. 'And I think he wants the break to be permanent.'

'He loves you,' objected Paula.

'It's been building a while, in hindsight,' said Amelia. 'Not just the money. We weren't talking, not properly. Not like we used to. He said he'd be there to support me more when I took on the promotion, but he stayed out as much as ever, perhaps more.'

'I had no idea.'

Amelia tapped her glass absent-mindedly with her fingernail. 'I can't believe he hasn't even been to visit Charlotte,' she said.

'Where's he staying? The moon?'

'With Steve,' said Amelia. 'You met him, at our garden party last year. Divorced.'

'Steve?' queried Paula. 'But he's gone to Australia.'

'What?' Amelia put down her glass.

'Yes. It turns out we knew a few people in common, and he'd dated my cousin for a bit. She's the one who told me he'd taken a transfer at work. A month ago.'

Amelia looked at her friend, feeling humiliation rise. She tried to swallow it back down.

'There's probably some explanation,' said Paula, looking alarmed.

'Yes,' said Amelia. Why would he lie about where he was staying, unless . . .?

'He didn't deserve you,' said Paula, and Amelia found herself grateful for the interruption to her thoughts. 'You or Charlotte.' She leaned in. 'I never liked him, you know? Not really. I always thought he was a bit . . . smarmy.'

Amelia took a deep breath. Had she been an idiot for all these years?

She looked at Paula. 'Does everyone in the team know about the break?'

'Not from me,' Paula said. 'But yes, I think they do.'

'I thought so,' said Amelia. She took another sip of wine, feeling embarrassment creep into her. All those people, gossiping about her. She'd been with her husband for twelve years, and now he was behaving like this. Lying about everything.

'People are worried about you,' said Paula, watching her friend.

'I'm tough,' said Amelia, feeling anything but.

'I know,' replied Paula.

Amelia took another breath. She couldn't face this subject any more. 'Enough about me,' she said. 'How's your little boy doing?'

'Better each day,' said Paula. 'Thanks again for all you've done.'

'You're entitled to that leave,' said Amelia, though she'd had to fight Paula's case before HR agreed with her.

'Another drink?'

She glanced at her watch. 'I'm sorry, I've got to go. If I miss the next train, I'll be back after Charlotte's already in bed.' She waved at the waiter, who nodded tacitly and delivered the bill on a small silver tray. Amelia tapped her card and the waiter frowned at the machine.

'Sorry,' he said. 'Must be something wrong with the reader. Try inserting it.'

She did so, feeling her colour rise as the card was rejected. 'I'll try another one,' she said, fumbling in her wallet.

'I'll get this,' said Paula quickly.

'Thanks,' muttered Amelia, not meeting the waiter's eye. He

took the payment and scuttled back to the bar. Yet another humiliation, courtesy of Tom.

'Amelia?'

'Yes?'

'Go easy on yourself. You've just had your heart broken.' Amelia opened her mouth to contradict her, but Paula waved her objections away as if swatting a fly. 'And your life turned upside down. You deserve a break.'

'I'm fine,' said Amelia. 'Like I said, I'm tough.' She picked up her glass, swallowing the final mouthful. 'Join the others,' she said. 'I'm working from home tomorrow. See you Monday.'

Chapter 7

Amelia got up from the desk in her bedroom and stretched. She couldn't focus on work, thinking about Tom. He'd said he was staying with Steve. She was sure he had.

Where was he?

She picked up her phone to call him and then put it down again.

Later.

No, now. She dialled, wondering what she'd say. She wouldn't go straight in with an accusation.

Yes, she would, she wouldn't be able to help herself.

The call went to voicemail. 'It's your wife,' she said. 'Call me.'

She hung up. That was enough, for now.

She flipped her laptop shut, deciding that she wouldn't sit around waiting for the phone to ring. She'd go for a lunchtime run. Action. That would make her feel better, or at least replace her emotional stress with something physical. She pulled off the shirt she wore for work calls and replaced it with a T-shirt. She was in her leggings already, one of the few joys of working from home. She crept down the stairs, trying to avoid her mother. She didn't want to talk about sandwiches again, a subject Grace often managed to work into the conversation.

'Are you having a good day?' Grace said, poking her head from around the kitchen door. It seemed she was always listening for any movement on the staircase.

'Fine,' said Amelia, really not in the mood for a conversation.

'All OK?'

'Fine,' she repeated, then immediately felt bad. Her mum was just being friendly, and she was snapping at her. 'Yes,' she added, her voice softer. 'Everything is OK.'

Grace paused. 'I'm so sorry about the homework,' she apologised again. 'Of course that's much more important than sausage rolls. I don't know what I was thinking.'

'She got it finished,' said Amelia, not wanting to argue about this again. Not now. 'You'll know next time.'

'I will,' said Grace, her voice eager. 'And you're sure you'll be OK tonight, on your own with Charlotte?'

'She is my daughter,' said Amelia. 'I've been looking after her perfectly well for the last eleven years.'

'Of course,' said Grace, looking upset. 'I'm sorry.'

'No, I'm sorry,' said Amelia, feeling guilty again. 'It's been a bit much.' She paused. 'Where did you say you were going tonight?' she asked, trying to sound interested.

'Nowhere really,' said Grace. Amelia looked at her. 'Somewhere,' Grace admitted, seeming flustered. 'A miniature club. Silly really, just a group of OAPs getting together to make little toys.'

'You're still doing the trains?' queried Amelia.

'Just since your father died,' said Grace. 'You know, to get me out of the house.'

Amelia nodded, unable to think of anything to say to that.

'But I could stay home if you like?' offered Grace. 'I don't need to go.'

'We're fine, Mum,' said Amelia. She'd been looking forward to some time, her and Charlotte, without her mother around. 'Enjoy yourself.'

'I've made vegetable stew,' said Grace. 'It's on the stove. You just have to heat it up, and there's bread in the bread bin for mopping up the juices. It's nice being able to get through a whole loaf without it going mouldy.'

Honestly, the things that made her mother happy. Was that the path Amelia herself was on now she was separated? Feeling a sense of achievement at not allowing the bread to go mouldy? 'OK,' she managed. 'Thanks.'

Her mother was standing in front of her, blocking her path to the door, looking like she still wanted to chat. 'I'm going for a run,' said Amelia, hoping to end the conversation.

'How nice,' said Grace. 'I still remember when you won the three-legged race at sports day that time. How old would you have been? You were partnered with Samantha, and she moved away when you were nine, so it must have been—'

'I have a call at one thirty that I need to be back for,' said Amelia.

'Oh, I'm sorry, was I rambling?' said Grace, stepping out of her way. 'Maybe you'd like me to bring you up a sandwich later? Or if you hang on a minute, I could make one for you now. A packed lunch for your run? You could eat it in the park. It's a beautiful sunny day today, though it is a bit cold still . . .'

'No thanks, Mum,' said Amelia, putting on her trainers. 'I need to get going.'

'It's no trouble.'

'I'm fine.' Amelia stepped out of the house. 'Bye.'

She closed the door behind her and started to run, feeling the cold air spread into her lungs. It felt good to be out of that house. She narrowly avoided trampling the neighbour's dog as it attempted to weave between her legs, and she gave the owner, a new mum who always looked overwhelmed, a small nod somewhere between acknowledgement, annoyance and sympathy.

The park. That's where she would go. She headed that way, her feet pounding heavily on the pavement as she hit her stride. Perhaps a few circuits around the duck pond was what she needed to clear her head.

She went fast, trying not to look at streets that were so redolent of her childhood. Most buildings were much the same as they had always been; a shop front changed here, an extension there, but not much to show for thirty years of progress. Her old neighbourhood back in London changed almost daily as people hurried to add value to their homes and businesses popped up to supply the ever-growing need for oat-milk lattes, continental jams and gluten-free pastries.

The park hadn't changed at all, except for the addition of a coffee van that Amelia eyed up for later. She ran through the grassy outskirts to the focal point, a lake that sustained a small population of moorhens, some very noisy ducks and a couple of angry geese.

The sun was out but only doing half its job; the day bright but still cold. Amelia squinted as the sunshine reflected off the lake and into her eyes, but she continued to run, circling the lake twice before finally pausing to catch her breath. She watched as a flock of ducks eyed her up and swam towards her. A paddling of ducks, she corrected herself, remembering Charlotte's enthusiastic phase of learning the collective nouns for groups of animals. They probably thought she had a sandwich, and she showed them her hands to demonstrate their emptiness. She realised she was hungry too, and for a moment regretted the decision not to let her mother pack her lunch.

She set off for the coffee van, deciding to treat herself to a drink and a muffin in the sunshine before she went home. Maybe she'd even share it with the ducks.

Not at those prices, she decided as she exchanged a sweaty ten-pound note from her pocket for a blueberry muffin, a latte and a couple of coins. She headed back to the lake, taking it slowly now as the exertion caught up with her. Sitting down on a bench, she took a sip of the drink and a bite of the muffin and tried to reclaim the sense of peace that she'd briefly obtained while running.

'Amelia?' She squinted up at the man addressing her. 'I thought it was you, but you were whizzing round the lake far too quickly for these old legs!'

'Patrick.' Amelia greeted her dad's old friend, silently marvelling at how bald he'd become. The reflected sunlight gleamed from his head.

'Here to feed the ducks? You and your dad used to keep them plenty plump back when you were about as tall as this bench. Best-fed ducks in Kent, I always said. Bet they'd have tasted good too.'

'Not today,' said Amelia, trying not to let the memories push their way into her head. 'I'm staying with my mum for a bit,' she told him. 'With Charlotte. I was just having a break from my run.'

'Good thing,' said Patrick, sitting down creakily next to her. 'Those ducks are on a diet these days, like the rest of the world. Grapes and oats, according to the sign. Pond slime too, I expect. Poor old dears. Talking of old dears, how is your mum?'

Amelia couldn't help but let a small and disloyal laugh slip out at hearing her mother described like that. 'She's well,' she said. Patrick looked at her expectantly, and to her shame, Amelia realised she didn't have much more to say on how her mum was. She hadn't really asked. 'She's going out tonight,' she added, to fill the silence.

'Good for her,' said Patrick. 'Broken, she was, after your dad passed. There's only so much loss one person can take.'

'We all miss him,' said Amelia, feeling that she was the one who missed him the most. Her mother hadn't even kept his old chair. For a moment she let herself think what it would be like if her dad were here, right now. He'd be teasing Patrick about the out-of-season festive socks she could see peeking from his trouser legs. Warming his hands on her overpriced coffee but refusing her offer to buy him one. He only drank tea, and wouldn't spend money to drink that out when he had a perfectly good kettle at home. He'd insist that the ducks had a share of her muffin, though, despite the prices and their diet.

Before she could help herself, she broke off a chunk and threw it into the water, where it floated for a moment before attracting the attention of the ducks. A hen pecked and missed, and a drake ungallantly snatched it in its beak and swallowed, quacking loudly for more.

'I bet she's pleased to have you home.'

Amelia was so caught up in the duck drama it took her a moment to realise who he was talking about. 'Mum? Yes,' she said. 'It's nice for her to spend some time with Charlotte,' she added.

'Must be,' he agreed. 'Gets lonely,' he added. 'On your own again. At our age.'

Amelia felt a fresh flood of guilt. The drake had clambered out of the pond and was waddling towards her expectantly, closely followed by the hen. 'It's been hard for me to come back,' she admitted. 'Without Dad here. I just look everywhere and see where he should be. It's like when . . .' She stopped herself, unable to say the words.

'I know,' said Patrick. She felt his gnarled hand close over hers for a moment, surprisingly warm. 'She knows too.'

Amelia nodded, but she wasn't sure her mum did know. How could she? They never talked about anything. They hadn't, not for years. Not since she was twelve.

But that was her mum's fault, she told herself, not her own.

She'd been a child, her mother had been an adult. At least she'd had her dad. They could talk about anything.

'I think you're going to have to finish that muffin quickly,' said Patrick, gesturing to the insistent ducks, 'if you want to keep your fingers.'

Amelia took a final bite and threw the remaining piece to the female duck, who swallowed it in one and quacked gratefully. The drake looked straight at Amelia, his gaze indignant.

'Your dad would be pleased you've come back,' said Patrick. 'For your mum's sake.' He grinned. 'And the ducks'.'

Amelia smiled back at him. 'Are you still in the same house?' she asked. He nodded. 'I'll bring Charlotte round to visit sometime, if you like?'

'I'd love that,' he replied. 'Bring your mum too. It's been too long.'

Amelia nodded, her gaze on the ducks as they realised her food was gone. They waddled back to the lake, gliding into the water.

Grace sat in the restaurant pretending not to be fazed by the menu. It was a long time since she'd eaten out. The miniature greengrocer shop that she'd been working on was encased in bubble wrap and safety tucked into her handbag, which she'd placed on her lap. She was particularly pleased with the display of tiny apples outside the shop, crafted from polymer clay and varnished till they sparkled.

Charlotte and Amelia were both at home and had told her they'd be fine without her. And since she'd been so insistent that she had a lively social life, she couldn't admit that she was a little scared of a restaurant and would much rather be with them making Charlotte's dinner.

So here she was. Sitting at a table in a restaurant for the first time in years, with Samir next to her, Toby and Ava sitting opposite. Ava was already waving to Luigi to bring them a bottle of wine. 'Four is a much better number,' she told them. 'It makes sense to get a bottle.'

'I don't drink,' said Samir. 'You know that.'

'Three then,' said Ava, undeterred. 'You can have the breadsticks.'

'I don't think I'll drink either,' said Grace.

'Yes, you will,' replied Ava. 'It's a special occasion.'

'Is it?'

'You're out with us,' Ava said, flashing a smile at Luigi as he twisted the cork from the bottle with a flourish. He smiled back at her. He was just a few years younger than them, at a guess, with a pleasant face and a comforting roundness to his belly. 'And we're not buying towels or painting tiny houses. That makes it a party.'

'It is nice to see you outside of the club, Grace,' said Toby. 'How's the ski lift coming along?'

'I haven't been able to work on my layout,' said Grace, with a heady mixture of shame and pride. 'My daughter and granddaughter are staying with me.'

'And you've not introduced me yet,' cut in Ava. 'The cool aunt.'

'They're still settling in,' replied Grace, taking a sip of the wine Ava had poured into her glass. She used to enjoy a drink, but she'd barely touched alcohol since Jonathan had become sick. It was more delicious than she remembered. She drank some more, realising that she was thirsty. Even though the white wine was chilled, it felt warm travelling down her throat, and she felt her face flush a little.

'Being a grandparent is better than being a parent,' declared Samir. 'All the love, none of the responsibility.'

'I don't know,' replied Grace. 'I think it might be worse.' She paused as Luigi approached again, notepad in hand. She took another sip of wine as she wondered what on earth to order.

'Have the spaghetti alle vongole,' Ava told her. Grace nodded, grateful to have the decision removed from her. 'Luigi gets his clams shipped from Napoli every day, don't you, Luigi?'

'Only the best for the best,' Luigi replied, and snuck a little wink at Ava. She grinned.

'How is being a grandparent worse?' asked Toby.

Grace drank some more wine and was surprised to see her glass almost empty. Ava refilled it. 'I don't just have to worry about whether I'm doing the right thing for Charlotte,' she said. 'I have to worry about whether I'm doing the right thing for Amelia. Because she's in charge, I'm just there trying not to get in the way.'

'It's your house,' said Ava.

'And her daughter.' Grace hiccuped and Samir offered her a breadstick. She took it and discovered that dried bread was more delicious than she'd anticipated. 'I have to decide what to do that is best for Charlotte and won't upset her mother, or be in any way critical, because she'll be upset if it looks like I'm saying she's not a good mother. And she is good and it's so hard for her right now.' Grace snapped her breadstick in two, sending crumbs flying into her lap. 'I have to be so careful all the time. It's exhausting.'

'How long are they staying?' asked Ava.

'It may sound odd, but I wish they'd stay forever,' said Grace, biting into her breadstick and aware of the contradiction. 'It's the best thing that's ever happened to me,' she added. 'I hear my daughter snoring and it just makes me so happy having her in the house. So happy and so nervous and so worried that I'll mess it up.'

'You won't mess it up,' said Ava, patting her hand. 'They're lucky to have you.'

They sat in silence for a moment. Grace crunched the remainder of her breadstick, feeling lucky to have met Ava.

'What does Charlotte think of your layout?' asked Toby.

'You and your trains!' scolded Ava. 'As if that matters.'

'I bet she's impressed,' he continued.

'I haven't shown her,' confessed Grace. 'It seems so silly, this train set in my shed. I'm a grown woman.'

'It's a miniature world!' said Toby. 'And you're so skilful in the club. I'd love to see it.'

Grace shrugged. 'Maybe I'll show her one day.' She tried to think of a way to change the subject, but her mind felt foggy, clouded already by the wine.

'Kids love that sort of thing,' said Toby. 'You should see the look in the eyes of the children who come to my shop. Usually the world is too big for them. They can't reach things, can't even open some doors. Then they see a model railway and they become the giants. They get to be in control. It's special.'

Grace didn't say anything, suddenly regretting the wine. She could feel her emotions too close to the surface, as if displaced from their usual hiding place by the alcohol.

'It could be a nice way to bond,' suggested Samir. 'I give everything I make to my grandson. He loves the trains the most; we're building the layout together.'

'Spaghetti alle vongole,' announced Luigi, and Grace found herself pleased to be distracted from the direction the conversation was taking. 'For the beautiful ladies. Pizza to follow for the gentlemen.'

In the clatter of plates and the refilling of glasses and the grinding of pepper, Grace was able to settle herself. By the time Luigi departed with instructions to bring more wine, she found herself gazing at a plate of spaghetti decorated with shells that looked as if they'd been collected from the beach. Confusion reigned for a moment, until she watched Ava lift one to her mouth and gently tip the contents inside. Grace carefully wound spaghetti around her fork and tried to transfer it to her mouth with minimal drippage.

It was delicious, she had to admit. She felt herself relaxing again. Cooking for her family was wonderful, but eating at a restaurant with friends certainly had its merits too. She decided not to refuse an invitation again. She took another sip of wine and allowed Ava to refill her glass.

Chapter 8

On Saturday morning, Charlotte was surprised that her grandmother wasn't out of bed to make her breakfast. Her mother had gone for a run, so Charlotte helped herself to a bowl of cornflakes, which she ate standing in the kitchen. She'd already told her mum that she was going out with Sammy this morning, so she put her bowl in the sink and went to find her shoes. As she left the house, she frowned at her grandmother's handbag, left casually on the floor with what looked like shiny seeds spilling out. The comfy leather shoes that Grace usually lined up neatly by the cupboard were kicked off at the bottom of the stairs and her coat was wrinkled on the floor.

Charlotte shrugged to herself, hung up the coat and headed out, waving to Sammy when she saw him standing on the corner. They fell into step together until they reached their destination. She clambered to the top of the metal fence. It was one of their many access points to the wilderness at the side of the train tracks, and the most challenging, but they didn't mind. She had to jump, catch the top of the fence at exactly the right point and then heave herself over. She swung her other leg up, then dropped to the bushes on the other side.

Sammy took the grubbier route, lying on his belly and shuffling under the fence, leaving a muddy mark on his already dirty T-shirt.

Both safely on the other side, Charlotte stopped to survey the expanse in front of her. Brambles and nettles were interspersed with crocuses and snowdrops. The last time she'd come, she'd seen a rabbit poking its head out of a large prickly bush. She and Sammy had watched it, transfixed, until it darted away again.

'Which bit shall we go to?' she mused out loud, but Sammy put his finger to his lips.

'It's time for the 10.10 to London Bridge,' he said. 'Can you hear it?'

Charlotte set off along the path they'd made the previous weekend, when they'd come prepared in thick coats and gloves, and wellington boots to trample down the nettles and brambles. The plants were already starting to grow back, and she stomped on an errant nettle lest it sting Sammy. She looked back at him, standing stock still and mesmerised by the train in the distance.

Sure enough, it rumbled past them. They stood well back from the tracks, but still Charlotte could feel a gust of wind as it went by.

Sammy watched it disappear around the corner and then ran to catch up with her, his breathing a little wheezy. 'Where's your inhaler?' she asked.

'Dropped it,' he said, wiping his nose on his sleeve. 'But I'm fine.'

'Don't you have a spare?'

'At home somewhere.'

'Shall we go back and fetch it?'

'Nah. Want to race?' He grinned at her.

'No,' said Charlotte, alarmed. 'And watch out for those brambles. You got horribly scratched last time.'

'I'm fine,' he said. 'I'm tougher than I look.'

Charlotte didn't reply at once. They hadn't been friends long, but already she wanted to wrap Sammy up in cotton wool with his inhaler in his mouth and keep him safe.

'Do you think the foxes have cubs yet?' she asked, instead.

'Maybe,' said Sammy. 'What do you call a baby fox with carrots in his ears?'

'I don't know,' said Charlotte, though of course she did.

'Anything you want,' said Sammy with a laugh. 'Because he can't hear you.'

Charlotte groaned, and the pair continued in comfortable silence.

'What's that?' Before she could stop him, Sammy had veered off the path and into the brambles.

'Come back,' she said, knowing it would have no effect. With a sigh, she put up her hood for protection and scrambled in after him.

There was more room than she'd thought inside the bush. The green leaves above them sheltered the earth and gave the area the feel of a secret cave. 'This can be our den,' announced Charlotte, very pleased with the find. 'We're completely hidden.'

Sammy was still rummaging around the edge of the bush. 'A ball,' he announced triumphantly, producing a well-weathered and rather sad-looking tennis ball. He threw it at Charlotte, who caught it instinctively then dropped it.

'It smells bad,' she said. 'And it's all sticky.'

'I'll give it to Ryan,' he said with a smirk. 'It smells just like him.'

Charlotte felt herself flush a little. She'd seen Sammy's oldest brother at school; fifteen and tall and confident, and found herself going red when he'd glanced at her. She prayed Sammy didn't notice. 'What was that sound?' she asked, grateful for a distraction.

'It's not time for another train,' said Sammy, tossing the ball into the air and trying to hit it with his head. 'Ouch.'

'Shush,' said Charlotte. She heard the sound again, a little squeak. Or a squawk. This time it came with the rustle of leaves, and she turned towards the movement.

Sammy must have heard it too, because he stopped throwing the ball and scrambled behind Charlotte. 'Could it be a fox cub?' he asked.

'I think it sounds feathery.'

'How can something sound feathery?'

'Shush.' Charlotte crawled forward and peered into the bushes.

A tiny eye peered back. Very carefully, Charlotte reached her hand into the undergrowth. 'Come on, little one,' she said. 'I just want to help you.' The creature didn't try to escape, and she gently took hold of it. The bird was pink and scrawny, with fluffy brown feathers poking out and a bright yellow beak. It was tiny and warm and she held it to her chest.

'What is that?' exclaimed Sammy.

'It's a baby bird,' said Charlotte. 'It must have fallen out of its nest. Look, there's its beak and a bit of feather.' Its wiry feet gripped her cupped fingers as if they were a branch, and its wing buds pushed against her palms. It was shaking, and she could feel its heart beating ever so fast. She held it a little tighter to offer reassurance. 'You'll be OK,' she told the bird, marvelling at how tiny it was. 'We'll look after you.'

'How?' asked Sammy. 'I bet your mum won't let you keep it. And it wouldn't last five minutes around my brothers.'

'It doesn't have anyone else,' she said. 'It must have got lost here. Maybe its parents abandoned it.'

She thought for a moment of her father. 'I'm going to take it home,' she said, cradling the bird in her hands. 'I saw a cardboard box by the fence. It can live in there under my bed and I'll feed it scraps from dinner. Grandma will help me.' The bird cheeped its assent, and Charlotte felt a little burst of pleasure in her heart. She was going to save this bird.

'It's eleven.' Grace blinked her eyes open to see her daughter, who'd opened the curtain and was looking at her, amusement spread over her face. 'Here's a glass of water.'

'What are you doing in my room?' asked Grace, lifting her head from the pillow and then sinking it back down again. She felt confused, not quite remembering her journey home. Was this the onset of Alzheimer's? Was another symptom the pain in her head and the terrible taste in her mouth?

'I thought you were making a vegetarian lasagne today?' said Amelia, sitting down on the bed. 'You were full of your plans when you got home last night.'

Last night.

'Apparently some guy called Luigi gave you a recipe.'

'Yes, of course,' said Grace, as it came back to her. 'Luigi's lasagne recipe.'

'And I thought it was Dad who liked his beer.'

'It was,' said Grace. 'But last night was . . . a special occasion.'

'I'll put the coffee on, party girl,' said Amelia with a laugh. 'But let's order pizza tonight, shall we?'

'Perhaps that would be best,' said Grace, though the thought of pizza made her stomach turn. 'I think maybe something I ate didn't agree with me.'

'Of course,' said Amelia as she left the room. 'Something you ate.'

Grace turned over and tried to get back to sleep. Her dreams had been full of days at the beach and toy trains and fresh apples from the greengrocer. She closed her eyes firmly, ignoring the insistence of a full bladder, hoping that the throbbing in her head would subside if she blocked out the light.

Days at the beach. One day in particular. Grace found memories bubbling up in her like the foam of a wave. 'Why are you wearing a shirt and tie?' she'd asked Jonathan, on that special holiday, years ago. 'I thought we were going for a stroll along the sand?'

'I can look smart, can't I?' Jonathan had objected.

'I suppose,' said Grace. 'It's winter in Margate, so I don't suppose we'll be swimming.'

'You do like it here, don't you?' said Jonathan, sounding suddenly anxious. 'Do you wish we'd gone on one of those package holidays to the Costa Blanca that they're doing now?'

'Of course I like it,' Grace replied, meaning it. They'd been together for almost a year at that point, and Jonathan had been planning this trip for weeks. The hotel was nicer than anywhere she'd stayed before, with a rather grand four-poster bed squeezed into the room as if Henry VIII had passed through before them. 'It's perfect.'

Jonathan grinned like a maniac at that comment. 'Come on then,' he'd said. 'Let's go for that walk on the beach now. It's meant to rain later.'

They walked. It was cold, the sea wind lashing at their faces, but Jonathan was sweating as if they had gone to Benidorm after all. It was hard going, their feet sinking into the sand with each step, as though they were walking on a planet with an extra gravitational pull.

They'd been down by the water, the grey waves echoing the colour of the sky. Jonathan was looking out to sea. Grace could feel the beginnings of rain kissing her cheeks, and she turned to him, about to suggest that they went back.

He wasn't there.

'Marry me,' came a voice, and she realised that he had sunk to one knee, right there on the wet sand. He was holding something in his hand, a box lined with plush red velvet housing a small diamond ring. 'I love you,' he said. 'I love you so much. Marry me.'

Grace found herself concerned for his trousers, surely getting damp down there. An overly enthusiastic wave was all it would take to soak him right through, maybe even wash away that ring.

'Get up,' she said. 'The tide's coming in.'

Jonathan didn't move. She watched his teeth close, biting on his lips. 'Is . . . is that a no?'

'No,' she replied, then saw his face contort. 'No, I mean, it's not a no. I love you!'

'It's a yes then,' he grinned, getting to his feet and enclosing her in a hug, which he released only to redirect his face from her neck to plant a kiss on her mouth. Grace kissed him back, a salty kiss that tasted of joy and the sea and ever so slightly of the kippers that Jonathan had eaten for breakfast. He took her hand and placed the ring on her finger. She felt it gripping her tightly, safe and firm and full of love as the rain continued.

The thought of rain was too much for Grace's bladder, and she pulled herself out of bed and hurried to the bathroom, fears for her hip replaced by the necessity of reaching the toilet in time.

Amelia smiled to herself as she made coffee, rather enjoying the role reversal. She remembered creeping back into the house as a teenager, trying not to slur her speech if her parents were still up and waiting for her. Attempting to tell a coherent and innocent version of her evening that certainly didn't include seven Bacardi Breezers and a snog with Rahul from the year above. Waking bleary-eyed at midday and finding a cool glass of water next to her bed.

She poured herself a cup of coffee, and one for her mother. She felt good this morning; she'd already been for a run, her second in two days, and she could feel the endorphins still pumping through her body. Much better than a hangover.

Charlotte seemed happier too, out with a new friend she'd made. It hadn't taken her long, and Amelia felt a flush of pride that her adaptable daughter was doing so well.

In the circumstances.

She glanced at her phone. Tom still hadn't called her back.

Unacceptable, she decided. She could hear her mother running water in the bathroom upstairs.

She'd try again.

He answered straight away this time. 'Hi, Amelia. I was just about to call you.' He paused. 'Listen. I'm sorry about our last chat. Quizzing you about shoes instead of asking after Charlotte. I've been under a lot of pressure, things are so tough here . . .'

Amelia knew how that felt. But then she also knew he had been lying. 'Tough with Steve?' she asked, unable to help herself.

'Tough everywhere,' he replied. 'How is Charlotte? How are you?'

'How is Steve?' she countered.

'What's this obsession with Steve?' he replied. 'I want to talk about my daughter.'

'Maybe I should bring her for a visit,' said Amelia. 'If Steve wouldn't mind. Because that's where you said you were staying, wasn't it? With Steve?'

'Yes,' said Tom. 'But you can't visit, I'm afraid.'

There it was. 'Because Steve is in Australia,' finished Amelia. 'And that means you are . . .?'

A pause. 'I'm flat-sitting for him while he's away.'

'What?'

'He's got an empty flat,' said Tom. 'And I needed a place to stay.' Amelia bit her lip, feeling like an idiot. Of course. That made sense. 'Why? What did you think?'

'Nothing,' she lied. She took a sip of coffee, thinking. 'So why can't we visit?'

'I need to go away,' said Tom. 'For work. I've got a potential investor in Scotland, and I need to spend some time with him.'

'Can you come and see Charlotte before you go?' asked Amelia. 'She misses you.' In truth, she wanted to see him too. Especially now she knew he hadn't been lying to her, at least about that. It changed things.

'I've got so much prep to do,' said Tom. 'And I need to leave on Monday.'

'Charlotte will be disappointed,' she said, wondering how she'd explain this to her daughter.

Tom hesitated. 'I'm sorry, Amelia, I really want to see her. But this is my chance to turn things around. I don't want to mess it up.'

'How long will you be gone for?'

'A few weeks? I'm not sure,' he replied. 'But I'll call. And Charley knows she can call me too. Any time.'

'Yes,' replied Amelia. She could hear her mother coming down the stairs. 'Well then,' she said. 'We'll see you when you get back.'

She hung up and thought a moment, then allowed herself a deep exhale. He hadn't been lying, not about this at least.

It wasn't much, and he wasn't going to win father of the year. But it still made her smile.

Sammy and Charlotte walked the long way to get out of the wilderness, going via the railway platform. Charlotte didn't want to clamber over the fence with her precious cargo. She held back the loose piece of wire and Sammy went through, then he did the same for her.

It was Saturday lunchtime now, and the platform was nearly empty. One man stood near the edge with his back to them, his grey raincoat blowing in the wind. There was something familiar about the coat, and Charlotte stopped to have a look at him.

'He'll be waiting a long time,' said Sammy. 'The next train doesn't stop here, it's fast all the way to Waterloo.'

The man turned at the sound of Sammy's voice.

'Mr Brown!' exclaimed Charlotte, delighted. 'What are you doing here?' Mr Brown blinked at them through his glasses in surprise. 'It's me,' she told him. 'Charlotte. And Sammy. I bet you don't recognise us outside of school.'

'Of course I do,' said Mr Brown. He seemed distracted. 'Hi, Sammy.'

Sammy grimaced. 'No teachers at the weekend,' he whispered to Charlotte. 'All week long is bad enough.'

'Where are you going?' asked Charlotte, ignoring him.

'Nowhere,' replied Mr Brown.

'But you're waiting for a train.'

'Oh yes,' he said, as if surprised to find himself at the station.

'There isn't one for . . .' Sammy looked at his watch, 'an hour and twenty minutes.'

'Oh,' said Mr Brown. 'Thank you.' He looked like he was going to leave. The bird cheeped from Charlotte's hands, but Mr Brown didn't seem to notice.

'Do you want to see what I'm holding?' asked Charlotte.

'It's a bit funny-looking,' said Sammy.

'It's a baby bird.' Charlotte held out her hands, opening them a fraction. The bird peeked out. 'I rescued it,' she told him. 'I'm going to nurse it back to health.'

Mr Brown looked at the bird and seemed to think for a few moments. 'I'm afraid that's not a very good idea,' he said. 'Its chances of survival would be very low. I'm sorry.'

Charlotte felt her eyes prickle with tears. 'Isn't there anything I can do? I promised I'd save it.'

'Sorry,' said Mr Brown. 'It's just too little to make it without its mum.'

'There must be something?'

Mr Brown hesitated again. 'Maybe,' he said. 'Did you see the nest?' Charlotte shook her head. 'But you remember where you found it?'

'Of course.'

'The best thing you can do is try and put it back in its nest. Its parents might still look after it.'

'But it smells like Charley now,' said Sammy.

'Birds have a poor sense of smell,' said Mr Brown. 'They won't mind.' He turned away.

'Come with us,' said Charlotte, eager to enlist every assistance for her bird. 'You can help.'

'I'm not sure I can.'

'What if the nest is up a tree and Sammy and I can't reach? You're much taller.'

'I can climb the tree,' said Sammy.

'Come on, sir, please? Your train isn't coming for ages,' she added. 'You might as well.'

Mr Brown cast a look back to the tracks. 'OK,' he said. Charlotte grinned at him.

It was a bit of a feat fitting Mr Brown through the gap in the loose wire fence. He wasn't fat and was fairly young by teacher standards, but he was a lot bigger than Charlotte and Sammy. They managed it eventually with only a small tear in his coat that he didn't seem to mind. He followed them through the wilderness and listened politely as Charlotte pointed out the landmarks: an old Doc Marten that housed a spider's nest, a fallen tree trunk that was very good for sitting on, and a hole that Charlotte suspected led to a rabbit warren.

They reached the bramble den, and Mr Brown peered around.

'There,' he said, finally, looking upwards. 'See that little collection of twigs?' Charlotte nodded. 'That must be its nest.' He paused. 'Hear that sound?' She nodded again. It was a frantic tweeting. 'That's its parents. They know it has gone and are looking for it. Blackbirds.'

'How do you know?'

'Each bird has its own call,' he replied.

'Every train sounds different too,' agreed Sammy.

Charlotte looked at Mr Brown. 'Can you reach?'

'No,' he said. 'Blackbirds tend to build their nests fairly low down, but that one is rather higher than usual.' He hesitated. 'Do you think you could climb on my shoulders?'

'I haven't been on anyone's shoulders since …' Charlotte stopped herself. Since her dad had left.

'Let's have a go.'

It was an awkward manoeuvre, but somehow Charlotte, clutching the bird with both hands and with her thighs wrapped around Mr Brown's neck, found herself lifted up into the tree. 'I see the nest,' she said. 'Just a little higher. Can you stand on tiptoe?'

They wobbled but managed it. Charlotte gave the bird a kiss. 'Good luck,' she said, and popped it back into the nest. It cheeped at her, and she heard a little chorus of other tweets too. Its brothers and sisters, sounding delighted to have their errant sibling back.

Mr Brown lowered her to the ground. 'We need to give them some space,' he said, his voice quiet. 'The mother won't come back while we're here.'

Charlotte threw her arms around his neck. His face felt stubbly and warm, just like her father's. He even smelled similar. 'Thank you,' she said. 'Thank you for saving the baby chick.'

'Yuck,' said Sammy. 'You kissed a teacher.'

Charlotte disentangled herself immediately, feeling horribly embarrassed at her actions. It was like when she'd once accidentally called a teacher 'Mum' at her old school and the whole class had laughed.

'Sorry, sir,' she mumbled.

'It's OK, Charlotte,' said Mr Brown. He paused. 'That bird is not out of the woods,' he added, 'but we've given it the best chance.' He smiled at her. 'You've saved a life today. Perhaps. Now let's leave the birds to it.'

'We can come back and check on it tomorrow,' said Charlotte.

Mr Brown didn't reply.

'Can't we?' she pushed. 'You too.'

'We'll see,' replied Mr Brown.

'Pizza time!' Amelia opened the box. She hadn't cooked, but for once she was responsible for their dinner, and in a small way, it felt empowering. It hadn't been easy, either. Deliveroo hadn't made it to this part of Kent, so she'd resorted to Google to find the best pizza in the area. 'Come get some while it's hot.'

Charlotte practically bounced into the room and Grace trudged behind her. 'Can we eat it straight from the box like at home?' her daughter asked, as Grace opened the cupboard to fetch plates.

'Sure,' said Amelia. 'Let's give the dishwasher a break.' She watched her mother as she took a slice of pizza awkwardly, clearly not used to eating a hot meal without a knife and fork. As she bit into it, the cheese slid off. She looked around, helpless for a moment, until Amelia handed her a paper towel. 'You seem much brighter, Mum,' she said. 'Have you recovered?'

'I'm not as young as I used to be,' said Grace, making Charlotte giggle. 'And the club isn't normally like that,' she added quickly. 'Ava insisted on a second bottle, and Samir doesn't drink, so it was just Ava, Toby and me, and then after dinner Luigi brought out this bright yellow bottle that reminded me of citrus cleaning fluid but was somehow also delicious.'

'Limoncello,' said Amelia, remembering a warm summer evening with Tom in Sorrento early in their marriage, gazing out at the sea as they sipped on the potent liquor that made her think of lemon blossom.

She reached out and took a piece of pizza to distract herself from the memories. It was greasier than the ones she was used to back in London, and the base wasn't even made from sourdough. She glanced at Charlotte, who was already starting on her second slice. 'I spoke to your dad earlier,' she said.

'When is he visiting?'

'Not for a while,' said Amelia carefully. 'He has to go to Scotland to see an investor.'

'Oh,' said Charlotte. She paused. 'When will he be back?'

'I don't know,' replied Amelia. 'But it's good news for the business,' she added weakly. She took another bite of her pizza. 'How was your day?' she asked, keen to get back to positive subjects.

'Brilliant,' her daughter replied. 'Sammy and I went to the wilderness like I told you we would, and we found a baby bird that had fallen out of its nest, and Mr Brown helped us save it.'

'Mr Brown?' queried Amelia. 'Your teacher was there?'

'My favourite teacher,' corrected Charlotte. 'He knows all about birds, as well as bats and dolphins.'

'But why was he with you?'

'He was waiting on the platform,' said Charlotte. 'And he said he'd come back and help us check on the bird again.'

'I don't know if you should be hanging around with strange men in isolated places,' said Amelia, making a mental note to talk to this Mr Brown.

'It's OK,' said Charlotte. 'He's a vegetarian.'

Amelia couldn't help but laugh at this. 'Even so,' she said.

'And Sammy was there too,' Charlotte added. 'And it's not like Mr Brown's a stranger.'

'Perhaps I'll come too, if your teacher will be there,' said Amelia. 'It would be nice to meet him.'

'I've met him,' said Grace. 'He seemed nice.'

'You'll like him,' Charlotte told her, and Amelia was pleased that she didn't seem fazed at the prospect of her mother joining her. 'I think he's even nicer than the teachers at my old school. He's quite young and he's cool.'

'Chilled,' contributed Grace, seeming pleased with herself.

Charlotte and Amelia looked at each other for a moment, then started to laugh. 'What's so funny?' asked Grace. 'I used it right, didn't I?'

'Well done, Mum,' said Amelia through her giggles. She took another slice of pizza. There was no buffalo mozzarella or sun-dried tomatoes, but it did taste good. Things might not be perfect back in her childhood home, but for a moment, with the taste of pizza filling her mouth and the sound of Charlotte's laughter in her ears, nothing seemed quite so bad.

Chapter 9

'Charlotte. Perhaps you can tell us?'

Charlotte tore her eyes from the window, where she'd been watching a blackbird plucking worms from the playground planters. The crocuses were emerging, the bright flowers reaching upwards as if they wanted to gulp down the sunshine. She wondered if her own bird was hungry.

Mr Brown hadn't come back to meet them. He hadn't been at school all last week either, and she hadn't known what to do for her bird.

Worms, of course.

She could catch worms and throw them up to it. They didn't seem terribly appetising to her, but each to their own. She knew that mother birds would normally eat the worms and then regurgitate them for their chicks, but was that stage in the process strictly necessary?

Mr Brown would know.

But where was he? He wasn't scheduled a holiday that she knew of, and the other teachers were filling in between supply teachers. No one seemed happy about the situation.

Sammy nudged her and Charlotte looked up. Mrs Varga was still looking at her, her face contorting into a frown. 'Earth to Charlotte?'

'What?'

'Exactly. What's the answer?'

'Sorry, miss, what was the question?'

Mrs Varga tutted. 'See me after class. Daniel, any ideas?'

The repugnant Daniel knew the answer, of course, which turned out to be igneous rock. For a moment, Charlotte wondered what the question had been, then she gave up and turned back to the window.

Sammy slipped a picture to her, and Charlotte smiled. It was recognisably Mrs Varga, but her pretty face was adorned with black teeth, a pointy hat and a bulbous wart on her nose. Normally Charlotte rather liked Mrs Varga, but she'd been in a bad mood for the last week or so.

The bell rang and everyone leapt up, even though Mrs Varga was still talking.

'Not you,' said Mrs Varga, as Charlotte tried to make her escape. The others left her to her fate. 'Not concentrating in class?' asked Mrs Varga, perching on the edge of Charlotte's desk. 'You've not been here long, but already I know that's not like you.' Her voice was softer than when she was teaching. Charlotte looked at her. She had dark circles under her eyes.

'Sorry, miss,' said Charlotte. She paused. 'When's Mr Brown coming back?' she asked. 'You're friends, aren't you? I've seen you together in the playground.'

'Watching us, are you?' Mrs Varga's voice had changed again. It was hard now, like chalk.

'Where's he gone?'

'He's taking some time off.'

'Why?'

Mrs Varga sighed. 'He's probably exhausted by you lot and your constant questions.'

'But why didn't he tell us he was going?'

'He doesn't need to ask your permission,' replied Mrs Varga. She paused. 'He's not himself,' she conceded.

'What does that mean?'

'I told you, he's taking some time off.'

'Is he sick?'

'Listen, I really don't think—'

'Is he abroad?'

'This really is none of your business.'

Charlotte opened her mouth to disagree, but something in Mrs Varga's face stopped her. 'Sorry, miss,' she said instead.

'Pay attention in class next time,' said the teacher, waving her from the room. Charlotte turned to look at her, watching as Mrs Varga sank into her chair. She looked sad.

Grace sat in her granddaughter's room and watched the stick insects. Charlotte had explained how to tell them apart. Apparently Hugo had a shorter body with a little kink at the end of his tail. Or was that one Pickle? Either way, they struck her as rather inadequate pets for Charlotte. She couldn't stroke them, not really, and taking them for a walk involved the insects crawling with some alarm from one of her hands to the other, their sticky feet defying the laws of gravity.

Still, they were better than nothing, and Grace often found herself in this room during the day, watching them munch on leaves, processing them through their bodies and then emitting the remains in neat little black pellets. She was otherwise alone in the house; Amelia went to the office most days, despite the long commute, and Charlotte was at school.

It wasn't like before, though. Her guests had been with her almost a month now, and there were signs of them everywhere. Grace cleaned, feeling like she was snooping as she made beds and fished dirty clothes from the laundry baskets, and cooked, building an ever-expanding repertoire of vegetarian delights. The things people could do with fungus these days had been eye-opening for her. The world had changed.

'I bet Charlotte's bird would rather eat you than a mushroom,' she told Pickle, or possibly Hugo, as one of the creatures crawled up the glass in her direction. Charlotte's obsession with that bird was matched only by her alarm at Mr Brown's failure to return to school. Grace had met him when she'd picked Charlotte up one day in her first week of school; a young, pleasant man with a nervous manner that made her think of Jonathan.

The sound of the neighbour's dog barking outside excited the stick insects, and they both started their balletic progress upwards. 'Marriage,' Grace had said all those years ago, when she accepted Jonathan's proposal, testing out the word and everything that came with it. A wedding, a house.

A baby.

'My career,' she'd said, twisting the ring on her finger.

'I'm not asking you to give anything up,' Jonathan had said, pulling her further from the sea, which had started to lap dangerously close to their shoes. 'I've thought about that.' He smiled at her. 'If anyone can do it all, it's you.' He grinned again. 'Us now.'

'But . . .'

'We'll make it work,' he said. 'I'll do whatever it takes to make you happy.'

He had. He'd done his best, at least.

Grace twisted the ring on her finger and watched the stick insects, who had paused in their walk and were as still as the sticks from which they took their name. She could practically taste the sea air, even now, as they'd made that decision. That was what love was, that was how husbands and fathers should be.

Amelia was on her own now. A wave of anger hit Grace that her daughter didn't have a worthy husband. He still hadn't visited Charlotte. Grace couldn't help but think that more than just guilt at bankrupting his family was keeping him away. She hoped she was wrong.

And she also found herself hoping that Mr Brown, at least, would come back soon. Charlotte was already missing her father; it didn't seem fair that another man had disappeared from her life, even if it was only a teacher.

Tom needed to visit; Charlotte needed her father. Frequently Grace wanted to ask Amelia when he'd be back

But she didn't. Was needing a father an old-fashioned notion? She knew that families came in different shapes and sizes these days. Amelia and Jonathan had doted on each other. Their relationship had seemed so simple, so easy. They'd loved one another, enjoyed each other's company, never seemed to argue. Grace loved Amelia with a ferocity that terrified her, but as she got older, she felt like her relationship with her daughter was fragile, as if she were walking above a ravine on a thin sheet of glass that could fracture at any moment.

The dog barked again, and an idea landed in her mind as if it had been flung there by one of the stick insects. She stood up so decisively that she knocked the tank and Pickle (or Hugo) fell from his leaf. She couldn't bring Tom back, but perhaps she could give Charlotte something else she wanted.

Maybe not quite what she wanted, but a trial run. A connection.

She apologised to the insects, then set off.

Charlotte and Sammy had gone to the wilderness by the tracks and Sammy was hacking at the soil as they searched for worms to feed to the bird.

He paused. 'That worm is wriggling all funny,' he said. 'And that one.'

They were digging underneath the tree that contained the nest.

The soil was still soft from recent rainfall, but Charlotte only had three worms in her bucket, a disappointing haul. She'd been practising her aim and was planning to fling them into the nest so that her baby bird and its siblings could gobble them up.

She came over to him. 'I think that used to be one worm,' she said, watching the panicked wriggle and abrupt ending of the two worm halves, mystified at their new situation. 'And you've chopped it in two with your spade when you were digging.'

Sammy looked as though he might be sick.

'The birds won't mind,' said Charlotte. 'And I'm not sure the worms understand.'

'Can't we go and watch the trains?'

'Let's get a few more first,' said Charlotte, wishing she'd thought of feeding worms to the baby birds earlier. 'They're probably so hungry.'

'But they've got their parents to feed them.'

'You never know,' said Charlotte. 'Maybe their parents are busy.'

'OK,' said Sammy. He went back to digging.

'We'll have to fling the worms into the nest,' said Charlotte. 'Are you any good at throwing?'

'No,' said Sammy. 'Are you?'

'Not really.' Charlotte paused. 'If Mr Brown was here, he could have lifted me up and I could have fed the birds by hand.' She loved that idea, checking on her bird, lowering the worm into its open beak.

'What did Mrs Varga say was wrong with him?'

'That he isn't himself,' said Charlotte. 'Whatever that means. Right. Here goes.'

Carefully she took hold of a large worm that was attempting to scale the bucket wall back to freedom. It recoiled from her fingers, but she held it firmly. 'Sorry,' she told it. 'But it is for a good cause.' She squinted upwards and flung it into the air.

It flew right over the nest and landed in the bushes on the other side.

'Oops,' said Sammy.

'I saw where it landed,' she said. 'I'll fetch it and try again. You watch the others.' She went to where she'd seen a leaf shake and crouched on the wet earth, peering under the bush.

Something else caught her eye, glinting in the sunlight. She reached in and grabbed it.

'Glasses,' said Sammy, as she pulled them out and peeled a leaf from the frame. The glass was covered in mud, which Charlotte wiped with her coat. Underneath, the lens was fractured. She ran her fingertip along the cracks, the shape echoing the pattern of a spider's web.

'Do you recognise them?' she asked.

'They do look familiar,' said Sammy.

'These are Mr Brown's glasses,' she said. 'I'm sure of it.' She looked at them again. 'Look, they even have that bit of Sellotape wrapped around the right side, from when he sat on them in class after Marlon sneaked them onto his chair. Remember?'

'You're right,' said Sammy.

'We were here with him,' she added. 'When he helped us save the bird. But they didn't fall off then. We'd have noticed.'

'He'd have noticed too,' said Sammy.

'He must have come back to check on the bird,' said Charlotte, feeling full of affection for her teacher. She'd known he wouldn't abandon them. 'These glasses are broken,' she said. 'Like they've been hit with some force.' She paused. 'Have you ever seen Mr Brown without his specs?' she asked, her voice anxious.

'No,' replied Sammy. 'Never.'

Charlotte and Sammy walked slowly back from the wilderness with their discovery. She'd wrapped the glasses in an empty

Sainsbury's bag that she'd pulled from the edge of the track, and she could feel their outline through the muddy orange plastic.

'You do realise this is a clue,' she said.

'What do you mean?'

'Mr Brown is meant to be sick. But people who are sick don't normally leave their glasses, smashed, under a bird's nest by the side of the train tracks. They leave them by their bed while they eat chicken soup and recover.'

'*You* don't eat chicken soup. You're vegetarian. And you said he was too.'

'Tomato, then,' said Charlotte. 'But you know what I mean.' She paused. 'It's suspicious.'

They stopped walking and looked at each other. 'He could have dropped them, trodden on them by accident and then went home feeling sick?' said Sammy.

'It's one of the possibilities,' said Charlotte. She thought of her adventure books. 'But there are others.'

'Like what?'

She paused. 'Something could have hit him, and he lost his memory and forgot where he lived,' she said. That had apparently happened to Drago before he started in *Love Shack.* He'd confessed it, teary-eyed, to Anita before he'd leaned in for a noisy kiss that had made Charlotte's stomach turn and had been the subject of intense analysis between her old friends at school the next day.

Sammy frowned at her.

'Or he could have been abducted, and the glasses lost in the process,' continued Charlotte, warming to her theme.

'When my dad left, it was because he went to prison,' said Sammy.

'Really?' asked Charlotte, stopping in her tracks.

'Not for murder or anything exciting,' elaborated Sammy. 'Something to do with some dodgy tellies.'

'Oh,' replied Charlotte, deciding not to tell her mum. She paused. 'I don't think Mr Brown would do anything like that,' she said.

'Probably not,' conceded Sammy.

'Maybe he has money trouble,' said Charlotte. 'And is having to work really hard with a Scottish investor.' She wasn't sure exactly what this entailed, but it did seem to involve being absent.

'But he's a teacher.'

She shrugged off the objection. Her mind was whirring; making connections.

'Well, see you tomorrow,' said Sammy as they reached the fork in the road.

'Come over,' suggested Charlotte, not ready to drop the topic just yet. 'We've got loads to talk about.'

'It's nearly dinner time.'

'My grandma is making vegetarian chicken and mushroom pie, with chocolate sponge for dessert.'

'My mum said we're having beans on toast again,' Sammy told her.

'Eat with us. You can call your mum from my place to check she doesn't mind.'

'She won't mind,' said Sammy, grinning at her. 'If your grandma won't?'

'Course not,' said Charlotte. She smiled back at him, feeling rather pleased to be able to invite a friend round, spur of the moment like this. In their old house, her mother pretended it was fine but always seemed put out, retreating into her bedroom with her laptop while Charlotte and her friends searched the cupboard for crisps.

It wouldn't be like that here. She could already visualise her grandma's face, welcoming and fussing around them and offering Sammy seconds of cake. 'And you can meet Pickle and Hugo,' she added. 'They can help us make our investigation plan.'

'Investigation plan?' queried Sammy.

'Yes,' replied Charlotte. 'For Operation Find Mr Brown.'

Grace was brushing egg yolk onto the rather magnificent pie she had made. She liked baking; it reminded her, in a somewhat roundabout way, of her old job. Experimenting with different materials, seeing how they reacted to one another, how heating them changed their state. She was just wondering whether she should try to fashion some stick insect decorations from the pastry trimmings when she heard Charlotte come through the door.

'Hi, Grandma. Can Sammy stay for tea?' she asked. Grace looked. Sure enough, behind Charlotte there stood a small boy, grinning at her.

'Of course,' she said, feeling rather proud that Charlotte wanted to invite a friend to her house. It meant she felt comfortable, and settled perhaps, and was maybe even a sign that she wasn't ashamed of her grandmother.

She smiled back at the boy. 'Hello, Sammy. I hope you like mock chicken pie.'

'I'm not sure,' he replied. 'But I definitely like chocolate sponge.'

Grace laughed. 'That's dessert,' she said.

'He's got to call his mum,' said Charlotte. 'And I want to show him Pickle and Hugo.'

Grace nodded as the children left the room, and wondered how this affected dinner plans. The pie was huge, but should she add a starter? More vegetables?

Little boys didn't like vegetables, she thought, remembering. Then she stopped herself. This little boy would likely be completely different. She was generalising. She looked in the fridge and fished out a head of broccoli, then, feeling indulgent, got the box of fish-shaped crackers from the cupboard and emptied them into a bowl.

She filled two glasses with apple juice and put them on a tray with the crackers to carry to Charlotte's bedroom. Dinner would be at least half an hour, and she didn't want them to get too hungry.

She knocked on the door, balancing the tray rather deftly on one hand, then pushed it open. Sammy was sitting on the bed with two stick insects dangling from his arm. He looked up and grinned at her again. He was a smiley thing, thought Grace, unable to help but smile back. 'I see you're an animal lover like Charlotte,' she said, setting down the tray. Charlotte was at her desk, writing something in her notebook with a very serious expression.

'Animals are OK,' he replied. 'But it's trains I love.'

'Trains?' repeated Grace.

'Yes,' said Sammy. 'I want to be a train driver when I'm older.'

'I'm going to be a vet,' chipped in Charlotte. 'Or maybe a detective.' She looked up and saw her grandmother's face. 'Are you OK?'

'I need to check on the pie,' said Grace, leaving the room.

Chapter 10

'I don't understand,' said Sammy, after school the next day. 'Why do I have to vomit?'

'You don't have to vomit,' explained Charlotte. 'You just have to pretend to have a stomach ache to distract Miss Conti while I creep into the office. I had a good peek earlier when I brought the register back and there's a filing cabinet over there that has "Teachers" written on the label. I just need a minute and hopefully I can get Mr Brown's address.' She'd thought long and hard about where to start her investigation, and checking that he wasn't at home in bed seemed a lot more straightforward than uncovering a kidnapping, even if it was somewhat less exciting.

'I probably could vomit,' offered Sammy. 'If I use my fingers.'

'No vomit,' said Charlotte, her voice firm. 'Come on.'

It was after school. Charlotte and Sammy had stayed late, ostensibly for art club but really so that they could sneak into the office while Miss Conti was alone. They had ten minutes before Charlotte's grandma was due to pick her up for whatever surprise she'd organised, and Charlotte was determined to use the time wisely.

'Gahahwah,' shouted Sammy, clutching his stomach.

'Miss Conti!' called Charlotte. 'Sammy's sick.'

'I'm going to vomit,' he said. Charlotte tried not to tut as she disappeared around a corner and peered back round.

Miss Conti looked up from painting her nails and sighed. 'Come on,' she said, giving her nails a quick blow. 'Let's get you on one of these comfy seats and find a bucket.' She glanced at her watch and sighed. 'The school nurse will have gone home.' She looked peeved at having sole responsibility for this.

'Blahahwah!' Sammy looked up. 'Can I have a glass of water?'

'OK.' Miss Conti made her way to the staff kitchen, the sound of her heels clacking along the industrial school flooring. Charlotte slipped into the office. She pulled on the drawer. It didn't open, and for a moment she worried it was locked. She tugged again, and it gave way. It was just an errant file blocking the drawer's smooth passage along its rail.

Miss Conti kept her files in impressive order, sorted alphabetically. It took Charlotte but a moment's leafing to find Mr Brown's. There it was. A thin brown folder. She opened it. She only had time to grab the first sheet and tuck it into her pocket when she heard Miss Conti returning.

She slipped out of the office, trying to look innocent.

'Your water,' said Miss Conti, handing the glass to Sammy. He gulped it down and looked at Charlotte, his face a question. She nodded and tapped her pocket.

'All better now,' he said with a grin. 'Thanks, miss.'

Miss Conti looked rather relieved at the miraculous recovery as she took back the glass and inspected her nails. 'Shall I call your mum?'

'I'll look after him,' said Charlotte sweetly, in a voice that she hoped suggested she would never dream of stealing a teacher's details. 'Goodbye, miss.'

*

Amelia sat at her desk, reviewing the material from the agency again. It was good. The campaign was developing brilliantly now, and they'd really paid attention to the notes she'd written so carefully. She closed her eyes a moment, visualising the campaign in her head. The adverts were so striking, and she could already imagine how strongly it would work on social media. She needed to present it to the board of trustees, but she could tell that with the right set-up, they'd love it as much as she did.

It was just the copy that needed tweaking. She began typing, trying to include the words that had tested so well in her audience research. It flowed out of her, as if the language had been sitting in her brain all this time, just waiting for a chance to escape.

She typed in the call to action with a flourish, then sat back to admire her words. It seemed so right to her, but she decided she needed a second opinion. 'Paula,' she called. 'Will you have a look at something for me?'

Paula came over and Amelia got up to allow her to sit down. She looked at her team, everyone apparently absorbed in their work. She glanced at the picture of Charlotte that she kept on her desk, and realised that she hadn't thought about what to do about Tom, or her situation, for at least an hour. That might be a new record. She hadn't heard from him again since he'd told her about Scotland, and didn't want to interrupt him while he was busy. It sounded like he might be able to turn things around, and although there was much more to their break than the money, she couldn't help but think that financial recovery could be the start of something else. Something slow, but something nonetheless.

She hadn't looked at her watch either, knowing that Grace had after-school plans for Charlotte. Say what she would about her mother, she was reliable. If she said she'd pick Charlotte up, she would. She might not get things quite right, but at least she'd be there when she said she would.

Amelia breathed out heavily, feeling a sense of freedom. Today she would stay at work until she'd completed everything she wanted to, no hurrying out to make a disappointing spaghetti bolognese or to search the local shops for non-existent veggie sausages.

'It's brilliant,' said Paula, looking up and smiling. 'A game-changer.'

'You really think so?' said Amelia, trying not to look too proud.

'The phone lines will be ringing off the hook,' Paula said. 'And before you say anything, it's just an expression. I know it's all online.' She laughed. 'You'll break the internet,' she added.

'I doubt that,' said Amelia. 'Not with our budget.' But she smiled. It felt good to have the time to devote to her work again; it made her feel more like herself, the self she'd been before she'd had to slow everything down to make time for her family. 'But thanks,' she added. 'I do like the campaign.'

'Everyone will,' said Paula confidently as she got up to allow Amelia to sit back in her chair. 'And you're coming to my fundraiser this time?'

'Of course,' said Amelia, confident that her mum would look after Charlotte.

'Great.'

Amelia looked at her screen again and began to type. Everything else faded away as she lost herself in her work.

Grace felt as though she was being pulled along like a kite. 'Calm down, Rex,' she said to the dog at the end of the lead. 'We're not running late. And you don't need to get me airborne.'

They were running, though, and Grace could already feel herself short of breath. 'I'm too old for you,' she said, wondering why she was having a conversation with a dog. 'And I'll be pleased to get you back to your owners.'

She'd borrowed Rex from the next-door neighbours. His owner, who also possessed a newborn baby, had been exceptionally pleased when she knocked on the door and asked if she and her granddaughter could take her dog for a walk. 'Any time you like,' she'd said, with a keenness that should have been a warning sign. The next warning sign was a wodge of small plastic bags that she pressed into Grace's hands, filling her with dread.

It was worth it, though, when she saw Charlotte's face as she waited at the school gates. She looked around for Sammy and saw a retreating back heading in the opposite direction. From behind, he could be any little boy, and she felt her mind drift for a moment.

She pulled her thoughts back. 'Don't get excited,' she managed to puff out. 'He's just borrowed from next door.'

Suddenly Charlotte and the dog were a mass of fur, hands and paws. Grace looked on, keeping a tight grip on the end of the leash, feeling the weight of responsibility for the animal as heavy as the chain. 'I thought we could all go to the park for a walk together.'

Charlotte extracted herself from the dog and Grace felt herself in a rather meaty-smelling hug. She realised the dog had already covered Charlotte in slobber. 'Thank you,' said her granddaughter. 'He's magnificent.'

'He's a bit of a mutt,' replied Grace, feeling the need to be modest on the dog's behalf. 'But he's certainly got quite a tongue.' In his excitement, the tongue almost dragged along the floor. 'Come on, let's get to the park. I hope the weather holds. Those clouds look rather ominous.' Talking about the weather made her feel a little calmer, and she allowed herself one final gaze after Sammy. He'd disappeared around a corner.

Progress was slower now, with Rex frequently stopping to look back at Charlotte or stop and sniff something. First a lamp post, where he cocked his leg and urinated to delighted encouragement from Charlotte. Then an abandoned water bottle, which he sniffed at and barked at; when it proved unperturbed by his attentions, he cocked his leg and urinated on that too. Then he picked it up in his mouth, urine and all, and carried it along with them until he saw a pigeon pecking away at an abandoned chip. The water bottle was forgotten and the pigeon was barked at and then chased, with Grace dragging along behind him. The pigeon waddled at first, trusting her to restrain the dog. When it realised which of them was actually in charge, it took flight, shooting Grace a dirty look in the process. Rex jumped up at it still, mouth open as if he could catch the bird, although by then it was safely perched on the top of a lamp post, watching them smugly.

'Maybe the next one, Rex,' Grace told him, pretty confident that all the pigeons in the area were very much safe. Rex barked at her anyway, as if in agreement, then turned his attention to the chip. He had much more success with the flightless fragment of potato, and swallowed it whole.

'Is he an Alsatian?' asked Charlotte as they reached the park.

'Mixed with something,' said Grace. She looked at him. He was sandy-coloured, with black splodges that reminded her of an oil slick.

'Labrador perhaps,' said Charlotte, making a mental note to look up dog breeds in great detail when she got home. 'There's a softness to him.'

'That water bottle didn't think so,' said Grace. 'Neither did the chip.' She handed Charlotte the lead. 'You can be in charge now,' she said. 'There're no cars. Sandra said we can let him off the lead once we're a bit further in.'

Charlotte took the lead solemnly and they walked across the park. 'Here should be fine,' said Grace, and Charlotte released the dog. The two of them immediately embarked on a rather complicated game of chase that soon also involved a large stick and a murmuration of alarmed starlings.

Grace sat down on her usual bench, though her emotions were far from usual. It was hard to believe that this was the same place where she'd come to sit, alone, so many times. She reached out to touch the wooden planks of the bench, as if to reassure herself that it was unchanged. It was. She was the one that was different.

Not alone.

She had Charlotte and Rex, and Amelia would be home later. She listened to Charlotte's laughter and Rex's barks, and ignored the first gentle drops of rain.

She felt as though she could smell more in the air. Was it cows that could smell rain? Yes, that was it. They sat down when they knew it was coming. Jonathan told her it was because they wanted to keep a patch of grass dry, though Grace couldn't see what was wrong with wet grass. Perhaps the mud?

She smiled. She'd never forget the hem of mud that was clinging to the bottom of her dress by the end of her wedding day. They'd got married in a church, pretty much everyone did those days, then had decamped to Jonathan's parents' garden for the party. Her own parents had offered to pay for a local hotel, something a bit swankier, but Grace wanted a simple wedding. Close friends, family, a buffet and a little dancing perhaps.

'It's not very fancy,' her father had complained, as he'd lowered his head to enter the small marquee that Jonathan's parents had had the wisdom to erect, ignoring Grace's suggestion that the whole event take place under the open skies.

'It's perfect,' her mother had said, smiling at Grace. 'And you look beautiful.'

'Thanks, Mum.'

'And the rain will clear later. I've already seen the sun peeping through.'

She'd been right. The sun emerged, its presence illuminating the ceiling of the marquee with a soft glow. Grace had gone outside to enjoy it and Jonathan had followed her. Standing there, hand in hand with her new husband, she felt the pressures of the day lift with the clouds, the enquiries about when the babies would come dissolve with the last drops of rain.

'It's been a perfect day,' Jonathan said. 'I wouldn't change a single thing. Not a single drop of rain that landed on my rented suit.'

'Not a single squidge of mud,' replied Grace, thinking that Jonathan's mother wouldn't feel the same way when the guests trudged inside to use her toilet.

The insistence of the rain on her head brought her rudely back to the present. She stood up, stretching out her back and her memories. Rex and Charlotte were both panting now. 'Let's head back,' she said.

'Run!'

They were almost home, but the heavens had opened and rain poured from the sky. Rex was jumping around, snapping his mouth at the raindrops, but Grace was determined to get him home before they were all soaked through.

'You go inside, I'll drop Rex off,' she said. Charlotte gave Rex a soggy hug, then obeyed, and Grace, feeling rather shamefaced, delivered a very wet dog to her neighbours.

'Hot showers,' she suggested when she got back. 'Then dressing gowns and hot chocolate.'

Once they were warm and dry, Charlotte and Grace sank comfortably into the sofa, clutching their drinks.

'What makes people disappear?' asked Charlotte all of a sudden.

Grace took a sip of her hot chocolate, buying herself some time before she answered. Was Charlotte asking about her father? That was something for Amelia to answer, surely. Perhaps Grace would mention that Charlotte was asking questions. Really tactfully, in the nicest way. She'd make that offer she'd been contemplating, that if Amelia wanted Tom to visit, that was fine by her, but equally if she didn't, that was fine too.

That wasn't saying anything, she realised, playing the conversation in her head as she so often did when she had to talk to her daughter about something tricky. She knew Amelia so well that she was often right about what she'd say. Yet at the same time, she still managed to irritate her daughter. She'd been polite, they both had, since she'd moved in. But she could see the annoyance in Amelia's eyes, hear it in her voice, sense it in the way she took a three-hour round trip to the office each day rather than be at home alone with her mother.

She'd not answered Charlotte's question. Grace started to panic, feeling her granddaughter's eyes on her, earnest as the dog's. Could she offer more whipped cream instead? Marshmallows maybe? She thought she had some in the back of her cupboard, pink and white and possibly mouldy, if marshmallows were even capable of growing mould. They seemed indestructible. If there were some world disaster, it would be just ants and marshmallows left to rule the earth.

She had to say something. 'All kinds of reasons,' she said, looking at the disappointment in Charlotte's face at the hazy answer. 'Would you like a marshmallow in your hot chocolate?'

'No thanks.' Charlotte took a sip of her drink. 'Mr Brown has been gone for almost three weeks,' she said. 'The teachers say he's taking time off.'

'That's where he is then,' said Grace, feeling relieved. Mr Brown. Of course.

'Maybe,' said Charlotte. 'I'm going to find out.'

'OK,' said Grace, surprised at the determination in her granddaughter's voice. She paused. 'Can I help?' She thought for a moment of what she could do. 'I could call the school,' she suggested. 'Perhaps they'd tell me more. I am a grown-up, after all.' It wasn't much of a credential, she realised, but it might help.

Charlotte wavered, unwilling to share her quest beyond the small circle of Sammy and herself. 'No,' she replied eventually. 'Sammy and I have it covered.'

'OK,' said Grace. 'He's a nice boy,' she said, carefully. 'Invite him round again if you like.'

'Thanks,' said Charlotte.

'I quite like trains myself, you know,' Grace added, remembering what Sammy had said when he came over for dinner. It had been a shock at the time, for reasons she didn't want to think about.

'Trains are OK,' said Charlotte. 'I don't really see the attraction.'

'Neither did your mother,' said Grace, then suddenly felt disloyal. She fished around for something to counter it. 'She liked making up songs,' she said.

'Really?' asked Charlotte.

'Her best ones were about a fairy princess,' continued Grace, starting to enjoy herself. 'Called Elizabeth. It was challenging, because not many things rhyme with Elizabeth. We tried to convince her to give her a different name, but she was determined.'

'That does sound like Mum,' said Charlotte.

'I might have a recording somewhere,' said Grandma. 'We definitely taped her singing it, on an old Fisher-Price tape machine.' She smiled and took another sip of her hot chocolate. 'I'll have a look in the attic next time I'm up there.'

They sat together, each silently musing on words that might rhyme with Fairy Princess Elizabeth.

Chapter 11

'Is this really where Mr Brown lives?' It was Saturday morning, and Charlotte and Sammy were looking up at the tower block doubtfully. 'It's not very teacher-y.'

'Did you expect him to live in a library?' asked Charlotte, though she was feeling the same. 'Come on,' she said, swallowing the unease she could feel rising in her. 'Let's go in.'

It wasn't as easy as that. They didn't have a key fob for the sensor at the main entrance and didn't know the code. They couldn't even get into the stairway. 'I'll ring the bell for Mr Brown,' said Charlotte, trying to sound confident, as she unfurled the paper she'd stolen from the school. 'I've got the number here.'

'But he's gone missing,' said Sammy. 'He won't answer.'

'Maybe he is just sick,' said Charlotte. 'And in bed.' She pressed the buttons carefully and they both listened as the bell rang.

No answer.

Charlotte repeated the action, then again.

'I guess we have to give up,' said Sammy, turning away. 'What were we going to do anyway if we got inside?'

'Peer in the windows,' said Charlotte. 'Look for clues. Interview the neighbours.' She had her plan all worked out. 'Find out who saw him last.' She nodded, agreeing to her own ideas. 'Then we'll know how long he's been gone,' she added. 'The police will want to know that.'

'The police?'

'We'll need to go to them.' She'd been reading up on it. 'And file a missing persons resort.'

'Resort?'

'Yes,' replied Charlotte, feeling a little less certain. 'It's police terminology,' she added, trying to sound wise.

'And what do we do if we can't get in the building?'

She hesitated. 'Maybe there's a fence we can climb over that will get us into an area at the back that will lead us to an open door,' she ventured. They were always finding secret passages in her Famous Five books.

'Let's try this first,' said Sammy. He stepped forward and started pressing buttons.

'What are you doing?' asked Charlotte in alarm.

'Someone is bound to let us in,' said Sammy. 'If we ring all the bells.' Sure enough, the door made a buzzing sound and they heard the lock unlatch. 'See?'

He pushed the door open and they both stepped inside.

'It's quite nice,' he said. 'Once you get in.'

Charlotte was surprised too. The lobby was pleasant, with a dried flower arrangement inside a glass case, the flowers peering back at her curiously. It smelt of incense, giving the hallway a heavy, church-like atmosphere.

'He's on the fifth floor,' she said, feeling more cheerful now they'd passed the first hurdle. 'Let's take the lift.'

When the lift arrived, a lady in her fifties emerged. She was wearing harem pants and had a dangly shell necklace that clinked when she walked. She smiled at the children and they stood to one side to allow her to pass before getting into the lift and pressing the button for the fifth floor.

They got out, and after a brief period spent speculating about which direction to turn, they found themselves standing outside number 512. Mr Brown's flat.

'What now?' asked Sammy.

'It's a real pain that he lives in a flat,' pointed out Charlotte. 'There's no window to peer through.' That had been how the children in her book had discovered their clue. She looked dubiously at the doors to either side.

'I suppose it's good that he's got neighbours right here, though,' said Sammy. 'We can interview them.'

Neither made any move. The conditioning not to talk to strangers was strong, and Charlotte imagined how horrified her mother would be if she knew that her daughter was knocking on random people's doors.

Still. Mr Brown was missing. This was an emergency, of sorts.

'Well, we need to try his door first,' she said, and gave it a firm rap with her knuckles. 'Just in case he is there.' There was no answer. She knocked again, even more loudly.

Nothing.

Then something.

A wail.

It sounded like an animal, howling in pain. Charlotte and Sammy looked at each other, and stepped away from the door.

'What was that?' asked Sammy.

Charlotte shook her head. She had no idea.

Grace was engrossed in the mechanism for her cable car, sorely neglected since her family had moved home. So many of the little engineering challenges in her world could be overcome using simple machines. Cogs and chains. Levers and pulleys. Throw in wheels and inclined planes, and the cable car ceased to be a challenge at all. Shrinking the scale to 1:43 made many things so much easier; there was no way a seventy-two-year-old woman, albeit one who had regularly been attending yoga, would be able to construct a cable car at life size, but in her world, anything was possible. It felt good to be able to do things for herself, prove her independence, even in miniature. She smiled as the cog spun round and the cable car set off on its inaugural journey above the slope of her mountain.

She loved the smell of the shed: pine walls and superglue. She ran her fingers along the workbench, feeling the indentations made by years spent here, carefully crafting her layout. The shed was large, too large for the garden really, but for her it had always been a sanctuary. It was peaceful, quiet except for the sound of the baby next door crying.

It took Grace back. Jonathan had insisted they build the shed when she was pregnant with Amelia. He'd already offered, to the astonishment of everyone they knew, to be a stay-at-home dad. When he'd promised that she wouldn't have to sacrifice her career, he'd meant it.

And so he'd built it for her, with careful adherence to all safety guidelines, of course. He hoped that she'd be able to bring projects home from work and it would mean that she'd be able to pop out to be with him and the baby whenever she took a break.

Of course, that hadn't happened. In her work, she needed to be on site. When she was pregnant, she'd taken on more paperwork, stayed away from where the action was, but the office left her bored and dissatisfied.

Then Amelia was born. Grace remembered the surprise she felt when the nurse handed her her daughter, as if she'd never really expected her pregnancy to result in a new little person at all. The eyes tightly shut, face locked in a scowl, as if angry at entering the world. The fingers, furling and unfurling as Amelia felt the air for the very first time, the tiny fingernails unnervingly long. The stern instruction from the midwife to support her head as Grace twisted in the bed to look at Jonathan.

'Her nose!' said Jonathan. 'It's just like yours.' Grace had noticed her daughter's nose for the first time, soft and squidgy and nothing like her own. Then Amelia had opened her eyes, one by one as if unsure whether she really wanted to see the outside world.

Her scowl had deepened and her skin flushed pink as she started to howl. Grace hadn't known what to do. 'What's wrong with her?' she'd asked.

'Nothing,' the midwife replied. 'She's perfect.'

'Hello?' The door next to Mr Brown's had opened and a frazzled-looking woman was standing there, bouncing a howling baby in her arms. Her hair was tangled and she had dark circles under her eyes. 'I'd just got Jonas to sleep.'

'We were looking for Mr Brown,' said Charlotte, relieved that the howling they'd heard could be assigned to a perfectly healthy-looking baby.

'Mr Brown?' queried the woman as she rubbed the baby's back and it gently gurgled in response, calmer now.

'Your neighbour,' said Charlotte.

'He's our teacher,' explained Sammy.

'Oh, you mean William. I'd rather like to find him myself.'

Charlotte tried to swallow the worry that had risen in her throat. 'He's not been home?' she asked.

'I haven't seen him in a while,' said the woman.

'Have you heard him moving around?' asked Sammy. 'In the flat?'

'I don't listen out for it,' replied the woman. 'But no. Not a peep. And he'd offered to put in a shift with this little monkey.' The little monkey burped, then rested his head on his mother's shoulder. Sammy and Charlotte both watched as he closed his eyes and drifted back to sleep.

'When was the last time you saw him?' asked Charlotte, her voice an exaggerated whisper.

'Oh gosh, now you're asking.' The woman gently swayed, stroking the baby's wispy hair. 'It's certainly been a week or two, maybe more. It's hard to keep track of time with a little one. Some nights last forever, but then days fly by all at once and Jonas is holding up his head all by himself, like a big boy.'

Charlotte tried not to tut at the irrelevance of the information. 'Any idea?' she pressed.

'Well, I went to stay with my mum for a bit after Jonas was born. That would have been about a month ago. I've been back for a fortnight and haven't seen him.'

Charlotte and Sammy exchanged meaningful glances. They'd last seen Mr Brown three weeks ago.

'And did he say anything,' she asked. 'About going away?'

'Definitely not,' replied the woman, her voice certain. 'I told him I was going to stay with my mother and he didn't mention a thing. Now, when was that?' She looked up to the ceiling, as if the answer might be found there. The ceiling didn't help. 'Sorry, not sure.'

'OK,' said Charlotte. 'Thanks,' she added, trying not to sound too unimpressed.

'I'm going to put Jonas down for his nap now,' said the woman, stepping back into the house. 'Tell Mr Brown to pay me a visit when he gets back. Kettle's always on for him.' She closed the door.

Sammy looked at Charlotte. 'What now?' he asked.

'Well, I think we can cross being in bed off the list,' said Charlotte.

'Unless he's dead there?'

'I'm going to try the neighbour on the other side,' she said, trying to keep her voice matter-of-fact and not think about that possibility. 'To see if they've got a better memory.'

'OK,' said Sammy, hanging back.

This door had a bell, which Charlotte rang, then rang again. No answer.

'Over here,' said Sammy. Charlotte looked at him; he was crouched at Mr Brown's letter box. 'I can see something,' he said. 'Take a look.'

'What is it?' asked Charlotte.

'See for yourself.'

She bent down to put her head next to Sammy's, wishing she'd thought of looking through the letter box herself. It was just wide enough for them to have one eye each in a position to see. Charlotte looked down at the doormat. There was a large pile of post.

'He's not been here for a while,' she said. 'His neighbour was telling the truth,' she added, as if it had been in doubt. She began to methodically index what she could see. She'd put the details in her notebook later. There wasn't much: a hallway with a tired beige carpet. The walls were white, with a framed print on one side. She squinted at it. It was a line drawing of some kind of bird in flight, a branch tightly clutched in its beak.

'Have you seen it yet?' asked Sammy. 'Do you think it's dead?'

'What?' asked Charlotte, feeling sick.

'There,' said Sammy, unhelpfully.

'Where?'

'On the table.'

Charlotte searched for a table. She could just about see into the kitchen at the end of the hallway. The door was ajar and she could make out a table. On it was a bowl, with some fruit. She strained her eyes. 'A rotten banana?' she queried.

'No,' said Sammy. 'The little table right by the front door.' He paused. 'Maybe you can't see from there.' He shifted over, giving Charlotte the letter box to herself. 'Is it dead?'

Her new field of vision meant that she could see a small end table just in front of a coat stand. On it sat a fish tank with a model ship inside, sunk to the bottom. A goldfish floated at the top, its body twisted and starting to disintegrate.

'Yes,' said Charlotte, moving back from the letter box. 'It is dead.'

Sammy and Charlotte walked back from the tower block in silence. The day had turned cold, clouds concealing the sun. It was raining. The sight of the fish had shocked them both, and they didn't feel like knocking on any more neighbours' doors after that. Sammy kicked an empty Coke can along the pavement and Charlotte tried not to visualise the fish's milky eyes, staring at her mournfully from the aquarium.

'How long can a fish live without food?' asked Sammy, finally.

'About two weeks, I think,' said Charlotte. 'Maybe three. They've got a pretty slow metabolism. Most animals would die of thirst before hunger,' she added. 'But that's not a problem for fish.'

'Oh,' replied Sammy. He kicked the can again and it skidded into the road. They both watched as it ricocheted off a car tyre and came to rest in a puddle. 'How long do you think that fish has been dead?'

Charlotte had been thinking about that herself. 'A while. Longer than a week, I think. Did you see the way the scales were peeling . . .' She stopped herself. 'A while,' she repeated.

'And when did we last see Mr Brown?'

'Exactly three weeks ago, by the railway,' replied Charlotte. 'That's the last time we know of that anyone saw him.'

'Perhaps he did get a train,' replied Sammy. 'That day. The 11.54 to Waterloo.' He hesitated. 'That's a big hub. He could have travelled anywhere from there.'

'He didn't have a suitcase,' said Charlotte. That had been playing on her mind. 'And wouldn't he have arranged for someone to feed his fish if he was going away? And told the school that he would be gone? And why were his glasses sitting there all smashed?'

They walked in silence again. Charlotte paused to pick up a worm that had been washed by the rain onto the pavement. She flung it gently back to the earth surrounding a tree. It wriggled gratefully and began to burrow back into the mud to safety.

Grace was humming to herself as she chopped an onion for the vegetable soup, enjoying the efficiency of cutting through the multiple layers, the satisfaction as the sphere became semicircles and then neat little squares. She heard the door open and close again.

'Charlotte, you're a bit early for lunch,' she said, pouring oil into a saucepan and turning on the gas. 'But I could make you a snack. Maybe some carrot sticks and dip to keep you going?' She turned around. 'What's the matter?'

Charlotte was biting her lip, anxiety painted over her face.

'I went to Mr Brown's flat,' she confessed.

'What?' Horrible newspaper headlines appeared unbidden in Grace's mind. Charlotte going to the home of a grown man, on her own.

'I went to try to find him,' Charlotte replied. 'But he wasn't there.'

'You shouldn't have done that,' Grace said. 'It's not safe.'

'Why?'

'Going to people's houses. Even if they are teachers. Anything could have happened.'

'It was a flat,' said Charlotte, as if that made it better. 'And I didn't go inside, I just went to see if he was there. Sammy was with me.'

'Still,' said Grace. 'We should probably tell your mother.'

'His fish was dead,' said Charlotte.

Grace wondered if she was giving this information as a distraction from the idea of telling Amelia. 'That's sad, but . . .' She paused. 'How did you even know where he lived?'

'I found out from the school office,' replied Charlotte, glossing over the details. 'But he hasn't been home in ages.'

'How do you know?' Grace was starting to find herself drawn in, despite her concerns.

'I saw through the letter box. The fish had been dead a while,' said Charlotte. 'Who leaves a dead fish in the tank if they're at home?'

Grace couldn't dispute the logic.

'I'm worried about him,' said Charlotte, her eyes on the chopped onions.

Grace turned the heat off under the saucepan. 'Come on,' she said. 'Let's sit down and you can tell me all about it.'

She listened to Charlotte's account: the baby bird, the smashed spectacles, the glassy-eyed fish. 'And you told me that Mrs Varga said he was taking some time off,' she said, her voice careful.

'Yes,' said Charlotte. 'But it doesn't make sense. He always wore those glasses. Always. And where is he if he isn't at home? And why didn't he get someone to feed his fish?' She paused. 'He loves animals,' she said. 'He knew all about blackbirds, and he showed us how dolphins use sonar. He wouldn't just leave his fish to starve; he's vegetarian.'

'No,' agreed Grace. 'It doesn't make sense.'

'I just want to make sure he's OK,' said Charlotte.

Grace looked at her clever granddaughter, so concerned for the safety of a teacher she barely knew. A little certainty in a tumultuous time. Surely she deserved that much.

'No more putting yourself in danger,' she said firmly. She

paused. 'But perhaps there is something I can do to help. First thing Monday, I'll call the school and see if they'll tell me any more than they would you. How does that sound?'

'Good,' replied Charlotte. 'It sounds good.'

Chapter 12

'I hope you're not going to leave a mess in your grandmother's kitchen.' Amelia was lingering in the doorway.

'I've almost finished it,' declared Charlotte. She wiped her hand across her forehead, leaving a chocolatey trail. A week had passed since she'd been to Mr Brown's flat, and Sammy's birthday had arrived.

'I think the icing is meant to go on the cake rather than your face,' pointed out her mother with a laugh. She took a paper towel and dabbed affectionately at Charlotte's forehead.

'It just needs one finishing touch,' said Charlotte, ignoring her mother's less than helpful advice. She unwrapped a mini chocolate Swiss roll from its packet and stuck it, with a flourish, on its end on the top of the rectangular cake.

'It looks very good,' said her mother. 'But aren't cakes usually round?'

'Not this one,' said Charlotte. 'It's special.'

'I'm sure your grandma would have loved to help you,' Amelia said. 'She used to make some rather amazing-looking cakes after I left home. Always the pride of the town bake fair, or so Dad said.'

Charlotte glanced at her. The words were complimentary, but

there was something about her tone that made Charlotte think it was meant as an insult.

'This cake will be amazing,' she said, deciding not to worry about it. 'And I wanted to do it all myself.'

'Why does it have Jammie Dodgers stuck on the side?'

'Are you joking?' asked Charlotte, an edge to her voice like a kitchen knife. She'd been baking and decorating for three hours. 'Can't you see?'

'Is it a caterpillar?' ventured Amelia.

'Caterpillars don't have wheels,' said Charlotte, exasperated. 'Or chimneys.'

Grace came into the kitchen and stood next to Amelia, trying to ignore the mess.

'Grandma, you can see what it is, can't you?'

'Well,' she said, 'I can see some Jammie Dodgers making very fine wheels, a Swiss roll chimney, which is an excellent idea, and I believe those Smarties are magnificent bumpers.' She smiled. 'So it's clearly a train. And a triumph.'

'I knew *you'd* know.' Charlotte gave her grandmother a hug, which Grace accepted with a nervous glance in Amelia's direction. 'You're the best.'

'Don't get your grandmother all covered in chocolate,' said Amelia.

'Do you see it now, Mum?' asked Charlotte.

'Of course,' said Amelia, smiling. 'I was only teasing,' she added, unconvincingly. 'Well done.'

'Sammy will love it,' said Grace. 'And you were right, you didn't need my help,' she added, trying to sound as though the perceived rejection hadn't made her fret all morning. 'You could do it on your own.'

'I'm brilliant at baking,' agreed Charlotte, licking her fingers. 'Will you give me a lift to Sammy's? I don't want a rail disaster on the way.'

Grace couldn't think of anything she'd rather do than drive Charlotte to Sammy's house while her granddaughter held the precious cargo. She'd help her carry the cake inside. Perhaps she'd even be invited in, for a slice and a rendition of 'Happy Birthday'. She could play detectives with the children, planning how she'd assist their investigation. She spent a moment wondering if she could spare something from her shed as a last-minute present for Sammy to complement the one she'd already helped Charlotte with. Then she glanced at Amelia's face and bit her lip.

'I've got my yoga class,' she said, although she'd have plenty of time for both. 'Maybe your mum would like to borrow the car?'

If Amelia was cognisant of Grace's sacrifice, she didn't let on. 'Clean up first,' she said to Charlotte. 'Then I'll drive you.'

Grace couldn't work out how Charlotte had managed to get chocolate icing on the ceiling. Gingerly she positioned a chair underneath the spot, grabbed a damp sponge and clambered on, thinking she was too old for such shenanigans. If she fell, she'd break that hip, or worse, and she'd have to admit that her incipient doom was all because she couldn't live with a fleck of brown goo on the kitchen ceiling.

She wiped it, the motion taking her back to the days of changing Amelia's nappies, the myth that baby poo wasn't offensive well and truly put to bed. She climbed back down, sighing with relief when her feet were safely back on the kitchen lino, and allowing her thoughts to drift.

Jonathan had been amazing with Amelia from the moment she'd been born. He didn't seem to mind the dirtier tasks, gently singing to her as he changed her nappy, blowing raspberries onto her little jelly belly in a way that made her gurgle with delight. Grace remembered when it was time for her to leave Amelia to go back to work. Every hormone in her body had told her to stay at home. Everyone she knew told her that too. Her mother, so supportive of her career, had suggested that the project could wait for her for another six months.

But Jonathan knew it was the right thing to do.

'It's not a sacrifice for me, Grace,' he'd said. 'Believe it or not, I don't have the same passion for safety inspections as you do for engineering.'

'You'll be the only man at the mother and baby groups,' said Grace.

'I'll be in demand,' he'd said, and smiled in a way that showed Grace she had nothing to worry about. 'You've been at home with the baby for six months now,' he said. 'And I can tell you're bored.' He stopped himself. 'Not that you're not a great mother,' he'd said. 'But you're not happy unless you're mixing bigger things than formula.'

She missed him so much and so often. He'd have made having Amelia home so much simpler. He'd have talked to her about Tom, about what had happened, in his straightforward way. He'd help, but not intrude. Grace didn't have the same knack. Jonathan was who they all needed; the oil that lubricated the family machine.

She picked up the broken eggshells that Charlotte had left on the counter. Her granddaughter wasn't a great one for cleaning up after herself, but then not many children were. Grace used to try to make it into a game for Amelia, but the girl had quickly seen through her attempts, and it had been quicker, easier and created less conflict if she just did it herself.

Her son had been different, right from the start.

*

Amelia climbed into the car and took a deep breath. Even after all these years, it still smelled like her father. Or maybe her father had always smelled like his car. The leather of the seats, the exhaust from the old engine. Tom's cars were fast but quiet, but her dad's car was noisy and slow. It was good for the local wildlife, he used to say. Cats, pigeons and foxes always had plenty of warning to get out of the way.

'This car reminds me of Grandpa,' said Charlotte, as if she could read Amelia's mind.

'Me too,' replied Amelia. She paused. 'I miss him.'

'And me,' said Charlotte. 'He used to carry me round on his shoulders and we'd pretend to be a giraffe.'

'I remember,' said Amelia, smiling at the thought. 'He used to do the same with me.'

'Really?'

'A long time ago. He was a great dad.' She bit her lip, wondering whether to bring up Tom. Time had been creeping by since they'd last spoken. Almost a month. She knew he was busy, but it was a long time for him not to see his daughter.

Or her.

'Have you talked to your dad much?' she asked. 'You know you can call him any time.'

'A little,' said Charlotte. 'He doesn't always answer.' Amelia gripped the steering wheel tightly at that news.

'Did he mention when he'd be back?' she asked, hating herself for using her daughter to get information.

'Soon, he said. He'll call when he is. He says he really wants to see me.'

'But you don't have a date?'

'It's OK,' continued Charlotte, adjusting the cake tin on her lap. 'Because I know he's busy. I've been busy too. With Sammy and our detective work.'

'You've been spending a lot of time with Sammy recently,' ventured Amelia, feeling she might say something she regretted if she continued to talk about Tom. 'We should invite him round. I'd like to meet him properly.'

'He's been round already,' said Charlotte. 'But you were at work.'

'Oh,' said Amelia, feeling the guilt that constantly assaulted her. Working when she should be with her daughter. Being with her daughter when she should be working. It seemed impossible to get the balance right. 'Let's have him over when I'm home,' she said, trying to be positive.

'He and Grandma get on so well,' continued Charlotte merrily.

'Really?' said Amelia, not sure why that annoyed her.

'Yes,' said Charlotte, adjusting one of the Jammie Dodgers. 'Because they both like trains.'

'Oh.' Amelia paused, remembering. 'But you don't like trains, do you?'

'Not as much as animals.'

'You don't feel left out?' she ventured.

'No. Of course not,' said Charlotte, with a laugh. 'Besides, trains are quite cool. Don't you think?'

'I suppose,' said Amelia.

'We're here,' said Charlotte. 'It's the one with the red door. Thanks for the lift.'

Amelia watched Charlotte clamber out carefully, carrying the cake and present. She smiled at her daughter. 'That cake is really very good,' she told her, determined to make up for her lack of enthusiasm earlier. 'He'll love it.'

'He will,' said Charlotte, with the confidence of youth.

Amelia waited until Charlotte was safely inside the house, then thought about returning home. The prospect wasn't appealing. Maybe she'd take a detour, she decided. A little drive along the motorway. Her mother's ageing battery could likely do with a proper charge.

She felt a rare sense of freedom as she pulled away.

She drove past the station, along the road that ran parallel with the train tracks. A train pulled alongside her, quickly gathering speed and overtaking her.

Trains.

What was it with her family and trains? She'd been pleased that Charlotte had never gone through that phase, always preferring animals and mystery stories to wheels and tracks and engines.

It was easier that way. Less painful.

Amelia shifted gears. It had been a while since she'd driven a manual. Not for the first time since she'd moved to her mother's house, she found herself tempted to not come back. Maybe she could pick up Charlotte and drive them both to the airport, find whichever flight was the cheapest and just get away from it all.

Of course she couldn't. She had responsibilities: funds to raise for her charity and debts to pay. Charlotte had school. And she needed to save money if she wanted to be able to move out again.

For a moment, she thought about what that would entail.

Being on her own. A single parent.

Or perhaps not.

'Ryan, stop that! Billy, it's your brother's cake. Get your fingers out of the icing!' Sammy's mother stopped shouting and turned to Charlotte, one eye still on the boys circling the cake, which was sitting on the kitchen counter looking vulnerable. 'What would you like to drink, dear?' she said, smiling at her. 'Orange squash?'

'Maybe we should put the candles on the cake, Mrs Doyle?' suggested Charlotte, nervous that Sammy, waiting in the living room, wouldn't even get to see her efforts before his brothers stole a wheel. 'And sing "Happy Birthday". While we still can.' She was surreptitiously trying to get a look at Ryan while studiously avoiding eye contact.

'Good idea,' said Sammy's mother. 'And what nice manners you have. I always say, if only at least one of my boys had been a girl, it would all be different. Sammy was my last hope.'

'He doesn't play football, so he might as well be a girl,' said Ryan, his fingers almost to the train's chimney.

'That's ridiculous,' said Charlotte, deciding that maybe he wasn't so handsome after all. 'And there is nothing wrong with being a girl.'

'Ryan, get away from that cake,' snapped his mum. 'And be nice to your brother. It's his birthday.' Ryan and Billy finally left the kitchen, tackling each other for control of a bruised apple that was being used as a football. 'I wanted to bake a cake myself,' said Mrs Doyle. 'But on my own, well, you know what it's like.'

Charlotte nodded, enjoying being spoken to like a grown-up, though of course she really had no idea what it was like.

'They didn't have any train cakes at Aldi,' Mrs Doyle continued. 'So it was the caterpillar or a football one. I'm glad you've come through.'

'It's no problem,' said Charlotte, starting to feel embarrassed.

'I've got him something special for his present, though,' his mother told her, leaning in. 'Couldn't afford it new, but God was smiling on me in the charity shop. Sammy is going to be over the moon.'

*

Sammy's mum passed him her present once they were all sitting, full of cake, in the living room. As he ripped off the paper, his mouth fell open. Charlotte leaned it to see what it was. 'Wow,' she said.

'A train set,' said Sammy, as if saying the words would make it more real. He turned to his mother and threw his arms around her neck.

'I don't know if it works,' she said, looking pleased and a little embarrassed. 'It's not brand new. But I . . .'

She'd lost his attention. He was opening the slightly scuffed box with shaking hands and sliding out the cardboard tray. Within it sat a small red train, three wagons of different colours and styles and a stack of tracks. 'A Hornby 00-gauge freight set,' he exclaimed. Ryan came up and tried to snatch it.

'Proper good, that,' he said.

'It's mine,' said Sammy, using his whole body to protect it from his brother's clutches. 'Thanks, Mum.'

'Leave your brother alone,' said Mrs Doyle. 'Glad you like it, son,' she said to Sammy. 'God bless.'

'Open mine,' said Charlotte, handing him her present. 'It's even better now you've got a train.'

Sammy put the train carefully in its box and set to work on Charlotte's gift. She'd made ample use of Sellotape, and opening it was no mean feat. His brothers got bored and disappeared with another chunk of cake each, kicking the unfortunate apple in front of them.

'It's not a train,' she told him. 'But I think it might go well with it.'

He finally managed to tear off the paper. 'It's a train driver's hat!' he squealed, and threw his arms around her in a massive hug.

'It's got your name on it,' added Charlotte. 'See?' Her grandmother's friend had made it for him.

'Let's set up the track,' said Sammy, putting on his hat and grinning at Charlotte. 'Come up to our room. Let's do it now, before my brothers get back.'

Chapter 13

'So did that little boy like the hat?' asked Ava, her head upside down and her necklace dangling as if trying to get into her mouth. 'It would have been better if you'd let me add some sequins.'

'I don't know yet,' muttered Grace. 'And I'll never get into downward dog if you keep distracting me.' Ava often tried to chat during yoga rather than focus on the class, even though it had been her idea to come. Grace was already in the teacher's bad books for arriving late after she'd lost track of time while cleaning the kitchen. She could see Yogi Padma watching them with a rather unblissful frown. 'But thank you,' she added, not wanting to sound ungrateful.

'I've got some news of my own,' said Ava. Grace contorted her neck to look at her friend. 'I've not lost my touch.'

'Gaze to your navel, Grace,' said Padma. 'And focus on your breath. It's your life force.'

Grace breathed in and out and looked at her belly, inadequately concealed by the loose T-shirt she'd allocated for yoga. She tried to lift a hand to tuck it into her jogging bottoms and wobbled precariously.

She could just about remember a time when her belly had been reasonably flat, many years ago, but it had never looked anything like Padma's. The teacher was wearing a top that was somewhere between a vest and a bra. It displayed a slender slice of tanned midriff, which, as if not gorgeous enough, was adorned with an intricate tattoo of a lotus blossom and finished with a gleaming jewel somehow balanced in her navel.

Tattoos didn't used to be like that, remembered Grace. They were crudely drawn affairs on burly men confirming their love for their mothers, girlfriends or football teams. Padma's creation looked like it was made of dark lace; fragile and delicate. Grace wondered if it hurt, then rather uncharitably wondered what it would look like stretched out, if Padma were to become pregnant.

'Rest in child's pose,' said Padma, and Grace sank back gratefully, feeling her soft belly against her wobbly thighs. Her stomach hadn't been the same since she'd had Amelia. If she sucked it in tightly, it was just a little saggy, but as soon as she ate anything, it would blow up like a balloon, as if the skin was reminiscing about the expanded joys of pregnancy.

Joy wouldn't have been the word that Grace used to describe her own pregnancies. She still vividly recalled the struggle she'd had to reach her feet to put socks on. Of course, that had seemed like nothing once the baby had come. The crying, the constant crying, yet with little clue as to what baby Amelia might need. Colic, the nurses had said, with a sympathetic nod. She just needed to grow out of it.

She was still waking in the night when Grace went back to work, trudging in like a zombie, longing for sleep. Sitting down at the office was a relief; drinking a cup of tea without little hands grabbing for it a treat. Guiltily, Grace had enjoyed her daytimes away from the baby, and sometimes she'd lingered at work longer than she needed, unwilling to go back to the small tyrant at home.

'Rise to all fours for cat-cow,' instructed Padma. 'Use extra cushioning if you need it.'

Grace slipped a folded blanket under her knees and tried to ignore the clicking sound as she arched her spine.

It had grown easier as time wore on. Jonathan was the one who would get up at night, and by the time Amelia could talk, it was him she cried out for. Grace had felt a small pang of jealousy, quickly overridden when she heard Jonathan pull himself out of bed to go to her daughter's room and she could snuggle back down under the covers.

'Now raise one arm to the sky for easy twist.' It wasn't so easy for Grace, but it gave her a chance to smuggle a look at Ava, who had managed to twist herself around like a corkscrew. She always had been rather bendy, as she frequently told anyone who would listen.

'So do you have a new admirer?' Grace whispered.

Ava glanced up at her. 'I'll tell you in the yoga café after,' she said, clearly relishing the suspense now she'd piqued Grace's interest. 'We don't want Padma to tell us off for talking in class.'

Grace put her forehead back to the floor and tried to take a serene yogic breath.

Grace sniffed her herbal tea. She remembered when the only herbal option you could get, even at the supermarket, was a nice bland chamomile. And here she was drinking something that tasted like it could be from a witch's cauldron. She looked up at the blackboard and read the ingredients again. Liquorice, ginseng and nettle. She took a sip and shuddered. Eye of newt and toe of frog, more like.

'It'll do wonders for your constitution,' Ava told her, drinking enthusiastically from her own cup and relaxing back into the beanbag. 'Trust me. I've got the digestion of a twenty-five-year-old.'

Grace shifted a little, feeling the thousands of little balls inside the beanbag sink beneath her. She was not a fan of the yoga studio café, she decided, and longed for a proper chair. She couldn't bear to think about how long it would take her to get up again. They'd probably have to stop the next class and have the yogis join forces to heave her out.

'Lucky you,' she said. She put her drink down on a low table. Whoever had designed the cup had definitely gone for beauty over functionality. It had no handle and hence was starting to burn her fingers. She leant forward, feeling the filling of the beanbag shift beneath her again. Chairs were so stolid and reliable in comparison. 'So go on then,' she said, feeling like a teenager, in conversation if not in body. 'What's your news?'

'I'm going on a date,' said Ava. Grace nodded. She'd guessed that. 'With . . . Luigi.'

'That's hardly a shock,' said Grace with a smile. 'He was clearly interested in you.' She looked up to see Padma enter. Apparently she'd been practising yoga for ten years, though she barely looked older than Charlotte. Womb yoga, thought Grace. That was probably the new craze.

'I did think he might be,' said Ava, sounding pleased and waving at Padma, who was engrossed in her phone.

'Why do you think he gives us so many breadsticks?'

'Well, I'll be eating for free there from now on, I expect,' said Ava. 'No need for early-bird specials. He's cute too, don't you think?'

Grace thought a moment. Luigi had a pleasant face and a comfortable body that spoke of a life enjoyed. 'Yes,' she said. 'I do.'

'And nice?'

'He gave me his lasagne recipe,' said Grace. 'So no complaints.'

'I'm glad you think so,' said Ava. 'I think he might be the one.'

'Have you actually been on a date yet?' asked Grace, trying not to sound doubtful.

'No,' said Ava. 'But you have to go into things full of confidence, don't you think?'

Grace didn't think so at all. 'I suppose,' she conceded. She picked up her cup absently and took a sip, then hurriedly put it down again. 'This is the tea of the devil,' she said. 'Why couldn't I have English Breakfast?'

'Expand your horizons, Grace,' said Ava.

Grace pulled a face. 'I'm too old for expanded horizons,' she said.

'You're never too old for broadening your mind.'

'Mine is definitely shrinking,' replied Grace. 'Yesterday I spent ten minutes looking for my reading glasses, only for Charlotte to point out that they were on my head.'

'Kids are always losing their glasses,' laughed Ava. 'It's just now you're a little more mature you read more into it.'

'I couldn't read anything without my glasses.'

Lost glasses. Grace still hadn't worked out what to do about Mr Brown. She decided to tell her friend. Ava listened, pausing only occasionally to take a sip of her drink. 'So I called the school,' finished Grace, 'but they wouldn't tell me anything. Muttered something about data protection and right to privacy.'

'Chief Constable Hopkins,' Ava announced.

'What?' asked Grace. 'You think I need to get the police involved?'

'Of course not,' said Ava. 'This Mr Brown is probably staying with a girlfriend, lucky devil. But don't you see? It's perfect.'

'What do you mean?'

'You need to show your granddaughter that you're taking this seriously,' said Ava. 'Hopkins is your man. Charming and kind. He'll be lovely to Charlotte, set her mind at rest, and you'll look incredibly cool.'

'I've never looked cool in my life,' said Grace. 'And I don't know any policemen at all, let alone this Hopkins man.'

'You are so lucky to have me as a friend,' said Ava, grinning. 'You do know I used to be a lawyer? Rather a good one at that. I still have my connections in the police department.'

'Really?'

'I'm very sure that if I put in a word, he'd meet with you and Charlotte.' She sat back in her beanbag, looking pleased with herself.

'Isn't wasting police time a crime?'

'Hopkins won't mind,' said Ava. 'And he owes me a favour.'

'I was going to start by meeting with Mrs Varga at the school,' said Grace. 'But I have to admit, your plan does have a bit more . . .'

'Glamour? Drama? Pizzazz? You're welcome.' Ava tipped the rest of her tea into her mouth. 'It doesn't taste the best when it's cold,' she admitted. 'The things we do for our bodies.'

'Proper coffee?' suggested Grace. 'And maybe a cake that isn't made from vegan courgettes and quinoa?'

'Let's go. I'll drop a message to the chief constable. He'll be thrilled to hear from me.'

'I'm sure we'll be able to get the train to work,' said Charlotte. Sammy was walking her home, his cap held dejectedly in his hand.

He kicked a stone, which skidded out in front of them for a few metres before settling to a halt at the edge of the kerb. 'Maybe,' he said.

'And it still looks cool.'

'I suppose.'

'What else did you get?' she asked, hoping the subject might cheer him up.

'Just a card from my dad,' he said.

'He remembered, then,' said Charlotte. Sammy had told her that he'd forgotten last year. 'That's good.'

'It said "Happy tenth birthday",' said Sammy, miserably. 'But I've just turned twelve. He doesn't even know how old I am any more.'

'I'm sorry,' said Charlotte, but it got her thinking about whether her own dad would forget her age. It had been a long time since she'd seen him. Was he going to end up like Sammy's father?

'But your cake was the best,' said Sammy. He grinned at her. 'Much better than the one my mum bought me.'

'That was yummy too,' said Charlotte, generously. She paused. 'My mum thought the cake I made was a caterpillar at first.'

'That's silly,' said Sammy. 'Caterpillars don't have chimneys.'

'Exactly,' said Charlotte. They fell into a comfortable silence and the stone received another kick.

'Want to plan some more investigations?' suggested Charlotte, watching it ricochet off a car tyre.

'Isn't your gran helping?'

'She tried ringing the school,' said Charlotte. 'But they wouldn't tell her anything.' She paused. 'I don't think she'll be as good a detective as we are.'

'We are pretty smart,' said Sammy, cheering up. 'What were you thinking?'

'Mr Brown isn't at his flat, which is where he was meant to have been. So we need to figure out where else he could be.' She thought a moment. 'What do we know about his habits?'

'He doesn't smoke,' volunteered Sammy.

'That's good,' said Charlotte. 'But I meant his routine. Where he goes. Who he hangs around with.' She paused. 'I haven't been at the school as long as you . . .'

'Sorry,' said Sammy. 'I never thought he was that interesting. Just a teacher.' He absent-mindedly plucked a leaf from an overhanging hedge as they walked. 'I think some of the others might know more.'

'Good plan,' said Charlotte, feeling a little fizz of excitement. 'We'll ask around on Monday.'

'I've got my chest check-up Monday.'

'Tuesday then,' said Charlotte. She looked at Sammy. 'Are you feeling OK?'

'Never better,' he said, taking a deep breath to demonstrate.

'OK,' said Charlotte. They reached her house and stood for a moment outside the front garden. Her grandmother came out holding a half-full rubbish bag.

'Hello there,' said Grace, who had spotted them walking along and had hurried out with the first excuse she could think of so she could chat to them. 'Just taking the rubbish out,' she said. 'How was your birthday, Sammy?'

'Mixed, to be honest,' said Sammy, in a grown-up way that made Grace want to laugh.

She resisted the urge. 'How so?'

'I got a Hornby 00-gauge train set,' he said.

'That's a fantastic little engine!' exclaimed Grace.

'But it doesn't work.'

She took a breath in, sharply. It wasn't her size, but still. 'Perhaps I could take a look at it for you?' she suggested. 'I might be able to help.'

'Really?' said Sammy.

'Really?' questioned Charlotte.

'I can do more than cook, you know,' Grace told her, annoyed at the doubt in her granddaughter's face. 'I used to be an engineer for Concorde.'

'Mum told me,' said Charlotte. 'She said that's why you called her Amelia. After a pilot who died.'

'Amelia Earhart was a pioneering explorer and feminist,' corrected Grace.

'And she said that Concorde was banned from the skies for crashing.'

'Concorde was an innovation,' said Grace, with dignity. 'But yes, there were some issues. Bring it over,' she said, turning to Sammy. 'I'll see what I can do.'

'Thanks, Mrs Sayers.'

'Call me Grace.' She paused. 'Will you join us for dinner? We're having a vegetarian lasagne. It's an authentic Italian recipe.'

'I can't. Mum's making egg and chips,' said Sammy.

'That sounds lovely,' said Grace. 'Pop the train set over any time. And Charlotte, I have an idea to talk to you about as well. I think you'll be rather excited.'

It was a good turnout, thought Amelia, looking around the fundraiser. Sipping champagne in a gorgeous orangery in one of London's nicest parks had been a strong draw, and Paula had managed to negotiate the use of the building free of charge. Amelia looked around for her friend to congratulate her, but instead caught an attractive waiter's eye and allowed her champagne flute to be refilled.

'There you are,' said Paula, appearing behind her. 'Not bad, eh? And I've told the waiters to keep the drinks flowing. Generous drinks make generous donors.'

'It's great,' replied Amelia. 'You've even got the weather onside.' It had been a gorgeous spring day, and still felt mild. Guests were spilling from the orangery into the gardens, admiring the abundant banks of rhododendron.

'I'm glad you could make it this time,' said Paula. 'Your mother must be a more reliable babysitter than Tom.'

'It's not babysitting when it's your child,' replied Amelia, automatically, remembering that she'd missed Paula's last event when Tom had called her with a crisis in his business just when she was meant to be heading out.

'Here's to that,' said Paula, chinking her glass. Amelia found to her surprise that it was nearly empty again, and the waiter was already refilling it.

'We're not donors,' she said to him pleasantly. 'You don't need to top us up as much.'

'We're working mothers on a night out,' corrected Paula. 'Even if it is a work event. Keep the drinks coming.'

'No problem,' he said with a smile. 'Enjoy yourselves, ladies.'

Paula looked him up and down. 'And *she's* single,' said Paula, giving Amelia a little push.

'Good to know,' replied the waiter, as Amelia resisted the urge to kick her friend in the shins.

'I'm not really,' she blurted out, feeling champagne-filled blood rush to her head. 'I'm married, but we're on a break, and I still think that . . . well, I don't know. But I wouldn't say single.' She shot a look at Paula as the waiter backed away.

'What are you doing?' asked Paula. 'He was cute.'

'He was young enough to be my son!' said Amelia. 'And I'm not single. I don't know what I am. But I'm certainly not picking up waiters at an event.'

'You're right,' replied Paula. 'Sorry. I don't know what I was thinking.'

'Thank you,' said Amelia.

'We should find you a nice rich donor instead.' Amelia looked at Paula in horror. 'Relax, I'm joking,' Paula added. 'Sorry. Maybe I should go easy on the champagne.'

'Maybe you should,' replied Amelia, not taking her own advice and instead taking a deep swig from her glass.

'What's going on with Tom, anyway?' asked Paula.

'I don't know,' replied Amelia. 'He's been away.'

'You haven't spoken?'

'I don't want to bother him. He'll call when he's back.' She smiled briefly. 'I was pleased when it turned out he was staying at Steve's place after all.'

Paula frowned at her. 'Do you miss him?'

'We've been married for so long,' said Amelia. 'We've shared so much. I know what he did was wrong, but . . .' She stopped herself. 'Yes,' she said instead. 'I miss him.'

'Tell him that,' said Paula.

'I don't know,' said Amelia.

'I'm not his greatest fan, but you can't stay on a break forever. You need to decide what you're going to do.'

'Maybe,' said Amelia. The waiter was back and she realised her glass must be empty again. She avoided eye contact this time. 'Anyway,' she said. 'I need to network, and you have an event to run. See you later.'

Amelia rested her head on a supportive tree as she took a drag on a cigarette she'd cadged from the waiter. She wasn't usually a smoker, but every now and then she felt like she couldn't manage without one. Even now, it made her feel like a naughty teenager, and she'd crept away from the end of the event to enjoy it in peace. The night air was cool and refreshing, and she felt like she was thinking more clearly than she had in a while.

Paula was right. She had to call Tom. He needed to come back and he needed to see Charlotte.

And they needed to talk.

Before she had a chance to change her mind, she got out her phone, blinking a little at the brightness of the screen, and dialled.

It went to voicemail, and she listened to Tom's message, the one she'd heard many times before. When she'd called him to check what time he'd be home, to tell him to buy bread. To tell him she loved him.

'Hi,' she began. 'It's me.' She paused. 'Your wife. Listen. Charlotte needs to see you. It's getting ridiculous, her being without her father so long. Scotland isn't that far away; you can get the train down and visit one weekend.' She paused again, wondering why he hadn't done so already. 'She misses you,' she added. 'She's been tracking down this missing teacher, you know how she gets, but it's you she needs. She misses you.' She'd said that already. Perhaps she shouldn't have called after a drink. Or six. 'I miss you too,' she said, the words slipping out of their own volition. Shit. 'Or maybe I don't. This break has gone on long enough,' she continued, not sure where she was heading. 'It's confusing for everyone. We need to decide what we're going to do.' She felt assertive now, like she was taking control. 'Whether we're ending things ...' She stopped herself, memories of the good times flooding her mind. 'Or not. Anyway, call me,' she finished, wishing she'd kept her phone in her bag. 'We need to talk.'

Quickly she hung up and looked around for the waiter. She needed another cigarette.

Chapter 14

'Well, here we are.' Grace stood in front of the police station, feeling as if her confidence had seeped into the nearest drain. She paused, not wanting to go in but aware that she had brought them here and she'd seem ridiculous in front of Charlotte if she backed down now. It had all happened rather quicker than she'd intended; Ava had texted Saturday evening telling her it was set up for Monday morning, before school.

It would be fine. They were meeting Ava's contact. Her friend had assured her that he'd been fully briefed and would help, if only by listening and treating Charlotte's concerns with respect. Who knows, perhaps he'd even be able to locate Mr Brown for them.

But standing here in front of the imposing red-brick building, Grace had a bad feeling.

'Come on, Grandma,' said Charlotte. 'Let's go in.' She'd been delighted at the offer of speaking to the police, and had wanted to schedule it for the following day so Sammy could come too. Grace had been tempted, but Ava had already set the date and she was worried about causing inconvenience by rearranging.

Grace followed her granddaughter, who pushed merrily through the revolving door. Grace disliked that type of door immensely;

it seemed designed to entrap people. She escaped the other side and put on an efficient smile that she hoped communicated to the police officer on reception that she was a law-abiding citizen not at all here to waste a senior officer's time.

'We've got an appointment with Chief Constable Hopkins,' she said. The man directed them to take a seat. Grace frowned at the rather suspicious-looking stains on the material, but her back was starting to hurt so she sat down anyway.

'These are the type of chairs you can't use as a weapon,' said Charlotte, rather excitedly. 'Look, they're stuck together and fixed to the floor so you can't chuck them around.'

'There goes my plan,' said Grace.

Charlotte laughed. The sound made Grace start to feel more relaxed, and she sat back in the chair. It was actually surprisingly comfortable.

'I've never been in a police station before,' said Charlotte.

'I have,' said Grace, rather dramatically, hoping Charlotte wouldn't ask any more.

'Really?' Charlotte looked excited. 'What had you done?'

'I found a wallet,' admitted Grace. 'So I handed it in.'

'Oh,' said Charlotte. Grace thought she heard the man on reception snigger.

They sat there for what seemed like ages. It was early on Monday morning, and a procession of people came and went, but no one seemed to have any interesting problems or crimes to report. Grace imagined that Friday and Saturday nights were when the station was most exciting, and was rather pleased that they'd found a sedate time. She even wished she'd brought a book to read, and was about to suggest that they go to the newsagent's she'd spotted around the corner for magazines when a young man in an ill-fitting uniform appeared.

'Grace Sayers?' he said, looking at them doubtfully.

'Yes,' said Grace. 'Are you taking us to Chief Constable Hopkins?'

'I'm afraid he's busy on urgent matters,' the man replied. 'I'm PC Kennedy and I've been instructed to deal with your case.'

'But we were meeting with Chief Constable Hopkins,' objected Grace. She was prepared for a chat with a pleasant older gentleman who had been carefully briefed by Ava on what to expect, and who might even let Charlotte try on his hat. This man didn't even seem like the kind to make her a cup of tea.

'Follow me, please,' he said.

There was nothing for it. Grace took a breath and stood up. She thought she'd done so rather gracefully, considering the lack of chair arms to use as props, but PC Kennedy looked at her in alarm and reached out an instinctive hand to assist her. 'I'm fine,' said Grace, then realised she sounded rather rude. 'Thank you,' she added. 'Anyway.'

Anyway. Now she sounded rude again. Was there anything worse than thanking someone *anyway*?

'Grandma is very sprightly,' said Charlotte, loyally.

Grace smiled at her, wondering where she'd picked up that word. 'Over-sixties yoga,' she told PC Kennedy. 'You should see my down dog.' PC Kennedy looked as if he had no idea what to do with that information. Grace fought the urge to giggle, and found herself looking forward to telling Ava the anecdote later.

'This way,' he managed, showing them into a small room with a tape recorder on the table. They all sat down. The machine looked like something from Grace's era, and she had to resist the urge to reach out and press one of the reassuringly large buttons. It would most likely make a very satisfying clicking noise.

'Grandma?' Charlotte was looking at her. As was PC Kennedy. She must have been concentrating on the tape recorder for longer than she'd realised.

'I'm sorry,' said Grace, feeling a little flustered. 'What was the question?'

PC Kennedy emitted an almost imperceptible sigh. 'You were going to explain why you've come.'

'Yes,' said Grace. 'Absolutely.' She paused. 'My granddaughter has reason to be concerned for the well-being of one of her teachers,' she said. 'Mr William Brown.' She looked at Charlotte. 'Charlotte, you've done all the work. Why don't you tell PC Kennedy what you've found out?'

Charlotte smiled, seeming pleased to have the opportunity. 'Shall we switch on the tape recorder?' she suggested.

'That won't be necessary,' said PC Kennedy, sounding slightly amused.

Charlotte looked a little put out. 'I'm sure PC Kennedy will take excellent notes,' said Grace, determined that her granddaughter would get the attention she deserved. 'Won't you?' she suggested, her voice firm.

'Of course,' said the policeman, looking a little surprised. He took a notepad and pen from his pocket.

Grace listened to Charlotte's account, feeling, as she often did, incredibly impressed with her granddaughter. She looked at PC Kennedy's face and saw the telltale grimace of a suppressed yawn. It was one thing her being ignored, but Charlotte? That was not on. She started to feel cross, then noticed that he had the beginnings of a cold sore at the edge of his lip and found herself feeling rather sorry for him. It was probably hard work being a junior officer, out on the streets day in, day out. She expected his mother worried about him all the time; Grace certainly would have. Putting himself in danger to keep the public safe.

Still, he could have offered her a cup of tea. Grace's hands were feeling cold. It would be nice to have a mug of tea to wrap them around. Never mind. Perhaps she and Charlotte could stop at a café on the way back to school and treat themselves.

'Thank you for your time,' said PC Kennedy, starting to get to his feet as soon as Charlotte had stopped talking.

Charlotte looked to Grace in alarm. Grace knew what those words meant; they were being fobbed off. 'What action are you going to take?' she asked him.

'I've got what I need,' he said. 'I don't think there's any reason to be concerned.'

'You've heard the reasons to be concerned,' said Grace. 'The glasses, the fish . . .' Even as she said the words, she heard how it must sound to this busy young policeman. An old woman and an eleven-year-old girl creating drama from a teacher on holiday.

'We'll handle it from here,' he added with a smile.

It wasn't a pleasant smile. It was patronising. He was talking down to her. And to Charlotte.

Grace took a breath. He was treating her like a silly old woman. In front of her granddaughter. Cold sore or no cold sore, it wasn't on.

'Thank you,' she found herself saying, remembering how she used to deal with the men who tried to patronise her at work. 'But I would like to know specifically what you will do to handle it.'

'Well . . .' PC Kennedy mumbled, seemingly surprised to be challenged. 'We'll—'

'I have a suggestion,' interrupted Grace. 'You should talk to the school and see if they will tell you more than they've told Charlotte and myself. Then you should check with his relatives to see whether they have heard from him. We need to establish if he is really missing or taking a deliberate break. And then you can file a missing person report and begin investigations in earnest.' She'd read up on that last bit online, using Amelia's laptop. 'At that point I will be able to tell my good friend Chief Constable Hopkins what an excellent job you have been doing.' The last bit was artistic licence, but PC Kennedy wasn't to know.

Grace paused for breath. The policeman and Charlotte were both staring at her.

'Perhaps you should write that down,' said Charlotte to PC Kennedy. 'In your notebook.'

Grace walked next to Charlotte, who was paying attention to avoiding cracks in the pavement, giving her step an irregularity punctuated by little jumps and hops. Grace had sympathy; she was always on the lookout for uneven paving slabs, the kind that might trip her, start the fall that she was always so paranoid about. Knowing her luck, it would be a banana peel and she'd have the kind of ridiculous slip that characters had in cartoons.

'Do you think he'll do all that?' asked Charlotte.

'I should hope so,' said Grace.

'Interviewing his family is a good idea,' said Charlotte. 'I'd quite like to do that myself.'

'We shouldn't bother his family,' said Grace, firmly. 'We should leave it to the police. You certainly shouldn't be talking to strangers on your own.'

'Oh,' said Charlotte, looking miserable. 'But . . .' She trailed off, stepping heavily on a crack in the pavement.

Grace thought a moment. She couldn't have her granddaughter putting herself in danger, of course not. But as long as her investigations were harmless, surely it was OK?

'How about you interview your classmates?' she suggested. 'See if they know any more about Mr Brown?'

Charlotte smiled. 'Yes,' she said, starting to hop around the cracks again. Grace found herself a little envious of the easy agility of youth. 'I was thinking that already. Tomorrow, when Sammy is back, we're going to find out his habits. We already know that he doesn't smoke.'

'And I'll talk to the school again,' offered Grace. 'Perhaps I should speak directly to Mrs Varga this time, in person. Just in case PC Kennedy doesn't get around to it.'

Grace had done her best, but she still wasn't sure the policeman had taken them seriously; after all, they were hardly *The Sweeney*. Though now she thought about it, the policeman had seemed too young to remember that show. What were the modern police dramas? Was *The Bill* still on? It seemed a while since she'd seen it.

'OK,' said Charlotte. She stopped and looked at her grandmother. 'Do you think something terrible has happened to him?'

'I don't think that's likely,' said Grace. 'But we'll certainly get to the bottom of it. Between us.'

The truth. That was what they all needed.

Grace decided to talk to Amelia about Tom. She knew that he and Charlotte had spoken on the phone a little, but he should visit.

She'd insist.

No, insist was too strong. It wasn't really her place.

Suggest, maybe. Hmm, that was a sure-fire way to put her daughter off an idea.

Perhaps a hint would have to do.

If she picked her moment carefully.

'Bye, Grandma,' said Charlotte as they reached the school gate. 'Love you.' She gave Grace a quick hug.

Grace watched as Charlotte went into the school, then turned around to walk home. She could still feel the echo of that hug, a warm circle wrapping her body. *Love you.*

The visit to the police station had been a good idea after all.

*

Amelia put down her heavy bag of shopping on the kitchen counter. She decided that braving the busy supermarket on a Monday evening meant she deserved a treat, and pulled the wine she'd added to her basket at the last minute from the bag. Opening it, she poured herself a large glass.

Right. Now she was ready.

'Are you sure you wouldn't like any help?' offered Grace, poking her head around the door.

'It's just a vegetable curry,' said Amelia. 'I can manage.'

'You are clever,' said Grace. 'I wouldn't know where to start.'

'I'm going to start by opening this jar,' said Amelia, taking out the ready-made jalfrezi sauce. 'Then I'm going to cut up a few vegetables and fry it all together, pop the naans in the oven and we're all set.' She sounded more confident than she felt. Back home, she'd order a curry from their local rather spectacular Indian restaurant, but here, the only curry house she'd found was down a rather sad-looking alleyway. She'd seen a dead mouse lying ominously on the front step.

'Aren't you going to peel the carrots first?' suggested Grace, as Amelia struggled awkwardly to chop them with her best knife.

'It's more authentic this way,' said Amelia.

'Really?' asked Grace.

'No idea,' said Amelia. She glanced at her mother, who looked confused for a moment, before both of them started to giggle.

'You've had a long day,' said Grace. 'Maybe I can be your assistant chef?' She pulled on her apron. 'You give me directions and I'll follow them.'

'OK,' said Amelia. She took a sip of her wine. 'Start by peeling the carrots.'

'Of course,' said Grace. She'd peeled all five before Amelia had unpacked the rest of the vegetables.

'Show-off,' said Amelia. 'Wine?'

'I don't think the sous chef should drink on the job,' replied Grace.

'We need to slow you down,' smiled Amelia, 'or you'll take my job.'

'In that case . . .' said Grace. Amelia poured her mother a drink and handed it to her. 'What's inspired all this?' Grace asked.

Amelia paused. She didn't want to say that she was sick of her mother's cooking. It was good, but after a while, she found herself craving more flavour. And feeding herself and her daughter made her feel more like a good mother. Someone who could cope if she had to be a single parent. Tom hadn't returned her call.

'Just a thank you,' she said instead. 'It's been good of you to put us up.'

'It's been a treat,' gushed Grace. 'And Charlotte is such a credit to you . . .'

Amelia listened as Grace praised her daughter. She'd never tire of hearing about Charlotte's talents and many kindnesses, and felt herself flushing with pleasure and the wine.

'I'll let her tell you about the police visit this morning,' continued Grace.

'Police visit?' queried Amelia.

'I told you, remember?' said Grace, though there was a little doubt in her voice. 'Chief Constable Hopkins? I'm sure I did, but with my memory . . .'

The name didn't ring a bell, but Amelia knew she often tuned out her mother's chatter, an art she'd perfected as a teenager. She could see Grace starting to look worried, so she nodded. 'Of course,' she said. She took a clove of garlic and tried to peel it with her fingernails. The garlic resisted.

'Can I help?' asked Charlotte, coming into the kitchen. 'If we're all cooking together?'

Amelia realised that was exactly what they were doing, and felt a moment of wholesomeness.

'Only if you've finished your homework,' said Grace, with a glance at Amelia.

'I have,' said Charlotte.

'Then come on,' said Amelia. 'You can peel the garlic.'

'Here's a trick,' said Grace, taking a clove and banging it with the flat of her knife. Amelia jumped in surprise and a little wine sloshed from her glass.

'Careful, Mum,' she said. 'You almost gave me a heart attack.'

'It worked,' said Charlotte, watching the peel fall away.

'Your grandma is a woman of many talents,' said Amelia. The wine was working and she could feel herself starting to relax. 'So tell me about this police visit.'

She listened as Charlotte enthusiastically recounted the events of her morning. She found her eyes flicking every now and again to Grace, who looked like she was trying not to beam with pride even as she chopped onions. Amelia didn't remember even having met this Mr Brown, whose whereabouts seemed to be taking up so much of her daughter's energy.

But she knew where this sudden interest in a missing teacher was coming from.

Tom.

Charlotte's absent father.

She grabbed a courgette and sliced into it aggressively. She'd thought he'd call right back after that message. She couldn't remember exactly what she'd said, but the thought of it, unreciprocated, made her wince. She continued slicing the courgette, waiting for a break in Charlotte's story.

'So now we're going to interview the other kids at school,' finished Charlotte. 'Because Grandma says we need to leave talking to strangers to the police.'

'She's quite right,' said Amelia. 'Safety first.' She paused, unable to think of a natural way to turn the conversation to Charlotte's father. 'Have you heard from your dad?'

'We spoke a couple of days ago,' said Charlotte. 'He said he's busy with work.'

Amelia gritted her teeth. 'He's never too busy for you,' she said, determined that it would be true. 'You know that.' She struggled with the jar of sauce, finally managing to open it with the assistance of a few firm taps on the counter and a dishcloth. She gave it a dubious sniff. 'I'll talk to him,' she said, deciding that she'd be completely sober this time. 'Set something up. Scotland isn't that far. He can come back for a visit.'

Charlotte didn't reply, and Amelia felt her heart break for her stoical daughter. Damn Tom and his stupidity. His selfishness. He was too much of a coward to see his daughter after what his mistakes had cost the family. Too much of a coward to even talk to his wife.

'Do I have time to call Sammy before dinner?' asked Charlotte, changing the subject. Perhaps for the best, thought Amelia, before she said something about her father that she'd regret. 'He missed it all because he had a hospital appointment.'

'If you're quick,' said Amelia, though she had no idea how long dinner would be now. Grace had stealthily taken over, and Amelia found the courgette and knife had both been removed from her vicinity.

'Ready in ten minutes,' said Grace, who was also sniffing the sauce suspiciously. 'All of it?' she queried.

'I suppose,' said Amelia. She took the jar from her mother and slopped it into the pan, immediately filling the kitchen with a rich, spicy aroma that made her feel like she was back in London, opening her favourite takeaway while Tom poured the wine.

But she wasn't. She paused, waiting to feel sad. Or angry. But actually, the anger was already starting to be superseded by other emotions. Amelia realised she was enjoying herself, cooking for her family with her mother and daughter.

Maybe things weren't so bad after all.

'OK,' said Charlotte, at lunch break on Tuesday. 'Interview time.' Sammy nodded. 'We'll ask the other kids in our class first. I'll take the girls,' she said, feeling a mixture of excitement and dread curdling with the surprisingly delicious peanut butter and banana sandwiches her grandmother had made her for lunch. 'You take the boys.'

'But they're all playing football.'

'Join in,' suggested Charlotte. 'Just for a minute,' she added, as she saw Sammy's face fall. She relented. 'Or maybe we can both talk to them tomorrow, while they're still queuing for lunch?'

'That's a much better idea,' said Sammy, brightening. He paused. 'I'll go and ask Kaval now, though,' he said, gesturing to a gloomy-looking boy who was sitting on a bench watching the football game intently. 'While his leg is broken.'

'OK,' said Charlotte again, but Sammy had already wandered off. She took out her notebook to write down the girls' answers, then worried she looked geeky and put it back in her bag. 'I've got this,' she said to herself, then realised she'd spoken out loud and quickly looked around to make sure no one had heard her. A pigeon glanced up at her disapprovingly, then waddled towards a puddle and proceeded to drink the murky water. Charlotte took her eyes from the pigeon and directed it back to the gaggle of girls. They had pulled four benches into a square so they all faced each other. It felt as impenetrable as a walled castle.

Still, she had to try.

'Hello,' she said, walking over.

No one turned around. Perhaps she hadn't been loud enough. She coughed ostentatiously, then tried again. 'Hello.'

The three girls with their backs to her turned around; the others looked up at her. 'Hey there,' said Erica, her voice friendly. She was a slight girl with an abundance of freckles. 'How are you settling in?'

'Fine,' replied Charlotte, surprised. 'I've been here a month now.'

'It's Charlotte, isn't it?' said Nia, taking charge. 'Anne-Marie, move over so Charlotte has room.'

'Oh,' said Charlotte. 'Thank you.' She smiled and took a seat.

'We were just talking about what happened in *Love Shack* yesterday,' said Nia. 'Did you see it?'

It was a test and Charlotte felt her heart sinking. She hadn't watched it for ages, reading up on animals instead. She'd found herself much happier as a result.

Until now.

'I missed the last few episodes,' she said hesitantly.

'It's been a bit boring recently,' said Erica. Charlotte smiled at her gratefully. 'Are you looking forward to the school trip?' Charlotte had barely thought about it, though she was vaguely aware it had been the subject of discussion amongst much of the class.

'I suppose,' she said. 'Where are we going?'

'Mrs Varga still won't say,' said Nia. 'I reckon Wales, but Anne-Marie thinks it will be Somerset.'

'Oh,' said Charlotte, unable to think of a better reply. She remembered her mission. 'I wanted to talk to you about Mr Brown,' she said. 'Since he disappeared.' She looked around.

Anne-Marie had put her magazine down. 'He's just on holiday, isn't he?' she asked.

'I don't think so,' replied Charlotte. She took a breath and decided to tell them about the abandoned pair of glasses she'd found at the railway line, and what she'd seen at his apartment. A hushed silence fell after she'd finished, the girls seemingly more impressed than PC Kennedy had been.

'Do you think he's dead?' asked Nia, her eyes shining.

'No,' said Charlotte quickly. 'Well, I don't know. It's a mystery.'

The girls all nodded in agreement.

'I can't believe you took his records and went to his house,' said Erica.

'You won't tell, will you?' said Charlotte, regretting sharing so much with these girls she barely knew.

'Course not,' said Nia. 'It's cool.'

Charlotte smiled. 'Sammy helped,' she added.

'Actually,' said Nia, her voice rather dramatic, 'I know something about Mr Brown too. But I'll be in big trouble if you tell I told, because I've been sworn to secrecy.' She looked pleased with herself.

The girls leaned in and Nia looked around carefully. Charlotte realised she was holding her breath. 'We'll keep it secret,' hissed Anne-Marie.

'What is it?' asked Charlotte, the words spilling out of her too quickly.

'Promise not to spread it?' said Nia.

They all solemnly nodded their heads.

'OK,' she said. 'Now, I know this is true because the lollipop lady told Rebecca who works at the supermarket with my sister Asha. She's working there to save up because she's off to university in the autumn.' The others looked at her. She lowered her voice to a whisper, her eyes shining with the special light that came with illicit gossip. 'Mr Brown has been having an affair.'

The girls collectively gasped.

'With . . .' she paused for effect, 'someone else at the school.'

'Who?'

'I can't say,' she replied, clearly enjoying herself. 'You have to guess.'

'Is it a teacher?'

'Sort of.'

They all looked at each other.

'Miss Conti,' declared Anne-Marie. 'The school secretary. She's the only single woman under the age of forty.'

Nia nodded. 'Got it in one,' she said.

'She's very pretty,' said Erica.

'Mr Brown is OK-looking,' said Anne-Marie. 'For a teacher.'

'They broke up,' said Nia. 'According to my sister. And that's why Mr Brown disappeared.'

'People don't disappear when they break up,' said Anne-Marie.

'My dad did,' said Charlotte. The words escaped her before she even realised she was saying them. The other girls were all looking at her. She tried to laugh it off, but it came out as more of a snort. She felt Erica's hand rest on her arm.

'Not a word to anyone,' said Nia, her voice stern. 'Remember.'

Of course, Sammy didn't count. She told him the minute she saw him, and now they were standing outside the school, waiting for Miss Conti to leave the office.

'So what's the plan?' asked Sammy.

'Follow her, of course,' replied Charlotte. 'Maybe she'll lead us right to Mr Brown.'

'I thought they'd broken up?'

'I don't think Nia knows as much as she said,' said Charlotte, thinking of the gleeful expression with which the girl had spread the gossip. 'She might have made some of it up.'

'Then we don't even know it's true.'

'Here she comes,' said Charlotte. They both watched as Miss Conti stepped out of the school, took a quick look around and lit up a cigarette. Then she waved at the lollipop lady and crossed the road. 'Let's follow her and see.'

They hurried after her, keeping as close as they dared. 'I wish we had disguises,' said Charlotte. 'We'll have to remember for next time.'

'I could come as a train driver,' said Sammy. 'That cap you gave me would be perfect.'

Miss Conti was making good speed for someone in high heels. Then all of a sudden, she turned around. Charlotte and Sammy scrambled to hide: Charlotte chose a nearby tree, Sammy flung himself behind a bin.

'I don't think she saw us,' said Charlotte, as Miss Conti continued on her journey. She realised she was rather enjoying herself. 'But let's hang back a bit, just in case.'

'It's all right for you,' said Sammy, stepping out of his hiding place, 'but it stinks back here.' He paused. 'Oh, she's with someone now. A man.'

Charlotte jumped out from behind her tree. 'Is it him?' she asked. 'Mr Brown?'

They gazed down the road. Miss Conti was holding the man's hand, but they both had their backs to them.

'I can't tell,' said Sammy.

'Come on,' said Charlotte. 'Let's follow them.'

Three blocks later, she was still none the wiser. It was starting to get dark, and Miss Conti and her friend had reached the outskirts of town and turned down a narrow alley. Charlotte watched as a fox ran from behind a bin, turned to look at them for a moment and then disappeared under a car.

'I don't think it's Mr Brown,' said Sammy, as they stood just outside the entrance to the alley. 'It's the wrong coat.'

'He might have a new one,' said Charlotte. But much as she wanted to find her teacher, it would be a bit of an anticlimax if he'd just left because of a girlfriend. 'We need to get closer,' she said. 'Come on.'

'They'll see us if we follow them down there.'

‘No they won’t,’ said Charlotte. ‘Just keep quiet.’

They crept around the corner and saw Miss Conti in a passionate kiss with the man.

She broke off the kiss and looked straight at Charlotte. ‘Are you following me?’ she said. The man stepped back.

He was not Mr Brown.

But he was angry, his face red. Charlotte noticed his bulging muscles and a tattoo of a skull across his knuckles.

She turned and ran.

She had reached the high street when she realised something.

Sammy wasn’t with her.

Chapter 15

Grace put Sammy's precious cardboard box on the workbench in front of her. It showed an image of a train speeding through the countryside, its carriages pulled along behind it. It was a 00-gauge engine, which was to say 76 times smaller than real life. The most common scale in the UK, and a good choice as a starter pack.

She'd always worked with ScaleSeven, which seemed colossal by comparison at 1:43. Less common, and harder to get off-the-shelf components, but she liked the larger size. It allowed for more detail. The people could have a wider range of expressions, the shops more detail. Not to mention more robust engines.

She took a deep breath and carefully slid out the contents of the box. She laid out each piece of track, checking the fishplates were in order first. The way the tracks connected to each other was vital – a little loose, and the electricity couldn't flow.

All fine. That was rare. When a train set was played with, a fishplate would often come loose. This had clearly not been used much; perhaps a child had had it foisted on them by an over-enthusiastic parent.

No, surely all children loved trains. Even Amelia had been interested for a while. Something about the magic of the movement was too hypnotic to resist.

Grace connected the tracks in a perfect oval on the flat work surface, placed the little engine on top and plugged in the transformer. Slowly she eased the dial round.

Nothing.

She checked the plug from the transformer to the controller. It was fine. She checked the other plug, from the controller to the power track. Fine.

It must be the engine itself.

She took her screwdriver and carefully unwound the screws to investigate the engine's innards. The mechanism was different to her trains, and she frowned at it, then used her tweezers to make a few adjustments.

She placed it back on the tracks.

Nothing.

Grace gritted her teeth. She was determined to fix this train set.

She felt sick at the thought of letting Sammy down, and sat for a moment looking at the engine. She needed to run more tests.

Despite the years of tests at school, and later at work, that word always brought to mind a pregnancy test. Back in her day, it hadn't been as easy as peeing on a stick. When she thought she was pregnant with Amelia, she'd been to the doctor, but the second time around, she'd missed two periods before buying a home testing kit.

It had looked like an elaborate chemistry experiment, but the results had been clear.

The thought of going through it all again had felt like too much. The pregnancy, the lack of sleep. Even having to leave another little baby to go back to work.

Jonathan had been delighted when she told him. He'd convinced her it would be OK. They knew what they were doing this time. No unrealistic expectations, not the same anxiety about whether they'd be able to keep the precious little creature alive. They'd done it once, and look how wonderful Amelia was.

They'd do it again.

Grace was less convinced, but Jonathan told her it was because she was the one carrying the extra burden. 'As soon as the baby is out, I'll do my share,' he told her. 'This will be amazing. And just think of how thrilled Amelia will be to have a little brother or sister.'

Grace gently levered the wheel and engine assembly out of the bodyshell. 'There you are,' she said to the train. 'There's your problem.' She used her tweezers to gently extract the broken cog. The teeth were worn down. In her storage section, hundreds of tiny little drawers were neatly labelled. Spare arms for her people, spare sheep for the farm, and many different components for her trains, her lighting, her music effects.

Nothing at 00 gauge, of course.

Grace smiled, an idea forming in her mind, even better than simply fixing and returning the train.

She'd take Charlotte and Sammy to a very special place.

Charlotte retraced her steps, but by then her legs were tired. It took her longer than she wanted to get back to the alleyway.

She stood at the entrance. It smelt spicy and exotic, likely from the Indian restaurant that backed onto it.

Deserted.

Then she heard a clatter. Another fox emerged from an upturned bin and stared at her accusingly, half a naan bread dangling from its jaws.

Charlotte looked at the bins and felt dread rising in her. 'Sammy!' she shouted. The fox fled at the panic in her voice. She should have looked for him earlier, checked that he was following her. That man, that angry man, must have grabbed him.

And now he was gone.

'I'm here.' Sammy poked his head out from behind a bin. He was sitting down. 'Did you see that fox? I didn't know foxes liked curry.'

'Thank God you're OK,' said Charlotte, wrapping her arms around him. 'I thought—'

'You ran,' said Sammy. 'You just left me to my fate.'

'I thought you were behind me,' said Charlotte, releasing him. 'I did, you have to believe me.'

'Of course I do,' said Sammy. He smiled. 'I was just joking.'

She smiled at her friend, feeling the guilt lift from her shoulders. 'What happened?'

'That man was pretty cross that we were following him. He said it was an invasion of Miss Conti's privacy. Then off they went. I sat down and had a little puff on my inhaler, then waited for you and watched that fox. I knew you'd come back.'

'You're OK?'

'Fine.' He grinned at her. 'You are such a worrier,' he added.

'No I'm not,' said Charlotte, feeling the worry evaporate now Sammy was in front of her. She sat down next to him. It did smell nice here, like spices and bananas. The back of an air-conditioning unit was exhaling hot air nearby with a loud whirr. 'So, what does it mean?'

'Seems like Mr Brown isn't having an affair with Miss Conti,' he said.

'Or he is,' replied Charlotte, 'and that man got angry at him.'

They looked at each other. 'He was pretty aggressive,' said Sammy. 'And all we did was follow him.'

'We'll need to investigate some more,' said Charlotte. 'The plot is thickening.'

'Now,' said Grace, 'don't get too excited, but I think you're going to like this place.' She'd picked Sammy and Charlotte up after school the next day in her rickety old car, and had even managed to park near the high street.

'The pet shop!' exclaimed Charlotte, her eyes shining.

'No,' said Grace, quickly. 'Not today,' she added, making a mental note to talk to Amelia about that idea as she carefully lifted a large bag-for-life from the boot of the car. She still hadn't managed to hint in any meaningful way about Charlotte's father, but maybe a pet would be a less contentious subject. 'Follow me.' She started to muse on the thought of an animal as they walked, the kids quickly overtaking her. Perhaps a guinea pig or a hamster would be rather wonderful. She and Charlotte had been for a few walks with Rex now, which was lovely, but Charlotte seemed so mournful when they had to return him.

She'd need Amelia to agree, but it was Grace's house, after all. She could keep the pet for them when they inevitably moved out (which she hoped would not be for a long while). It would give Charlotte a reason to come back, to visit. Amelia would bring her, and Grace would try to make another curry, and they'd share a lovely meal every week with the animal eating scraps from the table.

She just had to persuade her daughter.

She could practically hear the conversation already, with Grace promising that she'd look after the animal while Amelia scowled at her like a disbelieving parent. Still, it would be worth it to see the look on Charlotte's face, her eyes lighting up like headlights.

A rabbit perhaps. It could live outdoors then. She was pretty confident she could construct something that would fox the foxes, so to speak. She'd put it at the opposite end of the garden to her shed; the thought of gnawed cables and chewed tracks was too much to bear.

Wouldn't it like to roam around the garden? It seemed cruel not to allow it, just for the sake of her shed. Would the mouse-proofing system Jonathan had built for her years ago keep a rabbit out?

Maybe not a rabbit then. She'd heard somewhere that ferrets made good pets. Had Ava told her that? Seemed an odd piece of information for her friend to impart. Perhaps it had been Samir? Or had she seen it on television?

'OMG,' said Sammy, leaving Grace completely in the dark as to why he was spouting random letters, but drawing her back to the task at hand. 'It's a model train shop!'

'Grandma!' exclaimed Charlotte, and Grace was gratified to see that she was excited too.

They stood outside for a moment, soaking up the window. 'That one is 00 gauge, like yours,' said Grace, pointing to a small green train. 'Come on, let's go in. Toby is expecting us.'

She pushed the door, holding it open for the children, who weaved under her arms as if they were little maypole dancers. She took a deep breath, enjoying the distinctive smell. Glue, plastic and the metallic tang of electricity.

'It smells amazing in here,' said Sammy, as if reading her mind. 'Like heaven.'

'That's ozone, from the motors sparking,' said Toby, stepping out of the shadows. He held out his hand, and Sammy looked at it for a moment before taking it and shaking it solemnly. He shook Charlotte's hand too, and smiled at her. 'You've got your grandmother's lovely eyes,' he said.

Grace glanced at Charlotte. Her granddaughter raised an eyebrow at her, and Grace almost found herself blushing.

'So,' said Toby, breaking the moment. 'Show me the patient.'

'The patient?' echoed Sammy.

'It's here,' said Grace, taking the train box from the bag. 'I've found a faulty cog. You said you had a replacement?'

'Give me a minute,' said Toby. 'Why don't you take a look around?'

The children didn't need to be asked twice. Neither did Grace.

She watched as they drank it in. The front of the shop was devoted to displays, little worlds set up with their own dramas, characters and skies. Grace saw Charlotte pause to examine a scene at a zoo, marvelling at the tiny tiger, teeth bared at the monkey enclosure next door. A monkey was mid-swing in the branches of a scarily authentic tree, a tiny banana in its almost human hand.

Bananas. That took her back.

She remembered trying to scrape mashed banana from the wispy baby hairs on the top of Peter's little head. 'How did that get there?' she'd asked her baby son, who'd gurgled back at her, his eyes not quite focused. 'You're not even eating solids yet.'

Amelia stood next to him, banana peel clutched in her hands like a smoking gun. 'He likes bananas,' she said. 'They make him giggle.'

'You know he can't have anything but milk still.' Grace smiled at her daughter.

'He was only sniffing it,' insisted Amelia. 'And then he wanted to wear it as a hat.'

'You're late for school,' said Jonathan, sweeping in to pick up his daughter in a giant hug. 'And Mummy is late for work.' He looked at Peter. 'And you, little one, are late for the hairy banana hat party.'

Grace had laughed, an exhausted laugh. She'd thought it had been hard having one child and a job, but she realised now that was nothing. Two children were relentless. She felt like she was involved in an intricate balancing act, a human tower of constant lateness and sleepless nights, always on the brink of tipping over into disaster. As long as nothing went wrong, they could just about remain like this, a precarious stasis. Then Amelia would get a tummy bug, or Peter would start teething and stop sleeping, or there would be problems at work and she had to stay late, and their tower would come tumbling down.

But while things were smooth, they could cope. Enjoy themselves even, in a tired, slightly delirious way. 'Come on,' she said to Amelia, who was busy blowing raspberries at a delighted Peter. 'School.'

'We'll get her there, don't worry,' said Jonathan. 'You go to work. We can't have our breadwinner being late.' Grace had smiled at him, and leaned in for a kiss that tasted of bananas.

'Yuck,' said Amelia.

'Hiccup,' said Peter.

'See you later,' said Grace. 'I'll try not to be late.'

She refocused her eyes on the monkey in front of her, and looked around for Charlotte and Sammy, suddenly aware that she'd forgotten all about them. They were standing together at the front of the shop, still gazing at something.

'Look at that!' exclaimed Sammy.

Tracks circled past the sea, then followed a steep incline to take them over the doorway before making their way past the planes and through a tunnel into the aisles filled with thousands of boxed treasures at the back of the shop.

'I'll turn on Percy, shall I?' said Toby. 'Just a tick.'

He disappeared for a moment behind the shop counter, then they heard it.

A gentle sound, like horses' hooves in the far distance. The train, presumably Percy, had chugged into life. Sammy and Charlotte both turned to watch its progress along the track. It chuffed up the slope to travel over the doorway, then came whizzing down the tracks before stopping at a red signal.

'Wow,' said Sammy.

'It's so nice to see them enjoying the trains,' said Grace, looking at Toby.

Toby smiled. 'Nothing like the gleam in the eye of a child watching a train,' he said.

Grace felt a sadness deep inside. She knew that gleam well.

'Do you and Toby hang out together a lot?' asked Charlotte, interrupting her reverie. Her eyes had moved from the train to her grandmother and Toby. She was smiling.

'Just at the miniature club,' said Toby. 'And the occasional dinner with friends.' He smiled. 'Grace is the best miniaturist by far,' he said. 'Her inventions are really something to behold. I keep telling her she should patent her designs.'

'Nonsense,' said Grace, blushing a little. 'How's that cog coming along?'

'Come through to the back,' said Toby. 'There's better light in my workshop.'

They followed him. 'I'll do the honours, if that's OK with you, Sammy?' suggested Grace. Sammy nodded and they all watched as she worked. 'I'm just removing the gear and axle cover,' she told them, feeling like a surgeon. 'There's another recessed screw here,' she said, using a tiny screwdriver that Toby handed to her to remove it, her face solemn. 'With this gone, we can reveal the wheel axles, taking us to this broken cog.' She removed it, carefully slid the new one into place, then fastened the engine back together. 'That should do it,' she said. 'Shall we get it set up and check?'

Toby slid the tracks from the box. 'Now, young man, you need to slot the tracks together very precisely,' he said. 'Precision, routine and a flat surface. That's what you need if you are to be a model railroader.' He smiled at Sammy as the boy connected the final piece of track. 'That's right. You've got a steady hand.' Sammy beamed. 'Now, run your finger along the rail. If there's a little bump, it's not in correctly and the train will derail. You need it smooth.'

'It's smooth,' said Sammy, barely able to contain the excitement in his voice.

'Then go ahead,' said Toby, gesturing to the controls. 'Nice and gentle, ease her in.'

Sammy carefully turned the dial, a millimetre at a time.

Nothing happened.

'A little more,' said Toby. 'The light is on.'

Sammy continued to turn. Grace felt her heart sink as the train remained static.

She didn't think she could bear his disappointment.

All at once, as if it had been teasing them, the train sprang into action. Grace emitted a small squeal. 'Thank heavens for that,' she said.

Sammy turned the dial up a little more, and the train gathered speed. He looked to Toby.

'That's fine, keep her going,' he said. The train continued to speed up, until it was chugging cheerfully around the track. 'How about we put the carriages on too?' he suggested. 'You can reverse her into them by spinning the dial in the other direction and she'll pick them up. What do you say?'

Sammy simply nodded, words seemingly beyond him.

Grace felt a heady mixture of joy and utter sadness as she watched this little boy delight in the train on the track. Then she felt a hand coiled around her own and glanced down to see Charlotte smiling up at her. 'Look at how happy Sammy is,' she said. 'Thank you for bringing us here.'

'You're welcome,' said Grace, joy pushing out the sadness. She loved how much pleasure her granddaughter obtained from someone else's happiness.

Charlotte was special.

'For Christ's sake,' Amelia muttered to herself as she sat on the train listening to the mumbled announcement about delays.

'What did he say?' asked the annoying person next to her, who seemed to have half of McDonald's spread out in front of him on the table like a banquet, his pot of sweet chilli dip threatening Amelia's laptop.

'Delays,' said Amelia.

'Why?' he barked, as if her making out more of the announcement made her in some way culpable for what was happening.

'I don't know,' Amelia snapped back. 'Leaves on the track or something.'

The mood on the train, usually one of bored acceptance, was turning. It was crowded, people were irritated, and they'd been sitting here for twenty minutes already. The carriage smelled like the pickle in the man's burger, mingled with sweat and latent anger.

Amelia was feeling particularly annoyed, because she'd deliberately left the office early to spend some quality time with her daughter. Instead she was trying not to watch the man next to her shove chicken nuggets into his face.

He took a sip of his fizzy drink and burped softly without excusing himself. Amelia opened her laptop again and tried to connect to the Wi-Fi, which was cutting in and out like a motorbike in traffic.

Her phone rang, the sound loud and obnoxious, earning her a few tuts from other passengers. She hurried to answer it, realising too late that it was Tom.

For a moment she considered hanging up again and switching the phone to silent. The last thing she wanted was a conversation with her estranged husband in front of the carriage.

What if he wanted to talk about Charlotte? What if he wanted to talk about that voicemail?

'Hello,' she said, her voice clipped.

'Hi there,' he said. 'How's things?'

'Fine,' she replied, carefully. 'You?'

'Work is going better,' he said. 'Things are looking really positive here. Early days, but still . . .'

She listened to him chatting awkwardly and tried not to think about the way he used to kiss her neck. Unbidden, an image of him in bed sprang into her mind. She could almost feel the warmth from his body wrapping around hers.

He made a joke about something and Amelia found that she was smiling in spite of herself. She turned away from the other commuters and looked out of the window. The train was moving now, and already they had left the grey of London behind. She could see into suburban gardens, complete with children's trampolines and plastic slides, knocked over in the wind.

Families, together.

'It's nice to talk to you,' she ventured, her voice quiet so the man next to her couldn't hear. He was now tucking into an apple pie, and she could smell cinnamon, infusing a sweetness into the air.

'Yes,' Tom said, sounding nervous. 'It is.'

Amelia smiled. 'You got my message?'

'I did.' He paused a moment. 'I'm coming home soon,' he said. 'Well, not home, but I can visit. You know what I mean.'

'I do,' said Amelia. Finally.

'Actually,' he continued, 'I have something I need to tell you. Something important.'

'Go on,' she said, encouragingly. She felt like she could guess what it might be. About time.

Five minutes later, she ended the call and put her phone back in her handbag. She opened her laptop again and swore at the Wi-Fi.

She hadn't guessed that.

Chapter 16

There was no coming back from this. Amelia knew that. They'd been on a break, but it was still a shock. The pain felt physical, as if Tom had punched her in the stomach.

Over. It had to be now.

Even when he hadn't called, hadn't seen Charlotte, had been annoying about his shoes, she'd felt deep down as though the most likely outcome was a reconciliation. He needed to make it up to them, she needed time. But they needed each other.

Not any more.

She sat at the kitchen table, scowling at her cup of black coffee. It was early still; the sun hadn't yet risen, but she hadn't been able to sleep. How could she when her world was crumbling around her?

She glanced at the clock on her mother's oven. She could feasibly have a shower soon and head into the office for an early start. She didn't want to work from home today; she needed to be out in the world. Away from this house. Perhaps she'd be able to lose herself in work. Losing herself was the best she could hope for today.

Because she certainly didn't want to think about how she was going to break the news to Charlotte.

No.

How *he* was going to break the news. No way was she letting him get out of that. Not after he'd been lying for so long. And lying so pointlessly. He must have known he'd have to tell her eventually.

'You're up with the lark,' said Grace, coming into the kitchen. 'Did you want to get some work done before the meeting with the school later?'

'What meeting?'

'You know, with Mrs Varga. About how Charlotte's settling in. Eleven a.m.'

Damn. She'd forgotten. Amelia pictured her day. Lingering in the house. Avoiding her mother's sandwiches. Making polite small talk with a teacher. She just wasn't up to it. Not today.

'Actually, I wanted to ask you about that,' continued Grace, sounding nervous. 'Please say no if you'd rather I didn't, but I did actually have a little something I wanted to ask Mrs Varga about. It's about that teacher, Mr Brown, the one Charlotte has been looking for. I did offer to talk to her, and this seems like a good opportunity, if you wouldn't mind if I joined too . . .' She stopped herself, looking at Amelia. 'Are you OK?'

'Fine,' said Amelia. She paused, seeing her way out. 'Actually, Mum, I quite need to be in the office today. Would you mind taking the meeting?' She thought for a moment. 'I could dial in if she needs to speak to me?'

'Of course,' said Grace, looking relieved. 'And no, I wouldn't think we'd need to bother you. I can handle it,' she added, seeming pleased to be able to say those words. 'Charlotte's settling in fine, don't you think?'

Amelia nodded, and took another sip of her coffee. It tasted bitter, matching her mood. 'Yes,' she said. 'No concerns.' She looked at her mother, whose mouth was open as if she wanted to say something else but hadn't yet found the words. 'What is it?' she asked, trying not to sound impatient.

'I was thinking about ferrets,' said Grace. Amelia frowned at her. It seemed recently that everyone was full of surprises. 'It's just . . . I walked by the pet shop the other day, and you know how much Charlotte loves animals, and they are meant to be very clean creatures, very clever, and—'

'We can't get a ferret,' interrupted Amelia, wondering if her mother had finally lost the plot.

'It wouldn't have to be a ferret,' Grace continued, ploughing on. 'Maybe a puppy, or a rabbit or something?'

'The last thing I need is another life to be responsible for,' interrupted Amelia. She thought again of her phone call with Tom and felt her blood boiling like the water for her coffee.

'I'd look after it,' said Grace, sounding to Amelia like a pleading child. 'It wouldn't be any trouble.'

'It would be lots of trouble,' said Amelia. She paused, taking a breath. Her mother was just thinking of Charlotte. Amelia knew how much Charlotte wanted a pet. The stick insects had been positioned as a test to see if she could look after them, with a potential upgrade to something with fur and more complicated needs if she did well. She had, but then everything had changed.

And with the call last night, it had changed again.

'OK,' said Grace. 'Sorry.'

'Don't mention it to Charlotte for the moment,' said Amelia, collecting herself. 'We'll see how things go, shall we?' Her voice was as soft as she could manage, but she could tell she didn't sound right. 'Thanks for taking the meeting,' she added. 'It's a real help.'

'Are you sure you're feeling OK?' queried Grace, putting her hand on her daughter's forehead in a gesture that reminded Amelia of being five years old. She felt her temperature rise at the contact. 'You look pale.'

'I'm fine,' repeated Amelia, standing up. 'I just need to get to the office. That's all.'

Grace watched her daughter drain her cup and put it in the sink. She took a breath. 'It's not easy, you know,' she ventured, feeling for once as though she understood where Amelia was coming from. 'Working and being a mother. I did it too, you remember.'

'I remember,' said Amelia, her voice cold. She looked at her mother.

Something in her gaze made Grace nervous, but she'd started now. 'It means you can't be there for every event, every parent–teacher meeting. But your career is important. And you're setting a great example for Charlotte.'

'What are you saying?' asked Amelia.

'Just that you're doing a brilliant job,' said Grace, hastily. 'With everything that you've got going on.'

'I'm there for Charlotte as much as I can be,' said Amelia. 'She's my priority.'

'I know,' said Grace, wishing she'd kept her attempt at a compliment to herself. 'That's what I'm saying.' She paused, feeling the tension in the room rising like steam from the kettle. 'You're doing a much better job of it than I ever did. Just look at how wonderfully she's turning out,' she said, finally. 'She's a credit to you.'

Amelia couldn't help but smile at this, and Grace felt the tension start to evaporate. 'Yes,' she said. 'She is quite something.' She looked at her mother. 'Thanks again for today,' she said. 'I really appreciate it.'

'You're welcome,' Grace replied, relieved to have finally said something right.

'Who can tell me what the capital of Croatia is?' asked Mrs Varga, holding a pin in the air, ready to stick it into the map of Europe she'd Blu-Tacked to the wall. The class looked back at her blankly. 'I've just said it, moments ago,' she added, putting down her pin. 'Was anyone listening?'

No one was. The children couldn't concentrate in class, because the location of the school trip had been announced in assembly that morning.

There'd been speculation for weeks. The hot favourite was Wales, where the class of two years ago had been. The Lake District had also been rumoured, but when the Isle of Wight was announced, a cheer was raised. There was something very exciting about travelling to an island. It sounded distant, exotic, even though it was just across the Solent.

'OK,' said Mrs Varga, looking at the whispering class squirming with excitement. 'We'll come back to Zagreb later. I have some more details of the trip that I can share.'

Silence fell. Charlotte stopped scribbling a note to Sammy and he looked up from his drawing. 'Who has a question?'

A forest of hands shot up.

'Sammy,' said Mrs Varga.

'How will we get there?'

'Train,' replied Mrs Varga. Sammy grinned. 'Then ferry. Nia,' she said, moving along.

'How many to a room?' Nia asked. 'Because I want to share with Anne-Marie and Erica and—'

'There are no rooms,' interrupted Mrs Varga. She paused, seeming to enjoy the puzzled looks she received.

'Where will we sleep?' asked Marlon. 'We'll have to have beds.'

'No beds either,' replied Mrs Varga. She smiled. 'You're all paying attention to me now, aren't you?'

More hands were raised, several children reaching so high that their bottoms left their chairs. Mrs Varga paused, not selecting anyone to ask. Charlotte wondered if she liked the drama.

It was too much for several children, and comments started to fly unprompted.

'We'll freeze to death.'

'I'm not sleeping on the ground.'

'What if it rains?'

'Calm down, everyone,' said Mrs Varga, sitting down. 'We will be camping.'

More questions flew around the room. Mrs Varga raised a hand to silence them.

'There will be tents provided, but you will each need to bring your own sleeping bag. A letter is going home to your parents this week with the list of requirements along with your permission slips and booking forms.'

More hands shot up, but Mrs Varga waved them away. 'We'll be at a campsite near the beach. It will be May and you will not freeze to death inside sleeping bags. The tents will keep the rain off.' She looked at Kaval, who was waving his arm around desperately. 'Let me guess,' she said. 'Loos? There will be toilets at the campsite. And showers. Does that answer your question?'

'Yes, miss,' replied Kaval.

Nia's hand was up again. 'How many in a tent, then, miss?' she asked.

Mrs Varga referred to her notes. 'There are three tents of four, four of three and one of two,' she said. 'Plus two tents for the teachers.' She paused. 'Girls and boys will need to sleep in separate tents, of course.'

Charlotte and Sammy looked at each other in dismay, then both flung their own hands in the air. 'No exceptions,' pre-empted Mrs Varga. Charlotte opened her mouth to object. 'You'll have to share with other friends,' said Mrs Varga. 'It will do you both good. You can all decide who shares with whom amongst yourselves if you can do so nicely. If not, I will decide for you.'

Sammy and Charlotte began whispering urgently to each other while Mrs Varga continued to talk. So did many of the other children, trying to get first dibs on how the groups would divide. Mrs Varga, apparently realising that her words were being lost on the class, closed her eyes for a moment.

'We need to figure out a way to share a tent,' hissed Charlotte, her voice urgent. She paused for a moment. 'Maybe I should be with you in case you need some help with your inhaler?'

'They'll never go for that,' said Sammy mournfully.

The bell rang and the class jumped up.

'Come to my house tonight,' said Charlotte. 'We'll think of something. We have to.'

The classrooms looked much as Grace remembered from when Amelia was at school here. There'd still been blackboards and chalk back then, all replaced by screens now, but otherwise it had hardly changed. Different children's work adorned the walls, but in essence the displays were the same. Careful drawings of landmarks from around the world, stuck to the wall with Blu Tack. A map of Europe, capital cities marked with drawing pins. Tissue-paper lava erupting from sugar-paper volcanos. An oil spill, the slick black heads of seabirds poking up mournfully from the disastrous waters.

The room even smelled as she remembered. Ink, glue and

disinfectant, with the faint hint of baked beans that always seemed to linger in the air from school dinners.

'Sorry I'm late.' Mrs Varga hurried into the classroom, a harassed expression on her face, before looking in surprise at Grace. 'Is Charlotte's mother not joining us?' she asked.

'She's very busy with work,' replied Grace, feeling defensive. 'She's high up in an extremely important charity,' she added. 'They're curing cancer.'

'We can reschedule if that would be better?' Mrs Varga seemed less impressed than Grace had hoped with Amelia's career.

'No, it's fine,' replied Grace. She waved her notepad and pencil in Mrs Varga's direction. 'I'll take notes and fill her in.' She smiled, feeling competent. 'Shall we get started?'

'Of course,' said Mrs Varga. 'Apologies again for the delayed start,' she said. 'We're a bit short-staffed and one of the supply teachers arrived back late after break.'

Perfect. Grace had been wondering how to bring up Mr Brown. And here he was, innocently inserting himself into the conversation. 'Not a problem,' she said brightly, seizing her opportunity. 'Charlotte told me that one of the teachers was off. Mr Brown, isn't it?'

'That's right,' said Mrs Varga.

'I hope he's OK?' said Grace.

'Yes, he'll be fine.'

Grace paused. Fine. It meant nothing; a platitude. 'Can I ask what the matter with him was?' she said.

'I'm sorry,' said Mrs Varga, sounding irritated rather than sorry. 'It's not my place to say.'

A polite way of saying mind your own business, thought Grace. 'Of course,' she replied. She needed to be less direct.

'Now, let's talk about Charlotte.' Miss Varga smiled. 'I think this will be an easy meeting. She's a lovely child, very bright, well behaved, and she's formed such a strong bond with Sammy. I do think it will do her good to share a tent with some of the other girls on the school trip, though, and I hope it will be a positive influence for them too . . .'

Grace sat back and smiled as Mrs Varga praised her granddaughter. Yes, she was a bright girl, and kind, and a very good student. Amelia had been clever too, though not always as pliant in the classroom as the teachers would have wanted. Grace had been rather proud of that – her daughter, who thought for herself and didn't go along with things unless she could see the point. Of course, that made her more difficult at home too, never agreeing to anything unless she could see the benefit to herself. But still. Grace had always respected her for it, even when trying to wrestle her into a much-maligned car seat.

Peter hadn't been like that at all. Grace didn't know whether it was because he was the younger child, or just how he was, but he was happy to go along with whatever they were doing. Amelia used to dress him up as a princess when he was starting to walk, and he'd twirl around for her, happy as anything on his stocky little legs.

But wheels. Those were his passion. Toy cars, diggers, ambulances. Anything he could roll across the floor, chasing after it in his pink princess dress. That was what made him happy. Grace still remembered when he'd discovered Amelia's long-discarded wooden tracks and train. He'd built a little loop, and pushed that train around and around for hours, merrily choo-chooing to himself. Amelia had snatched it back, of course, even though she never played with it any more. But gradually Peter wore her down and she allowed the tracks to change ownership.

Mrs Varga coughed gently into her elbow, in the way the children had been taught in the pandemic. Grace remembered being told to cover her mouth with her hand when she coughed, which was of course the least hygienic place to choose, what with all the hand-shaking in which she was also encouraged to partake. She realised that the cough was meant to signal that their meeting was at an end.

Not yet.

'You've been so helpful,' said Grace. 'I feel very reassured. I'm sure her mother will be too, when I pass all this on.' She paused, taking in Mrs Varga's pretty face. It had only been a couple of months since she'd first met her, when Charlotte had started at the school, but she looked different, like she'd aged several years. 'It's good to see that Charlotte has such a lovely teacher looking out for her,' Grace continued, determined to find out something at least.

'We do our best,' said Mrs Varga, starting to look distracted now, as if she were thinking about what she needed to do next.

'Charlotte has been lucky with her teachers,' said Grace. 'I feel like she and Mr Brown had already formed a bond in those first weeks she was here. He helped her save a baby bird.'

She watched as Mrs Varga's fingers went to fiddle with her wedding ring. 'That does sound like Mr Brown,' she said.

'He seemed so nice,' said Grace.

'He's a great teacher,' said Mrs Varga, shifting uncomfortably in her chair. She didn't meet Grace's eye, instead gazing up at the volcano display and frowning as if she'd just noticed a spelling mistake.

'It must be difficult,' said Grace, watching Mrs Varga's face cloud over. 'Managing without him.'

She had the teacher's attention now, the volcano display forgotten. 'It's been challenging,' Mrs Varga said, looking straight at her. 'But we've coped.'

'I do hope he's OK,' said Grace.

'He will be,' said Mrs Varga, twisting her ring around her

finger. Grace didn't push her, knowing from experience that often people would say more than they wanted to if the alternative was an awkward silence.

'I haven't told the children yet . . .' continued Mrs Varga. Grace leaned forward, to catch the words as they came out. '. . . just in case. But all being well, he's going to join us on the school trip.'

Grace had to hold in a giant sigh of relief. He was OK. Mr Brown was OK. He was coming back.

She couldn't wait to tell Charlotte.

'Charlotte will be so pleased,' she said. 'Thank you.'

'If you wouldn't mind, perhaps don't tell her yet,' said Mrs Varga. 'Like I said, it's provisional.'

'OK,' said Grace, who wasn't sure whether she could hold in that information. She smiled again. 'It's such a relief,' she said.

'Yes,' replied Mrs Varga. 'It is.'

Grace found herself humming as she walked home. An old tune, one she couldn't quite place, but she knew it was one of Jonathan's favourites. She'd dawdled on the way, treating herself to a relaxed lunch out and even a walk around the park.

Mr Brown was OK. Grace didn't know where he'd been, but at least she could reassure Charlotte that he'd be returning soon. She wouldn't specify the trip; she had Mrs Varga's confidence to honour. But she could tell her that he would be coming back, that was something.

Charlotte still hadn't seen her father, but at least one absent man was returning. Perhaps it was finally time for Grace to talk to Amelia about a visit from Tom. Her conversation with Mrs Varga had gone so well that she was feeling full to the brim with confidence.

Mrs Varga. Grace didn't know the details, but she felt sure she had more to do with Mr Brown than just as colleagues. The way she'd looked, fiddled with her ring. She knew what had happened to him. And Grace felt it wasn't simply an unscheduled holiday. She'd seen it in Mrs Varga's face, as clearly as if it had been written there in felt-tip pen.

Grace had seen Charlotte, briefly, in the playground, and her granddaughter had asked if Sammy could come to their house this evening. The thought made Grace feel even happier, and she decided that she'd bake cookies for the two of them.

She was still humming when she came through the door and tripped on the trainers left just inside.

She righted herself. Did no one but her worry for her hip?

Amelia.

It meant Amelia was home early.

'Hello,' she called.

'Hey,' said a voice from the kitchen. The kitchen had the best Wi-Fi in the house and Amelia sometimes sat there to make calls when she was at home, muttering swear words under her breath at her working conditions. It always made Grace feel uncomfortable, trying to prepare dinner or make tea without disturbing her. Loading the dishwasher was a minefield; leaving dishes around felt like polluting her workspace, but tidying up made such a racket. Amelia never complained, but the clatter Grace couldn't help but make as she put plates in their slots caused her daughter's jaw to tighten, the vein in her forehead to quiver like it used to when she was a child on the brink of a tantrum.

But no. Today was a good day. Grace went confidently into the kitchen. 'I didn't expect you to be back yet,' she began brightly. 'This is a treat.'

'The trains were up the spout.' Amelia spoke without taking her eyes from her screen, her fingers still typing. Grace found herself impressed by her daughter's ability to multitask. These days she herself often felt like she'd forgotten what she was doing halfway through, and that was without any distractions. 'I got in OK, but all the later trains back were cancelled, so here I am. Just what I needed, today of all days.'

'Wrong sort of leaves,' said Grace, with an attempt at light-heartedness. Her daughter still sounded strange. 'I expect.' She paused. 'Cup of tea?' she offered.

'OK,' said Amelia. Grace smiled. This was unexpected, and a good start. She felt the acceptance gave her permission to be in the kitchen, and she pottered around tidying things away while she waited for the kettle to boil.

'The meeting went well,' she offered.

'Oh yes?'

'Mrs Varga said that Charlotte is a star pupil,' said Grace, editorialising a little. 'And very happy.'

Amelia looked at her. 'That's great,' she said, seeming distracted still. 'Thanks again for going.'

'No problem,' said Grace. 'Biscuit?' she offered.

'No thanks.'

Not a surprise, and Grace didn't let it bother her. 'These ones are past their best now,' she said, popping one into her mouth anyway. 'I thought I'd bake some fresh cookies this afternoon.'

'Good,' said Amelia, her attention still on her screen. Then she looked straight at Grace, as if seeing her for the first time. 'What's that you're humming?' she asked, her voice sharp.

'Oh,' said Grace, unaware that she had been. 'I can't quite remember what it's called. One of your dad's favourites.'

'Hum it again.'

Grace did so. 'Recognise it?'

'Almost,' said Amelia. She seemed to soften a little, and joined in.

Grace closed her eyes. For a moment, she felt herself transported back to Amelia's childhood. To seven-year-old Amelia duetting with Jonathan, both of them wearing pink tiaras, while Grace, their audience, sat on the sofa, Peter's warm body snuggled into her. She could practically see his Thomas the Tank Engine-slipper-encased feet, tapping in time to the dubiously keyed rendition of Fairy Princess Elizabeth.

'"How Deep Is Your Love"!' declared Amelia, a note of triumph in her voice. 'I can't believe it took us so long to get it.'

'That's it,' said Grace. 'Your dad fancied himself as a bit of a Bee Gee.'

'He really couldn't sing,' said Amelia. 'He couldn't even stay in tune with Fairy Princess Elizabeth.'

Grace beamed at the memory. 'I loved her,' she said. 'You really were so talented.'

'Luckily for the world of music, I gave up songwriting at the age of eight,' Amelia said. 'It really was hard to find a rhyme for Elizabeth.' She paused. 'Now I come to think about it, there's always meth. And death. Not sure why I didn't come up with that at the time.'

'I told you to call her Mary,' ventured Grace. 'You could have rhymed her with . . .'

'Hairy,' said Amelia.

'Fairy?'

'Wary.' Amelia gave a small cackle. 'I'm not sure either song would have been one of the greats.'

The kettle boiled, and Grace made two cups of tea, brewing them for longer than usual. She didn't want to leave the kitchen now. This was the nicest conversation she'd had with Amelia for ages. Was it the ideal opportunity to ask about Tom? Or would it ruin it all?

'I'm thinking about inviting Tom over,' said Amelia, as if she could read her mother's mind. 'There's something he needs to talk to Charlotte about. Would that be OK?'

'He's Charlotte's father,' said Grace. 'Of course it's OK.' She paused. 'This is your home too,' she said. 'You don't need to ask my permission to have visitors.'

'I know,' said Amelia.

Grace took a breath. Even though she'd been about to suggest that Tom visit, the fact that it had come from Amelia gave her misgivings.

'Here's your tea,' she said instead, sliding it over to Amelia as she gathered her thoughts. She hesitated. 'You aren't getting back together, are you?'

'What?'

'Because I think it would be a bad idea,' said Grace, wishing that Jonathan was here to have this conversation. 'I know how hard it is to cope alone. I lost my husband too,' she managed. 'And I know you probably don't want my advice, but—'

'Tom isn't dead, he betrayed us,' said Amelia, all signs of humming stopping right there. 'It's not like Dad at all.'

'What?'

'Dad didn't leave,' continued Amelia. 'He died.'

'Yes, but it meant I was on my own . . .'

'You can't blame him for that.'

'I wasn't.' Grace looked at Amelia in surprise. That wasn't what she'd meant at all. 'I just—'

'You'll want to get started on your cookies,' said Amelia, pulling together her papers. 'I'll get out of your way.'

'You're never in the way,' said Grace. But Amelia was already gone, leaving her tea, undrunk, steaming on the kitchen table.

Grace had everything ready. She'd made lemonade and baked cookies, the chocolate chip ones that Sammy and Charlotte both declared their favourites. Amelia had clattered about upstairs for a while, then headed out to a café where she knew the Wi-Fi and the coffee were both strong.

It was a beautiful spring afternoon, and Grace went into the garden. Her daffodils were late this year, but they had started to unfurl their flowers, opening up to absorb the sunshine. She smiled at them, remembering planting the bulbs all those years ago. Peter had been making noises like an excavator as he used a small shovel to dig, and Amelia had placed the bulbs in the centre of each hole, carefully covering them in earth. Both children had been coated in mud. Amelia had even plucked a small worm from the earth and waved it in Peter's face, to his shrieks and intense amusement.

The clematis that grew up the shed was starting to bloom as well, the star-shaped flowers milky white as the moon. Rex started to bark just as Grace was debating whether she had time to do a spot of work on her layout. No. She'd begun to realise that the dog barked when he heard Charlotte come home, excited at the prospect of a potential walk with his favourite human.

She hurried indoors, feeling as excited as Rex to see Charlotte.

'We're going to the Isle of Wight,' announced Charlotte as soon as she was inside.

'And Mrs Varga won't let us share a tent,' said Sammy.

'I've made cookies,' offered Grace. 'And lemonade. Let's have them in the garden. I have news of my own.'

Charlotte didn't need to be asked twice. 'We need a plan,' she said, getting three glasses from the cupboard and the lemonade jug from the fridge. Sammy grabbed the plate of cookies and they all went outside and settled themselves at Grace's little wooden table. 'It's discrimination,' said Charlotte.

'It's not my fault I'm a boy,' added Sammy.

'Perhaps it will do you good,' said Grace, remembering what Mrs Varga had said. 'You can make some new friends.'

'I don't want new friends,' said Sammy. 'I just want Charlotte.'

'And what if none of the girls want to share with me?' said Charlotte. 'I'll be going tent to tent like a stray dog.'

'Of course they'll want to share with you,' said Grace. 'You're lovely. In fact, Mrs Varga was telling me that today.' She smiled. 'Among other things. Including your missing teacher.'

She had their attention now. 'Mr Brown?' asked Charlotte. 'What did she tell you?'

'He's coming back,' Grace said. 'Soon.'

She found herself in a three-way hug, two small sets of arms wrapped around her. Then the questions started, so fast that she found herself a little dizzy.

'Where has he been?'

'Was he sick?'

'Was he kidnapped?'

'Was it Miss Conti's boyfriend?'

Grace disentangled herself to better deal with the barrage. 'I'm afraid I don't know the answer to any of that,' she said. 'All I know is that Mr Brown is coming back.'

Charlotte took a breath. 'You don't know why he was gone?'

'No,' said Grace, feeling a little less pleased with her discovery. 'I'm sorry.'

'Then there is still detection work to be done,' said Sammy, his voice bright as a daffodil. He grinned. 'We can follow the evidence, see where the case leads.'

Charlotte nodded, and Grace realised that they didn't want to abandon their quest. 'Do be gentle with Mr Brown when he's back,' she warned.

'Well, we're not just going to ask him where he's been,' said Charlotte. 'That would be silly.'

'Exactly,' said Sammy.

'And you mustn't go to his flat again,' warned Grace.

'Of course not,' said Charlotte. She smiled at Sammy. 'We'll come up with something much cleverer than that.'

'Of course you will,' said Grace.

Chapter 17

Charlotte and Sammy were sitting in their favourite spot in the school. It was a bench just like any other, except it was where the school caretaker had made less of an effort at cutting back the bushes that lined the otherwise concrete playground. As such, it was more likely to attract the interest of bees and other passing insects, had a slight air of privacy, and provided a small degree of protection from misdirected footballs.

'So what's the plan?' asked Sammy.

'Well, I still think that Miss Conti's boyfriend is Suspect Number One,' Charlotte said. 'Maybe he did something to Mr Brown that meant he couldn't come to school.'

'Like kept him prisoner?' suggested Sammy.

'Kept who prisoner?' That was the problem with this bench. People could sneak up on them without Charlotte and Sammy realising. Luckily, they didn't often bother, but today Nia stepped into view.

'No one,' said Charlotte quickly.

'If you say so,' said Nia, in a very grown-up manner. 'Charley.' She paused and smiled at Charlotte with the expression of someone who knew they were about to offer something momentous. 'I'd like to invite you to share a tent with us. On the island.'

'What?' asked Charlotte, concerned that she hadn't heard correctly.

'That's right. With me, Anne-Marie and Erica. We want one of the fours because we've heard they're loads bigger, and Anne-Marie won't share with Aariya because of the hairbrush incident.'

Charlotte suppressed the small squeal that was rising inside her, but she couldn't do anything about the blush that turned her features pink. She beamed. 'You want to share with me?'

'Actually,' began Sammy. Charlotte turned to look at him. 'Oh,' he said, and was silent.

Charlotte looked at his expression and took a deep breath. 'I was still going to try to share with Sammy,' she said, pushing the words out reluctantly. 'I know they said boys and girls couldn't, but . . .'

'If you need to think about it,' said Nia, looking put out, 'you can, but Anne-Marie wanted to ask Tisha, so . . .'

'It's fine,' said Sammy. 'Share with them if you like.'

Charlotte looked back at Nia, who was now twizzling a strand of hair between her fingers. 'I'd love to,' she said, her voice much higher-pitched than she'd intended.

'Cool,' said Nia. 'Island crew.'

'You don't mind?' asked Charlotte when she'd gone. 'We couldn't share anyway; we'd never have won. And this means we don't have to go on hunger strike.' She opened her bag of crisps and offered Sammy one.

He declined. 'Like I said, it's fine. I'll see if Marlon has room in his tent.'

*

Amelia sat across the table from Charlotte after school, trying to act naturally. But she found she didn't know what to do with her hands. Her fingers tapped the table as if of their own volition, so she put them on her lap, but that felt wrong too, so she used them to scratch at her neck. Grace was at her miniature club meeting, so it was just the two of them. She'd deliberately chosen this time to talk to Charlotte, but now she couldn't help but wish Grace was pottering around the kitchen, dispelling the tension with offers of tea and home-made biscuits.

'Are you OK, Mum?' asked Charlotte. 'You're all fidgety, like you've picked up Rex's fleas.'

'I've invited your dad over,' said Amelia. 'Tomorrow.'

'Oh,' said Charlotte. She paused. 'Does this mean the break is over?'

'No,' said Amelia, not sure what else to say. 'But he needs to see you. I know it's overdue,' she added, wincing at her choice of words. 'But he's your father, and no matter what, he loves you.'

'No matter what?' queried Charlotte.

Amelia bit her lip. She was making things worse, she knew. 'The important thing is that he loves you,' she reiterated.

'I know that,' said Charlotte, giving Amelia a funny look. Amelia wondered what else to say. She'd decided that the news itself had to come from Tom, and she couldn't exactly tell her daughter that he had something to impart that had devastated her, then make her wait till the following day to find out what it was. But Charlotte was still looking at her, and she had to say something.

'I thought I'd pop out while he's here, get some work done,' she said. 'To give you two some time together.'

'It's Saturday tomorrow.'

'I've a lot to catch up on,' said Amelia defensively.

'Don't you want to see him too?'

'Your grandma will be here,' replied Amelia.

'OK,' said Charlotte. 'I can tell him all about my school trip. You'll never guess who I'm sharing a tent with . . .'

Amelia listened to her daughter merrily chatting away. Perhaps it would be OK. Sometimes it seemed like children were Teflon-coated, able to withstand pressures that adults could not. Charlotte had her school trip to look forward to, time away with her friends.

Amelia felt a moment of jealousy. A holiday with friends to take her mind off things. That would be fantastic.

No. It would take more than a holiday to take her mind off this news.

She found her fingers tapping on the table again, but when she looked down, she saw that they weren't just tapping. They'd left little indentations in the wood, like angry crescent moons.

She took her hands away and set them on her knees, under the table.

Thankfully Charlotte hadn't noticed.

'I can't join you all for dinner tonight,' announced Ava as she tried to thread the string for her swing set into the appropriate hole. 'Luigi is taking me into town.'

'I thought you were looking even more glamorous than usual,' said Grace, taking in her friend's freshly coiffed hair, and heels that seemed perilously high to her, though they were probably only two inches.

'Thank you,' said Ava. She smiled. 'I did think about missing the club tonight to spend more time getting ready, but then I thought no. He can take me as I am.' Grace couldn't imagine how Ava still had the energy and enthusiasm for dating. The thought of it made her feel exhausted.

'You look very nice,' said Samir. 'But your girls are crooked.'

'I beg your pardon?' Ava frowned at him, adjusting her top.

'On the swings,' said Grace, quickly; she'd noticed the same thing herself. 'The children on your swings are not sitting straight.'

Ava burst out laughing, sending strings and paintbrushes and the dyed green sand they used for grass flying everywhere. Grace looked at her a moment, then couldn't help but join in.

'You are making a terrible mess,' complained Samir. 'And I don't see what was so funny.'

'I didn't think you had it in you, Samir,' said Ava, wiping the corners of her eyes. 'My girls!' she said, and snorted into giggles again. 'Gosh, I needed that.'

'I hope you have fun tonight,' said Grace, pulling herself together.

'You know me,' said Ava. 'I always do.'

Grace smiled at her friend, feeling relieved again that her dating days were behind her.

She and Jonathan had given up on dates when Amelia was born, and were just rekindling hope of being able to go out, just the two of them again, when Peter came along. They didn't mind, not really. It was nice being the four of them, and she and Jonathan still had the end of the evenings together, the quiet, tired hours when the kids were sleeping. They'd snuggle on the sofa, glass of wine in hand, and chat about their day. Inevitably it would be the kids they'd talk about, dissecting the nuances of Amelia's latest school report, or worrying about how Peter seemed to have lost his appetite.

Of course, it was a sign, though they hadn't known it till later.

'You should come next time!' said Ava. Grace looked up at her; she'd almost forgotten where she was. It took over sometimes, even all these years later. She'd think about Peter and it was as if it was all happening again.

'I'll ask Luigi if he knows anyone.'

'No thanks,' said Grace.

'It's about time you got back out there,' said Ava. 'Met some nice men.'

'There are nice men here,' said Toby. Both women turned to look at him. Ava raised an eyebrow. 'I just meant . . .' he continued, stumbling over his words, sounding surprised that he'd spoken up, 'if you wanted to step out some time, I would be happy to oblige.'

'They're all coming out of the woodwork tonight,' said Ava with a smile. 'Must be something in the tea.'

'I don't know . . .' began Grace, feeling suddenly awkward as she became aware of everyone looking at her.

'All of us, I meant,' said Toby. 'A group excursion.' He was red now, and Grace could see a trickle of sweat making a dash for it down his forehead. 'To see a train. Ride a train. The model village in Bekonscot,' he said finally, finding his stride. 'We should all go for an outing to ride the real miniature train.' He looked at Grace. 'And see the model village. What do you think?'

'That sounds lovely,' said Grace, feeling relieved. 'A group excursion. Just the ticket.' *Just the ticket?* She was glad no one under sixty was here to hear her say such words.

'I'll invite Luigi,' said Ava.

'I'll bring my grandson.' said Samir. 'He'd love it.'

'All settled then,' said Toby, smiling. 'I'll make the arrangements.'

Grace lingered behind after the club to help Toby tidy up. 'Your see-saw is very impressive,' he told her as she rinsed paintbrushes in the small museum sink.

'It's a very simple weighted mechanism,' said Grace.

'You should do something with your designs,' said Toby. 'They really are so elegant.'

'I just do it for pleasure,' said Grace. 'And it has lots of memories for me,' she added.

There was a moment's silence, then Toby began to sweep up the green sand that Ava had scattered when she started to laugh. 'I hope Ava has a nice date,' he said.

'I'm sure she will,' said Grace. 'She's good at dating.'

'I wish I was,' said Toby. He looked at Grace, who looked back at her brushes. The water was running clear now, but she continued to scrub them for something to do. 'I've never been very good at it,' he said. 'The only time it seemed easy was with my wife.'

'Oh,' said Grace, not knowing what else to say.

'Seven years ago, she died,' continued Toby, unusually talkative. 'We couldn't have kids, it turned out, so it was always just the two of us. When she knew it was the end, she told me to try to meet someone else once she was gone. But it's not that easy, is it?'

'No,' said Grace.

'Anyway, I'm sorry I put you on the spot like that.'

'No, I'm sorry . . .'

'We'll have a lovely time riding the trains, at least. It's a great little place, lots of fun.'

'Yes.' Grace finally turned off the tap, feeling suddenly bad about wasting water. She started to dry the brushes. Toby came and took them from her. For a moment it was their hands that brushed, and Grace was surprised to feel something at the touch of his skin. A tingle.

'Thanks for helping,' said Toby.

'You're welcome.' Grace fiddled with her hair. She felt his eyes on her. 'Thank you for helping with Sammy's train.'

'A pleasure,' said Toby. 'Any time.'

Grace said goodbye and left the museum, thinking for the first time in a long while about how she looked from behind as she walked.

Like an old lady, she told herself, but even so, she allowed herself a slight sway to her hips.

Charlotte felt weird in her stomach, as if it were her that had swallowed worms, not the baby blackbird she'd tried to rescue. Her grandmother was being weird too, fussing around cleaning the house as though it were royalty they were expecting.

It wasn't. It was her father. And he was late.

Her mother had gone out already. She'd seemed strange when she mentioned her father was coming, tapping out an odd rhythm on the table with her fingertips.

Charlotte adjusted the jeans she was wearing. They had a big tear at the knee and she'd had to convince her grandmother that they were meant to be like that, and that no, her knee wouldn't get cold. They were the kind all the girls were wearing out of school now. She knew, because she'd been to Nia's house at the weekend with the others. These girls weren't that different to her old friends, she realised, and she felt like if she was careful, she could be a permanent part of the group soon.

Accepted.

She pulled at the end of one of the strands of fabric on her knee, and felt a slight resistance as the hole grew bigger.

She heard the doorbell ring, followed by a small crash as her grandmother dropped something. She stood up, then sat down again, then stood up. She looked at Pickle, who was absolutely still, but couldn't see Hugo. He was probably at the bottom somewhere, scrabbling around in the wet oasis foam she used to keep the privet fresh. She took a deep breath and left her room to greet her father.

Grace stood awkwardly next to the kettle, which was taking an inexplicably long time to boil. She'd offered tea, which she was planning to make, and then she was going to do some carefully choreographed work in the garden. Enough to make her seem busy, to get her out of the way, but keeping her available and not muddy if she was needed inside again.

Instead, she was here, held hostage by this stubborn kitchen appliance, which apparently had not got the memo.

The memo. She'd seen too much American TV. Charlotte had been watching *Love Shack* these last few days, and Grace had joined in, despite her worries about it rotting both their brains. From what she could make out, a group of skinny, tanned American girls hung around together talking about their feelings for a group of boys with tattoos they'd regret in later life, who clearly just wanted to lift weights and style their hair. Occasionally two of the members would couple up and go on a date somewhere with a picnic basket, not touch the food, loudly kiss and then return to report back on the experience to the others.

'So how have you been?' Tom was asking a question, and she realised it was directed at her rather than his daughter, who was busy being fascinated by the hole in the knee of her jeans.

What could she say? That it had been the best of times and the worst of times? That if he cared about how anyone other than himself was doing, he would have visited weeks ago? That having his wife and daughter living in her house had made her feel alive in a way that she no longer believed to be possible?

'Good,' she replied, with a nod to confirm the veracity of her answer. 'You?'

'Good,' he said.

She felt his answer fill her with rage, but the kettle took that moment to finally boil, so she picked it up and filled his tea cup. Deciding he didn't deserve nicely brewed tea, she splashed in some milk, removed the bag before it had a chance to properly release its flavour and slid it over to him. The ultimate act of British vengeance.

'Are you OK?' she asked Charlotte. The girl looked up from her jeans and nodded. 'I'll just be outside, I've got some gardening to do,' she said casually, as if she hadn't rehearsed those lines.

'The garden is looking very nice,' said Tom. 'I like the yellow tulips.' He gestured outside.

'Those are daffodils,' said Grace, with thinly disguised disgust.

'Very pretty.'

'I'll be outside,' repeated Grace, loudly.

'See you in a bit, Grandma,' said Charlotte.

Charlotte looked at her father as her grandmother clattered out of the room. He looked well. She'd kind of been expecting blood-shot eyes, messy hair and crumpled, unwashed clothing. Wasn't that how men were supposed to look when they were separated from their families? Heartbroken? She'd seen it on television. Her father was clean-shaven, smart. He smiled at her. Were his teeth a little bit whiter than she remembered?

'It's so good to see you, princess,' he said. 'I've missed you.' He came over to where she was sitting and gave her a hug. Charlotte breathed in deeply. She'd missed him so much, but all she could think was that he smelled different. 'You look all grown up,' he said. 'In just a couple of weeks.'

'It's been almost two months,' said Charlotte, instantly regretting the harshness in her tone.

'I would have come to see you sooner,' he said. 'I wanted to. But you know what your mother is like. And the business needed my attention.'

Charlotte looked at him. 'Is it . . .'

'Things are looking up,' he said. 'I've found an investor.'

'That's promising,' she said, using words she'd heard from him in the past.

'And you're happy here?' She nodded. 'I've missed you so much,' he said.

'I could come and visit now you're back in London? The train from here, it goes into Waterloo . . .'

'Soon,' he replied, lifting the tea to his mouth.

'When?'

'It's a bit complicated right now.' He transferred the cup from one hand to the other and then put it back down.

'What do you mean?'

He took a breath. 'Listen,' he said, although that was what Charlotte was doing already. He coughed. 'You know . . . you'll always be my number one priority. You know that.' She looked at him. 'I've met someone,' he added, the words quick. 'I'm staying with her. She's very nice. You'll really like her. She can't wait to meet you.'

Charlotte opened her mouth, then closed it again. She tried a second time, her brain whirring. 'Like a . . . girlfriend?' she asked, disbelieving.

'Like that, yes,' said her dad, sounding relieved that she understood.

'But Mum . . . It was a break . . . You still could . . .'

'It was difficult, with your mum,' he said, clearly feeling for the words. 'It had been for a while. And you'll really like Julia. You will.'

'Julia?'

'Yes.' He bit his lip. 'And listen, there's something else. Your mum thought I should be the one to tell you.' He hesitated. 'Good news, really.' Charlotte waited. 'You know how you always said you wanted a little brother?'

'A puppy,' she corrected, feeling like she was going to be sick. 'I wanted a puppy.'

'Yes,' said her dad, suddenly fascinated by the contents of his tea cup. 'Well, this is even better.' He looked up at her. 'You're going to be a big sister.'

Grace snipped the branch of buddleia that overhung the kitchen window and tried to get a glimpse inside without being spotted. She'd seen them hug, and then watched what was clearly an awkward chat, Tom mainly addressing his weak cup of tea.

She glanced in again, and saw Charlotte's face. She looked like she was going to be sick.

It was time to intervene.

'Don't mind me,' she said, clattering in so she couldn't be accused of eavesdropping. 'I just need some twine.' She was pleased she'd thought of a reason in advance and placed the twine on the kitchen counter. 'That jasmine just won't go where I want it to. It's like it's set on invading the rose bush, even though there's a perfectly good fence for it to climb. That's how wars start . . .' She stopped, realising that she had gone a bit too far with that explanation, and looked at Charlotte. She looked shaken, her face pale as a jasmine blossom. Grace fought the urge to throw Tom out of her house.

She didn't need to. 'I should be going,' he said.

'Already?' The word was laden with criticism, despite the fact that Grace was pleased he was leaving.

'It's a long train ride back to town,' he replied. 'But we should do this again soon, shouldn't we, kiddo?'

'I'm not a kid,' muttered Charlotte, but she accepted the hug he offered. He looked at Grace for a moment, as if wondering whether to hug her too; then, reading her face, gave her a half-nod instead.

'Thanks for the tea,' he said, nodding to the mug also.

'Safe journey,' said Grace, following him to the front door. She watched him fumble with the latch for a moment, then he was gone, shutting the door with a bang behind him.

Grace hurried back to her granddaughter. 'Did you know?' asked Charlotte.

'Know what?' said Grace.

It was too much for Charlotte, who put her head in her hands. Grace rushed over and wrapped her arms around her, and they sat like that, Grace silently speculating on what had happened, until Charlotte finally took her face from her grandmother's cardigan and told her about the baby boy who was on his way.

Grace didn't know what to say, so she gave Charlotte another hug to avoid talking. Her own thoughts started to wander, back to her own little boy.

'But he's so healthy,' she'd said to the doctor when he'd told her, his face stern. 'He just looks so healthy. Anyone can see it.'

Jonathan had taken her hand. 'He has been tired a lot,' he said. 'And his appetite isn't what it was.'

'Yes, but it was nothing to worry about,' said Grace. 'You said. He just wasn't sleeping well. Or all that hungry.'

'I know it's a lot to take in,' said the doctor. 'And we need to run more tests. The more we understand about his precise condition, the better his prognosis will be.'

Grace had watched Peter that evening. His cheeks weren't rosy any more. They were pale. He was tired, too tired to play with his sister, so Amelia had been sent to stay with her grandmother, just for a few days. Just while they worked out what to do.

She should have noticed earlier. Jonathan had done his best, but if Grace had been around more, she would have spotted it. She knew she would have. She would have taken him to the doctor earlier, it would never have got to this stage.

It was all her fault. It didn't matter that the doctor told her not to blame herself, that it could happen to anyone, that they couldn't have done any more than they had. She knew it was her fault.

'He'll get through this,' said Jonathan. 'The doctor said the chances were good.'

Grace had nodded, forcing herself to believe. Because the alternative was impossible to contemplate.

She felt her granddaughter wriggle in her arms, so she released her. 'Why would he do this?' asked Charlotte.

'No idea,' replied Grace. She fished for words of comfort and found nothing that seemed suitable. Then she caught sight of a box of cocoa powder sitting out on the counter. 'How about we make biscuits?' she said, trying to rid her mind of her own thoughts. 'To cheer ourselves up.'

'I'm not sure . . .'

'Come on. We can't just sit here being miserable.'

Charlotte thought a moment. 'Chocolate bourbons,' she said. 'They're Mum's favourite.'

'Then chocolate bourbons it is.'

Amelia sat on the wobbly café stool, staring past her laptop and through the glass in front of her. She shouldn't have had that second flat white. She could feel her heart beating a little faster than it should. It was the caffeine, certainly not the fact that she'd just seen the man who would soon become her ex-husband walk past her on his way to the train station.

Having left his bombshell behind, no doubt.

She flicked her laptop shut without even pressing 'save'. She hadn't done any work anyway. She'd been staring through the window, watching pigeons pecking up the remains of a vegan bar a toddler had tossed out of his buggy in a fit of disgust.

She needed to get back now, to pick up the pieces. She stood up and left the café. She should have been there when Tom told Charlotte. She knew that was the right thing to do.

But it was still too raw. What if she cried? Right there in front of him. In front of Charlotte. She couldn't bear to hear the words from his mouth again. To see his face as he spoke them. There would be shame there, of course there would. But what if there was pride too? It was another life that he was bringing into the world.

Another child. She still couldn't believe it. She felt indignation build up with each step she took. She and Tom had even discussed having a second child, the two of them, a few years ago. She'd been all for it at first. The thought of a little brother or sister for Charlotte. It brought back some of the happiest memories of her childhood, before Peter was sick. She'd wanted Charlotte to feel that; there was nothing quite like it.

But Tom had said they had so much going on in their lives. Her work. His business. Enjoying alone time, the two of them. Charlotte was enough, and she deserved all their attention.

Amelia had found herself nodding at that point. Charlotte *was* enough, and Amelia had remembered other aspects of what it had been like having a sibling, always fighting for attention and so rarely being the outright victor.

And now he'd done this. Betrayed them all, and put a new baby in the middle of the mess.

She stood outside her mother's front door for a moment, steeling herself for what she was going to find inside, before she put her key in the lock and turned it.

She was ready for tears and disbelief.

She wasn't ready for the sight of her daughter with powdered chocolate all over her face and clothes.

'What's happened?' she asked.

'We were making chocolate biscuits and had a cocoa powder disaster,' said her mother. 'You don't need to look so horrified; it'll come out easily enough in the wash.'

Amelia looked at them both. 'Charlotte,' she said. 'Did your dad speak to you about . . . what's happening?'

'Yes,' said Charlotte. 'He's having another baby.'

Amelia took a deep breath at hearing her daughter speak the words. 'We need to talk about it,' she said. She looked at Charlotte and could see the hurt curdling beneath the cocoa powder. 'But first, how about a hug?' She held open her arms and stepped forward.

'I'm still a bit chocolatey,' said Charlotte, stepping back.

Amelia put her arms down again, trying not to let herself feel rejected. They stood in silence for a moment, watching each other.

'We were feeling a bit down, weren't we, Charlotte?' said Grace, answering a question no one had asked. 'And I thought it would help if we had something to do.'

'So we started baking your favourites,' added Charlotte. 'Chocolate bourbons.'

Amelia felt sadness creeping up in her. She didn't know if it was the caffeine, the sight of her husband or the way that Charlotte was starting to sound like Grace. But it felt like too much. Could no one sit down and talk about how they felt? Rolling out dough was no substitute for dealing with emotions, but it was what she'd had to put up with from her mother for what seemed like forever. And now her mother was spreading it to Charlotte like a virus. She looked at Grace, who was in turn looking at the biscuits in the oven as if her primary concern was whether they would burn.

'For goodness' sake, Mum,' she said. 'Forget the biscuits.' The words came out louder than she'd intended and seemed to startle them all. 'Sorry,' she added, trying to calm herself down. It wasn't like any of this was Grace's fault, and the last thing Charlotte needed to deal with was an angry mother. 'I didn't mean to snap.'

'That's OK,' said Grace. She unravelled a length of paper towel, wetted it slightly and mopped at Charlotte's face. 'I'll just clean her up,' she said. 'And then I'll get out of your way.'

'Thank you,' said Amelia. 'Charlotte, let's sit on the sofa and have a proper chat. OK?'

'Dad told me all about it while you were out,' replied Charlotte.

Amelia stepped back as she realised something. Chocolate bourbons. Coffee. Baking when they should be talking. Being in a café when she should have been holding her daughter's hand. It was just different ways of avoiding the issue, of backing away from what needed to be done, what needed to be said.

Actually, not even that different. She felt flooded by shame at her actions.

At her absence.

No. She wasn't going to make the same mistakes as her mother. Not with Charlotte. She wasn't. Not again.

Out of the corner of her eye, she saw Grace reaching for an oven glove, and she tried not to let it irritate her. 'You can leave the biscuits, Mum,' she said, her voice as gentle as she could manage. 'We need to focus on what matters. We need to talk about what's happening.'

'What's there to say?' said Charlotte, all of a sudden. 'Dad's got a new family.'

'It doesn't mean he's going to stop loving you,' said Amelia. He'd stopped loving *her*, Amelia. She was the one he didn't want any more. It didn't matter that she'd thrown him out; it didn't make the rejection any less bitter.

'It was meant to be a break,' said Charlotte.

'I thought so too,' replied Amelia.

'But now he's going to have a new baby.'

Amelia took a breath. 'Yes,' she said. She'd thought about what to say to comfort Charlotte. *He still loves you. Families come in all shapes and sizes these days, but they always love each other.* It all sounded hollow in her head, platitudes when what she really wanted to do was scream at Tom for doing this to his daughter. To all of them.

'It's fine to feel angry,' she finally managed. 'I know I am. Angry and hurt and betrayed and . . .' She stopped herself. 'Angry,' she repeated. 'But we'll get through this.' She took Charlotte's hand, chocolatey as it was, and held it in her own. 'Together.'

'But we're not together,' said Charlotte. 'You and Dad and me.'

'I know, but . . .' Amelia found her voice breaking. Charlotte was right. Their old life was gone, the chasm forever cemented by the new life that was growing inside *Julia*.

'He's not going to have time for me,' continued Charlotte.

'He is,' managed Amelia, though she wasn't sure that was true.

'Plenty of people have more than one child,' said Grace, the words cracking a little as they came out. 'It doesn't mean they love the ones they already have any less.'

Amelia turned to stare at her.

'What's the matter?' asked Charlotte, her eyes on her mother.

For a moment, Amelia couldn't speak. And when she could, it came out angrier than she was expecting. 'Why don't you ever talk about him?'

'What?' said Grace. 'We're talking about Tom right now.'

'You just went back to work,' said Amelia. 'You locked up the shed and that was it.'

'Oh,' said Grace. She sat down.

'What's going on?' asked Charlotte.

'I think your mother wants to talk about Peter,' said Grace, her voice quiet.

'Who is Peter?'

'He was my little brother,' said Amelia. 'He died when I was twelve.'

Chapter 18

The biscuits were burnt, but they ate them anyway, straight from the baking tray, as they sat around the kitchen table.

'I had an uncle?' said Charlotte.

'He died thirty years ago,' said Amelia.

'Thirty-one years,' said Grace. The hurt of it never seemed to dull.

'Why didn't you tell me?'

'Your grandmother doesn't like to talk about it,' said Amelia, who was starting to look as if she wished she hadn't said anything. 'She loved him very much.' She paused. 'We all did.'

'I'm sorry, Grandma,' said Charlotte. Grace felt her granddaughter's fingers wrap around her own, giving her hand a soft squeeze that made her think of a small set of hands from years ago.

'Thank you, Charlotte.' Grace reached out and took another biscuit with her free hand, just for something to do.

'He liked trains,' said Amelia. 'It's why your grandma started building her models. When he got sick, they built them together.'

'We all did,' said Grace. She took a bite of the biscuit as they all sat in silence. It was bitter in her mouth.

She, Amelia and Peter used to sit in the shed. She'd put a comfy chair in there, wrap a blanket around him and they'd build the layout together. Even Amelia would help, though she was always more interested in the little people than the mechanics. Peter was all about how things worked; the dynamics of transformers and voltage and current. He was only five years old, but he'd listen, fascinated, to Grace as she explained.

One day he was restless, sitting there in the shed. 'I want to go to the seaside,' he'd said. Grace had looked at him in surprise.

'It's the middle of winter,' she said. 'It'll be covered in snow.'

'Maybe we could go in the summer,' suggested Amelia. Grace had looked at her, watching as Amelia's face changed. 'Oh,' her daughter said, as if it hadn't sunk in until now.

'I want to feed the seagulls,' Peter insisted. 'Build a sandcastle. Go for a swim.'

'I'm sorry,' Grace said, looking at his pale face. 'I really think . . .'

'We could take the train there,' he suggested.

No one spoke, perhaps all realising the impossibility of that idea. It was all they could do to move Peter from his bedroom to the shed.

'We'll bring the beach here,' declared Amelia, determination flooding her voice. 'A model beach.'

And they had, starting the very next day. Grace had brought sand and resin and crafted a sea, adding tiny shells and little figures in bathing suits. Amelia suspended seagulls from the ceiling using fishing wire, and even recreated something of the smell, with a concoction of essential oils mixed with coconut oil.

Peter had loved it, running his fingers through the sand. Amelia found a large shell and he held it to his ear, listening to the sounds of the sea emanating from within.

After that, wherever he said he wanted to go, Grace and Amelia would build it for him in miniature.

But after he died, Grace found she couldn't bear to be in the shed. For years, she locked it up, unwilling to deal with the memories. The life that hadn't been. She'd gone back to work, dedicating herself to her career. She'd even found some purpose again, although of course she'd never felt the same unadulterated happiness that she used to enjoy from the coil of a spring, the gliding of a perfectly fitted ball bearing. Not after what she'd lost.

'What happened to the models?' asked Charlotte, breaking her reverie.

'Your grandmother didn't have time for them any more after Peter died,' said Amelia. 'She went back to work.'

Grace looked at her daughter. 'They're still in the shed,' she said. For a moment, she thought of offering to take Charlotte there right now. Then she saw Amelia's face. 'But this isn't about the trains,' she said.

'No,' said Amelia. 'It's about you, Charley. Listen, darling,' she said. 'Your dad has made a mistake, and he's going to have to deal with the consequences. But he still loves you. You know that.'

'I suppose,' muttered Charlotte.

'And if you ever want to talk, about anything, you know I'm always here for you.'

'And Grandma,' said Charlotte.

Amelia picked up another biscuit and took a bite. 'Yes,' she said. 'Grandma too.'

Grace stood up. 'I'm going to get started on the dishes,' she said. She'd spoken more about Peter in the last hour than she had in the previous ten years, and she thought another word might break her. 'Would anyone like me to get them anything? Charlotte, maybe some milk?'

'No thanks,' replied Charlotte. She paused. 'I have some homework to do.'

'I've got work to finish too,' said Amelia. She looked at her daughter. 'How about we both work in my bed? It'll be cosy.'

'Will you be OK, Grandma?'

'Oh, don't worry about me,' said Grace, with an attempt at a laugh at the lie she was about to tell. 'I'll feel better when the kitchen is clean.'

Charlotte snuggled up to Amelia on the single bed. Her mother was warm and smelled of coffee and burnt biscuits. Her workbook and her mum's laptop both sat on the bedside table, unopened. Nothing seemed quite as bad as it had an hour ago, but Charlotte still felt queasy and unsettled right down to her stomach. It reminded her of when she'd eaten too much liquorice at her old friend Claire's birthday party and had spent all evening on the toilet.

'Quite a day,' said Amelia, breaking the silence they'd fallen into. 'You must have questions.'

Charlotte didn't even know where to start.

'What's it like?' she asked finally. 'Having a little brother?'

Amelia bit her lip. She used to talk to her dad about Peter all the time. They'd remember him together: his obsession with wheels spinning, with how things worked, his love for trains that surpassed all else.

But since her father had died, all discussion had stopped. Her memories were still there, still vivid, but talking about them felt like driving an old car, rusty from disuse.

'Infuriating and wonderful,' she said, after a pause. 'He used to take my things apart to see how they worked. I still remember when he dismantled my toy ice-cream cart, my prized possession, to examine the mechanism inside. He declared that it didn't even contain a functional freezer and that all my ice cream would melt within the hour.' She'd been livid, screaming at him that the ice creams were plastic anyway but the cart was ruined. 'He put it back together for me,' she said. 'Piece for piece.' She smiled. 'He was clever that way, like Grandma. She adored him.'

She looked at Charlotte, who was examining the pattern of swirls on the duvet cover. 'She must miss him a lot,' said Charlotte, without looking up.

'Yes,' said Amelia. She thought of the time after Peter died. Grace had barely smiled, going to work and getting home late and looking with a glazed expression at the endless drawings and report cards with which Amelia proudly presented her. She took a deep breath. 'We all did.' She paused, wincing at the cliché that was about to come out of her mouth, but unable to find other words that would describe it. 'He lit up our lives.'

Charlotte took a moment, tracing the concentric circles on the pillow with her fingertip. 'You loved your brother.'

'Of course,' said Amelia. She put her hand on Charlotte's and said words that hurt her as they came out. 'And you'll love your brother too,' she said. 'Half-brother,' she added, not able to help herself.

'No I won't,' said Charlotte. 'He means you and Dad won't get back together.'

'It's more complicated than that,' said Amelia. 'There are lots of reasons why your father and I can't be together, but it doesn't mean that either of us loves you any less.'

Charlotte nodded, not really believing it. Her father would have a new baby, a little boy. They'd never go on holiday, the three of them, again. He wouldn't be home to help her with homework, to tickle the stick insects, to laugh with her at her mother when she screamed at a spider lurking in the corner of her bedroom.

'I love *him* a bit less,' she said.

Amelia didn't know what to say to that. It made her so sad that her daughter had to go through this. And it made her angry too, that this man she had loved, who a little bit of her still loved, could do this to their family. 'That's OK,' she said. 'But he's your father. I know he'll do his best to make it up to you.' Even as she said it, she didn't really believe it. But what else could she say? 'And you'll always have me,' she added.

'And Grandma,' said Charlotte.

Amelia nodded. 'Grandma too.'

'What was the brand of sleeping bag you said you wanted?' Grace was staring at the shelves in the camping shop.

'Kelty Cosmic' said Charlotte. 'It's what Nia and Anne-Marie have.'

'It's a pity Sammy can't share a tent with you too,' said Grace. 'Did you want me to have a word with the teachers?'

'No thank you,' said Charlotte, quickly. 'We don't mind.'

'It's nice to have girlfriends too,' said Grace. 'There aren't many women who come to our club, but meeting Ava has been fantastic for me. You two really must meet soon. She's utterly fabulous, as she'll tell you herself.'

'Did you tell her about Peter?' asked Charlotte.

Grace picked a sleeping bag from the shelf. 'This one's a nice colour,' she said. 'The yellow of a cornfield.' She could feel Charlotte's eyes on her. What was she doing? She took a breath. 'No,' she said. 'It wasn't a secret, what happened to him, but . . .' She put the sleeping bag down again. 'It's just, sometimes when something is so very, very awful . . .' She stopped again, feeling tears gathering at the edges of her eyes. She couldn't cry here. Not in Mountain Warehouse.

Charlotte looked at her grandmother. 'You know, if you ever want to talk about it . . .'

'Thank you,' said Grace. She looked close to tears.

'I do like the yellow,' said Charlotte quickly, even though she didn't really. 'Shall we get this one?'

Grace took the opportunity to change the subject. 'Yes,' she said gratefully. She looked around. 'Now,' she said. 'What else is on our list?'

The conversation came back to the safe topics of wellies and waterproof trousers. Grace found she could gradually breathe more easily again, and she helped Charlotte gather up a selection of Gore-Tex clothing that rustled as she took it into the fitting room.

Grace took a seat on a small and incredibly uncomfortable stool just outside the cubicle and gazed idly at the display tent that was set up in the middle of the shop. She probably still had Amelia's old waterproofs in the attic, she thought, and there was definitely a sleeping bag there. She hadn't even looked for it, though. For one thing, she didn't like to use the ladder, not at her age. For another, children liked new things, and she wanted to treat Charlotte. She'd been so excited about this trip, Grace wanted her to have whatever accessories she felt she needed to make the most of it.

'Do these ones make me look fat?' asked Charlotte, stepping gingerly from the changing room.

'Not at all,' said Grace, perturbed at such a question from an eleven-year-old. 'And I love the colour.'

'They're navy,' said Charlotte, as if that were a colour no one could love.

'They're perfect,' said Grace. 'Let's get them. Then I think it's time for a treat as we've done so well. Let's go to a café and I'll get you something delicious.'

'Let's have another look at the sleeping bags first,' said Charlotte, deciding to choose a different colour now her grandmother seemed happier. 'And then I thought maybe we could look for some things that aren't on the list. Jeans and stuff?' She had gone through her wardrobe and rejected most of her clothes for the trip.

'Of course,' said Grace, wondering how many pairs of jeans her granddaughter needed. 'Lead the way.'

*

Charlotte sat with the girls in class and watched Sammy at the next table. They'd been put into their island groups to start a 'life skills' team project they'd been assigned: building a catapult for an egg out of a wooden spoon, two bricks and a handful of elastic bands. Even Charlotte couldn't work out how that would ever be a useful skill in life.

'Oh my God,' exclaimed Nia, jumping away from the bricks. 'There's a spider! Miss, miss!'

'Charlotte will rescue it,' called out Sammy.

Charlotte frowned. 'No I won't,' she said quickly, trying to sound convincing. 'Yuck.' She couldn't help having a look at it, though. She leaned over. A tiny red clover mite, no bigger than a pinhead, was crawling across the brick. 'That's not a spider, it's a . . .' She bit her lip, not wanting to be known as an insect expert.

Mrs Varga came over and dispatched the creature with a flick of her notepad. 'There'll be worse than that at the campsite,' she commented.

'Crabs,' contributed Marlon, snapping his fingers in the direction of the girls. 'Coming to pinch your noses in the middle of the night.' Kaval started giggling.

Nia rolled her eyes and raised her hand. 'I want a clean brick, please, miss,' she requested. 'And a tent a long way from Marlon.'

'I'll see what I can do,' said Mrs Varga with a sigh.

Charlotte watched Sammy drawing something but didn't peer over to see what it was. They'd barely spoken since they'd been put into different groups. She hadn't even told him about the baby. A pang of anger hit her, as if someone were flicking one of the elastic bands on her bare skin. She wasn't sure where to direct it, and found it seeping into how she felt about her friend. It wasn't her fault they couldn't share a tent, though he was making her feel like it was.

'Guess what happened at break.' She turned to see Nia

whispering to her. 'I saw Marlon pinch Sandra right on her bottom.'

'Really?' said Charlotte, grateful for the distraction.

'Do you think he fancies her?'

'Maybe,' said Charlotte. 'Did she tell on him?'

'She told Tabitha, who told Tisha, who told Anne-Marie. So it must be true.'

'Oh,' said Charlotte, not quite following.

'Hey,' said Nia, as Mrs Varga went to the far end of the room to help clean up the remains of an egg that had rolled off Kaval's table and smashed dramatically on the floor. 'Did you ever find out what happened to Mr Brown?'

'No,' replied Charlotte. 'But I do know he's coming back soon.'

'Probably just a holiday then,' said Nia.

'Yes,' said Charlotte.

'I don't see much of a catapult at this table,' said Mrs Varga, making them all jump as she appeared behind them. 'How will your eggs fly?'

Nia and Anne-Marie started to giggle.

'This is going to be a long trip,' sighed Mrs Varga.

Grace carefully folded Charlotte's waterproof trousers, thinking about the baby that was on the way. They were sitting on Charlotte's bed, packing for her trip.

Grace didn't want to bring it up. Apart from anything else, she didn't think she could handle a discussion about how babies were made. Charlotte must know; they taught them that kind of thing younger and younger these days. For Grace, it had been a mystery until she was well into her teens. A friend had broken the news to her in the end, a garbled account that left her feeling rather shaky. Amelia had given her a matter-of-fact and scarily accurate explanation while she was still in primary school.

'When will the baby be born?' asked Charlotte, all of a sudden.

'Oh,' said Grace, taken aback. 'I don't know, I'm afraid.'

'Will Mum know?'

'I expect so,' said Grace. She paused. 'She'll be home soon. She said she wanted to help you finish packing.' She thought of her daughter, of all she was going through. 'Maybe don't ask her just yet,' she added, worried that such a question would upset Amelia, and maybe prompt some anger at the person asking. She thought a moment; Charlotte should know, though, so she could prepare herself. 'I could ask her for you, if you like?' she offered, selflessly.

'I don't really care anyway,' said Charlotte.

A new baby, thought Grace. She and Jonathan had gone to meet Charlotte when she was four days old. Even waiting that long had seemed impossible, but Jonathan had been insistent that they give the new family time to settle before they visited. Grace had been so excited, barely able to sleep. Amelia had looked tired and pale but happy, clutching the baby girl to her chest as Charlotte suckled, cheeks puffed, skin still red from the shock of the air, having spent so long enclosed in amniotic fluid. Amelia had smiled up at them, gently unlatching the baby so they could admire Charlotte's scrunched-up little face. Charlotte's mouth had opened and shut, found no more food forthcoming and started to scream with an intensity that left Grace stunned.

It had been the most special moment.

'I'm sure you'll want to meet him when he comes along,' she said.

'I won't,' said Charlotte.

'It's up to you,' said Grace.

'None of this was up to me,' replied Charlotte.

Grace realised that she had said the wrong thing. What was the matter with her? 'I'm sorry.' She looked at Charlotte, who was just about holding it together.

Be practical. That was the answer. 'How many pairs of socks shall I pack?' she asked. 'You're there for seven days, so maybe ten, to give you some spares?'

'OK.' Charlotte smiled, seemingly relieved at the change of subject.

'I'll put twelve in,' said Grace decisively. 'There's nothing worse than wet socks.'

'Isn't there?'

Grace was saved from answering by the sound of the door. 'That'll be your mum,' she said. 'Why don't you pick which hair-bands you want to take while I have a quick word, then she'll come up and help you finish off.'

Grace left Charlotte flicking though her box of bits and bobs and went to the kitchen. Amelia was unpacking her laptop from her bag. 'How's it going?'

'We've made a good start on the packing,' said Grace. 'But there's plenty more to do.'

'It will do her good to get away,' said Amelia. 'I'll miss her, though.'

Grace looked at her daughter. She wondered whether to offer a hug, opening her arms in a gesture somewhere between an invitation and a stretch, just in case.

'I'll go up and help her,' Amelia said, fussing with her laptop bag and appearing not to notice her mother's stance.

Grace put her arms down again. 'Is there anything I can do?' she asked.

'Have you packed enough underwear for her?'

'Anything for you, I meant,' said Grace. She went over and put a hand on her daughter's shoulder. 'It must be hard.' She paused, wondering whether to ask her question. Better she ask than Charlotte, she decided. 'When's it due?'

Amelia shrugged the hand off, but for a second her voice wavered. 'June,' she said. 'You can do the maths.'

Grace silently did so, unsure what else she could say. 'I've packed Charlotte some extra socks,' she said.

'How is she?' asked Amelia.

'Confused,' said Grace. 'Have you spoken to her about it all?'

Amelia looked at her, and Grace felt the disdain burn into her.

'Of course I have. Families need to talk about big things that happen.'

Amelia watched as Grace winced at her comment, but found she didn't regret it. Her mind went back to the days when she and Grace and Peter had sat in that shed, building a perfect little world together, a world where any affliction could be repaired with a bit of glue and a dash of paint. Everything seemed possible then, even the most perfect beach, complete with the smell of the sea.

But real life hadn't been like that.

Peter had died.

Amelia had wanted to go back to the shed, to sit there with her mother and talk about her brother. About what had happened. Maybe even continue to build the world they had started for him. But Grace had locked it up and gone back to work, staying later than ever before. It was just Amelia and her father. Two where there had been four. That was when Amelia realised the shed hadn't been for all of them.

It was just for Peter. Her mother's favourite child.

And with him gone, there was no space for Amelia.

Her mother was talking. 'Charlotte is in her room,' she said. 'I've made a list of everything she'll need. Make sure she checks it all off.'

Amelia made a decision. 'By the way,' she said, 'my finances are looking better. I think I'll have the debts cleared by next month.'

'That's brilliant news,' said Grace, her voice catching a little. 'Congratulations.'

'So Charlotte and I will be moving out as soon as I can find a new place. I'll line up some viewings after work next week.'

'Oh,' said Grace. 'There's no rush.'

'No,' replied Amelia. 'But I think it will be better when we're out of your hair.'

'You're not in my hair,' said Grace.

'You know what I mean.' Amelia looked at her mother, who nodded back dutifully. Amelia couldn't stand the look in her eyes. 'Right,' she said, eager for an escape. 'I'll go and help Charlotte.'

Chapter 19

Charlotte could practically taste the excitement floating on the breeze. The class were standing on the platform, chatting and laughing, their bags piled high on a tired metal bench. Tightly coiled sleeping bags had been compared, the ominous clouds in the sky fretted over and train tickets lost and then discovered again, lurking in pockets or decorating the concrete. Parents had been reticently kissed goodbye, though Charlotte knew her mum would still be sitting in the car, waiting to wave at the train as it left.

They were ready.

Most of the children were in their tent teams, but Sammy had positioned himself next to Charlotte. 'I can't wait for this trip,' he said, the first words he'd spoken to her for ages.

'I bet you're just excited to see the tunnel at Barnham,' said Charlotte, taking the olive branch.

'Too right,' said Sammy, with a laugh. 'We go through that tunnel, then at Chichester we go over a bridge. And then the train will separate. I'm hoping Mrs Varga will let us get out so we can see the separation.' He smiled at her. 'But you can have the window seat if you like.'

Charlotte smiled back at him. 'You take it,' she said.

'Thanks,' he replied. He looked at her. 'I've missed you,' he said. 'You've been weird. What's wrong?'

Charlotte hesitated. She didn't want to talk about her dad. She didn't even want to think about him. But she couldn't sit with Sammy for hours and not tell him. He already knew something was up. 'I'll tell you on the train,' she said.

Nia came over, providing a welcome distraction. 'Hey, Charley,' she said. 'Nice jeans.'

'Thanks,' said Charlotte. 'Yours are cool too.'

'The fast train to Waterloo is due in two minutes,' interrupted Sammy. 'It doesn't stop here. I'm going to watch it from the footbridge. You coming?'

'No thanks,' said Charlotte, feeling Nia's eyes on her.

'You'll sit with us on the train, Charley?' offered Nia.

'She's going to sit with me,' said Sammy. 'We'll get out to see the train separate at Havant.'

'Boring,' said Nia. 'Charley, wouldn't you rather sit with us? You can share my EarPods.'

EarPods. Music. Giggling and gossip. Charlotte paused a moment, looking at Sammy, who looked back at her, his face hard to read.

'I'd quite like to listen to music,' she said, her voice tentative. 'And we are meant to stay in our groups.'

'Cool.' Nia smiled at her, then went to rejoin the others. Sammy stared at his shoes.

'You don't mind, do you?' asked Charlotte quietly, regret creeping up on her already.

'It's up to you where you sit,' said Sammy, seemingly talking to his trainer. 'Are you really not even coming to see the train go past?'

'No,' said Charlotte. 'I'm going to go to the loo. Nia said the ones on the train have automatic doors that can open at any point while you're sitting on the toilet, then the whole class will see you pee.' She shuddered with horror at the thought.

'Be quick,' said Sammy. 'It's only five minutes till our train is due to arrive.'

Charlotte watched guiltily as he wandered over to the bridge and started to trudge up the steps. She walked along the platform to the loo.

When she came out, she stopped.

A sound had caught her attention in the bushes, just on the other side of the fence.

A sound in her wilderness, to the right of the platform.

It was just a cat. A ginger tabby she'd seen several times around there before, and once briefly mistaken for a small fox. She went to move on, but then the cat paused and stared at her.

There was something in its mouth.

Something black. And feathered.

Charlotte didn't hesitate. She quickly turned to check that the teachers weren't looking her way – she couldn't risk them stopping her. They weren't. It appeared that the excitement was too much for someone, and the platform was splattered with vomit. All four teachers were distracted.

Charlotte rushed to the loose piece of fence that she knew so well and slipped through.

She crept as quietly as she could towards where the cat was sitting, its jaw still wrapped tightly around the bird. The cat looked at her and made a hissing sound, aware that she was after its prize.

'It's OK,' she said, her voice gentle. 'It's your instinct.' She crept a little closer. 'That's a lovely collar,' she said. 'But you don't need that bird, you'll have lots of nice cat food waiting for you at home.' She tried to see whether the bird was alive. It wasn't struggling, but there still seemed to be the light of life in its eyes.

She reached out, towards the bird, but the cat sprang back. Charlotte had anticipated that, and flung herself onto the animal. It squirmed and wriggled and scratched, but she didn't let go.

In the background, she heard the sound of the train approaching. Then Mrs Varga's voice, rounding up the children. 'Everyone in your groups,' she called. 'We'll get ready to board.'

Charlotte reached down for the cat's mouth, trying to prise out the bird. The cat howled in objection, the movement loosening its grip.

All of a sudden, the bird was in Charlotte's hand. She lifted herself from the cat. Freed, it shot off and disappeared into the bushes.

'In your groups,' called Mrs Varga again. 'Right, let's count you. Keep still. Still, I said. This is impossible. Miss Conti, can you help, please?'

Charlotte ignored her teacher's voice and looked at the bird in her hands. It was shaking, but warm. It was a young blackbird, its feathers shiny. A little juvenile plumage still showed through.

'Are you OK?' she asked it, her voice gentle. The bird looked straight into her eyes, and Charlotte felt a flicker of recognition. Could it be the same one she'd rescued before?

There was no time to wonder. The bird was wriggling in her palms, trying to free itself.

Charlotte opened her hands. The bird hesitated for a moment, then hopped onto her knee. She watched as it opened its wings and flew up into an oak tree, disappearing amongst the leaves.

'Come on!' Sammy had run over and was standing by their hole in the fence. 'It's time!'

'Coming,' said Charlotte, getting to her feet. She grinned at him. 'You'll never guess who I just saw,' she said.

'Tell me later,' said Sammy. 'We can't miss this train.'

*

'So that's Charlotte safely off?' asked Grace, pleased to see Amelia sitting at the kitchen table, laptop open. 'Her first trip since starting at the new school. Quite an adventure for her.'

'She's been going abroad with us since she was six months old,' said Amelia.

'It's different, though, isn't it?' replied Grace. 'Going with your friends rather than your parents.' Amelia didn't look up from her laptop, so Grace continued. 'I remember your first school trip. You were about Charlotte's age. So excited. Worried about whether you had the right type of sleeping bag, just like she was.'

'I'd stayed away from home plenty of times,' said Amelia, frowning.

'With my parents,' said Grace, worried that she'd somehow stumbled onto sensitive ground. 'It's different with your friends.'

'Yes,' said Amelia. 'You said.'

The five days Charlotte would be away suddenly seemed like an eternity to Grace. Just her and her daughter now. Together. Alone. No lovely eleven-year-old to chat about her day and her teachers and birds and stick insects. To break the tension, to give them all safe ground on which to interact.

Grace realised she was dreading it. At the realisation, guilt started to seep into her emotions. She should be looking forward to this. Mother–daughter bonding time. The chance to reconnect. Get closer.

She took a deep breath. 'So, with the vegetarian out of the house,' she started brightly, 'anything special you fancy to eat?'

'Whatever,' replied Amelia, and Grace was reminded of her daughter's teenage years again.

'Maybe something you miss from your childhood?' she suggested. 'Isn't there anything I used to make that you'd like again?'

'Dad did most of the cooking,' said Amelia. 'You were at work.'

'Yes, but . . .' Grace paused, biting her lip. 'There must be something.'

'I'm actually really busy with work this week,' said Amelia. 'I'll probably be back late most nights, and I'm trying to get some viewings in. You go ahead and eat without me. I'll sort myself out.'

'Oh,' said Grace. She tried not to look upset. 'It was just a thought,' she added.

Amelia looked at her. 'Don't be like that,' she said. 'We're looking at a massive deficit and need to raise millions if the labs are to continue their work. I've still got all of next year's budgets to be approved, a new campaign to finalise, and the board of trustees is breathing down my neck about demonstrating return on investment, so I need to put some extra hours in. You understand.'

Grace understood very little of that, but she nodded. 'No problem,' she said, fishing around for something to say to prove she wasn't upset. 'I'll be busy too,' she announced. 'The club is going on an outing and I'm in charge of the picnic.'

Amelia didn't respond and Grace didn't blame her. In charge of the picnic? Here was Amelia, with her daughter away, her husband having a baby with another woman, and a high-pressure job to worry about, and Grace was telling her about preparing a few sausage rolls. Maybe a quiche.

Her daughter needed help. Support. Someone to talk to about what was happening in her life. For a moment, Grace wished she could be that person. She'd love to be.

I'm a great listener, she would say.

No you're not, her daughter would reply.

And she hadn't been. Not straight after it happened. Amelia was right. She'd locked up the shed and gone back to work. She had to – they had bills to pay, and she'd taken almost a year off while Peter was sick. A part of her had wanted to spend every minute with Amelia, but there was another part that still enjoyed her job. The moments, absorbed in her task, when she wasn't thinking about what she'd lost. She couldn't bring herself to talk about Peter; the pain was too much.

Jonathan had talked with Amelia about her brother, she knew he had. So Grace had just carried on, in the only way she knew. It was all she could do. Amelia must understand that, surely? She opened her mouth to say something more, but no words came out. 'Cup of tea?' she found herself saying instead.

'No thanks,' said Amelia, picking up her laptop. 'I'm going to work in my room.'

Charlotte gazed out at the sea. It was a strip of dark blue, with the lighter blue of the sky fading to white above. She took a breath of the salty air, which seemed to explore deeper into her lungs than the inland air ever did. Her hands idly pulled through the sand, the grains gently caressing her fingers, leaving swirly patterns in their wake.

'Pretty cool here, don't you think?' Sammy sat on the sand next to her.

'It's OK,' said Charlotte. She paused, feeling a little anxiety. 'Nia was sitting there, though.'

'Even the air smells nice,' said Sammy, ignoring her.

Nia and the other girls approached. 'I asked you to save my place,' said Nia, her voice petulant.

'Could you move over a bit, Sammy?' said Charlotte.

'You're meant to sit in your tent groups,' said Anne-Marie.

'Go on the other side of Charlotte,' said Sammy. 'There's lots of room.'

Nia and Anne-Marie sat down on the other side with a humph.

'Everyone gather round now,' called Miss Varga to the class. 'Where Charlotte is, on the sand. It's time to tell you the rules of the campsite and the beach. It's very important that you all listen carefully.'

The class sat cross-legged on the beach, the campsite behind them and the sea in front. The tents were more permanent constructions than Charlotte had been expecting, and contained camp beds. Showers, already strewn with long black hairs, were in a building to their right, along with the toilets. The only reason they could leave their tents at night was to use the loo, and the path there was lit. They must put all rubbish in the bin and leave the campsite as pristine as they had found it, if not more so. Charlotte imagined that last bit was a reference to the hairy showers. Sammy poked her and mimed at her to turn around, but Charlotte ignored him, lost in her own thoughts.

Because all she could think about was her father. The new child. The one he'd chosen over her. Why wasn't she enough? She'd been a good daughter, or at least she thought she had. She loved her father, she'd never been too naughty, not compared to many of her friends.

Or had she?

Her mind went back to an argument she'd had with her dad when he wouldn't buy her a second ice cream. She must have been four or five, and it was coming up to dinner time. She'd thrown herself on the floor and wailed, and told him she didn't love him any more.

Was that when he'd decided to have another child? A better one?

Other memories flooded back, lapping at her mind like the waves lapped the sand. Times when she'd shouted at him. Times when she'd sided with her mother. The time when she told him she hated him because they'd run out of ketchup for her chips.

She frowned at Sammy, who was starting to whisper in her ear again. His warm breath tickled her, but she couldn't make out what he was saying. Mrs Varga was talking about the tides now. They had to stay on this stretch of beach because the tides moved quickly, and they must only go to the caves on the supervised trips at the times allocated. 'Shh,' hissed Charlotte, noticing Mrs Varga's eyes on them. 'Leave me alone.'

'Turn around,' insisted Sammy, more loudly now.

'Did you have something you wanted to share with the class, Sammy?' asked Mrs Varga. Sammy shook his head quickly. 'Good,' said Mrs Varga. 'In that case, leave the talking to me.' She looked different on the island. She was wearing jeans with a rip in the knee, and looked much younger out of her teaching clothes. Her hair had gone a little frizzy in the sea air, and already her face was starting to show a faint tan from the May sunshine.

Mrs Varga started outlining their itinerary. Charlotte smiled to hear that they'd be visiting the zoo as well as a farm where they'd be able to feed the lambs. Sammy beamed when Mrs Varga mentioned the steam train ride they'd be taking later in the week.

It was Nia's turn to whisper in her ear now. 'This is so lame,' she said.

'I know,' said Charlotte. She looked back at the sea. The sun was lower in the sky now, an orange haze lighting up the clouds, reflected back and dancing in the waves. It would be dark soon, and she'd be sleeping in a tent for the first time in her life. She felt a little flash of gratitude that she hadn't missed the train, thinking about the alternative. Back at home with her mother and grandmother, trying not to talk about her father's new family.

New family.

Charlotte hated those words. She felt her gratitude evaporate like water from the sea, forming clouds about her head. It took her a moment to notice that Mrs Varga had stopped talking, and everyone around her was starting to get up. What were they meant to be doing? She saw Nia and the other girls starting to walk towards their tent, already arguing about who would get which camp bed. She went to hurry after them, but felt a hand grab her elbow. She turned around.

'What is it, Sammy?' she asked. 'You almost got us in trouble with Mrs Varga.'

'Why wouldn't you listen to me?'

'I was trying to pay attention,' she lied.

'Are you angry with me?'

'What?'

'I know you had to share a tent with the girls. It's OK.'

Charlotte felt guilt creep up on her. Sammy hadn't done anything wrong. Not really. 'It's not that,' she said. 'It's . . .' She paused, looking for a reason not to tell him about the baby. 'What did you want to say?'

'I can't believe you haven't noticed!' he said.

'Noticed what?'

'Look over there.'

Charlotte followed the direction of Sammy's finger. A man was standing with his back to them. 'What?' she asked.

He turned around.

Charlotte gasped.

'Exactly,' said Sammy. 'It's Mr Brown.'

Chapter 20

Amelia blinked. She'd been staring at the numbers on the screen for so long her eyes were stinging. She liked spreadsheets, the order they provided, the good sense that could be extracted from them. When she worked on them for too long, she even started to dream in little boxes, her unconscious moving deftly from one compartment to another.

She made a change to one of the numbers and watched the repercussions spread across the chart; the complicated matrix of formulas that she'd asked Max in accounts to build for her paying off. She was almost there. The metrics were starting to add up in the way she wanted them to.

'Amelia.' She looked up to see Paula standing next to her, her jacket on, bag over her shoulder.

'Sorry,' said Amelia, remembering the Outlook reminders she'd been dismissing. 'I'm too busy for our lunch today. Let's take a rain check.'

'You need to eat.'

'I'll grab a sandwich later,' she lied.

'No you won't,' said Paula. 'Come on, let's get some air. It's a beautiful day, we'll find a table outdoors.'

‘I really . . .’ Amelia’s voice trailed off. She realised she was hungry, tired, and wanted to talk to someone who wasn’t her mother or her daughter. Someone who wasn’t involved but would listen. She’d already told Paula in a garbled phone call what had happened, but they hadn’t discussed it in person yet. She felt like she needed to.

She hit ‘save’ and locked her screen, standing up. ‘Come on then,’ she said. ‘But no alcohol. I have a meeting with Clive later.’

‘He won’t mind if you cancel,’ said Paula. ‘Let’s see how we feel.’

They shared the customary silence in the lift to the ground floor, then stepped out of reception into the brightly lit spring day. ‘It is nice,’ said Amelia in surprise, rummaging in her handbag for her sunglasses.

‘That window desk is wasted on you,’ laughed Paula.

They walked through one of the urban squares, which was littered with small groups of office workers lounging on the grass, sitting cross-legged in circles like children, their shoes kicked off. Amelia recognised some members of her own team and nodded in their direction. They waved back.

‘Thai?’ suggested Paula. Amelia nodded. She missed the trips to Asia she’d taken with Tom before they’d had Charlotte. She paused for a moment, wondering how long he’d been unfaithful to her. Had he always been cheating?

Not always, surely. He’d loved her. She knew he had. She thought back to their trip to Langkawi, the two of them sharing a day bed, their bodies intertwined despite the heat as they watched macaque monkeys play what seemed to be a game of chicken by the waterfalls at the edge of the infinity pool. She could almost feel his hand gently stroking her hair.

She stopped her train of thought as abruptly as she could. She was torturing herself. She nodded to a waiter and slipped into the chair he pulled back for her at a table outside their favourite lunchtime restaurant. She tried to appreciate the feel of the sun on her face while she held a menu she knew by heart.

'Do you want to talk about it?' asked Paula. 'I mean Tom, of course, not the curry.' She looked at Amelia. 'Sorry, lame joke.'

Amelia attempted a smile and failed. 'It had been going on for months,' she said, knowing that Paula needed no more context. 'At least that's what he tells me. It could have been years for all I know. It's not like I can trust a word that comes out of his mouth. He could have told me ages ago what was going on, when we first went on the break. But he kept up the lies.'

'Wine,' said Paula, beckoning the waiter. 'We need a bottle.'

'I told you, I have a meeting.'

'To hell with the meeting,' said Paula. 'You need a drink.'

Amelia nodded. Perhaps she did. 'And he said she was the only one too,' she added. 'But again, who knows?' She picked up a prawn cracker from the bowl, twizzling it round in her fingers before taking a bite. Crumbs flew over the table like snowflakes. 'I feel like such an idiot.'

'You're not an idiot,' said Paula, filling Amelia's glass and then her own. 'You were in love.'

'You know she's twenty-seven?' said Amelia, taking a gulp from her glass. 'Twenty-fucking-seven. And she's wealthy, apparently. She's bailed out his business already.'

'Then she won't be wealthy for long,' said Paula. The waiter came to take their order and they both asked for their usual. Amelia a green chicken curry with sticky rice, Paula a pad thai.

'She must have been the mystery investor,' said Amelia. 'But he wasn't in Scotland. That was an excuse so he didn't have to face us. I don't know why he didn't just tell us sooner.'

'He's a coward,' said Paula. 'And he wasn't staying at Steve's place?'

'Another lie, I suppose,' said Amelia. 'He was probably with her the whole time.'

'I wouldn't wish him on anyone,' said Paula. 'He'll probably do it to her too, a couple of years down the line.'

Amelia dipped her prawn cracker in the sweet chilli sauce. 'You know what the worst thing is?' she asked. 'It's what it's doing to Charlotte. How's she going to have a healthy relationship with men now?' She paused. 'Things that happen when you're a kid,' she added, 'they screw you up for life. I should know.'

'She's got you,' said Paula. 'She's lucky.'

'I'm forty-two, on the brink of divorce and living with my mother,' said Amelia. 'I'm hardly a role model.'

'You're clever and successful and independent,' said Paula. It was her turn to pause, staring at the prawn cracker in her hand for a moment. 'It's a good thing this has happened to you.'

'What the hell?' Amelia found herself reeling.

'That came out wrong,' said Paula quickly. 'What I mean is, you're better equipped to deal with this than anyone else I know. Look at you. You haven't had a breakdown. You haven't even missed a day of work. You can cope with this. Most people couldn't.'

I don't want to cope, thought Amelia. I want to live in a nice house with a happy daughter and a loving husband and take exotic family holidays together.

But that wasn't how things were panning out. Not any more.

'Maybe,' she acknowledged. She paused. 'I have to be practical,' she said. 'Hold myself together. For Charlotte's sake, if nothing else.'

'What does she think of all this?'

'She's upset,' said Amelia. 'But she's on her school trip now. I hope that will do her good.' A bit of distance, a break. She shuddered at that word. A break. Broken.

When Charlotte got back, they'd have to deal with what would happen next. She took a sip of her wine, not looking forward to the future.

'And isn't it a little bit exciting, the idea of dating again?' Paula suggested. 'When you're ready. Maybe someone better is right around the corner.'

'Or someone worse,' said Amelia. She knew Paula was trying to cheer her up, but the thought of having to date again was horrifying. 'It was hard enough at thirty. Now I'm in my forties, a single mother, and I hate men.'

'Not all men.'

'All men,' said Amelia. She paused. 'No, I can't go through that again. Maybe I won't even bother getting my own apartment. I'll just live at home with my mother, getting fat. Then she'll move to an old people's home, Charlotte will go to university, and I'll choke on a chocolate bourbon and be eaten by the neighbour's dog.'

'Usually it's a cat,' said Paula.

Despite herself, Amelia felt amusement tugging insistently at her lips. 'My mum wants to get a ferret,' she said with a laugh. 'Perhaps that will do the honours.'

'Urgh,' said Paula, shuddering. 'Ferrets are like extra-large rats.' Then she smiled. 'It's nice to hear you laugh again,' she said. 'Things will get better; you do know that?'

Amelia breathed in the steam from the curry in front of her, enjoying the scent of lemongrass and coriander. 'I hope so,' she said, picking up her fork. 'They can't get any worse.'

The bald ibis pecked at the entrails of a dead rat. Charlotte watched as a long string of guts emerged from the rat and the enormous bird swung back its head in an attempt to swallow them whole, as if sucking up spaghetti.

'Yuck,' said Nia. 'That's disgusting.'

'It is,' agreed Charlotte, fascinated.

'Let's go see the lions again,' said Anne-Marie. 'Maybe they'll be awake by now.'

Charlotte knew that was unlikely; lions slept for most of the time, especially after meals, and she'd seen various carcasses littering their enclosure. 'Sure,' she said, deciding not to volunteer that information. She followed the other girls.

Sammy ran up to her, wheezing a little. 'Cool zoo,' he said. 'Did you see those rat guts?'

Charlotte nodded.

'I thought I'd *swing* by the monkeys next,' he said. 'Get it?'

Charlotte smiled, but then she saw Nia turn back and roll her eyes at them. Charlotte forced a bored expression onto her face and Nia nodded approvingly. 'Aren't you in a different group?' she said to Sammy.

'I'm a rebel,' said Sammy, with a laugh.

Nia rolled her eyes again, a facial manoeuvre she'd likely practised in the mirror and decided suited her. 'Don't get us in trouble,' she said.

Sammy pulled at Charlotte's sleeve. 'Have you spoken to him?' he asked.

'Who?' asked Charlotte, though of course she knew who he was talking about.

'Mr Brown.'

'No,' she said, her attention caught by an owl peering out of its enclosure. It blinked at her, its amber eyes seeming to glow in the low light of the aviary. She wondered if it could roll its eyes as skilfully as Nia. 'He's back now,' she said. 'There's nothing to investigate.'

'But we don't know where he was,' said Sammy.

'He was probably just on holiday,' said Charlotte. Since her dad's news, she found it difficult to remain interested in other people's lives.

'He's not tanned,' said Sammy. 'He's all pale-looking, and he has those dark circles under his eyes. It's like the morning after my mum has a night out with Auntie Lisa.'

'Maybe he was with your Auntie Lisa,' said Nia, turning around. The girls all laughed. They stopped in front of the lynx enclosure, and peered in at what looked like a large cat, fast asleep.

'That's a cute baby lion,' said Erica.

'It's a Eurasian lynx,' said Charlotte, before she could stop herself.

'Did I hear you guys talking about Mr Brown?' asked Anne-Marie, as they all started walking again.

'No,' said Charlotte.

'Yes,' said Sammy.

'Because when I called my mum, I told her he was on the trip,' said Anne-Marie, with the cryptic smile that preceded gossip. 'And guess what she said?' They stopped, and a wallaby, perhaps sensing the excitement, jumped closer to the wire fence to watch them.

'That he had bad weather on holiday?' asked Nia, looking bored.

'She said I should stay away from him,' said Anne-Marie. 'She said she can't believe he's being allowed to come. That he shouldn't be around kids.'

'What do you mean? He's a teacher,' objected Erica.

'She said he wasn't fit to teach,' Anne-Marie said, eyes gleaming.

They all stood in silence for a moment. In the distance, an eagle shrieked. The wallaby hopped away, deciding they were actually rather dull.

'He teaches science, not PE,' said Sammy. 'He doesn't have to be fit.'

'Think about it,' said Anne-Marie, with a knowing look. She

didn't elaborate, and Charlotte decided she probably didn't know any more than the rest of them. 'And take a guess.'

'We don't need to guess,' said Sammy, frowning at her. 'Because we're going to find out. Aren't we, Charlotte?'

'You should stay away from him,' said Anne-Marie.

'It's boring anyway,' said Nia. 'He's just a silly teacher. Come on, let's go to the café. I'm hungry.'

'Charlotte?' said Sammy.

Charlotte looked at him, and then at the group of girls, already heading towards the café. 'You're in a different group,' she said, hurrying after her new friends. 'You'd better find them before you get in trouble.' She could see that Sammy wanted to talk more to her, and she knew she was being mean. But she couldn't help it. She wanted to be with the girls, talking about nothing and everything and keeping her mind occupied.

Sammy turned around and walked away, kicking an empty Coke can as he went.

Grace laid out all the ingredients in front of her and tried not to feel overwhelmed. This was just a picnic. She was going to make sausage rolls, sandwiches and a few cupcakes. Enough to feed eight people: herself, Toby, Samir and Bilal his grandson, Ava and Luigi, plus a couple of other members of the miniature club that she didn't know as well. She could do it standing on her head.

On her head. Grace doubted anyone could really do anything on their head, over and above watching television, and who wanted to watch TV upside down? Perhaps Padma, but she didn't seem the type to make sausage rolls. Or watch TV, come to think of it.

She got started on her tasks, slitting the sausage skins and squeezing the filling into a bowl to combine with chopped onions, sage and parsley from the garden and a little grated parmesan cheese. She'd decided when she hit seventy that she didn't have enough life left to make her own puff pastry, and the ready-rolled packets stared back at her as if full of accusations. 'I'm making the filling,' she said defensively, thankful for once that there was no one around to overhear her.

It was rather nice to use real meat for a change. The veggie sausages didn't have the same texture, and Grace squeezed the mixture between her fingers to combine it smoothly with the other ingredients.

The motion took her back. When the kids were little, she'd make a huge effort for birthdays. Even if she'd missed other events, she'd be sure to book time off work and make the maximum fuss there could be. It was simpler when they were young, content with a picnic in the park and a few friends, some of their mother's special sausage rolls and too much cake.

The parties became more elaborate and more expensive each year as Amelia got older. Bouncy castles were hired for the garden, entertainers came dressed as whichever Disney movie character was the favourite at the time. Party bags were filled and squabbled over. Then came the era of activities: trampolining, ice skating, bowling.

When Amelia hit her teens, the parties stopped, at least for Grace. Even though Grace and Jonathan did their best to make birthdays fun for Amelia, after the death of her brother she didn't want her parents there any more. Friends would come over with sleeping bags and videos. They didn't want to be cooked for; they wanted pizza delivered in boxes on a motorbike, and to lock themselves in the living room, giggling.

'It's natural,' said Jonathan, as he and Grace perched in the kitchen, excluded. 'And a good sign. She's getting more independent. Growing up.'

'I don't want her to grow up,' said Grace. Then she thought of the alternative and felt sick.

'Of course you do,' said Jonathan. He grabbed a beer, and Grace wondered if he was thinking the same as her.

'More fizzy drinks, please, Dad,' said Amelia, emerging from the living room with pink streaks in her hair. 'Relax, Mum,' she said, casting a glance at Grace. 'It washes out.'

'I should hope so,' said Grace, who then bit her tongue. Even then, she sounded old in her own ears.

'Any sweets?'

'I've baked a cake. Do you want that now?'

'No, we want Haribos.'

'I've got candles, we could sing—'

'Here you go,' said Jonathan, throwing a bag over to her. 'I'll bring in some more cans from the fridge.'

'Cheers,' said Amelia, and she was gone again.

Grace reached out and took a sip of Jonathan's beer, then coughed. She'd never understood the appeal of beer, but Jonathan had always loved it.

'And she's barely even a teenager,' Jonathan had said, filling his arms with cans of soft drink. 'We've got much more to look forward to.'

The doorbell rang and Grace looked at her hands, coated in sausage meat. She scraped what she could back into the bowl and then scrubbed the rest off under the tap before going to answer the door.

'Ava!'

'You took your time.'

'I wasn't expecting you today,' said Grace, wiping her hands on her apron. She could still feel bits of sausage clinging stubbornly to her fingers. 'I'm right in the middle of making the food for tomorrow.'

'Perfect,' said Ava. 'Listen, I told Luigi I could cook, and I was planning to just pass off the picnic food as a team effort, but then I thought it would be more authentic if I did actually help, so we could talk about cooking together. So here I am. To help.'

'Oh,' said Grace, feeling exhausted by the rather complicated subterfuge. 'You know it's just a few sandwiches and sausage rolls.'

'Perfect. When you've been dating as long as I have, you remember to keep the lies simple,' said Ava with a smile. 'It makes you more believable.'

'I'll put the kettle on,' said Grace, as Ava followed her into the kitchen and settled down at the table.

'Any biscuits going?' she asked.

'I was just getting ready to put the sausage meat in the pastry, if you wanted to help?' Grace offered.

'No, no,' said Ava. 'I don't want to get in the way.'

'You could start slicing the cheese? I'm making the sandwiches in the morning, but I want to get it all prepared now.'

'No need,' said Ava. 'I already know how to slice cheese.'

Grace sighed and passed Ava the biscuit tin. She carefully spooned out her filling into the pre-prepared pastry, brushing the edges with egg to make them bond together.

'So, are you looking forward to the outing?' asked Ava.

'I suppose so,' said Grace.

'You do realise it's your first date?'

'What?'

'We all know Toby is organising this for you. He just invited the rest of us because he chickened out of one-on-one.'

'Nonsense,' said Grace. 'Besides, he sees me every week.'

'He's cute,' said Ava, dipping her biscuit in the tea Grace handed her. 'If you like that elbow-patches look. Although being chicken isn't the most attractive of male attributes.'

'He's not chicken,' said Grace, surprised to find herself blushing.

'I knew it!' said Ava. 'You like him.'

'He's a very nice man,' said Grace. 'But I was married for forty years. I'm not going to start again now.'

'This is brilliant,' said Ava, ignoring her. 'We can double-date.'

'I just told you I'm not going to—'

'I wonder if he plays golf. Luigi is a member of the local club. It has a lovely spa. You and I can relax there while the boys play, and then we can all meet for drinks after at the nineteenth.'

'The boys? They're both in their seventies.'

'You know what I mean.' Ava smiled at her. 'I can't believe I didn't think of it sooner. I suppose because Toby's a bit frumpy, but then you're not exactly the trendiest, are you?'

'Have you just come here to insult me?' asked Grace. She put the last sausage roll on the baking tray and looked up.

Ava was still grinning at her. 'Of course not. I'm here to give you a pep talk.'

'A pep talk?' Grace felt as if she were Ava's echo today.

'Exactly. It will be fun. Don't mess it up.'

'Start cutting tomatoes,' said Grace with a laugh. 'You're in charge of sandwiches.'

'But—'

'Or I'll ask you in front of Luigi how you make sausage rolls.'

'Fine,' said Ava, standing up sulkily. 'But I'm taking credit for the cupcakes.'

Charlotte liked the rock pools. At first glance, they appeared empty, save for seaweed, dancing as the breeze hit the pool. But on closer inspection, she found crabs, scuttling sideways with their pincers in the air, tiny fish the colour of sand, and sea anemones, sticky red tentacles reaching out greedily.

'It's so slippery,' exclaimed Nia, teetering on a seaweed-coated rock. 'And what's that smell?'

'It's the sea,' said Charlotte, giving Nia back one of her eye-rolls. They both laughed and Charlotte felt herself relaxing.

'Have we found everything on the list?' asked Erica, looking into their bucket.

'I've caught a normal crab, but no hermit crabs yet,' said Charlotte. 'Or shrimps. And I've seen a fish, but it was too quick for me to catch in the net.'

'I'm bored. I want to go back,' said Anne-Marie. 'Let's just pretend we dropped the bucket.'

'Mrs Varga said we have another hour until our lunch break,' said Charlotte. 'If we go back now, she'll just send us out again.'

'I'm not risking my life clambering over those rocks two extra times to go back and then get sent out again,' said Nia, finding the least seaweed-coated rock she could and settling down. 'Let's just wait.' Anne-Marie joined her. Erica and Charlotte continued to investigate the pools, Charlotte keeping her net poised.

'Those boys are disgusting,' said Anne-Marie, looking at Marlon, Kaval and Sammy. Charlotte glanced up. They had all put seaweed on their heads, like shaggy green wigs, and were chasing each other, arms outstretched. She tried not to laugh. Sammy saw her watching and waved, the seaweed slipping over his eyes.

'Sammy fancies you,' declared Anne-Marie.

'He's a bit short,' said Nia, crinkling her nose in disapproval. 'And pale.'

'We're just friends,' said Charlotte. 'He's like a brother.' She paused, the word bringing back thoughts of her dad and Julia. *Julia*. Even the name made her feel cross.

'That's what they all say,' said Anne-Marie in a teasing tone.

'He seems nice,' said Erica. 'When I left my book in the classroom last week, he brought it out to me.'

'Ooh, you've got competition, Charley,' laughed Anne-Marie. 'He's a dark horse.'

'Shut up,' said Erica. 'That's not what I meant.'

'He's coming over.'

Charlotte inwardly cursed the girls and felt strangely self-conscious. She bent down and peered into a rock pool, pretending not to notice Sammy.

'Hello, Sammy,' said Anne-Marie, in a flirtatious voice. 'How's it going?'

'Fine,' said Sammy, sounding tentative, as if he were expecting a trap. 'Charley, I need to show you something.'

The girls all giggled. Charlotte stood up. 'What is it?' she asked, trying not to sound interested.

'It's private,' said Sammy.

'I bet it is,' said Anne-Marie. They all giggled some more.

'You can show all of us,' said Charlotte, wishing the rock pool would swallow her up.

'Erica wants to see it,' said Nia.

'No I don't,' said Erica, who was starting to blush.

'Come on, Charlotte,' said Sammy, ignoring them. 'There's something I really need to tell you.'

Charlotte looked at him for a moment, then back at the girls. 'OK,' she said. 'Let's go over there. We can look for hermit crabs at the same time.'

'Is that what they call it now?' called Anne-Marie, her innuendoes making less and less sense.

Charlotte and Sammy made slow progress over the rocks, and Charlotte had to use her hands on the ground at times so as not to slip over. 'This is far enough,' she said when they reached a small patch of sand that felt relatively stable. 'What is it?'

'I saw Mr Brown,' said Sammy, his voice urgent. 'He's gone off on a walk along the beach with a strange woman.'

'So?'

'I've never seen her before,' he said. 'She might have something to do with his disappearance.'

'She probably doesn't.'

'Maybe they'll be talking about where he's been.'

'Maybe,' said Charlotte. 'But probably not.'

'Come on. We're meant to be detectives.'

'We're meant to be collecting rock-pool life.'

'Suit yourself,' said Sammy. 'If you're going to be like that, I'll follow them by myself.'

Charlotte hesitated for a moment and Sammy seemed to sense it. 'They went just behind those big rocks, to the other side of the beach,' he told her. 'Come on. It will be fun.'

'Mrs Varga is watching,' warned Charlotte, gesturing to the teacher, who was sitting on a deckchair on the sand, looking cold. 'And she said to stay away from those rocks.'

'I've got a plan,' said Sammy, his eyes shining. 'I'm going to tell her that I forgot my inhaler and have to fetch it from my tent. She can't leave you all with just Miss Conti, and it's only a minute away, so she'll have to let me go.'

'But Mr Brown went the other way.'

'You can get down to the beach from up there,' said Sammy, pointing. 'If you scramble a bit. Mrs Varga won't see where I went.'

'It's a good plan,' admitted Charlotte.

'Come with me,' urged Sammy.

Charlotte looked back at him, then at the girls. Anne-Marie was smirking, Nia was frowning and Erica was poking at the seaweed with her net, her face still pink. Charlotte looked at the crab in her bucket. It waved its pincers back at her. It didn't matter to her where Mr Brown had been any more.

He was back; the mystery was over.

'Come on, Charlotte,' said Sammy. 'It will be fun.'

'No thanks,' she said.

'Really?' The look on his face almost changed her mind.

But not quite.

'I haven't found any hermit crabs yet,' she said. 'Or shrimps.'

'Fine,' said Sammy. 'I'll go on my own.' He set off decisively towards Mrs Varga, stumbling on the drying seaweed as he went.

Chapter 21

'So the scale of the light railway is 1:3,' said Toby, 'and the train is powered by an electrical circuit, rather than steam. There are three carriages on this engine, and just enough room for us all to board together.' He looked at Bilal, Samir's grandson. 'Please stand back from the platform edge, young man. The train can pick up quite a speed.'

'You do realise we could have got to the outlet mall in the time it's taken to get here,' whispered Ava. 'We could be in Prada right now.'

'Shush,' said Grace. 'Toby's gone to a lot of trouble to organise this. You'll hurt his feelings.'

'You seem very interested in his feelings,' said Ava, raising an eyebrow.

'Sausage rolls,' warned Grace. 'Luigi will be back from fetching that coffee soon.'

'We'll do a circuit of this track first,' said Toby. 'And then we'll have our picnic, before moving on to the model village itself.' He smiled. 'It really is quite spectacular, the largest of its kind in the UK.'

The train arrived at the platform, driven by a teenager in a cap a little like the one Ava had made for Sammy. Grace looked at it in horror. 'Carriages' had been a bit of an exaggeration. There was no roof, and the seats were just cushioned planks of wood that they had to straddle, single file.

Toby climbed on, surprisingly sprightly.

'Go on, Grace,' said Ava. 'Sit behind Toby. I want to wait for Luigi.'

'I'm not sure I can make it on there,' said Grace. 'My hip . . .'

'You'll be fine,' said Ava. 'Go on.'

Grace stepped forward. She could see Toby turning to watch, and she swung her leg over with as much dignity as she could muster. She scooted backwards to allow a decent space between them, but even so, she was aware of her breath on the back of Toby's neck. It was studded with little white hairs, like snowdrop flowers emerging from the earth.

'Budge up,' said Ava. 'Luigi's here.' Grace scooted forward a fraction.

'It's a beautiful train,' said Luigi appreciatively.

Ava hopped on behind Grace with a flourish. 'Yoga's paying off,' she said, smiling as she swung her leg across elegantly.

'It is,' said Luigi. 'But you all need to move up. I am afraid I cannot fit in that little space.'

They all scooted forward some more and Luigi sat down with a thud. The whole carriage tilted backwards, drawing Toby's corduroyed bottom rather closer to Grace's crotch than she considered proper. She could smell his shampoo: apples and coconuts.

'Sorry about this,' Toby said, turning as much as he could, giving Grace rather a good view of his large ear. 'I thought it would be fun.'

'It is fun,' Grace told the ear, and smiled at it. The ear moved a little, and she realised that Toby must be smiling back. She remembered reading somewhere that ears were one part of the body that never stopped growing.

The train lurched into motion. Grace grabbed on to Toby's waist to keep her balance, then quickly released him, embarrassed. Ava had no such scruples, and Grace could feel her friend's fingernails clutching her ample waist. The train gathered speed and the journey became smoother. Grace felt the soft stroke of a breeze against her skin. Ava's grip released.

It was beautiful. The garden they were travelling through was carefully coiffed to be in scale with the railway, made up of plants with small leaves and flowers: thyme, oregano and heather. Little box hedges had been trimmed into topiary animals. They passed a small maze, and then circled a large pond, complete with a fountain featuring a statue of a little boy peeing delicately into the water. Grace spotted a frog sitting on a rock, eyeing the proceedings with disapproval.

They went up an incline, giving them a view of the model village. It was spectacular, and Grace felt pleased that she had come.

'Isn't this fantastic?' exclaimed Toby. 'I can feel the wind in my hair.'

'What's left of it,' muttered Ava.

'Shush,' hissed Grace. But Toby couldn't hear. Grace smiled at the back of his head, watching the silvery wisps blowing in the breeze.

Charlotte hovered over the rock pool, net in hand. She could barely make out the fish; it was too well camouflaged, its skin mottled like the patterns of the sand. But she could see two eyes, black and round, a clue to its location. It reminded her of a cartoon darkness, where only eyes gave away a character's whereabouts.

The girls had forgotten about Sammy now and were chatting about *Love Shack* again. The school trip had fallen at a key moment, and they were desperate to get back to watch it on catch-up. Drago was going on a date with Olivia, even though he'd given a commitment bracelet to Sandy.

Charlotte hadn't forgotten. The look in Sammy's eyes lingered in her mind even as she watched the fish. So what if she didn't want to find out about Mr Brown any more? Her friend still did, and she should have gone with him. The girls would have teased her, but they'd have become bored with that soon enough.

She lowered the net, slowly, slowly, at a fair distance from the fish. It was caught in a small pool with little cover from seaweed and few places to hide. Charlotte scraped her net along the bottom in its direction, picking up sand as she went.

'Have you got one yet?' asked Nia.

'Almost,' said Charlotte. She managed to get the net under the fish, and then in one smooth stroke lifted it from the water and carefully tipped the contents into her bucket. She peered inside, but with the sand swirling around, it was impossible to tell if she'd caught the fish or not.

Why was she bothering? The other girls didn't care. All the animals would be kept for an hour or two, be drawn by a reluctant class who just wanted to have ice cream, then be released back into the sea.

And all this time, Sammy was alone, out of sight behind the rocks, investigating. An investigation that Charlotte had started because she'd needed to know the truth. Once upon a time.

The sand settled at the bottom of the bucket. Charlotte looked in. The fish was there, darting around, ricocheting off the sides. The crab seemed to be stalking the shrimp she'd caught, and the hermit crab had retreated inside its shell.

'Here,' she said, passing the bucket to Erica. 'We've got everything now. I've even got a hermit crab.'

'Where are you going?'

'I don't feel well,' she lied. 'I'm going to see if Mrs Varga will let me go back to the campsite.'

'We'll check on you later,' said Erica.

'Thanks,' replied Charlotte. She set off, the sound of the girls giggling mingling with the waves, lapping at the edge of the rocks.

Charlotte looked at the vast stretch of beach in front of her, wondering where to start. Mrs Varga had been easy to convince, barely even listening to her excuses as she waved her back to the campsite. Charlotte had headed in that direction, then swerved back, scrambling down the dunes on the other side of the rocks, just as Sammy had suggested.

The beach was different here. No rock pools, just tiny pebbles, their edges blunted by the caress of the sea. As she looked ahead, she could see the cliffs, gradually increasing in height as the gradient grew steeper.

What she could not see was Sammy, or even Mr Brown and his mysterious female friend.

She carried on walking, enjoying the crunch that her footsteps made on the shingle. The sound gave her an idea, and she scoured the beach for other footprints.

They were harder to see than on the sand, but she eventually found a trail of impressions. Two sets, heading along the beach close to the water's edge. Mr Brown and the woman, it must be. She followed them, still unable to see anyone in front of her, save a couple of seagulls paddling in the waves. She could see no prints that might be Sammy's.

Clouds were starting to fill the sky, and Charlotte felt the first drops of rain. She was grateful for her waterproofs, and felt a moment's longing to be back at her grandmother's house, curled up on the sofa with a hot chocolate. Sleeping in the tent had been cold and uncomfortable these last two nights, even when the days had been warm. She dreaded trying to get to sleep with the rain pounding down above her head.

After she'd been walking for about fifteen minutes, the footprints stopped, then snaked around, taking her up to the caves and then back along the shore in the direction she'd come from. Disappointed, she realised that they must have come back before she'd even set off. She cursed herself for hesitating, for catching that insignificant little fish instead of going with Sammy.

Where was he? With another flicker of guilt, Charlotte wondered if he'd abandoned the whole plan when she hadn't come with him. He was probably back in his tent, napping or sulking.

Then she saw another set of footprints. Shallower and smaller than the rest, and right at the foot of the cliffs. Of course, that made sense. He would have been following them from here, where he'd be less likely to be spotted. Charlotte shivered, looking at the sharp rocks jutting out like giants' teeth, and pulled her coat more tightly around her.

She hurried along, following Sammy's footprints. She'd likely missed all the action and they would take her back to the campsite, but she kept track of them nonetheless, getting a certain satisfaction from putting her own feet exactly where his had been. She noticed that the pebbles were still wet here where they'd been shaded by the cliff.

The sun started to peek out from the clouds, right at the highest point in the sky, and the shingle glistened, basking in the light. She stopped a moment to look out at the sea, turning from grey to blue as the sun shone down on it, the sunbeams dancing in the waves. It was beautiful.

She was so busy looking out at the sea that she walked for a while before realising that Sammy's footprints had stopped. She stopped too, looking around her. She retraced her steps, then paused and listened.

That sound. Not a seagull. Not the sea.

Gasping.

Wheezing.

Sammy.

'Those sausage rolls were delicious,' declared Luigi. 'You are a woman of many talents.'

'Thank you,' said Ava, shooting a glance at Grace. 'It's my own recipe.'

'I should make you a chef in my restaurant,' said Luigi.

Grace allowed herself a small smile at the look of horror on Ava's face. They were sitting at the picnic benches at the edge of the park, finishing off the last of their lunch. Samir's grandson, Bilal, was next to her, his eyes on the remaining cupcake. 'Is he allowed another?' asked Grace, looking to Samir for approval.

'While he is with Grandpa, he can have whatever he wants,' proclaimed Samir rather grandly, and Bilal reached up to snatch the cake from Grace's Tupperware. Samir turned to his grandson and raised a finger of warning. 'Just don't tell your mum.'

'I won't,' said Bilal, his mouth already full of cake, the icing smearing his face.

Grace felt a little pang. She missed Charlotte. She hoped her granddaughter was having fun on her trip.

'Would you like to take a turn around the model village with me?' asked Toby, smiling at her.

'There's the picnic things to clear up first,' said Grace.

'I'll do it,' said Ava, probably the first time in seventy-some years that she'd offered to do a chore. 'You two kids have fun.' Grace scowled at her friend, who all but winked at her.

'OK,' said Grace. 'If you're sure.'

Toby offered her his arm, which Grace took, feeling faintly

ridiculous. They'd grown up in the 1960s, not the Victorian era. But actually, her arm felt rather comfortable nestled there, and the two of them began to stroll.

The model village was magnificent. Set in the 1930s, it was delightful, with real plants, a small lake and the most charming little details Grace could imagine. There was a tiny pub, with outdoor seating. A miniature couple sat hand in hand, gazing into each other's eyes. At the next table over, a frazzled-looking woman appeared to be telling off a small child. Her husband was standing up, leaning over precariously, beer in hand.

They continued. 'Charlotte would like that zoo,' commented Grace, looking at the penguins, paused mid-skid across the ice, watched by a polar bear standing up on its hind legs.

'In real life, a polar bear would never see a penguin, living as they do at different poles,' said Toby. 'Even in a zoo it bothers me.'

'Polar bears shouldn't really be kept in captivity at all,' said Grace. 'They're one of the species that doesn't do well. Even in the best zoos it's rather controversial.' She smiled. 'Charlotte told me that.'

'Then she should see a toy bear in miniature instead,' said Toby. 'We should bring her here. Sammy too. I bet this place would be his idea of heaven.'

Grace thought for a moment of another little boy who would have loved it here, and bit her lip.

'Look!' exclaimed Toby, as a red train emerged from a tunnel. 'That's Arthur, one of the original engines.'

'He's a beauty.'

'How about we go to the town square?' he suggested. 'It's my favourite part. The mechanisms they have in place are really quite something.'

'Sure,' said Grace.

Toby was telling her about the plants: the honeysuckle,

snapdragons and Japanese cedar. 'Much lovelier than the replica trees in my shop,' he said. 'Though higher maintenance. And I love the real water here too,' he continued, a nervous tone to his chatter. 'And the fish. Those koi have grown quite out of scale with the rest of the place, like whales swimming around in the pool. Not that the scale is terribly accurate. The trains are 1:32 and the buildings and people are more like 1:12. To allow for more details, I suppose, but it's not something I altogether condone. What do you think?'

Grace smiled at him. It had been a long time since a man had seemed nervous in her company, and it was rather flattering. 'I think a little leeway is OK,' she said.

'I tried to use real water in my shop,' he told her. 'For the boat display. But ironically enough, it didn't look real. Isn't that odd?' This time, he didn't wait for a reply. 'I tried Perspex first, that was a disaster, then glass, which was a little better, before finally settling for resin.' He paused and looked at her. 'I'm sorry, I'm gabbling, aren't I?' He didn't give her a chance to reply. 'Anyway, here's the square. Magnificent, eh?'

Grace looked. There was a small man up a ladder painting a sign. The ladder wobbled and started to fall back; his companion, who was meant to be holding said ladder, was instead kissing a lady wearing a bottle-green coat. Then the mechanism sprang back and the ladder righted itself. Grace found herself wondering whether the man considered himself unlucky – always on the brink of damage – or whether it was actually rather satisfying never to hit the ground.

'It's lovely here,' she told Toby. 'Let's bring Charlotte and Sammy next time.' She paused for a moment, unable to imagine anyone not having the best of days here. 'Maybe even Amelia.'

*

'Sammy!' Charlotte ran inside the cave. It was deeper than she expected, curving round so at the back there was barely any light at all.

It took a moment for her eyes to adjust to the darkness, and she almost stumbled over Sammy, lying curled on the sand as he struggled to breathe.

'Sit up,' she said, bending down to help him. 'That will give your lungs more room.' She thought for a moment. What else could she advise? 'And stay calm,' she barked at him, feeling panic flood through her. 'Where's your inhaler?'

'I . . . dropped it.'

'Where?' she asked, feeling her anxiety rise like the tide. It could be anywhere on the beach, in the sea, in a rock pool, floating useless as a dead crab.

'I had it,' managed Sammy, but that was all the speaking he could do.

Charlotte decided to take that as meaning he'd had it in the cave. 'Don't worry,' she commanded. 'I'll find it. You concentrate on breathing, OK? Everything is going to be fine. Stay calm.' She started feeling around on the ground, but her fingers grasped at nothing but sand. Sammy was still gasping.

What would help? Charlotte took a deep breath herself. It was fairly dark in the cave, but she would be able to make out an inhaler if it was on the open ground, so it must be at the shady edges. She looked at the ground again, noticing a slight incline. If Sammy had dropped it, it could have rolled down to the lower edge.

'Sit up straight,' she told him again, in the calmest voice she could muster. 'I can see your inhaler,' she lied, hoping that would calm him down.

It did, a little. Charlotte noticed the wheezing lighten off, by maybe half a degree. She searched with her eyes and her hands at the base of the rocks.

There it was, the plastic smooth in her hand. She closed her fingers around it and dashed to Sammy, thrusting it into his mouth.

He took a deep inhale, then another. 'Easy does it,' said Charlotte, who'd read up about how to help an asthma sufferer the evening after their first excursion to the railway line. 'One puff every thirty to sixty seconds,' she instructed.

Sammy nodded at her. Already his colour was better, and the wheezing was starting to subside. He tried to say something.

'Concentrate on breathing,' she said, putting her hand on his back. It felt warm to the touch and somehow reassuring. 'You're OK,' she said. 'You're going to be fine.'

They sat in silence, Charlotte rubbing Sammy's back. His breathing was almost normal now, and every now and then he would take a short puff on the inhaler. 'Not too much,' warned Charlotte. 'You've already had more than your ten.' It had taken him an alarming amount of time to recover; Charlotte felt like they'd been in this cave forever. It was hard to tell how long had passed, in the darkness with the sun blocked out.

'OK,' said Sammy. He lowered the inhaler. 'Thanks,' he said, smiling at her.

'Thank God you're all right,' she said.

'I'm tough,' replied Sammy, with a laugh that set him off coughing again.

'No laughing!' commanded Charlotte in alarm.

They sat there for a while longer, Sammy's breathing starting to take on a more regular rhythm.

'Sorry I didn't come with you,' said Charlotte.

'You're here now.'

'I should have come when you asked.'

'That's OK,' said Sammy. 'I couldn't hear what they were saying anyway.'

'It doesn't matter,' said Charlotte. 'You need to stay calm. You don't want to have another attack.'

'I followed them,' said Sammy. 'And hid behind rocks, creeping along like a proper spy.'

'I don't think that's what proper spies do,' said Charlotte, though it was starting to feel quite Famous Five.

'But with the sound of the waves, I couldn't hear anything, so I crept a bit closer and then I heard them say it was time to turn back, so I legged it and ducked in here to hide. They didn't see me, though.'

'You need to be more careful,' said Charlotte, her voice affectionate. 'I need you.' She paused, watching him. 'Listen,' she added. 'I really am sorry. I haven't been very nice to you.'

'I know,' said Sammy. 'It's OK, though.'

'It's not.' Charlotte took a deep breath, feeling her lungs inflate in a way Sammy's still couldn't. 'I had some bad news about my dad, and I took it out on you.'

'Your dad? What's happened?'

'He's OK,' replied Charlotte hurriedly, not wanting to worry Sammy. 'But he's not getting back together with my mum.' She paused again. 'He's having a new baby,' she added. 'With another woman. A boy.'

'Brothers are the worst,' said Sammy sympathetically. 'At least yours won't live with you, will he?'

'I don't think so,' replied Charlotte. 'But anyway. I'm sorry. Friends again?'

'Course,' replied Sammy.

He grinned at her, and Charlotte found herself feeling much lighter. 'Now, let's get you back to the campsite,' she said, standing up. 'Save your energy for the journey. Can you walk?'

'I think so,' said Sammy. 'I was OK at first, after the run. But it's so much colder in here, and that sets me off sometimes. I started to struggle, so I tried to shout to them, but by then they were already miles up the beach and mustn't have been able to hear me.'

'Don't worry about that now,' said Charlotte, who wouldn't feel better until Sammy was back at the camp, preferably with a doctor. 'Let's get you up.'

She helped him to his feet. 'Not too fast,' she said, continuing to hold his hand as they walked forward.

They stepped into the light together. 'What the ...?' began Charlotte.

The beach was gone.

In its place was the sea. Surrounding them.

Chapter 22

Amelia was in the middle of a presentation to the trustees about her new campaign. She'd outlined the strategy and watched them nod agreement. Now it was time to reveal the work. She knew excitement was creeping into her voice and she could tell it was infectious, the trustees sitting a little straighter in their chairs. Some were even leaning forward, as if to get a peek at the concepts all the sooner.

Her phone rang. 'Sorry about that,' she said, feeling a flicker of embarrassment as she flipped it to silent. The number was one she didn't recognise. 'I should put a message on my voicemail. "I don't owe any taxes and I don't want a free upgrade."' There was a polite murmur of laughter. Things were back on track.

She was just about to flick the presentation to her favourite slide when her assistant peered around the door, looking apologetic. 'Sorry,' she said, nervously.

'What is it, Sarah?' Amelia asked, trying not to sound impatient.

'It's a call for you. It sounds urgent.'

'Take a message and I'll call them back,' said Amelia. Sarah had very little sense of what was urgent, and had once taken her out of an important meeting with a key donor to answer a cold call from a telemarketer.

'It's about your daughter,' said Sarah. Amelia rose to her feet at that, but before she could motion to Sarah that she was on her way, her assistant had blurted out the rest. 'She's gone missing.'

Charlotte looked at the water. How had it come up so far, so fast? A wave rose and crashed against the rocks, answering her question. She felt a splatter of salty droplets hit her face, and looking down, she realised that the water was already seeping into the sand on which she stood. She took a step further out, grateful for her new wellingtons, to see if there was still a shingle path against the cliff face.

Nothing.

She took a step back.

'The water won't come inside the cave, will it?' asked Sammy.

'Yes,' said Charlotte. 'It's coming in already.'

'But it won't get all the way to the back, will it? If we stay at the back, we'll be safe?'

'I don't know,' said Charlotte. She looked down again. Already the water was almost to her ankles. Mrs Varga's warning about the tide rang in her ears again.

But it was too late.

She tried to squeeze the panic out of her mind and think. 'We have three choices,' she said. 'We could wait here and hope that the water doesn't come too far back and too high.'

'That's the only choice, isn't it?' said Sammy.

'Or we could try to climb the cliff.'

He looked at her in alarm. 'Didn't you see it? It's a sheer face.'

Charlotte nodded. 'But we're both good climbers.'

'Trees, not cliffs,' said Sammy. 'And my asthma . . .'

'Then I think we need to swim back,' said Charlotte.

'Swim?'

She looked out. 'It might not be that deep all the way along,' she said. 'We could maybe wade some of the way, if we're quick.'

'But there are waves,' said Sammy. 'And look at the rocks.' He moved further back into the cave. His wheezing started again. 'I'm not very good at swimming,' he added. 'I usually have armbands.'

'Armbands?' said Charlotte. 'You're twelve.' He looked back at her. He was terrified. She realised that she was too.

'I'm sorry,' she said. 'Swimming isn't easy.'

'Maybe the water won't come up too high,' said Sammy hopefully. 'If we stay in here.'

'It's too big a risk,' said Charlotte. 'If we wait, and it does come up . . .' She couldn't erase the mental image she had of the two of them trapped in the cave with the water over their heads, unable to breathe.

'Someone might rescue us?' suggested Sammy. 'I bet the teachers will have realised we're gone by now.'

'They have no idea where we are,' said Charlotte. 'I used the same trick you did.'

He took a deep breath. 'I'm sorry, Charlotte,' he said. 'This is all my fault. My stupid idea.'

'It's *my* fault. If I'd come with you in the first place . . .' She stopped herself. 'I don't know why I didn't. The girls were teasing me, and—'

'It's not your fault,' said Sammy. 'You're brilliant.' He looked at her. 'You know, you're the best friend I've ever had.'

Charlotte smiled at him, despite the rising water. 'You too,' she said. 'By miles.' She reached out to hug him, and felt her hand brush the edge of the rocks, dry and hard.

'I wish we knew how far up the water was going to come,' she said.

'I wish we had a phone.' Neither of them owned a phone, but

even the children who did had to keep them locked up in the campsite safe.

Charlotte thought for a moment. The rock pools. They were covered in life: seaweed, mussels, barnacles, anemones. Higher up, the rocks were barren.

'I know,' she said. 'Come feel the back of the cave.'

'Feel it?'

'It's pretty dark, so there won't be seaweed, I don't think, but there might be algae if the water comes right up. If there isn't, or it's just moss and stuff, then the walls probably stay dry and we should be safe here.'

They both hurried to the back. Charlotte wondered if she was wasting precious time, but making Sammy swim or climb in those conditions seemed too dangerous, if there was any alternative.

'Quickly,' she said. It was too dark to see, so she used her hands, feeling the rocks and praying for them to be bare.

'I've found something,' said Sammy. 'I don't know what it is.'

'Where?' Charlotte joined him and he put his hand on hers and guided it to about the height of their heads.

Charlotte felt it. It was a plant, no doubt, but was it moss or algae? She grabbed it, ripping it from the rock, and rushed over to the light at the mouth of the cave. The water was almost as high as her wellingtons now, and a wave washed some inside her boots, chilling her feet and her heart.

'I think it's algae,' she said, examining the stringy green substance in her hands. She looked at Sammy. 'We can't stay here.'

Another wave came in, filling Charlotte's wellies with more water. She made to take a step, but the weighted-down boots were too heavy now. She slipped them off, her socks already soaked, and tipped them out. Both children moved further back in the cave.

'I can't swim out there,' said Sammy. 'There's currents and waves and rocks and . . .' His voice trailed off.

'You have to,' said Charlotte. 'If we stay . . .' She stopped herself. 'It's not safe.'

Sammy began to wheeze again. 'We're going to drown,' he said. 'We're going to die.'

'We're not,' said Charlotte. 'Where's your inhaler?'

He raised it to his mouth. Charlotte watched him. He couldn't swim to safety. She didn't even know if she could. But she could try.

'I'm going to get help,' she said.

'How?'

'I'll swim out and raise the alarm.'

'You can't leave me.'

'Hold on to your inhaler,' she instructed. 'Whatever you do, don't drop it.' She looked to the back of the cave. There was a small ledge that would give him an extra metre or so in height. 'Climb up there,' she said. 'I'll bring back help.'

'You'll die.' The panic in his voice was infectious.

'No I won't,' said Charlotte, the water around her knees as she waded out. She paused, then undressed down to her T-shirt and underwear. She was freezing cold, but she knew the extra weight from the clothes would be the last thing she needed. 'I'm a good swimmer,' she said. 'I'll be fine.' She went back and hugged Sammy. He squeezed her back, and they stood there together, intertwined, until Charlotte unravelled herself.

She turned around and went back to the mouth of the cave, wading until the water was too deep, then she threw herself forward and started to swim for her life.

For both their lives.

'What do you mean, missing?' Amelia was shouting down the phone, not caring that everyone in the office was staring at her.

'She's eleven. She's on a school trip. In your care. Why weren't you watching her?'

Mrs Varga didn't have a good explanation. How could she? This was negligence.

And her daughter was missing.

'I'm coming there right now,' said Amelia. She took her mouth away from the phone to call to her assistant. 'Sarah. Get me on the next crossing to the Isle of Wight.' Mrs Varga was still talking. 'Yes, I do think it's necessary for me to come ... Well, you had better hope she shows up.' She listened for a moment. 'OK,' she said. 'The coastguards ...' A vision of her daughter, white-faced and wet-haired and washed up on the shore, suddenly came unbidden to her mind. All the other terrible things that could happen to a girl on her own came too, and jostled for position alongside that image. 'And the police too,' she instructed. 'At once.' She listened, her eyes on Sarah, who was on the phone, presumably trying to get tickets. 'The catamaran will be quickest,' she called out. 'And Sammy too?' She paused, feeling a thread of comfort and clinging to it. If her daughter was with her friend, it was a little more likely that they had gone somewhere together.

But it wasn't like Charlotte to run away.

She had been taken; she must have been. Amelia felt the comfort snap.

She needed to get to the Isle of Wight. She needed to be there, looking for her daughter. She put down the phone and looked at Sarah, who was already speaking. 'You're booked on the catamaran from Portsmouth Harbour to Ryde. The quickest way is by train, you can get the 14.57 if you leave now.'

Amelia glanced at her watch, grabbed her handbag and ran from the office.

*

Grace sat on the coach, staring out of the window. The glass was murky, covered in the echoes of dirty raindrops that reminded her of dried tears. The scene outside was little better; a grey day on the M25, the edge of the road punctuated with the corpses of animals that had ventured too near the traffic: foxes, rabbits, even a small deer.

She glanced away from the window to look at her fellow passengers. She was sitting on her own. Ava and Luigi were at the back, chatting and giggling like naughty schoolchildren. Samir and Bilal were both fast asleep, matching mouths open.

Toby was sitting across from her, staring out of the window.

Grace turned back to her window. It was starting to rain; that gentle British rain that was almost mist. Tiny droplets settled on the glass, catching the light like jewels. They were much more glamorous than the grubby ghosts of their dried-up predecessors.

'Guess what?' exclaimed Ava, her eyes sparkling like the raindrops as she plopped herself into the seat next to Grace.

'You shouldn't be walking around on a moving vehicle,' said Grace. 'What if you fell?'

'But I have fallen,' said Ava.

Grace looked at her in alarm, her eyes dropping to Ava's legs. She didn't seem in pain, but her feet were encased in rather impractical shoes. It was no wonder this had happened.

'You really should consider footwear with better grip. Especially if you're going to be walking around in moving vehicles.'

'Not that type of fall,' laughed Ava, then paused for dramatic effect. 'I have fallen in love.'

'What?' said Grace.

'With Luigi,' clarified Ava. She leaned in closer to Grace, who could smell a hint of the vanilla buttercream she'd used to ice the cupcakes on her friend's breath. 'And I just told him so.'

'Why?' asked Grace, still reeling.

'Because I do, of course.'

'But you've been dating for what, three weeks?' Grace's mind went back to her own courtship with Jonathan, her only context. Months of dancing around their feelings, dropping half-hints and wistful smiles. And she'd considered herself forward and liberated at the time. She'd invited him on their first date, for goodness' sake.

But a declaration of love after a few weeks?

'Retirement years are like cat years,' explained Ava. 'Things need to move faster now we're . . .' she paused, fishing for the right word, 'mature.'

'And you just came out and said it?'

Ava giggled, any maturity seemingly evaporating. 'Of course,' she said. She smiled. 'And it worked, because he said it right back. I even told him I hadn't really made the sausage rolls, and he didn't care.'

Grace found her friend's smile infectious. 'I'm happy for you,' she said, wondering what it would be like to think something and just say it, without worrying about the repercussions and judgement.

'And of course, it means I'll get free olives.'

'I hope that's not all you'll be getting,' said Grace.

'Me too.' Ava winked. Both of them got the giggles, and Grace found herself grateful for Padma's pelvic floor exercises as she tried not to let her bladder join in the excitement.

'But seriously,' said Ava, as their laughter subsided, 'he's kind and sweet and wonderful. I'm lucky to have found him.'

'And he's lucky to have found you,' replied Grace.

'The olives are just the cherry on the top,' added Ava.

'But saltier,' said Grace with a laugh. She glanced at Toby. He caught her eye for a moment, smiled, and then looked back at the rain battering the window.

'Toby is rather wonderful too,' commented Ava, her voice low for once. 'The same could be said of him.'

Except it hadn't. Because Grace hadn't said it.

'One of you should say how you feel,' said Ava, seeming to read her mind. 'He's fancied you for ages.'

'No one has fancied me for years.'

'Nonsense. You're fabulous. But the two of you are hopeless. What with his stiff upper lip and you keeping your chin up, it's no wonder you can barely speak to each other. You're not even sitting together, though you clearly both want to.'

'I don't know . . .'

'All I'm saying,' added Ava, 'is that if you want someone to know how you feel, you have to tell them. Organising group excursions and making models and baking cupcakes is all well and good, but it doesn't actually get you what you want and it's very much open to misinterpretation.'

Grace nodded. It sounded so sensible, so easy. Just to say what you felt. But it wasn't like that. Not for her. Not any more.

'I'd better get back to Luigi,' said Ava, giving Grace's hand a squeeze. 'You think about it.'

Grace squeezed back. 'I will.'

She looked at Toby as Ava left. 'Good thing we left when we did,' he ventured. 'Look at that rain.'

'Yes,' she agreed. She thought for a moment. 'It was a good trip,' she said. 'I enjoyed spending time with you.'

Toby beamed. 'As did I,' he said. 'With you.'

The cold came as a shock to Charlotte. She had already been in the water up to her knees, but the sea hit her body like a block of ice. She tried to ignore it, telling herself it would be fine soon, she'd get used to it. It was only the Solent, after all, not the Arctic

Ocean. She swam forward, casting a nervous look back at Sammy, who was watching her from inside the cave. A wave washed her back towards the cliffs, and she fought to continue. Another wave came, but she was ready for this one and closed her eyes, pushing her body upwards to rise with the water. She tried not to look out to sea, focusing instead on the cliff face. She realised that she wouldn't be able to swim far, not in these conditions. She needed to hope for shallower water soon, or to find somewhere she could get a grip and climb out.

Another wave hit her, hard, and she felt herself submerged beneath the sea. A force seemed to pull her deeper and deeper and further away from the cliffs. She struggled back to the surface and took a deep gulp of air. Another wave, stronger than the first, picked her up and thrust her against the rocks.

She cried out in pain, but the sea swallowed the noise and the current dragged her back under.

Another wave, and another.

Charlotte felt her head crashing against the rocks.

Then she felt nothing.

Nothing at all.

Chapter 23

Grace was pleased to be home, but she didn't feel right. She put the kettle on, but was uneasy, cold, even in her warmest cardigan. She went to the thermostat and turned up the heating. Jonathan hated an overheated house, especially in the spring, but he didn't get a say any more.

After her day out, she found herself longing for more company. She looked at her watch. Amelia wouldn't be back for hours. A perk of a trip planned by and for OAPs was that they were all well aware of their energy limitations and arranged to be safely back home by four.

She made a cup of tea, and decided to check on the stick insects while she drank it. She'd been left in charge of their care, and had diligently replaced their privet every day, choosing the choicest sprigs from her new plant. She entered Charlotte's room and clamped her mouth shut to avoid greeting them by name. Even if there was no one else to hear her talk to an insect, she would know, and then she'd worry about her own sanity.

Instead, she smiled at them as they munched on leaves, blissfully unaware of their owner's absence. 'It's only five more days now,' she said, deciding that it was OK to speak out loud because she was talking to herself more than to them. 'Then she'll be home. I can't wait.'

Grace realised she was exhausted. Even on pensioner's time, it had been a long day for her. She looked at Charlotte's bed, unslept in for two nights, and decided to settle there for a quick lie-down. Charlotte wouldn't mind, and Grace missed her so much. She lay down, breathing in the scent of her granddaughter's shampoo lingering on her pillowcase, and closed her eyes for a moment.

She couldn't relax.

She couldn't shake the feeling she had.

The feeling that something wasn't right.

It was probably just the excursion, she decided. The model village, the trains. It brought it all back.

That was why she felt like this. The heaviness in her stomach. The bile in her mouth. The twitch at the corner of her eye.

It was how she'd felt that day thirty-one years ago.

She'd never forget the moment in the doctor's office. *It has spread.* The three words she dreaded more than any others. She had known from the doctor's face that it wasn't going to be good news. But this? This was too much. She'd heard Jonathan's voice, discussing treatment plans and palliative care, but it all seemed so distant. So impossible.

This wasn't what was going to happen to her son. It wasn't.

Not five-year-old Peter. Peter who had been perfect from the moment he'd been born. Peter who she'd curled up next to at night, who knew everything there was to be known about trains. Peter who could have done anything he'd wanted to with his life. Funny, clever, kind Peter. There couldn't be a world without him. Grace couldn't exist in a world without him.

But here she was.

She remembered the phone calls she used to get from her friends and family. *Is Peter doing OK? He's a fighter. He'll pull through.* Well meaning, but awful to answer. People expected her to provide good news, and when she couldn't, no one knew what to say.

Amelia stood on the deck of the catamaran. It was raining in earnest, but she barely noticed the rain lashing against her face as she stared out at the sea, the cliffs in the distance.

Charlotte. Her little girl. Missing.

Amelia had never been an anxious parent; she'd made it her mission not to be. She still remembered her dad carefully inspecting each piece of equipment in the playground for safety before allowing her to climb. Her embarrassment in the park when her mother lost sight of her and was frantically calling, panic seeping out of her voice, when Amelia was simply on the other side of a tree. Or the humiliation of Grace insisting on walking her to school on her rare days off when all her friends came in on their own. Of having the earliest curfew, her dad dragging himself out of bed, groggy-eyed, to pick her up from a party when it had barely started, a coat over his pyjamas.

No. She'd been relaxed with Charlotte, laughing when other parents worried about whether their babies were getting enough milk or analysed their offspring's poo for reassurance of their health. Toddler Charlotte had been allowed to cruise along the furniture in restaurants, the occasional bump on the head accepted as a necessary part of growing up. She had made it easy for Amelia as she grew older. Sensible, caring, studious. Amelia had felt vindicated, smug even; her parenting had rewarded her with an easy child, even if Charlotte was a little prone to anxiety. Amelia had even been relaxed about that. It was a stage; she'd grow out of it.

And now here it was. The punishment for her hubris.

Her eyes scoured the sea as if she would spot Charlotte in the water and could throw her a life ring.

She tried to channel her usual self. The sensible person who would tell her that Charlotte and Sammy had run off to look after a stray dog and would be back soon, confused by the panic they'd caused.

But it didn't work.

She was filled with dread. All the terrible things that happened to missing children. All the children who were never found.

She tried to stop thinking about it. She pulled out her phone, willing it to ring with good news.

It didn't.

She paused a moment, looking at the phone. She'd left a garbled voicemail for Tom, but she should tell her mother what was happening. She'd avoided it on the train, blaming tunnels and bad reception, but in fact, it was because she felt that saying the words out loud would make Charlotte feel further away, her disappearance all the more real.

That was nonsense, she told herself. Reluctantly she scrolled through her numbers to her mother's. She had to tell her what was happening.

'Hello, Mum?'

'Oh good,' said Grace, pleased to hear her daughter's voice, even if she did sound a little odd. A chat was just what she needed to stop her unwelcome thoughts. A chat about dinner and pies and maybe Amelia coming home early. Yes, a meal with her daughter. 'I know steak pie is best if you leave the filling overnight,' she began, to fill what was starting to sound like an awkward silence. 'But I've got some stew in the freezer and I thought that if I added some stock, it would probably still be perfectly serviceable in pastry.' She paused. 'For dinner,' she added. 'If you'll be home in time tonight.'

The line was bad, or Grace's ears were playing up. 'Are you

somewhere windy?' she asked, unable to decipher what Amelia was saying. 'I hope you're not out in the rain,' she added. 'It's pouring down here.'

The whistling sound of the wind suddenly disappeared. 'That's better,' said Grace. 'Did you go inside? Where are you?'

'I'm on a catamaran,' her daughter replied. 'I've gone into the cabin. Listen, there's something I need to tell you.'

In a few swift sentences, Grace felt her world disintegrate.

'I'm coming,' she said, already reaching for her handbag. 'I'll be on the next boat.'

'No,' said Amelia. 'There's no need.'

'I want to be there,' Grace replied. 'You shouldn't be on your own. I'll help.'

'You can't help.'

'Yes I can,' said Grace, determined. 'I can look for her, I can ask around. I can . . .'

'Don't come. The best thing you can do is stay home, wait and see if she calls.'

Grace didn't argue. Not any more. Not with what was going on. This wasn't about her.

It was about Charlotte. And a terrified mother.

'OK,' she said, her voice as calm as she could manage. 'You know what's best.'

'I need to keep the line free,' said Amelia.

'Call me if you need anything,' said Grace.

Amelia had already hung up.

Charlotte's eyes flickered open, but darkness was all that greeted her. Her head was pounding and she was freezing. She reached up to touch her head, but banged her elbow on something sharp and hard. She cried out in pain.

'Charlotte?' She felt a hand touch her ankle.

'Sammy?' she said, her voice croaky.

'Oh, thank God,' said Sammy. 'I thought you might be . . .'

'What's happening?' asked Charlotte. She tried to sit up, but discovered it was not just her head that hurt. Everywhere did.

'Stay where you are,' commanded Sammy. 'I don't think I could lift you back up here again if you fell.'

Charlotte raised her head a fraction and could just make out Sammy sitting with his arms wrapped around his legs, shivering. 'Where are we?'

'Still in the cave. On the ledge.'

'How did I get here?'

'The wave washed you right back in,' he said. 'So I waded out and pulled you back and managed to get you up here.' He paused. 'You were bleeding quite a lot,' he said. 'And I might have bumped you even more. Sorry.'

'You saved me,' said Charlotte.

'You saved me first,' said Sammy.

She tried to sit up again, but her ears were making a funny sound, as if they had water gushing through them. She felt a few drops splash her face. She reached out her hand and felt around her.

Cold water.

The sea was still rising, and quickly.

'We'll be OK here,' said Sammy. 'Won't we?'

Charlotte used her other hand to touch the side of the cave, near her head. It was coated in something soft and damp.

Algae.

'I hope so,' she said. But as the water rose, she knew they had no hope at all.

Chapter 24

'We really are doing everything we can, Mrs Sayers,' said the policeman. 'Charlotte and Samuel's photos have been issued to every officer on the island. The coastguard are searching the nearest beaches and caves – all the usual places. We'll find them.'

'They will, God willing.' Sammy's mother clasped Amelia's hand again. 'We've just got to pray.'

Amelia shook the hand off. This woman was insufferable. If she mentioned God one more time, Amelia felt like she was going to scream. Even though he'd been awful recently, she wished Tom was with her. He'd be useful. He'd have ideas, he'd charm more resources from the police, he'd be practical.

'There must be more,' she said. 'Have you called in the police from the mainland?'

The policeman bristled. 'We're perfectly well equipped to deal with this on the island,' he said. 'I'm sure your daughter will turn up soon.'

'Amen,' said Sammy's mother.

Amelia turned away from them. She didn't think that antagonising the police or Sammy's mum would help, but she was ready to fight when she needed to. In the meantime, she took a deep breath, her eyes scanning the campsite one more time.

Mrs Varga was sitting hunched in a ball outside one of the tents. Mr Brown had his arms round her. Something about the two of them, together, made her feel another moment of longing for Tom. She'd left him several voicemails but heard nothing. He was probably busy with his new girlfriend, puffing through antenatal classes.

The thought made her angrier, and she decided to go and shout at Mrs Varga again. The teacher had been negligent, letting the children out of her sight even for a moment. She walked over, but a look from Mr Brown made her pause. There was something in his eyes that suggested gentleness. Sadness.

Loss.

Amelia found that instead of shouting, she was near to tears. She opened her mouth to try to channel her emotions back to anger, back to something she could control, but instead a sob came out.

Then all of a sudden, Sammy's mother had enclosed her in the hug Amelia had been trying to avoid since she arrived, and Amelia found herself crying into the woman's soft polyester scarf.

The hug was warm against the cold outside, and it reminded her of a time she'd fallen off her scooter when she was young. The pain in her knee had been overwhelming, and she'd howled. Her mother had set Peter back down in his pram and come running over to her, scooping her into her arms, reassuring her that everything would be OK.

Amelia realised it wasn't Tom that she wanted after all.

It was her mum.

'Mrs Sayers, Mrs Doyle?' Amelia looked up. The policeman was talking to them. She released herself from the hug and stepped back, trying to understand what he was saying.

'They've been found,' he said, but he wasn't smiling. 'The coastguard have them.'

'Thank the Lord,' said Sammy's mum.

'Are they OK?' asked Amelia.

'The ambulance will meet them when they get back to land,' said the policeman. 'You two had better come with me.'

Grace paced around the house for a while, then googled *Isle of Wight dangers* on her phone. It didn't seem like a hotbed of crime, but the warnings about red-flag beaches worried her. She almost phoned Amelia back to ask her if she'd called the coastguard, but then remembered what she'd said about keeping the line free. They would have thought of the coastguard, of course they would. She'd be interfering.

Getting in the way.

Don't come.

She was a burden. She knew she was. All old people were, eventually. Either they outlived their usefulness and someone had to care for them, or they died and someone had to arrange their funeral, sort through their possessions.

And here she was thinking of herself again. Her mind went back to Charlotte.

No, she couldn't think about her. Not in danger, not missing.

Amelia didn't want her there. Grace understood. She remembered coming back from Peter's funeral and going into the bathroom, locking the door. She'd needed to be alone.

'Mum,' Amelia had called. 'Where are you?'

Grace hadn't answered. She'd sunk to the bathroom floor, the tiles cold and still a little damp from her shower earlier. She could barely believe she'd managed to wash, to get dressed, to watch her boy's casket disappear forever into a hole in the ground.

'Your mother just needs a minute,' she heard Jonathan say. 'You come with me, we'll put the kettle on.'

'I want Mum!' Amelia had said, her voice shattering like broken glass as she banged on the door. 'Please come out!'

It was too much. Grace had doubled over, sobs finally overtaking her. She couldn't open the door, she couldn't let her little girl see her like this.

It had been hours before she'd emerged; cold, stiff and exhausted. Amelia was asleep on the sofa, Jonathan stroking her hair. 'She needed you,' he'd said.

'I couldn't,' replied Grace. 'I just couldn't . . .'

She hadn't been there for her daughter.

And now, thirty years later, her daughter didn't want her.

Grace unlocked the back door, ignoring Rex's barking, and went into her shed. She flicked the switch and tried to watch the train as it travelled through her world.

For years, she'd kept the shed closed up. She'd gone back to work and they'd carried on. Eventually Amelia left home for university, and it was just her and Jonathan left.

Twenty years later, Jonathan died and Grace found herself alone.

Coming back after his funeral to her empty house, she had decided it was time to go back into the shed. To clear it out. She was more aware than ever that day of her own mortality. If she died, Amelia would have to deal with the shed. And it wasn't as if the day of her husband's funeral could get any worse.

But when she unlocked the door, something surprising happened. Her day started to get better.

The beach. The village. The train, which still worked, chugging through the tunnel as she turned the dial.

It was so full of joy, a joy that was infectious. It gave her the feeling that perhaps she had more to do than wait for death. She had mountains to build, ski lifts to engineer, a farmyard to populate.

Suddenly her phone made a noise. Grace grabbed it. A message from Amelia.

Charlotte had been found. The comfort of those words lasted but a second, while she read the rest of the message.

Critical condition.

She grabbed her handbag and put on her coat. She had to help. She *could* help, no matter what Amelia said. She knew she could.

She had to be there. This time, she had to be there for her daughter.

And for Charlotte.

Grace took one step up the stairs on the boat and stopped, clutching the handrail as the wind blew at her aggressively. People all around her were fine, practically skipping up the stairs despite the way the boat was lurching. She'd felt a little better on the train, like she was doing something useful instead of hiding in her shed. But the train was familiar ground; the boat was not.

She stepped down again, deciding that she wouldn't go up to the top deck after all. It was evening now, the sun low. The sea around her looked a deep purple against a lilac sky, but Grace barely noticed the colours. Or the chill in the air, or the fatigue in her body.

She just had to make it there.

She had wanted to watch as the island came into view. In her mind, she would see Charlotte immediately. The confusion resolved, her granddaughter perfectly fine and thrilled to see her.

Her daughter too. 'It was all a fuss about nothing,' Amelia would say. 'But I'm glad you came.'

'I'm glad too,' Grace would say. 'Because I knew I could be useful. And I have something I wanted to say to you, to both of you.' And then she'd say it. How much she loved the two of them. How happy she was that they were living with her and how there were times when only the thought of Amelia had made her want to carry on living.

But she couldn't even climb the stairs. She held the handrail still, realising that to turn around and get back to her seat, she'd have to let go of all support.

Maybe she'd just stay here, holding on, until the boat reached the shore.

Her bladder disagreed.

Perhaps Amelia had been right. She shouldn't have come. Maybe she would be a burden; an incontinent old woman who couldn't even climb the stairs on a gentle ferry journey across the Solent.

'You OK there, love?'

Grace looked at the man standing next to her, concern flooding his eyes. He was tall, probably about Amelia's age, and had a pleasant, ruddy face that suggested he spent a lot of time outdoors. He was wearing muddy wellies. He probably took little rowboats out in storms to go fishing and would think she was a silly little old lady making a fuss on the ferry steps.

'I'm fine,' she said, her bladder cursing her pride.

'It's a bit choppy today,' he replied. 'How about you take my hand?'

Grace bit her lip, looking at the steady, strong-seeming hand. It was a tempting proposition. She would be no use to anyone with a broken hip.

'OK,' she said. 'Thank you.' She felt sturdy fingers encase her own.

'I'm Henry,' he said.

'Grace,' she replied.

'Going up, Grace?'

'No, thank you. To the ladies' room, please.'

Grace tried to pull herself together in the loos. She was going to be strong. She was.

When she came out, she was surprised to see Henry still there. 'Thought I'd escort you back to your seat,' he said. 'Till you get your sea legs.'

She took his hand again, and he walked her to a comfortable chair, which she sank into gratefully. He sat down opposite her. 'What brings you to the island?' he asked. 'I can tell you're not from round here.'

Grace didn't know what to say. This man was just trying to be polite; he hadn't signed up to hear about her injured granddaughter, even if Grace did want to talk about her. Which she didn't. But she couldn't bring herself to lie either, pretend she was going on holiday. Could she say that she didn't want to discuss it? It sounded so rude, after he'd been so kind. She looked at him and realised she'd already gone too long without answering. He probably thought she'd forgotten the question. That she had dementia.

Then she felt even worse. Worrying what a stranger thought of her while her granddaughter was in hospital. Self-obsessed, that was what she was.

'I've been over to visit my son in Southampton,' offered Henry instead, seeming to realise that Grace wasn't going to be forthcoming. He smiled at her. 'He was bored of the island, can you imagine? Wanted the bright lights of the city. He's at uni now. Even got himself a mainlander girlfriend.'

'Really?' said Grace, feeling a modicum of relief at hearing about someone else's family.

'Oh yes,' he replied, clearly on one of his favourite subjects. 'Pretty grand she is. City type. Thought tomatoes grew underground, like potatoes.' He leaned back, laughing. Grace tried to smile, but her mouth was too tense.

'You OK, love?' he asked again.

'No,' Grace replied. 'Not at all.'

'Maybe it would help to talk about it?'

Grace paused a moment. Maybe it would.

*

Grace lingered outside the hospital door.

'This is definitely the right place,' said Henry.

'Yes,' said Grace. 'I'm sure it is.' Henry had been amazing. Once they were off the ferry, he'd insisted on driving her to the hospital, claiming he couldn't leave her alone in the dark. And now here she was. Standing outside. Too afraid to go in, but too embarrassed to tell him that after coming all this way, she wasn't sure she should be here at all.

'Do you want me to come in with you?'

'No,' replied Grace, though that was exactly what she would like. 'I'll be fine from here.'

'I'll come,' he said, stepping forward and pushing the revolving door. 'It can be tricky navigating these hospitals. I'll make sure you find Charlotte.'

Grace stopped herself from telling him she was very familiar with hospitals; first for Peter and later for Jonathan. That in fact it was her familiarity with hospitals and what happened in them that was part of the problem, part of the reason she didn't want to step inside.

She knew what could happen.

'Come on.'

'OK,' said Grace. Not going in wouldn't help anyone. She took a deep breath and stepped through the door.

Henry spoke to the lady on reception. He knew all the details by now, allowing Grace to look around.

It was a different hospital, but it smelled the same. Disinfectant, the rubber of the floors. A hint of nervous sweat.

'This way.'

She followed him through a labyrinth of corridors punctuated by fire doors. He diligently held each one open for her. 'This should be it,' he said as they approached a small room.

Grace stepped inside and saw Amelia, her face puffy, look up at her from where she was sitting next to a bed. Charlotte lay there, eyes closed, face pale, a worrying selection of tubes protruding from her. She saw Amelia's eyes briefly rest on Henry, then go back to her. 'I know you said not to come, but . . .'

'Stop,' said Amelia. She stood up, and for a moment Grace thought she was going to throw her out. Instead, she found herself in an embrace. 'I'm glad you're here, Mum,' said Amelia. 'I'm so scared.'

Chapter 25

'Well.' Amelia looked at the man speaking. He was tall, with an open face, but seemed uncomfortable, shifting from one foot to the other. Her mother seemed to have acquired him along the way somewhere. 'I'll leave you to it,' he said. 'I hope your little girl gets better.'

'She will, won't she?' said Grace, as Henry left.

'There's a head injury,' said Amelia, her voice low. 'But they have her hypothermia under control.' She repeated the words the doctor had said to her, trying not to burst into tears as she spoke. 'We just need to wait and hope she wakes up.'

Waiting. Hoping. It was all so uncertain, so passive. Amelia wanted more action from the doctors. She looked around, wanting something she could control.

'Would you like some tea?' said Grace, her eyes never leaving Charlotte's body, lying there filled with tubes. Amelia felt as though the tubes were strangling her own heart.

'No,' she said.

Grace glanced up. 'When Peter was sick,' she began, 'people were always trying to fill me with tea.'

Amelia nodded. It was the first time her mother had brought up the subject of Peter for as long as she could remember.

'Sit down,' she offered. 'You must be tired.'

'They were always trying to make me sit down as well,' said Grace, taking a seat. 'Sit down and drink tea.' She paused. 'It seems a funny recipe for recovery, but I don't suppose anyone's thought of anything better.'

Amelia sat down too. She put one hand on Charlotte and Grace took her other one. Memories of holding her mum's hand on the way home from school flooded back to Amelia; talking about her day and her friends and what she wanted for dinner, all while squeezing her mother's fingers in her own.

Grace took a deep breath. 'I thought I'd know what to say,' she said. 'I've been through this, and worse. But there really isn't anything. Not when it's your child. There aren't any words that can help. I wish there were and I wish I could say them.'

Amelia looked at her. Losing her brother had always seemed like a tragedy in her own life; she'd barely thought at the time about her mother's loss, too young to really understand what other people had been going through.

But the full force of it hit her now.

The sense of powerlessness when her child was in danger. The feeling of being responsible, because it was the mother's job to keep her child alive.

And having to watch as her child grew weaker and weaker.

Amelia gently squeezed Charlotte's fingers. They felt warm now and had lost the blueish tinge that had terrified her earlier. She could just be sleeping.

'She looks like she's sleeping, doesn't she?' said Grace, as if reading her mind.

'I never understood why you stopped talking about Peter,' said Amelia, her voice soft. 'Not when I was little. But now . . .

I can't believe you made it through at all. Losing your favourite child.'

Grace's eyes flicked up to her. 'What?'

'I'm sorry,' said Amelia. 'I'm not jealous. I shouldn't be. I understand now what you were going through.'

'You know I loved you both,' said Grace. 'Just as much.'

'You didn't,' said Amelia. 'But it's OK.'

'It's not OK,' said Grace. She gripped her daughter's hand tightly. 'You mean so much to me.'

'You went back to work,' said Amelia. 'After he died. And you stopped playing with me.'

Grace shook her head. 'I never stopped playing with you,' she said.

'You locked up the shed. Closed the world we all shared. It made me realise that it was never for all of us, that time we spent together. It was just for him.'

Grace bit her lip. 'Those memories,' she began, 'are the most precious things to me. And it *was* all of us. All of us made them. Peter is gone, and yes, I miss him every day. But if I hadn't had you, I don't think I would have got through it.' She took a deep breath. 'I love you so much, and I am so proud of you. You gave me a reason to carry on. You still do. Maybe I shouldn't have gone back to work so soon, but it seemed like the only way I could cope.'

Amelia nodded, finding herself understanding. Work could be a respite when home was too hard. For them both. She'd never made that connection before.

'I should have talked about him more,' continued Grace. 'But saying his name felt like it filled my throat with broken glass.' She paused. 'You lost your brother. We were all so . . . lost. I should have been the strong one. I should have known what to do . . .' She stopped herself. 'I'm sorry,' she said. 'I'm sorry for shutting you out, for making you feel second best. You never were. I just couldn't cope.' She stopped talking, thinking for the first time about the damage she might have done to her daughter. 'I'm sorry,' she repeated.

'There is no right way to deal with something as terrible as losing a child,' said Amelia. 'I can't even imagine . . .'

'Don't,' said Grace. 'Don't try to imagine.'

A sob escaped Amelia, and she found herself pulled into an embrace, pressed into her mother's coat. She smelled of the sea, of coffee, of cakes baked on a rainy afternoon.

Of childhood. Of home.

Charlotte felt her head pounding as she forced her eyes open. The light was too bright, and she closed them again. She wasn't in the cave any more. There was a beeping sound, regular and rhythmic, and she could smell antiseptic. She moved her fingers, gently stroking something soft underneath her where rocks had been. She was warm and she was dry and she seemed to be in a bed. Carefully and slowly she opened her eyes again and blinked.

She could just make out a silhouette. A person, seated, blocking the worst of the light from her eyes. She blinked again.

'Mum?' she said.

'Charlotte!'

She found herself covered by her mother's face; kisses planted over her cheeks.

'I'll call the doctor,' said another voice.

'Grandma?' said Charlotte.

'Yes,' Grace replied. 'I'm here too.'

'Oh, thank goodness,' said her mother, lifting her face from Charlotte's and inspecting her carefully. 'Thank you.'

Charlotte blinked again, confused. Why was her mother thanking her? 'What for?'

'For being alive,' said Amelia. 'For waking up.'

'You're welcome.' Charlotte lay back, trying to remember how she'd got here. There was nothing in her memory, empty as a cave.

The cave.

Sammy.

She tried to pull herself up, to look around.

'Where is he?' she asked.

'Who?' asked her mother.

'Sammy,' she said. 'Where is Sammy?'

'He came in with you,' said Amelia.

'And he's OK?'

'I expect so,' said Amelia. Charlotte watched as she cast a concerned glance in her grandmother's direction.

'I'll go and see if I can track him down,' said Grace. She smiled at her granddaughter. 'I'm so pleased you're OK,' she said, bending to give her a kiss.

Charlotte stood by the bed, watching Sammy. He had an oxygen mask over his mouth, and numerous tubes coming from various points on his body. She gently took his hand in her own and squeezed it. 'You'll be OK,' she said, her voice soft. 'We saved each other.'

It was three days since she'd woken up in hospital. She was wearing some new pyjamas her grandma had bought for her at a local shop, and was wrapped in a fluffy terrycloth robe. She'd be going home the next day, almost recovered but for a few stitches that had yet to heal on her forehead. Sammy had to stay here until he was well enough to be moved, but even then he'd need to go to another hospital, his mother had said. He'd caught pneumonia, further damaging his already weak lungs, and he needed help to breathe.

His eyes flickered open; he'd been coming in and out of

consciousness for the last day. His hands went up to his mask, but Charlotte shook her head. He made a tiny nod of understanding, and they stayed there in silence.

'Please get better,' said Charlotte, quietly. 'Please.'

There was a tap at the door. 'There's some girls here to see you,' said Sammy's mother, Moira, coming inside. 'They're waiting in your room. I'll stay with Sammy.'

'I'd rather be with him,' replied Charlotte.

'He's not much company right now, bless him,' said Moira, coming to stand next to her.

'Yes, he is.'

They both looked at Sammy, who'd drifted back into something between unconsciousness and sleep, his eyelids flickering.

'You get on, talk to your friends. It will do you good. I expect they've been worried about you.'

Charlotte bit her lip. 'I'll be right back,' she told Sammy. 'Don't worry.'

'He's not going anywhere,' said Moira.

Charlotte nodded. That was the problem. 'Call me if anything changes,' she said, in her most adult voice.

'Of course I will, dear.' Moira smiled at her and shooed her out.

Charlotte opened the door to her room to find Erica, Nia and Anne-Marie sitting on her bed, giggling and eating grapes from the enormous fruit basket her dad had sent. He'd called her to check she was OK and to apologise for not visiting. Apparently he didn't want to leave Julia while she was in her third trimester.

The girls fell silent at the sight of Charlotte, and Erica stood up to make room for her on the bed.

'I've never met anyone who almost died before,' said Anne-Marie, respect in her voice. 'What was it like?'

Charlotte picked a grape up from where it had fallen on the bed and sat down. 'Cold,' she said. 'And wet.'

'When my sister Asha had appendicitis, she saw her whole life flash in front of her eyes,' said Nia. 'Did you?'

'No,' said Charlotte. 'I mainly saw water.' She paused. 'And Sammy.' She looked at them. 'He saved me, pulling me out of the sea when I got hurt on the rocks.'

'The coastguard saved you really,' said Anne-Marie. 'They told us those caves are pretty common places to get stuck, so that was one of the first places they looked. If it hadn't been for them, you'd both have drowned.'

Charlotte shrugged. 'I don't really remember that bit,' she said. 'I just woke up here, with a bandage on my head.'

Erica reached for her hand. 'We're so glad you're OK,' she said. 'We were worried.'

'What were you up to?' asked Anne-Marie. 'In the caves, on your own?' She raised an eyebrow.

'Sammy saw Mr Brown with a strange woman,' said Charlotte defensively. 'We wanted to see what they were doing.'

'It was his sister,' said Nia. 'She lives on the island. Mrs Varga told me.'

'Oh,' said Charlotte.

'Will you have a scar?' asked Anne-Marie, pointing at Charlotte's head.

'I don't know,' she said. 'Maybe.'

'You'll need to grow a fringe,' Nia told her. 'That's what Asha did back when she had acne.'

'It would suit you,' said Anne-Marie approvingly. 'Because you've got a big forehead.'

Charlotte didn't really know what to say to that. 'I'm actually pretty tired,' she said.

The girls looked at her for a moment, before getting off the bed so Charlotte could swing her feet up. Erica tucked the blanket around her.

‘We can’t visit again,’ said Nia, ‘because we’re going home tomorrow.’

‘That’s OK,’ said Charlotte.

‘But we’ll see you at school, once you’re well enough,’ said Erica.

‘I’ve got to rest next week,’ said Charlotte. ‘But I’m coming back the week after.’

‘Not much of a break for almost dying!’ said Anne-Marie.

‘Asha was off for six weeks when she had appendicitis,’ added Nia.

‘This is different,’ said Charlotte. She watched as Anne-Marie helped herself to a shiny red apple from the fruit basket and took an enormous bite.

They said their goodbyes, each giving her a hug. Charlotte watched them go, the door closing behind them. She let her head rest back on the pillow.

Amelia stood in the hospital corridor and nodded at the girls as they left. Grace re-entered the room, but Amelia hesitated a moment. She’d been to see Sammy while the girls were visiting Charlotte, and she hadn’t liked how he looked. Not at all. Although Charlotte was getting better, she could tell that Sammy wasn’t. His mother had been pacing back and forth between his room and the hospital chapel. Amelia had even popped in herself to light a candle for him, feeling rather hypocritical as she did so. But Moira had taken her hand and squeezed it, and Amelia knew that it meant a lot to this woman she barely knew but with whom she had shared the worst moments of her life.

‘Oh, there you are.’ She turned around to see a man who looked ever-so-slightly familiar. He was wearing wellies that had left muddy footprints along the hospital linoleum.

'Hello,' she said, wondering if he was one of Charlotte's teachers. He held out a big hand, and she shook it, surprised at its warmth.

'Grace told me Charley was doing much better,' he said. 'I'm glad.' He looked at her again, seeming to register her blank expression. 'Henry,' he told her, helpfully. 'I met your mother on the boat.'

'Of course,' said Amelia. She paused. 'Thank you for helping her.'

'You're welcome,' he said with a smile. 'She's brilliant, isn't she? You're lucky to have her.'

'I am,' agreed Amelia, realising that she meant it.

'My mum passed away last year,' he said. 'I miss her.'

'I'm sorry,' said Amelia. They stood in silence for a moment while Amelia wondered what he was doing here.

'You work in the hospital?' she suggested doubtfully, glancing at his boots.

'Oh no, I just popped in to see how you were all doing,' he said cheerfully.

'That's very kind of you,' said Amelia.

'I'm not a doctor,' he explained, as if there'd been a misunderstanding. 'But I am a vet. Livestock mainly, but some well-loved pets too.'

'OK,' said Amelia.

'Anyway, I'm glad Charley is doing well,' he said. Amelia looked at him again, curious as to why a stranger was so interested. Genuine, honest eyes gazed back at her from his pleasant face. He smiled, then she saw an idea light up his face.

'I'll give you my card,' he said, rummaging in various pockets. 'In case you need anything else while you're here.' He dug out a dog-eared card, wiped it on his trousers and handed it to her. 'Just call,' he said. 'Any time.'

'Thank you,' said Amelia, a little confused.

'Not as a vet or anything,' he clarified. 'I know the island, that's all. And I have a car. In case you need driving anywhere. I could make some suggestions, if you like. Places to visit. I could even take you.'

'We're going home soon,' said Amelia.

'That's a shame.'

'Is it?'

'Yes,' he replied. 'It is.' He paused a moment. 'The island is really beautiful,' he said, the words coming out fast. 'And you've probably not really had the best impression, what with your daughter getting stuck in a cave and all.' He stopped himself, looking horrified at his words. 'I didn't mean to bring that up. Sorry. My wife ... my ex-wife, I mean, was always telling me I talk too much when I'm nervous. Oh God, and here I am, bringing up my ex while I'm trying to talk to an attractive woman.'

Amelia frowned to cover the surprised pleasure she felt at the 'attractive' comment.

'Sorry,' he said. 'I'll just go home and die alone and be eaten by my cat.'

'At least you've got a cat,' said Amelia. 'I'm going to be eaten by my mum's neighbour's dog. Unless she has her way and we get a ferret, that is.'

'Lovely animals,' Henry said. 'Very intelligent.' He laughed, the sound nervous but genuine. 'So anyway, if there's anything you need ...'

Amelia hesitated for a moment, looking at his card. 'I could do with a nice cup of coffee,' she said, putting the card carefully in her pocket. 'A flat white. I'm sick of hospital tea.'

'I know just the place,' he replied. 'I'll fetch you a cup. I'll be twenty minutes or so, it's a bit of a walk.'

'Hang on,' said Amelia, feeling impulsive. She opened the

door to Charlotte's room and glanced inside. Charlotte and Grace were sitting on the bed, a large book with pictures of the rainforest open in front of them. Both were engrossed. 'Let's go together.'

'Really?'

'I could do with the fresh air,' she said. 'And the company.'

'Freshest you'll find in the United Kingdom,' he told her with pride. 'And I'll do my best with the company.'

Chapter 26

'Maybe walking Rex again would help,' said Grace.

'I hardly think a dog walk is the answer,' replied Amelia.

'She liked it before.'

'Maybe I need to find a therapist.'

'She can talk to us.'

'But she isn't.'

Grace nodded. Charlotte had barely spoken to them since she'd returned from the Isle of Wight. She'd pretty much stayed in her room for the first week. They'd hoped that going back to school would help, but it hadn't. She'd go out, come home, pick at her food, then go to her room again and close the door. 'She's just worried about Sammy,' said Grace. 'We all are.'

'And that's why she should talk to someone.'

Grace flicked on the kettle switch. 'Tea?'

'Yes please,' said Amelia.

Grace smiled. Her daughter was spending much more time with her now. Partly she was working from home to be there for Charlotte, of course, but Grace liked to think she was enjoying her company a little more too.

'What about Mr Brown?' she asked. 'Maybe he could have a word with her.'

'I'll pay a professional,' said Amelia. Then she relented. 'But yes,' she added, 'she did seem rather fond of him.'

Grace smiled, pleased to have had a good idea.

'And maybe you're right about that dog from next door,' added Amelia. 'Dogs are meant to be good for stress, aren't they?'

'And blood pressure,' said Grace.

'Yes.' Amelia paused. 'Let's go for the human solution first. Do you want to see what Mr Brown says?'

'Consider it done.'

Charlotte watched as a bee crawled up the glass inside the classroom window. It was a bumblebee, fluffy as a kitten. She wondered what it felt like to stroke, but she kept her hands firmly to herself, not wanting to scare the creature or get stung. It was the end of her first week back at school, without Sammy, and she had hated every minute of it. At least it was the final lesson of the day.

She looked at Erica, sitting next to her and laughing at Mr Brown climbing into a box, trying to impersonate a hermit crab moving into a new shell. Everyone was laughing, she realised. Laughing as if nothing had happened.

Sammy would have done a beautiful drawing of that bee. Charlotte started to sketch it, trying to capture the six articulated legs and the fluffy thorax, but it looked like an alien. She tried harder, grabbing a yellow pencil to bring the creature to life. If she could do it well enough, she'd take it with her on her next visit and prop it up next to Sammy's bed. The last time she'd seen him, she'd overheard that he was still on oxygen and strong antibiotics, and there'd been talk of permanent damage to his lungs from the pneumonia. Her mother had told her that Sammy's mother had phoned to say that he was starting to recover and was allowed home, but Charlotte wouldn't believe it until she saw for herself.

It was no good. The bee looked ridiculous. She crumpled the paper and threw it at the window. The bee, alarmed, left the glass and buzzed through the room, leaving children's screams in its wake.

'I thought that picture was really good,' said Erica, taking advantage of the bee distraction to chat to Charlotte. 'I've never thought of a bee as cute before.'

'It wasn't meant to be cute,' said Charlotte. 'It was meant to be anatomically accurate.'

The bell rang and the class jumped up. Charlotte started packing her bag. 'Can I have the picture?' asked Erica. 'I really like it.'

'No,' said Charlotte. 'It's for Sammy.' She picked it up again and smoothed it out. She wasn't sure whether she'd give it to him, but she certainly wouldn't let anyone else take it.

'Hey there.' Nia had sidled up to her. 'A few of us are going for pizza after school. Fancy joining?'

'You can tell us more about what happened in the cave,' added Anne-Marie. They'd already pumped her for the gory details, but Charlotte had remained tight-lipped.

'No thanks,' said Charlotte.

The bee took this opportunity to fly straight at Nia's head. She screamed and waved her arms around ineffectually. 'Kill it!' she yelled. Anne-Marie grabbed her notebook.

'No!' Charlotte snatched the notebook from her, chucking it to the floor. 'Let it be.'

All the girls stepped back and Charlotte realised she'd shouted.

'What's up with you?' asked Anne-Marie.

'Charlotte liked that bee,' said Erica. Charlotte felt a hand on her shoulder. 'She did a lovely drawing of it.' Erica bent down and picked up the notebook, handing it to Anne-Marie, who muttered something under her breath.

'Time to leave, girls,' said Mr Brown.

'Last chance for pizza,' said Nia.

'No thanks,' said Charlotte again.

'See you next week,' said Erica.

Charlotte watched them leave, but lingered for a moment, looking for something to use to rescue the bee from its classroom prison.

'Are you OK?' asked Mr Brown. 'I know you've been through a lot.' The bee buzzed past his face, and Charlotte watched as he tipped out a pencil pot and grabbed a piece of paper from his desk. The bee landed back on the window, and he gently placed the pot over it and slid the paper under.

Without speaking, Charlotte opened the other window, and Mr Brown released the insect into the playground.

'Thanks, sir,' she said.

'No problem,' he replied. He looked at her. 'How's Sammy?'

'At home, but still on oxygen. His mum said I can visit him at the weekend.' Charlotte looked out of the window at the students laughing and playing together, walking home in twos or groups. She'd travel alone today.

'And how's your bird?'

'What do you mean?'

'The bird you saved,' said Mr Brown. 'Just before . . .' He paused. 'Before I had to leave. I've been wondering about it.'

'I'm not sure,' said Charlotte, surprised that he remembered. 'I thought I might have seen it once . . .'

She looked out of the window again and saw her grandmother waving at the gate. 'I've got to go,' she said.

'Come on then,' said Mr Brown.

'What? I need to get home.'

'Your grandmother invited me to take a walk with the two of you,' said Mr Brown. 'If you have no objection?'

Charlotte frowned at him and put her bag on her shoulder. 'Why?'

'Just to chat.' He followed her out.

'Charlotte!' Grace called out, waving. Charlotte saw the other kids turning to look at her. Walking home with not just a grandmother, but a teacher. Sammy had better get well soon, because she'd never make another friend.

'I thought we'd go to that bit of wilderness you like by the railway line,' said Grace. 'See if we can find your bird. What do you say?'

Charlotte wanted to say no, to go home and lie in her room in the dark, like she had done every evening this week. 'I suppose,' she said, reluctantly. 'But all the birds look the same. How will we even know if we find it?'

'We'll know,' said Mr Brown. 'Let's go.'

'Oh,' said Grace, looking at the fence. 'Is there another way in?'

'Sorry,' said Charlotte, already halfway up. 'I didn't think.' She jumped down on the other side. 'I can hold it up?'

'Works for me,' said Mr Brown, getting down on all fours and crawling under.

'There's another entrance over there,' said Charlotte, gesturing for her grandmother's benefit. 'But it's also a bit scrabbly.'

'I think I'll wait here,' said Grace, sitting down on a well-placed bench. 'Take a picture of the bird for me. And don't wander too far.'

Charlotte hadn't been back here since she'd waited on the platform for the train to go on the school trip. That was only a few weeks ago, but it felt like a lifetime. The place looked different. The May sunshine had coaxed the flowers from their buds and the ground was coated in daisies and forget-me-nots.

'I came back to check on the bird,' said Mr Brown, as they walked along the path that Sammy and Charlotte had made, overgrown now. 'Before I left. I dropped my glasses and accidentally trod on them.'

'Oh,' said Charlotte. She paused. 'Sammy thought that was what had happened,' she said. 'When we found them.' A squirrel scuttled past and they both paused to watched it climb a tree, winding around it like a maypole dancer.

'You found them?'

'I gave them to the school office,' said Charlotte. 'I think they're in lost property.'

'Then I'll never get them back.' Mr Brown smiled. 'That place is like a black hole, swallowing everything that enters it.'

Charlotte didn't return the smile. 'Why didn't you just pick them up?' she asked. 'They could have been repaired.'

'There didn't seem any point,' said Mr Brown. 'There didn't seem much point to anything.' She looked at him, confusion clouding her face. 'I wasn't in a great place,' he added.

'You were here,' she said with a frown as she looked around her. 'It's beautiful.' She thought a moment. 'Was it raining or something?'

'No,' replied Mr Brown. 'I don't think it was.'

'Then why?'

'Let's sit,' said Mr Brown. 'We don't want to get too far from your grandmother. And then we'll watch for the birds.' He sat down on a log and Charlotte came to join him, choosing a spot on a soft patch of grass. Absent-mindedly she started to pick daisies, splitting their stems and threading them through to start a daisy chain.

She heard a sound in the distance and out of habit glanced at her watch. 'It's the 15.56 to Rochester,' she said. 'That was the first train Sammy and I used to see, when we came here after school.'

'You miss him,' said Mr Brown. 'He'll be OK, you do know that?'

'No one knows that,' said Charlotte. She put the daisy chain down. Mr Brown was right. There didn't seem to be any point to anything.

'He'll like your bee picture.'

'My bee picture is rubbish.' She saw an ant muddling its way through the grass. It climbed to the top of one of the blades and waved its front two legs around, as if looking for solid earth again. When it found nothing but air, it turned around and went back down to the ground. Sammy would have loved that, but he wasn't here to see it. She was here, but he wasn't. He'd waded into the water to pull her out. That was why he'd been so very cold. That was why he'd caught pneumonia.

'It's not your fault, you know,' said Mr Brown, as if following her thoughts.

'That I can't draw?'

'That Sammy isn't well,' he said. 'It sounds like you saved him.'

'I didn't do a very good job,' said Charlotte. 'He's on oxygen.'

'He's alive.' Mr Brown looked up, and then put his fingers to his lips. Overhead, they both heard the distinctive call of a blackbird. 'See what you did?' he said, his voice a whisper. 'You saved that bird, too.'

'It could be any blackbird,' said Charlotte. She paused, remembering the feeling she'd had when she'd almost missed the train. It had felt like her bird. But that was nonsense. They heard another song and watched as the bird flew to a tree nearby and proceeded to peck at berries.

'It wasn't just the bird you saved,' said Mr Brown. 'That day.'

'What do you mean?'

He shifted on the log and stretched out his legs. 'Charlotte, I feel like I can trust you,' he said. 'Can I?'

Charlotte felt the conversation was suddenly very serious. 'Yes,' she said.

'I'm going to tell you this because I know you've had a really hard time recently,' he said. 'And I've had a hard time too. Sometimes hard times are easier when they're shared. Talked about together. It makes us feel less alone.'

Charlotte nodded.

'When you saw me on the platform over there, I wasn't feeling too good about myself.' He paused. 'I lost my grandma in the pandemic,' he said. 'We'd been really close. And then I made some bad . . . personal choices, and . . . things were such a mess. My life was a mess. I couldn't go on, not without the people I loved.'

'I know how that feels,' said Charlotte.

'Even my goldfish was dying,' added Mr Brown. The image of the goldfish came back to Charlotte, floating twisted in the tank. 'And then you came,' he continued. 'And we saved that bird. This bird.' He gestured to the tree. 'Afterwards, I went home. And when I came back to check on it, I realised it had a chance. And that maybe I had a chance as well. Life isn't always great, but it's all we've got.'

Charlotte looked at him, not quite understanding. 'What?'

'I went away to get the help I needed. You saved me, Charlotte,' he continued. 'You saved me and you saved this bird and you saved Sammy.' He smiled. 'Thank you, Charlotte,' he said. 'We all have reasons to be grateful to you.'

Grace sat on the bench, enjoying the sunshine warming her face. She could just make out Charlotte's red coat through the trees. Her granddaughter was sitting down and looked deep in conversation with Mr Brown.

Grace still wasn't sure what had happened with Mr Brown, but she felt like she had a good idea. She remembered how cagey Mrs Varga had been about him when she'd met with her. There had been something going on between them; something that would never work out for the best.

For some reason, it had made her think that he'd be able to get through to Charlotte in her current state of mind. It was worth a try.

'Nice walk, you two?' she said as they emerged.

'We didn't get a photo of the bird,' said Charlotte.

'We think we heard it singing, though.' Mr Brown smiled. 'Didn't we?'

'Possibly,' conceded Charlotte. She looked at him. 'Thanks,' she said.

Grace smiled at them both. 'Let's get you home,' she said to Charlotte. 'I need to start on dinner.' She looked at Mr Brown, who nodded at her. 'Thank you,' she said.

'My pleasure,' he replied. He took a deep breath, and raised his face to the sun.

'So how was it?'

Grace and Charlotte had walked home in a comfortable silence that Grace decided to break only once they were inside.

'OK,' said Charlotte. Grace took that as a good sign. They both went into the kitchen. It was the first time her granddaughter hadn't gone straight to her room since she'd been back. Charlotte sat down and Grace poured her a glass of milk, which she delivered to her with a cookie on the side. 'Mr Brown said something weird,' said Charlotte.

'Oh yes?' said Grace. She sat down across from her granddaughter.

'Why do people feel it isn't worth carrying on?'

'Is that what he said?' She wondered if asking Mr Brown to talk to Charlotte had been the right move.

'Not exactly,' said Charlotte. 'But he'd thought that. He said it seemed like there was no point in anything. Not without the people you love. And I love Sammy.'

'Sammy is going to be fine,' said Grace.

'That's what everyone keeps saying,' said Charlotte. 'But no one knows for sure. Not even the doctors. Why do they say it?'

Grace took a breath. 'Because it's all they *can* say,' she said. 'Because we all want everything to be OK.' She looked at Charlotte. 'And it doesn't always work out.'

Charlotte looked back at her. 'And then what?'

Grace paused. 'We carry on,' she said. 'We have to.'

'Why?'

'Because there are other people that matter too.' She took another breath. 'When Peter died, it felt as if my world had crumbled. No, not crumbled. Crashed in around me, hurting every cell in my body. But I had your mother. And your grandfather. I carried on for them. And every day I'm glad I did. Your mother brings me so much joy. And so do you.' She paused. 'We were so scared, your mum and me, when you were missing. But here you are. Perfect.'

'I'm not perfect.'

'No,' said Grace. 'None of us are. But that's OK.'

Charlotte nodded. They sat in silence for a moment, then Grace stood up. 'I want to show you something,' she said. 'Outside.'

'I don't want to go out again,' said Charlotte.

'It's just in the garden,' said Grace. She paused, listening. 'Actually, is your mother home?'

'I don't know,' said Charlotte.

Grace opened the kitchen door to go and find Amelia. 'It's something I'd like to share with her again too,' she said. 'And I think it's something you might like to tell Sammy about, when you see him. It helped a sick little boy many years ago. It helped all of us. And I hope perhaps it will do so again.'

Charlotte stood just inside the shed, next to her mother. She opened her mouth and then closed it again. It was like stepping into a magical world that became more glorious with each switch her grandmother flicked. Lights came on in tiny homes. Music played. And the trains started their journey, merrily circulating through the perfect world in which they found themselves.

'I'm still working on it,' muttered her grandmother. 'But I thought . . .'

Charlotte wasn't listening. She was watching, enthralled, as the nearest train trundled along the track. The village lights switched on, and the choir in the church started to sing, the sound projecting from tiny speakers. She was distracted by a funfair: the big wheel circled, the carousel went round and she noticed, as she approached, that the sound of the choir was replaced by that of jangly fairground music. She peered at a couple of small children holding candy floss made from dyed cotton wool carefully stuck onto toothpicks.

Her eyes shifted focus and she took in the scale of the world, from the village to the woods to the mountain to the sea.

'Grandma,' said Charlotte, turning to Grace, 'did you build all this?'

'Some of it is from kits,' said Grace, trying not to look too pleased. 'But yes. Amelia and Peter and I built it together.'

'It's much bigger than I remember.' Amelia stood absolutely still, her eyes drinking it all in. 'Everything in the house looks smaller,' she added. 'But not this.'

'After your father died, I began adding to it again,' said Grace. 'What do you think?'

'It's magnificent,' Amelia replied.

Charlotte looked back at the miniature world. In the near distance, the train passed through a small wilderness area at the side of the track populated with tiny trees, their leaves a rich burnt umber for the constant autumn in which they lived. At the bottom she saw moss, replicating wild grasses. A tiny blackbird sat in a bramble bush, its mouth open in song. A surprised fox perched on its haunches to watch the train go past.

'That bird,' she said, pointing. 'It's so small, but I can still tell it's singing.'

'Yes,' said Grace. 'It's not just the engineering that you need to concern yourself with in a layout like this. It's the expressions, the characters, the drama.' She looked at her daughter. 'Amelia was always the best at that side of things,' she said.

'Really?' asked Charlotte.

'Yes,' said Grace. She hesitated a moment. 'I'm sorry, Amelia. I should never have closed it up. We should have continued with it. Together.'

'We all do what we need to,' replied Amelia. 'To survive when the worst happens.' She paused. 'I do forgive you, you know,' she added, looking at Grace. 'I didn't at the time, but now I understand.'

Grace took her daughter's hand. 'Thank you,' she said.

Charlotte wasn't listening. She watched the train travelling through a picturesque little village. Even the tiny apples were polished and perfectly arranged in front of the greengrocer's shop. Pigeons pecked around the cobbled streets, which were lined with other charming shops: a bakery, a dressmaker and a toy store.

'It's coming to one of my favourite spots now,' said Grace. They both watched it approach the village school. The gates were closed, but a boy and a girl stood at the fence, watching the train wind its way past them and into the first of the many tunnels through Grace's world.

'Grandma, it's amazing,' said Charlotte. 'Sammy would love it.' She paused a moment. 'But why haven't you shown it to us before?' she asked.

Grace hesitated. 'I don't know,' she said. 'Your mother is so busy and important and I'm a silly old woman with a train set.'

'Mum, I'm a mess,' replied Amelia with a laugh. 'Look at my life.'

'I couldn't be prouder of you.'

Charlotte nodded. 'You are pretty awesome, Mum,' she said.

Amelia looked from her daughter to her mother. 'I think,' she said, 'that perhaps it runs in the family.'

Chapter 27

Grace opened the door of the shop and stepped inside. It took a moment for her eyes to adjust to the comparative darkness, but when they did, she smiled. The layout was really quite something; she felt impressed anew every time she came. She looked at Toby's resin sea, and admired the artistry and skill with which he'd crafted the boats. For the first time, she noticed the diorama playing out on the ocean: the seagulls circling a fishing boat, the nets full as a hefty fisherman heaved them out, one colleague helping, another sneaking a cigarette at the back of the boat.

'Grace,' exclaimed Toby, appearing from behind the counter. 'It's so good to see you. How's Charlotte?'

'She's back at school,' said Grace. 'But she's not quite herself yet.'

'Sorry to hear that,' said Toby. He placed a hand on Grace's. She was surprised to feel a flicker of something, like a small electric current. He must have felt it too, because he withdrew his hand. 'I must have had my other hand on the track,' he said with a laugh.

'Sparks flying,' joked Grace, then instantly regretted it, feeling horribly embarrassed.

'I like your explanation,' said Toby. 'Listen . . . I was wondering—'

The bell rang at the front of the shop as two children entered, interrupting whatever he was going to say. 'Wow,' said one of them, watching the train power up the tracks by the doorway, gather momentum and then speed back down the other side.

Toby grinned at them and whispered to Grace, 'Nothing like the first time a child sees a model railway,' he said.

Grace watched, remembering. 'Except the second time,' she said. 'And the third.'

'And every time after that.' Toby smiled. 'Do you mind if I head to the front and see if they need any help?'

'Of course,' said Grace. She was here for a gift for Sammy. She thought that if Charlotte had something special to take him for her visit, perhaps it might make it easier. But what to get?

He had an engine already, and the basics of a track. She closed her eyes for a moment, remembering what Peter had enjoyed. A tunnel came to mind, and she thought of his face, illuminating like a signal tower as he watched the train travel in through one end and out the other. She smiled as she realised something. Usually, thoughts of Peter filled her with sadness, but this memory hadn't been clouded. It was joyful.

She selected a tunnel, small and with intricately carved brick-work. Sammy could assemble it himself, when he was able, or she'd teach Charlotte how to do it if he wasn't quite up to it.

'They were just browsing,' said Toby, approaching her again as the boys left. 'I told them they're welcome any time.' He looked at the box in her hands.

'It's a gift for Sammy,' she said. 'A get-well-soon sort of thing.'

'That's very kind,' said Toby. He paused a moment. '*You're* very kind.'

Grace flushed, a little taken aback.

'You are kind,' he repeated. 'And lovely. And you're the best miniature engineer I've ever come across.' He smiled at her. 'And very beautiful.'

'I'd hardly say that,' she said. 'Not any more.'

'Well, I would.'

Grace looked at him and hesitated, but only for a moment.

'How about dinner?' she said.

'What?'

'Not now,' she added hurriedly. It was barely noon; too early even for an early-bird special. 'Later.' She paused. 'Just the two of us.'

He looked at her, his face incredulous. 'A date?' he clarified. 'Grace Sayers, are you asking me on a date?'

Grace grinned at him. 'Absolutely,' she said. 'What do you say?'

Charlotte felt nervous as she stood at Sammy's front door, squeezing her mother's hand. It was as though her grandmother's model trains were circulating inside her stomach. The last time she'd seen him, he'd been lying flat on his hospital bed, using an oxygen mask to breathe. It had hardly been like Sammy at all, more like a bad drawing of him.

Thinking of bad drawings, Charlotte glanced inside the bag-for-life her grandmother had provided her with. Her drawing of a bee was within, along with a Tupperware full of chocolate chip cookies they had baked together, and a model tunnel that Grace had bought and wrapped for Sammy.

'Moira!' Charlotte was surprised to see her mother lean forward and embrace Sammy's mum as she opened the door.

'It's so good to see you,' said Moira. 'Charlotte, you look so well.'

Charlotte felt a shard of guilt. She was well and Sammy was not.

'We're so pleased that Sammy is home from hospital,' said Amelia. 'Your prayers have been answered.'

Charlotte looked at her mother. Was she feeling all right?

'Yes, these last few days he's just got so much better. It's more than we could have hoped for,' said Moira. 'Come inside. Sammy will be thrilled to see Charlotte.'

Charlotte wondered if that was an exaggeration. Sammy would be lying there unable to speak, and his thrilled state would be expressed by a tiny movement of his little finger.

'Is that Charlotte?' Sammy's voice rang out.

At the sound, Charlotte pushed past Sammy's brothers, lingering in the hall, and ran to his room. He was sitting up in bed, looking for all the world like her old friend. She flung herself on top of him and hugged him, her tears wetting his pillow.

'Good to see you too,' he said with a laugh.

'You're fine,' she said. 'They said you were getting better, but they didn't tell me you were fine.'

'I'm not,' said Sammy. 'I have to stay in this stupid bed for two more weeks and I'm already so bored. And apparently I'm not allowed to take part in any sport for six months.' He grinned at her. 'Especially football.'

'What a hardship,' said Charlotte.

'So what's been happening?' asked Sammy.

Charlotte started to talk, the words spilling out of her so quickly it was as if she had no control over them. Bees, girls, birds. The shed.

Mr Brown.

She told him everything. Sammy listened, his face puckered up with concentration. 'He was going to jump in front of a train?'

'What?' said Charlotte, who hadn't thought about the mechanics. 'No, I don't think that's what he . . .' She trailed off.

Of course. Sammy was right. 'I don't think he would have gone through with it,' she said, somewhat lamely.

'It's a good thing we stopped him,' said Sammy. 'You do know the disruption something like that would cause to the network?'

'It's not a joke,' said Charlotte.

'No,' said Sammy. 'I'm sorry.' He looked at her. 'Are you going to tell your friends?'

'What friends?'

'The girls. Anne-Marie and Nia would love to know something like that.'

'No,' said Charlotte. 'I don't think we should. It's enough that we know what happened.'

'And that he's OK now,' said Sammy.

'That we all are,' said Charlotte, smiling.

'Now,' said Sammy. 'Down to business. What's in that bag?'

Charlotte emptied the contents on the bed, and they laughed at her drawing together before Sammy opened his present, to a gasp of wonder.

'That's nothing,' said Charlotte. 'Just wait till you see what my grandmother has in her shed.'

Amelia took her suit from where it had been hanging in the wardrobe and folded it carefully, placing it in her suitcase. The house sale had gone through, the bank repaid, and she'd saved enough over the last couple of months to clear most of the debts with her name attached. Without that looming over her head, she had decided that it was time for her and Charlotte to have their own space again, and she'd arranged to rent a two-bedroom flat. Nothing fancy, nothing grand.

But hers. Hers and her daughter's.

She could hear Charlotte in the room next door, talking to the stick insects as she packed away her own things. It was a happy-sounding chatter, not like the last time they'd moved. Amelia had made sure to discuss the decision together, and although Charlotte had been reluctant at first to leave her grandmother's house, she'd eventually agreed.

Because they weren't moving far; she'd found a place a ten-minute walk from her mother's house. She couldn't uproot Charlotte, not again, so she'd be attending the same school and could still see Sammy every day.

'Cup of tea?' Grace called up.

'Yes please,' said Amelia. 'I'll come down.' If she was honest with herself, she wanted to be near her mother.

For Charlotte.

No. Not just for Charlotte.

For herself.

She felt less like a single parent when she had her mother around. It gave her the freedom to dedicate the time she needed to actually enjoy her job again, rather than suffering the endless spiral of working-mother guilt. Neglecting work to be with her daughter. Neglecting her daughter to do her work. It was exhausting.

Grace was the circuit-breaker in that cycle. Amelia had to forgive her mother to really accept the help that she needed.

And she had.

Plus she had discovered, to her surprise, that she was enjoying her mother's company. And she felt as though it would be even easier to enjoy her mother's company when she also had her own space. She needed her independence back.

'And a juice for you, Charlotte?' called Grace.

'Yes please.' Charlotte and her mother met on the staircase and descended together.

'I'll have to start buying the small loaves of bread again,' said

Grace when they reached the kitchen, handing Amelia a cup of tea and Charlotte an orange juice. They sat around the table in their customary chairs.

'Is that your way of saying you'll miss us?' asked Amelia, amused.

'No,' said Grace. 'My way of saying I'll miss you is that I'll miss you.'

Amelia placed a hand on her mother's. It felt warm. 'We'll not be far,' she replied.

'Thank you for that,' said Grace. The two women sat in silence for a moment, each blowing on their tea.

Charlotte mirrored them, blowing gentle bubbles through her straw into her juice. 'I'll miss you right back,' she said.

'We'll visit often,' said Amelia. 'Plus, you know that three days a week when I'm in the office, you'll come to Grandma's house after school.'

Charlotte nodded. 'We're going to create the perfect vegetarian sausage roll together,' she said. 'Aren't we, Grandma?'

'After you've finished your homework,' said Grace firmly, taking a sip of tea to punctuate that statement.

'And you will tell us if you get lonely, won't you?' persisted Charlotte.

'Don't worry,' said Amelia, mischievously. 'Your grandma has Toby to keep her company now.'

'I don't *have* him,' replied Grace, though Amelia was rather sure she did. 'And he's no comparison to my two favourite girls.'

'He is nice, though,' said Amelia.

'I'm glad you approve,' said Grace. She paused a moment. 'I hope you're taking the stick insects with you,' she added.

'I thought you liked them,' said Amelia. 'I sometimes hear you talking to them when I walk past Charlotte's room.'

'That's just me going doolally,' said Grace quickly.

They all laughed. Amelia wondered how it had been so hard for them to talk for so long. It felt so natural, so easy now.

'I'm going to finish packing,' said Charlotte, standing up. 'I've got lots of pairs of jeans to fold.'

'I'll come and help you in a minute,' said Amelia, still sipping her tea. She watched her daughter bounce out of the room and up the stairs.

'So,' began Grace when Charlotte had gone, 'Charlotte tells me you're thinking of taking another trip to the Isle of Wight?'

'We'll be staying inland,' said Amelia. 'No caving.'

'Certainly not.' Grace paused. 'Might I ask why you're going back?' A hint of a smile was playing at her lips.

'Charlotte missed quite a lot of the trip,' said Amelia. 'And she very much wants to feed the lambs on that farm.'

'And I hear someone has offered to show you around?'

'You have good ears for a seventy-two-year-old,' said Amelia. 'But yes. We do have a local tour guide.'

'A good find from me,' said Grace. 'On the boat.'

'We'll see,' said Amelia. She smiled, feeling more hopeful than she had in a long time. And with hope, she realised she'd found some forgiveness, too. 'Actually,' she added, 'there was something I wanted to ask your advice about.' Tom's baby had been born. A picture of a red-faced, wrinkled infant had appeared in her messages. She'd shown Charlotte, but her daughter had shrugged, appearing uninterested.

Grace looked at her, surprise registering on her features. 'My advice?'

'Yes,' said Amelia. 'About Tom.' She paused, watching Grace's surprise morph into a frown. 'Well, Milo really.'

'I can't believe we named you after a pioneering aviator and they named him after a milky drink,' said Grace, shaking her head.

Amelia couldn't help a snigger. 'Mum, I'm trying to say something serious.'

'Sorry,' said Grace. 'Please go on.'

She took a breath. 'It's not how I'd choose for Charlotte to have a brother,' she continued. 'A half-brother. It's messy. Far from perfect. But he is family. And a sibling is so precious ...' Memories started to flood into her mind. 'I think, if Charlotte wants to, that perhaps I should encourage her to spend some time with him.' She stopped, looking at her mother.

'I think that's a lovely idea,' said Grace. She hesitated too, then reached out and placed a hand on her daughter's. 'And kind,' she added. 'He'll be lucky to have Charlotte as a sister.'

'I'm not sure I'm quite up to visiting Tom and Julia,' began Amelia. 'Not yet.'

'I'd be happy to take her,' offered Grace. 'In fact,' she added, 'I'd like to see Tom again.' She smiled. 'I'll tell him about your new man.'

Amelia laughed. 'Throw in that he's six foot three and gorgeous and solvent.'

'And a vet,' said Grace, also laughing. 'And Charlotte adores him.' She paused. 'You're doing the right thing,' she said, her voice serious again.

'I don't think Charlotte will regret having a brother,' said Amelia. 'Whatever happens. I never did.'

Grace nodded and held her daughter's hand a little more tightly. The pain of the past was no longer a wedge, not now that they could finally talk about it.

It was a bond.

Grace sat in the kitchen. She could hear Charlotte and Amelia packing upstairs, their chatter reverberating through her home. It would be quiet without them. She tried to imagine going back to her old life. A lonely ham sandwich eaten in front of the television to avoid looking at the empty places around the table.

No. That was not what it would be like. This time, her fridge would be full. And her life would be too.

Her granddaughter would be there often, and Amelia would visit too. She'd promised she would, and Grace believed her. Because she felt now as though Amelia would actually want to come. She wanted to see Grace, to spend time with her, and not just out of duty.

Grace smiled to herself as she cleared away the empty cups.

Toby would come too. Grace felt a teenage flash of excitement at the thought of their next date. Ava wanted them to double-date, but just for the moment, Grace was keeping him to herself. She'd thought it would feel awkward, dating again at her age, but actually, it was fun.

She went into the hallway again and looked at the stack of her daughter's things, already lined up by the front door. Toby was no substitute for Amelia and Charlotte, there every day when she woke up, and still clattering around downstairs as she went to bed.

Much as she would miss them, she knew that her daughter moving out was the right thing to do. She could feel in her bones that Amelia needed her own space, her independence. She'd always been like that, sometimes wanting a little distance from her mother as they walked home from school, requiring a few moments alone in her room to process the day before joining the family. It was good for her to have that again, and Grace knew she had to respect her decision.

'Here we are,' said Amelia, banging a suitcase down the stairs behind her. 'The final one.'

'The final one,' repeated Grace, looking at the possessions in front of her. It felt like they were taking much less than they'd arrived with. Charlotte hopped down after her mother. 'I'm leaving some stuff here,' she said. 'For me to change into after school and stuff.'

'Me too,' added Amelia. 'For, you know, visits and things. I hope you don't mind.'

Grace smiled. They were leaving behind a lot more than they realised. 'No,' she replied. 'I don't mind at all.'

Chapter 28

'I don't know what possessed you to get that old thing, Mum,' said Amelia, sitting in the sunshine in Grace's back garden.

'My hearing aid is on, you know,' said Toby, coming into the garden from the kitchen.

Amelia laughed. 'You know I mean the dog,' she said. 'He must be well over a hundred in dog years.'

'There is nothing wrong with being old,' said Grace, carrying out a tray with a jug of home-made lemonade and a plate of biscuits. 'And as a bulldog, by my calculations Edison is only in his sixties. A spring chicken. See how well he's playing fetch.'

They all watched. Sammy had thrown the ball and Charlotte was on her knees looking for it in the privet while Edison sniffed her feet, tail wagging. 'Here it is,' she declared. She tossed it a short distance down the garden. Edison turned to look at it, then looked back at her, tongue hanging out, before waddling merrily after it, stopping a few feet short and looking confused. Rex gave an encouraging bark from next door, immensely excited at the new arrival and the smells and noises it provided.

'There you go, Eddy,' said Sammy, picking up the ball and placing it by Edison's paws. Edison took it in his mouth, then dropped it again and lay down heavily, instantly dozing off. A soft snore emitted from his contented body.

'Can we play in the shed now, Mrs Sayers?' asked Sammy.

'Of course,' said Grace. 'Charlotte, do you want me to help you put in the new animals for the zoo?'

'We've got it covered,' said Charlotte.

'Don't touch the wheels on the workbench,' said Grace. 'They are in precise alignment.'

'We won't.'

'You're still working on that contraption?' asked Amelia, pouring herself a glass of lemonade.

'That contraption could be your inheritance, young lady,' said Toby. 'I'm going to help Grace distribute it once it's perfected.'

'It might not work,' said Grace, though she was quite sure that it would. She'd been spending a little less time on her model world recently, allowing Sammy and Charlotte to add features and trying to ignore when they wobbled or the angles were askew.

Instead, she was developing a new kind of toy motor. It was like a pull-back mechanism, but she had an idea for a modified coil spring that would be much more effective than any toy that currently existed. She was even thinking of installing a solar panel that could power sound effects, maybe some lights. Hardly Concorde, but she was rather proud of it. It was nice to work on something that could have a life outside of her shed.

'But if it *does* work,' she continued, 'it could go inside any kind of toy vehicle. Even a train. And the vehicle could travel for up to fifty times the length of the pull-back.'

'And with the chassis Grace has designed,' added Toby, his voice full of pride, 'it can redirect itself upon hitting an obstacle and right itself if it flips. It can travel over any surface; with the right kind of tyre, it could even take on a puddle or a small pond.'

'I have every faith,' smiled Amelia. 'But I won't hold my breath on an inheritance, what with the upkeep you'll be paying for with this elderly gentleman. And by that I mean Edison,' she added. 'Not you, Toby.' They all watched as Edison pedalled his feet in his sleep, as if in his dreams he could ride a bicycle.

'It would be convenient if we had a vet in the family,' said Grace with a smile. 'Remind me where your next holiday is? Malaysia?'

'The Isle of Wight,' confessed Amelia. 'Again.' They'd been every month since May. 'I'm still economising,' she said.

'Is that why you didn't stay in a hotel?' Grace teased. 'Charlotte told me.' She paused. 'She's rather taken with him.'

'She's a blabbermouth,' laughed Amelia. 'And of course she likes him, he's a vet. She's still hoping that he'll convince me to get a puppy.' She smiled. It was more than that, she knew. Henry and Charlotte had a lot in common, anyone could see it. 'But we're not taking that dog of yours for a free check-up, if that's what you're thinking.'

'I wouldn't dream of it,' said Grace. 'We pay our own way, don't we, Edison?'

Edison made a slight whinnying sound at hearing his name, then rolled over, displaying his belly to the air.

'He's a good dog, eh?' said Toby. He put his hand on hers. It was warm, and Grace intertwined her fingers with his. Encouraged, Toby leaned forward and planted a soft kiss on her lips. She returned the favour.

'Yuck,' said Sammy, coming out of the shed at the wrong moment. He turned around and went back in.

'He'll soon change his tune,' said Toby with a laugh.

'Don't say that,' said Amelia. 'I'm already dreading the teenage years.'

'We all are,' said Grace. But she wasn't, not at all. She was looking forward to the future.

*

Grace settled down on her chair by the workbench and tested the wheels of her prototype. They responded with a merry hum, and she watched as they spun round and round, continuing for much longer than any other model she'd seen. It was almost ready.

Edison watched from the old armchair she'd installed in the shed for him to sit on. She'd adopted the dog mainly for Charlotte's benefit, although he wasn't the puppy Charlotte craved. Grace had been determined to get an older animal; she didn't want to leave a creature homeless when her time came, or burden Amelia with a dog. The animal shelter told her that Edison had already outlived one owner. Grace recognised the sadness of loss in his coffee-coloured eyes.

But it was not over for him.

He had a second chance to belong.

They both did.

She stood up from the workbench, content with her prototype. She could work on the next stage of the design in the morning. Tomorrow. Something to look forward to.

She inspected the miniature zoo on which Charlotte and Sammy had been working. The animals were hand-painted, the zebra more grey than striped, and all were horribly out of scale, but she loved them despite their imperfections.

'Come on, Eddy,' she said. He looked back at her, tongue lolling out. 'Let's show the passengers on this train Charlotte's zoo.'

She flicked the switch. A familiar sounded filled the room, like tiny horses galloping, as the train chugged into motion. It gathered speed as it entered the village and whizzed past the school.

The boy and the girl in the school yard watched its progress.

The train entered a tunnel.

And came out the other side.

Acknowledgements

I'm very lucky to have a wonderful team of people who helped me to see the light at the end of the tunnel as I wrote this book.

The fantastic team at Little, Brown have kept this novel on track – special thanks to Anna Boatman, Emma Beswetherick, Amanda Keats, Kate Byrne, Lucie Sharpe and Henry Lord. Thank you also to my brilliant agent Euan Thorneycroft and the team at A.M. Heath.

I'm grateful to Philippa Pride, my mentor, who, together with Otter and the other members of the Next Chapter writing group, have always made sure that I don't run out of steam.

My mother Susan always helps me to make my books so much better – thanks to her for her insight, ideas and support at every stage of this journey. She and my father Roger make the best parents (and grandparents) there could be.

Special thanks go to my husband and kids for helping me play with train sets in the name of research.

When Amy Ashton's world fell apart eleven years ago, she started a collection.

Just a few keepsakes of happier times: some honeysuckle to remind herself of the boy she loved, a chipped china bird, an old terracotta pot . . . Things that others might throw away, but to Amy, represent a life that could have been.

Now her house is overflowing with the objects she loves – soon there'll be no room for Amy at all. But when a family move in next door, a chance discovery unearths a mystery, and Amy's carefully curated life begins to unravel. If she can find the courage to face her past, might the future she thought she'd lost still be hers for the taking?

Perfect for fans of *Eleanor Oliphant* and *The Keeper of Lost Things*, this exquisitely told, uplifting novel shows us that, however hopeless things might feel, beauty can be found in the most unexpected of places.